MW00883898

Novels and novellas by Holly Tierney-Bedord

Sweet Hollow Women
Surviving Valencia
Bellamy's Redemption
Run Away Baby
Right Under Your Nose: A Christmas Story
Ring in the New Year
The Snowflake Valley Advice Fairy
Murder at Mistletoe Manor
Carnage at the Christmas Party
The Pinky Bean Chronicles
Zeke and Angelique
Coached
Sunflowers and Second Chances
Boots on the Ground: A Wrestling with Romance Novella
Dogged by Love
The Miraculous Power of Butter Cookies
Weekend Immune System

Holly Tierney-Bedord

ISBN: 9781983102950

Prologue

Saturday, June 29, 2013

The Night of the Port Elspeth Tragedy

Holly Tierney-Bedord

Evangeline Maddingly

"You promised me the doctor would be here soon. It's been over an hour," Evangeline said. Her greasy hair clung to her face. She smelled like sweat and the putrid-sweet hand lotion she'd received a week earlier for her birthday. Somehow, through everything she'd been through in the four days since she'd generously, carelessly applied it, its ginger lime fragrance still clung to her like remnants of smoke or shame. Normally so composed and pulled-together, the Maddinglys' youngest daughter was nearly unrecognizable tonight.

"Relax. He's just running a little late. It's hard to find this place after dark. Lay your head back down on the pillow and put this wet cloth on your forehead. You'll feel better." Only, the rag was dirty and mostly dry, having been dampened with the remains of a bottle of mineral water.

"I don't want that stupid rag," Evangeline said, twisting away from it. "What do you mean *he's* running late? You said the doctor would be a woman."

"I said that? I guess I thought the doctor was a woman, but it turns out, he's a man. Does it really make a difference?"

"I don't *care* if the doctor is a man or a woman," she said, her voice shrill with fear and frustration. "That's

5

not the point. I'm just trying to understand why your story changed."

"My story didn't change."

"Is a doctor even coming?" Evangeline asked. A drop of sweat from her hairline trickled down her temple, past her ear, tickling her face. It must have been a hundred degrees in there. "There isn't any doctor, is there?" she asked weakly. "There was never a doctor."

"Put your head back. You're making yourself upset. Why would you want to make yourself upset?"

And then with the petting. Evangeline hated the petting. She twisted her face away from the unwelcome smoothing of her hair and forehead. "Please don't touch me," she whispered.

'But I want to," her captor said in the soothing, gushing tone that used to give her comfort but now made her wretch. "I love you."

"Please stop telling me that," she said, taking in humid little gasps of air through her mouth, willing herself not to gag.

"I imagined us becoming a family someday. I think there was a time that you did, too. Tell me you did."

"I could never belong to you," Evangeline said, not bothering to hide her disgust. She'd tried a hundred different tactics, from making promises she had no intention of keeping to making threats. She was getting too exhausted to bother playing games that weren't working. "I'll never belong to anyone," she added defiantly.

"You're probably right," her captor said sadly.

"Is a doctor coming or not?"

"Of course not. We both know that it's not a doctor you need."

"I do though! I need a doctor. I need a doctor tonight. I can't wait until tomorrow," she said, beginning to cry. The tears, this time, were genuine. "Please. You said you'd help me."

"I *am* helping you."

"No, you're not! What was all this for if there isn't any doctor?" she asked through her tears, gesturing with her chin at the predicament she was in.

"The doctor was going to come, but he got called away on another appointment and he can't make it tonight, but I'm going to help you instead."

"Really?" Evangeline asked. She so desperately wanted to believe it that she almost did.

"That's right," said her captor, letting one finger trace down Evangeline's temple, down along her delicate jawline. She thought, for a moment, she smelled fireworks. Or a smell that reminded her of a trip she took many years earlier when she was just a little girl on one of her parents' learning trips that she and her sisters so despised. A trip to an iron mine in Canada.

"You're so beautiful," said her captor.

"Stop. Please. Please stop touching me like that. How are you going to help me?"

"I can fix you," said her captor.

"How? I don't believe you," she said.

"You need to trust me. It's your best option."

"I *did* trust you," she said. "I trusted you more than just about anyone. How stupid of me," she added, meaning it, but also thinking that perhaps showing that she recognized she'd lost might be all it would take to win again.

"You're not stupid. You're brilliant."

She shook her head, fighting her urge to throw up. This repulsive flattery. She tried to brush it away and focus instead on her dire circumstances. "What time is it?" she asked through her tears.

"What difference does it make? I think you should calm down and rest. You're getting worked up. It's not good for you."

"It matters to me. What time is it?" she asked again.

7

"Shhhh. Stop asking so many questions." Her captor placed both warm, sweaty palms over her eyes and mouth for a moment and whispered, "I need you to stop looking at me like that and stop talking. You don't need to glare at me. You don't need to talk to me like this."

Evangeline struggled away from the suffocating, unwelcome touch, instantly recognizing that what she'd been smelling was gunpowder. A whole new level of desperation came over her.

"Why are you doing this?" she cried. Staggering, jolting waves of tears were overtaking her ability to string words together. "We could get along again. We could start this whole thing over... Are you listening to me? Everything can be...however you want it again. I'll talk to my parents and tell them...nothing bad happened. I'd do that for you. But not unless we..." she coughed through her tears, "totally start over? Okay? A total re-do. ...Please? I'll do it if you'll do it. No hard feelings. None, I mean it. I swear! ...That sounds really good, right? Say it does and then I'll relax. I promise," she said. "I'm begging you! Let's undo all of this."

"No. Enough negotiating. Take a deep breath. Close your eyes. Try to get some sleep if you can. Everything will be better tomorrow."

"I'm not staying here again. How could I possibly fall asleep?" she said. "I'm going to scream if you don't let me go right now."

"You can scream all you want, but why bother? It's just making things worse. I, for one, find it very upsetting."

She opened her mouth to scream, but the only sounds that came out were sobs of defeat.

Five Years Later

~

Friday, February 9, 2018

An Invitation

Chapter 1

Cadence Sommerset

Hello, friends and neighbors!

I'm new to the area and I'm planning to take part in the Port Elspeth City Fundraiser coming up in April. However, to reserve a booth, I'll need to have $1,000 worth of inventory in handmade products to sell and donate. All proceeds will go to build the new Port Elspeth city park! My plan is to make jewelry, but I need some help to produce enough in such a short amount of time. Who's with me?

I've dabbled in jewelry making in the past and already have many of the tools and supplies we'll need. Please join me at my home at 1456 Piccadilly Lane on Tuesday, Feb. 20 at 7:00 pm if you're interested in getting involved. No experience necessary.

PS ~ There will be wine and snacks!

Warm regards,

Cadence Sommerset

Cadence reread her message two more times. Then she clicked on 'post' and held her breath, half-hoping it would magically disappear into cyberspace. An introvert by nature, she had to push herself out of her comfort zone to make new friends. Starting over in a new city over a thousand miles away from her hometown of Springwater, Arkansas, was going to require a little extra effort if she wanted to fit in. A fraction of a second later, her posting manifested itself onto her local community's social media site.

"There it is. Well, I guess it's really happening," she said to herself.

She looked around, taking in her bright, beachy home, wishing she was more excited about it. It made no sense to her that she wasn't ecstatic. This was their fresh start—and in a home that anyone would envy.

Cadence had always been house-obsessed. While her childhood friends had torn out pictures of wedding gowns and hairstyles from magazines, she'd raided her parents' *Architectural Digests*, saving the inspiration she'd found on those glossy pages.

She and her husband of four years, Dave, had unpacked the last of the moving boxes two days earlier and everything was now in its place.

"There won't be anything for you to do but sit back and relax," he'd told her, as the last packing box had been flattened and the final books and vases had been artfully placed on the built-in shelves.

"That sounds great. And maybe a little boring," she'd laughed, as they'd settled down outside on their Adirondack chairs, each with a blanket and a glass of champagne, and toasted to their new home.

"Before you know it, we'll have a family and you'll wish you had extra time on your hands," he'd assured her. "We're living the good life. Sit back and enjoy it!"

"No, I know. I mean, I realize how lucky I am."

"I still can't believe how much they're paying me," he'd said, shaking his head. "No more forty-five or fifty-hour workweeks for you. No more workweeks at all!"

"What a relief."

"You were getting so stressed out at your old job," he'd said, squeezing her hand.

"I sure was," she'd agreed.

"That's probably why it hadn't happened yet. But now it will. I have a good feeling about it. And we aren't getting any younger!"

"Thirty-four isn't exactly over-the-hill," she'd reminded him.

"Well, I'm thirty-seven."

"I know, old man," she'd teased.

"Can't you see this being the place where we raise our family?"

She'd nodded. "Of course. I can't imagine anything nicer. I'm sure it'll happen soon. You're right that I'd better enjoy this quiet time while it lasts."

They'd clinked glasses again and he'd leaned over and given her a kiss. Except for the unseasonably-cold wind coming off the waves, it had been a perfect scene.

Now she fixed herself a cup of coffee and checked the posting again to see if there were any responses. So far, nothing. Out her kitchen and breakfast room windows, the ocean glimmered a deep sparkly blue. It was the first time in days that the sky hadn't been overcast.

"It's so gorgeous outside that I'm going to go for a walk," she decided, pouring her coffee into a travel mug.

First things first, though. She removed a glass from one of the shelves in her kitchen and filled it with some tap water. She then went over to where her purse was hanging on the hook by the back door and unzipped the inside pocket. What she loved about this purse was that it had an inside pocket hiding *inside* the inside pocket. The perfect place to stash little things. She unzipped the secret pocket and popped out one tiny pink pill from within its plastic container. She put the pill on her tongue and took a big gulp of water to wash it down, trying not to gag. It always felt like an awkward production to her, which was one of the reasons she did it in secret. She'd never been fond of taking pills, even one as tiny as a birth control pill.

Chapter 2

Vivienne Van Heusen-Prescott

"Maybe if you had some friends you wouldn't be so concerned about mine," Olivia Prescott told her mother.

"There *has* to be a better choice than those druggie twins you've been hanging around with," Vivienne said. She'd come to hate the sound of her own voice. The way she'd catch herself screeching instead of talking. It reminded her of how her own mother had yelled at her when she was a teenager.

"Ada and Lila aren't *druggies*, they're *emo*. Haven't you heard that you're not supposed to judge people on their appearance?" Olivia twirled her once-blonde, now green and gray-streaked hair, sneering mockingly at her mother. "If you don't like them, too bad. They're pretty much my only option. It's not like I can have my pick of friends. And that's all because of you."

"I'm very tired of you talking to me like this. We can continue this conversation this evening. You're already late for school again, for—what? The second time this month? Or is it the third time?"

"I'm not keeping track."

"You told your father if he got you a car you wouldn't have that problem anymore," Vivienne reminded her sixteen-year-old daughter. Outside on their white gravel driveway—Neil Prescott insisted on it instead of concrete because he was convinced the crunching sound made when walking or driving on it was a deterrent to burglars— Olivia's white 2017 BMW x5 sat parked where she'd left it when she'd arrived home at eleven o'clock the prior evening, despite that she was grounded. The Prescotts had a parking stall for her, of course, but she rarely used it since she had a phobia of squeezing through the twelve-foot-wide garage door.

The morning sun shone on what looked like a fresh ding in the driver's side door of the vehicle, but Vivienne bit her lip. She simply didn't have the energy to comment on it.

"I'm late because of *you*, Mom! I'm late because you're bitching at me! Can I go now?"

"Please do," Vivienne said.

"Good riddance," Olivia said, stomping out the door.

Vivienne watched her drive away, sadness as well as a guilty flood of relief slowly seeping in and taking the place of the anger and anxiety that her only remaining child ignited in her.

"It wasn't supposed to be this way," she told herself. She couldn't admit this to Neil, but if she could do it over again, she would never have had kids. This was a reality she wrestled with every day. She'd decided it years earlier and was still waiting for something to change her mind. Olivia's behavior was only serving to strengthen the feeling.

Yes, her daughter certainly knew how to push her buttons. The comment about not having friends, for instance. It was so cutting and rude and true.

Vivienne had been an active part of several local clubs, including the nearly-impossible-to-get-into Port Elspeth Women's Club, until five years earlier. She'd been on her way to becoming one of the town's alpha-women. She'd just gotten a reserved parking space at the top secret ladies-only afternoon tea club, and, like all the Mortenson and Van Pelt women, she'd even started her own lifestyle blog. Then, in one moment, the Prescotts had gone from being one of Port Elspeth's model families to excommunicated untouchables.

Neil traveled so much that he could get buried in his work and pretend not to notice. Vivienne knew he felt it, too, though. His Saturdays used to be spent golfing with the guys. The Prescotts had also been members of the Port Elspeth Country Club and Good News Society, a local organization devoted to causes like making sure Port Elspeth had more hanging baskets adorning their sidewalk cafes in the downtown than any other small town in the area.

Now it all seemed like nonsense. Nonsense she missed terribly. She watched with a mixture of jealousy and contempt from the sidelines as her former friends carried on with their frivolous, smug ways without her.

"We need to move away," she'd told Neil, soon after they'd buried their son.

"It's not that easy," he'd told her. "I can't just up and leave my job."

"It's the only way we're going to have any chance at happiness again. We can't stay here. *Her* family has already gone. They knew better than to stay here."

"I don't want to talk about this."

"But you need to hear me! How can Olivia spend her teenage years here? At least think of her."

Back then Olivia had still been a sweet, loving child. Not even eleven years old yet. She'd been a completely different person than who she was today. Her bedroom had been filled with horseback riding ribbons and sailing club trophies. Her clothes had been bright and cute and colorful. Every year since she was four she'd been on the cover of the *Port Elspeth Gourmet Goodies to Your Door* catalog. It had been assumed that she'd be their cover girl until she graduated from high school. There hadn't been any fathomable reason for them to stop featuring her. After all, it seemed she was only getting prettier with each passing year.

"Give it six months," Neil had said. "Let me at least wrap up the McMurray project. They're our biggest account."

"Six months. But only six months," Vivienne had agreed.

"By then, things might start getting back to normal. No one holds what happened against us."

"But they do. Of course they do. Look around! Don't pretend you don't see it! People are avoiding us! They're never going to get over it." *And I don't blame them*, she added in her head.

"Six months," Neil had said again.

But six months later, when things were worse than ever, when Vivienne hadn't left the house in weeks except to visit her psychiatrist Dr. Eisley, and when her once-bubbly daughter had stopped getting invitations to friends' parties and homes, Neil needed another six months.

"We've got problems at the plant in China," he'd told her. "I have to go there and work things out. This would be a terrible time for me to leave."

"Fine," Vivienne had said, "but once that's all cleared up, can we please get serious about starting over somewhere new? Things are only getting harder."

"Maybe it's not as bad as you're imagining. Have you tried reaching out to your old friends?"

"They avoid me in the grocery store. They all unfriended me on Facebook. Neil, I can't take this. You know how important my social standing used to be. You *know* how hard we worked to get where we were."

"It's going to get better. For now, though, I've got to pack for China."

The China project ended up taking over a year. It was followed immediately by an expansion at the Sandusky plant that Neil had to oversee. (Vivienne had been so desperate that she'd said she'd even move to Ohio; Neil had said he wasn't giving up his ocean-front property to live in a cornfield.) That had been followed by new issues that had to be resolved at the facility in Bangladesh.

In the meantime, things around Port Elspeth got even worse. Especially for Olivia. There was no more horseback riding for her. No more sailing club. Those doors were closed now. She'd been slowly edged out, in that subtle, arrogant way that barely seemed to be happening, until one day she was standing so far outside the circle that it was hard to believe she'd ever once been a part of it. These days, Olivia Prescott wasn't even welcome at the shoddy Port Elspeth School of Dance.

Vivienne hated to think who her daughter might have become and the opportunities that would have been laid out before her, if their lives had only stayed on the proper track.

"They can't stay mad forever," Neil had unreasonably reasoned during years three and four of Vivienne's begging and nagging for them to relocate. "Try to focus on something positive for a while. Maybe you could pull Olivia out of school and take a little trip?"

"She's about to flunk out and she hates me. Taking a trip together would be a disaster."

"So then, keep her in school and you find something just for you."

"Like what? Nothing interests me."

"You could get back into lady bodybuilding."

"I don't want to be all bulky again! How could you have let me look like that? I want to be pretttty," she wailed, beginning to weep.

"How about if you go to the spa a little more? That'll relax you, and maybe those lotions they put on you will make you feel even more beautiful. Do they have a weekly pass? A rewards card? A punch card?"

"I don't know, Neil."

"Well, look into it, Punkin. I have that new project in Turkey monopolizing all my time. We can talk seriously about moving once that's under control. Put it on the calendar for May."

This was how the Prescotts functioned; keeping unhappily busy until the next scheduled talk that, at best, went nowhere.

Vivienne sighed and started pulling fruits and vegetables out of her refrigerator. Carrots. Kale. Apples. Part of a lemon left over from the day before. It was all organic, so she didn't get overly fussy about rinsing it off. After a distracted pass beneath the filtered drinking water spigot beside the sink, it all went straight into her Robot Coupe J100 Ultra juicer. She and her family may not have been part of the Port Elspeth high society anymore, but she was ready for them to rejoin at any time, and that meant always looking her best. She started each morning with fresh-pressed juice, vitamins, a handful of fiber capsules, two Xanax pills, and an intake of social media, which, at this point, was mainly just stalking people online. She settled down on the sofa and logged into her neighborhood's public bulletin site and saw that someone new had joined and was trying to find people to help her supply a booth with handmade jewelry at the town's upcoming fundraiser fair.

Vivienne sipped her juice, reading the woman's posting, a small line of concentration forming on her forehead. "Darn it," she murmured to herself, pressing the smooth, cool edge of her juice glass against the little wrinkle in an attempt to make it disappear. "Time to get more Botox."

19

This woman—her name was Cadence—honestly thought she was getting into the event that the Port Elspeth Women's Club was holding that spring. "Fat chance," Vivienne said, laughing out loud. No one got a booth there unless they had old money and connections. In all her time of social climbing—and she'd made it far—she'd never made it *that* far.

Just then, Vivienne's cellphone rang. She picked it up and saw it was Olivia's school calling. She groaned but answered it. "Hello," she drawled, making it clear from the start the call was a bother. "Vivienne Van Heusen-Prescott speaking."

"Hi, Vivienne. This is Joan Benson," said the school vice-principal.

"Joan! How *are* you? Is everything okay with Olivia?"

"Well, that's why I'm calling. It's going on ten o'clock and we haven't seen her yet today. Her tardiness is becoming a problem. Do you know if we can expect her soon?"

"She did get a late start this morning—" Vivienne began.

"And why is that?" Joan Benson interrupted. "You realize that it's up to you and your husband to see that she gets to school on time. With all due respect, Mrs. Prescott, it's the law."

"I realize that," Vivienne said curtly, recalling a time when some frumpy nobody like Joan Benson wouldn't have had the nerve to talk to her this way, "but I'm sure my daughter will be there soon. Maybe she stopped off for breakfast on her way."

"Which would be totally unacceptable," said Joan Benson.

"She gets headaches," Vivienne lied, "and when she does, she needs to eat. You could be more understanding, Joan. It's a health issue, not a choice."

Joan sighed with exaggerated annoyance.

"I'll give her a call," said Vivienne.

"Please call me back after you hear from her. Oh, wait. Would you look at that. She's walking in the door now," Joan Benson said.

"Then I guess the problem's solved. Good day, Joan," Vivienne said, ending the call. She exhaled and picked up her smoothie. Now it wasn't as cold as she liked. She set it back down on the counter top, a little too hard, and it splashed onto the sleeve of her silk pajamas. And that was the last straw. Tears began streaming down her face.

"Damn it," she whispered, getting up and wetting some paper towels. "Damn it all to hell. I can't take any more. I can't take it. I just can't take it."

She wiped up the spilled liquid and then pulled off her pajama top and threw it into the kitchen sink. She filled the sink with water so she could loosen the stain before it set in. There was a time when she wouldn't have walked around her house topless, but it wasn't like she got any visitors these days. Then she picked up her phone and texted her husband:

Something has to change. I can't do this much longer.

She waited.

Of course he didn't respond. He rarely responded to her texts when he was working.

She tried again:

Please don't ignore me. I know you have your phone with you all the time.

Please. I'm really at my wits' end.

Still nothing, so she tried a different approach:

If I was Pierre calling from the Strasbourg branch I know you would've responded to me by now.

Finally, feeling desperate, she took a picture of her naked torso and hit send.

Two seconds later Neil replied:

Are you crazy? What are you doing? Was this meant for me?

This actually made Vivienne laugh out loud. Her own laughter was a breathy, foreign sound she hadn't heard herself make in she-didn't-know-how-long. She responded with:

Yes, it was meant for you. Our daughter is driving me crazy. The school just called about her and I made up a dumb lie to cover for her. I'm so sick of everything! I really need some support around here please!!!

Neil texted back:

Okay. I hear you. I'll talk to her tonight. Now you've gotten me all distracted from my work.

She texted:

Glad I can still do something right. See you tonight.

Neil responded:

Have a good day, Punkin. I love you.

She signed off with:

I love you too. Bye.

Vivienne set her phone down. The morsel of attention from her husband had lightened her mood considerably and given her some hope. She turned back to the neighborhood message board and found herself unexpectedly inspired to compose the following message to Cadence:

Hi Cadence,

My name is Vivienne Van Heusen-Prescott. I live at 8555 Wild Rose Circle (the brick house with the black shutters and the four-car garage). Welcome to Port Elspeth! It's such a warm, friendly, close-knit community. You'll love it here!

I'm very interested in joining your jewelry making club. Please let me know what I can bring. I've probably got whatever gemstones or tools you'd need and I'm more than happy to share them with you.

Looking forward to it!

~Vivienne

She closed her computer and headed upstairs to take a shower and get ready for a trip to the craft store. She hoped someone there would be able to steer her in the right direction. After all, she'd never made jewelry in her life and didn't even know where to begin.

Chapter 3

Audra Fleming

"Okay, class, now I'd like you to dip your brushes into the glass of dirty rinse water on your left. Yes, Kelsie, that one. Swirl your brushes around; don't mash them into the bottom of the glass or you'll ruin them. Nice job, everyone. Now dip your brushes into your other glass of clean water. Great! Now you're ready to choose another color to paint with."

Audra Fleming smiled wearily, straining to keep positive. She yanked on the collar of the old concert t-shirt she was wearing, stretching it out, pressing it against her jaw, and distractedly using it to hide half her face. Then she twisted the cord of her necklace around her finger over and over until there was no more room to twist. At that point, she pulled her hand away and let the necklace unravel back into place. These were awkward habits she'd had all her life; when she was anxious they came back. She forced herself to control her hands, but now the neckline of her t-shirt was twice as big as it was supposed to be. She glanced at the clock on the wall, calculating everything that had to happen before class wrapped up.

"I like blue best," Aidan Lucas called out. Immediately all the children in the class began calling out their favorite colors.

Audra nodded encouragingly at her class of kindergarteners, deciding to let them roll with their little outburst of expression. "You're all doing such a nice job," she told them again, once they'd quieted down and returned to painting.

"Miss Fleming, are we your best class?" Aidan yelled.

"One of them," Audra told him, nodding.

The class liked that. They oohed and ahhed. Audra couldn't help but smile at their cute reactions.

"Okay, everyone," she told them after a few more minutes had passed. "It's getting to be clean-up time. I'd like all of you to carefully stand up and pick up your two glasses of water. Then form two single-file lines by the sinks in the back of the room. Right now, everyone. Get moving."

As much as she loved her job as the Middleford Pre-K through fourth grade art teacher, so much of it was more about crowd control and time management than actually creating art or fostering creativity. She wouldn't have minded a little more adult contact. Her afternoon break in the teacher's lounge and the Thursday night trivia league she ran were often the only times each week that she had any live, one-on-one conversation with people over age twelve.

She looked at the clock on the wall again. It was quarter to two. She'd told the kids to start clean-up extra early, in part because painting was inherently disastrous for five-year-olds, but mainly because she couldn't wait to see Ben Harrison.

Ben was a couple years older than Audra, taught English to fifth and sixth graders, and had recently broken off his engagement to his childhood sweetheart. He was the most gorgeous specimen of human maleness that Audra had ever seen. He could have been a model or an actor, as far as she was concerned. And on Fridays, his lounge break ran from 1:45-2:20. She didn't want to miss a minute of time with him.

"Okay, you're doing a fantastic job," she told her students. "Now, put your paintings in the drying rack, being extra careful not to let your painting touch your neighbor's painting."

The clock said 1:53 now. Time was quickly evaporating and the room still looked like a disaster.

"Smocks go on the pegs in the back of the room. Come on, class, you all know that by now. Go ahead, take them off and hang them up."

"Miss Fleming?" her student Madeline said, coming up and tugging on the hem of Audra's t-shirt, "I have to ask you something. In private."

"Okay, hold on for a second," she said to her student. She then turned to address the rest of the class who had stopped working to see why their classmate was up at the teacher's desk while they were supposed to be cleaning up. "Everyone, pay attention to your own business and keep working," Audra instructed. "Wipe up your work areas."

"Carlie and Alyssa are being mean to me," Madeline said when Audra turned back to her. "I think I need you to get them in trouble, please."

Audra sighed. It was now 1:57. Just then she heard the loud, animated voice of Christina Petermont, the music teacher, trilling in from the hallway outside the art room. Wherever Christina went, all eyes were on her. She never hesitated to break out into showtunes whenever she felt like it. Her hair was brassy blonde, her cocktail ring-covered hands were gigantic, and her personality was even bigger. She dressed in tight, printed capri pants, fifties-style blouses with bows at the neck, and stiletto heels. If she hadn't also been blatantly obsessed with Ben Harrison, she and Audra might have been friends. But, as it was, they were both after the same man and there wasn't room enough at Middleford Grade School for both of them.

"Carlie and Alyssa, over here," Audra said, snapping her fingers. "Everyone else, line up by the door."

"But there's still paint smeared on the tables," one of the students whined.

"Just get in line," Audra said. Their homeroom teacher was waiting in the doorway with a tired grimace on her face. Audra turned back to the three little faces in front of her. "Girls," she whispered. "Do you know what today is?"

"No. What is it?" asked Alyssa.

"It's National Be Nice Day. Everyone has to be nice to everyone else for the whole day. The reason you may not have heard about this day is because it's a secret. So, just between us, today's the day to be nice. Understand?"

"I've never heard of 'Be Nice' day," said Carlie.

"She just said that's because it's a secret," Alyssa told her.

"Class dismissed," Audra called to the rest of the kindergartners. "You three go ahead, too. See you next week!"

Madeline lingered for a moment, a skeptical frown on her face. "That was the best you could do?" she asked her teacher.

"That's all I've got," Audra said, shrugging.

"Well, okay. See you next week, Miss Fleming."

As soon as her students were on their way, Audra ran off to the teachers' lounge. As she approached it, she could hear Christina in there, belting out *Give My Regards to Broadway.*

Audra opened the door and stepped inside. Christina's singing devolved into a tumble of giggles. "I can't do it with Audra in here. She's too serious," Christina told her small audience of Ben and Sandra Donnelly, the junior high science teacher.

"I'm not that serious. You can keep singing," Audra said.

"No, no. You ruined it. Just kidding. They've already heard enough."

"I can't argue with that," Ben said, laughing. "There's room over here, Audra," he said, setting aside one of the pillows from the sagging sofa and patting a spot beside him.

"Oh, sure. Thanks, Ben," Audra said, trying to sound casual.

"Hey, Audra, I saw something this morning that I think might interest you," Sandra said.

"Oh? What's that?" Audra asked, simultaneously picking up on Ben's distractingly sexy presence and Christina's glowering breaths.

"Someone in my neighborhood is looking for people to make jewelry for a fundraiser. You're really good at that. I thought you might want to get involved."

"Oh, well, maybe," Audra said, instinctively reaching for the handmade cabochon necklace hanging around her neck. She forced her hand back down to her side so she wouldn't play with it. "You live up in Port Elspeth, right?"

"That's right," said Sandra.

"That's *so* far away," said Christina. "And everyone up there is *such* a snob. Not you, of course, Sandra. You're great. But most of the people in that town are stuck-up and rich."

"I subbed there the year after I graduated from college, before I got my job here," Ben said. "Their school looks like a palace compared to ours."

"People in Port Elspeth aren't *that* stuck up, and it's only thirty minutes from here," Sandra said. She was in her late thirties, whereas the other three in the teachers' lounge were all still in their twenties. Sandra might not have thought the people in Port Elspeth were stuck-up, but Audra was fairly certain they were living completely different existences than her own cramped one-bedroom lifestyle.

"I *know* how far it is," said Christina. "I'm rehearsing for a play there. I go there all the time lately."

"Well," said Sandra, "if you ask me, it's actually a nice drive. I love it. I listen to books on CD. And most of the people who live there are nice. Anyway," she turned back to Audra, "I thought you might be interested. In fact, I printed it out for you." She reached into her pocket and took out a folded slip of paper and passed it to Ben. As he passed it on to Audra, their fingers touched and a jolt of electricity shot straight through Audra.

"Thank you," Audra said. "I think I'll do it. I've been wanting a little more adult contact." And as she said that, somehow, she found the nerve to look right at Ben. For a second, their eyes locked.

"I have to get back to class," Sandra moaned. "One more hour and then it's time for the weekend." She went over to the sink to rinse out her coffee mug. According to the clock, both Ben and Christina needed to get back to class too, but neither was moving. Audra sensed that Ben was waiting for Sandra and Christina to go ahead so he could talk with her alone, but Christina seemed determined to stay planted right where she was.

"See you next week," Sandra said, heading out the door and closing it behind her.

"So, Ben, like I was telling you, dress rehearsals are this weekend and the following weekend is the play. Are you coming to it?"

"Um, I don't know."

"Come on," Christina said. "Say you're coming to it."

"I'm planning on going to Christina's play," Audra boldly decided, even though she wasn't even sure which play it was. "Why don't you come with me, Ben?"

Christina glared at Audra, but what could she say?

"Sure, Audra," Ben said, looking not-at-all displeased. "I'd love to go with you."

"Well then," Audra said, her heart racing, "I guess it's a date."

Chapter 4

Pearl Quincy

Pearl Quincy had lived for seven decades and called four men her husband, but she still couldn't make a decent pot of soup from scratch.

"Are you using water instead of stock?" her daughter Margo asked her.

"No, Miss Smarty-Pants. I know you think I'm losing my mind in my old age, but I'm still pretty sharp. I did not use *water*; I used that whole carton of vegetable stock you gave me."

Margo tasted the soup again and wrinkled her nose, setting the spoon daintily back onto the saucer beside the stove. Pearl had noticed that ever since she'd returned from living in France, Margo was more finnicky than ever.

"You know, Mom," Margo said, "maybe you'd have more luck with a cream-based soup."

"No, I don't think so. I'm sticking with lighter foods these days. I'm trying to lose weight," Pearl said.

"At your age, why bother?"

"Because I want to be healthy!"

"Oh. Okay. I was afraid you were going say you're trying to snag another man."

"I never 'snagged' any man. They all snagged me! And for your information, I wouldn't mind getting married again." Aside from marriage number one, which had been ill-thought-out and just about over when her husband Gene had crashed into a tree after one too many drinks with his friends, Pearl's other three husbands had all died of natural causes after many happy years with her. She couldn't be blamed for her track record.

"Oh, Mom," said Margo, a product of marriage number three, "give it a rest. Back to the soup, have you tried adding more garlic?"

Pearl nodded. "I already tried that."

"What about a little flour?"

"Tried that too."

"Corn starch?" asked Margo.

"I haven't tried it, but if the flour didn't help, I don't know that corn starch would."

"I don't know," Margo said. "Why don't you just give up?"

"Didn't you pick up any secrets in Paris?"

"None that I can share with you."

"I meant cooking secrets."

"Well," Margo said, "maybe." She took another spoonful of the soup, thoughtfully letting it swirl on her tongue like it was wine.

"Are you figuring it out?" asked her mother.

"I think it's a texture thing. The French love fat, but not greasiness. In America, we're so extreme. It's one thing or the other. The French think that a little cheese here, a little wine there, makes a meal richer. Here in the States, we're more like 'deep-fry everything' or 'never eat any fat' and this is why we don't have a healthy, happy, tasty balance."

"Oh, listen to you, my little expatriate. 'Here in the States,'" laughed Pearl. "I should have known when I named you Margaret and you decided when you were twelve that you'd rather be Margo, that this would be your life someday."

"I was born to be French," Margo agreed.

"You were. I know they do everything better there, but America has its upsides as well. We're not all bad here."

"Sorry, I didn't mean to lecture you," Margo said. "I love it here. There wasn't a day that went by that I didn't miss something about home. I'm just saying, maybe add some butter or oil to it."

"And make it more fattening?"

"Or keep doing what you're doing and keep wondering why it's not working."

"I'll give it a try," Pearl said, adding several capfuls of vegetable oil to the simmering pot of soup and giving it a good stir. Then she and Margo each tried another spoonful.

"Wow! Instantly better," Margo said.

"You aren't kidding," said Pearl.

They high-fived.

"I'm glad you're back," Pearl told her daughter. She refrained from asking her how long she planned to stay. Margo had returned home because her relationship with her girlfriend Lisette had 'gone stale.' That was what she called it, anyway. To Pearl, it wasn't much of an explanation and sounded very French. Maybe because she associated it with baguettes.

"I'm glad to be back, too," Margo said. "Thanks for letting me stay here."

"It's good to have you around the house again. It feels like old times."

"I was thinking," Margo said, "that along with finding a job, I need to make some friends. I want new, different friends. No one from the past. Do you have any ideas?"

Pearl stirred the soup, considering her daughter's request. A job? New friends? Apparently, she was planning on staying for quite a while. "Things with you and Lisette are definitely over?" she asked.

"I think so."

"Honey, you two were together for four years. Please don't take this the wrong way, but you don't seem very upset about it."

"I'm upset. It's just that this has been coming for a while. To you, it's fresh and surprising, but to me, I've already done a lot of grieving. I'm kind of relieved to be back home and not in the midst of it anymore."

Pearl nodded. "I get it."

"We can talk more about it later," said Margo. "For now, I'd rather not think about it too much."

"Here's an idea for you," Pearl said, going over to the computer on the desk in her kitchen. "Someone here in town wants people to help her make jewelry. You're artsy. You could help her with that."

"It's probably one of the Mortensons or the Van Pelts, or someone from some other rich family that was horrible to me in high school. No thanks."

"It isn't anyone you know. She says she just moved to town. Her name is Cadence. Isn't that a pretty name?"

"I guess so. I knew someone in Paris named that."

"Oh! A connection already!"

"Not exactly," said Margo.

"Here's her contact information if you want to get in touch with her. I'm already logged in. You can use my account."

"I don't think so."

"Margo! Just a minute ago you said you wanted to make some friends."

"Well... Maybe I'll do it if you come along with me."

"I don't know anything about making jewelry," said Pearl.

"I'll teach you."

Pearl sighed. "I guess you *did* solve my age-old soup dilemma just like that. Maybe you could teach me to make jewelry. Fine. I'm signing us both up!"

Saturday, February 17, 2018

Date Night

Chapter 5

Vivienne Van Heusen-Prescott

Vivienne watched her daughter backing out of the driveway, smiling and waving at her father. Olivia came about an inch from hitting their mailbox, slammed on the brakes, and covered her mouth in a faux-gasp that made Neil throw back his head in laughter.

"I've had it with both of them," Vivienne muttered to herself, finding no humor in the situation. Despite that Olivia was supposed to grounded, Neil had crumbled, yet again, and told her she could go out with her friends.

As he finished his busywork of picking up downed twigs from the yard, he stood up and looked toward the house. His eyes met hers. Vivienne glared at him and shook her head. She turned away, back to the beads and tools on her kitchen table that she was separating into her new craft carrier and a variety of fancy jelly jars. She'd discreetly, casually scuffed the craft carrier against the gravel in their driveway earlier that morning. The elegant little jelly jars had been purchased a couple days earlier at Ginger's Fine Imported Foods. At the time of purchase, the jars had been full of seventy-seven dollars' worth of organic preserves that she'd blasély dumped down the sink so she could reuse them for this sole purpose.

The jewelry making meeting was just a few days away and she wanted to give everything she was bringing a properly broken-in look.

She pretended not to hear Neil coming in the back door and putting his coat and shoes in the closet. He came up behind her, wrapped his arms around her waist, and said, "I took a half-day today so we could spend more time together, so why don't we?"

She ignored him, picking up a spool of wire (she had no idea what a person would use it for, but the woman at the craft store had added it to her basket of jewelry-making necessities) and pretended to be enthralled with it.

Neil removed it from her hand and it set it on the table. Vivienne picked up a pair of tweezers instead.

"Come on, my sexy little Punky-Wunky. Let's go upstairs," he suggested.

She spun around. "How could you let her go out with her friends again? She's never going to learn to behave herself if there are never any consequences to her actions!"

"You two have been going at it all day, as usual. Why don't you enjoy the peace and quiet?"

"Because knowing she's out with those idiots, getting into God-knows-what kind of trouble, further humiliating our already destroyed family, isn't at all relaxing! If she was at home where she's supposed to be, we would at least know what she's up to. We're supposed to be a united front. You always make me the bad guy!"

"There aren't good guys and bad guys. That includes our daughter. We're all just stressed out. Come on now, Punkin." Neil tilted Vivienne's face toward his own with the tip of his finger.

She let him do so, but she refused to make eye contact with him.

"Punkin…" he tried again.

"Why do you have to sound so cute and flirty?" she said with a sigh. She crossed her arms against her strategically bony ribcage. It took a consistent pattern of consuming never more than twelve hundred fifty calories a day to stay so thin. "I'm not giving in to you," she told him.

"Then at least hear me out. Olivia's not a bad kid and her friends aren't so bad either," Neil continued. "Personally, I don't care if her friends aren't in the sailing club and don't go to Immersive French Camp each summer. Just because they're different from her old friends doesn't mean they're bad kids."

"But they *are* bad kids," said Vivienne. "I'm not making this a class thing. They're weirdos and brats!"

"They are not," said Neil. "We need to try to let her be a normal sixteen-year-old. She needs friends, she needs fun, she needs a life outside of this house."

"If we hadn't given Oliver so much freedom, maybe he'd still be here," Vivienne said.

Neil's face hardened. "I don't want to hear that. It's not true."

Vivienne turned away. She didn't respond.

"Let's go upstairs," Neil tried again.

"I'm not in the mood! I want to move away from this town. If you won't leave your job, I'm going to have to leave you. I can't stay here for the rest of my life. I just can't."

Neil's jaw dropped. Never in their twenty-five-year marriage had his wife ever said she'd leave him. Vivienne looked and felt as shocked as he did to hear these words come out of her own mouth.

"Do you really feel that way?" Neil asked her.

"Yes," she said. "I do. I have for a while. And," she said, deciding she might as well put all her cards on the table, "if I do go, I think Olivia should stay with you. You two actually get along. And I may not like her friends, but she does. She's not going to want to leave them."

"Wow," Neil said. He took several steps back. His face was white.

Vivienne couldn't believe the rush of relief that had come over her. *Wow,* she thought, too, but it was accompanied by an entirely different emotion. The feeling of a thousand pounds of weight lifting from her shoulders. The feeling of freedom and hope and potential. It was so powerful that it drowned out any guilt toward her husband and daughter. It felt, simply, wonderful.

"I can't believe you'd want to leave us," Neil said. His voice sounded hollow and far away. He shook his head.

"But I don't want to leave you," she said. "That's not what I'm saying at all. I just want to be *happy*. And I can't be happy here."

"Okay," Neil said. "Okay, I get it."

"What do you mean by that?"

"I'll quit my job. I really will," he said.

"Are you serious?"

"Yes," he said. "Yes, I mean it. But, I'm going to have to finish up some big projects..."

"No. Stop. Not that again. You always say that."

"Hear me out. I'm taking you seriously, but we still need to have a plan. Okay?"

"Okay. I'm listening," said Vivienne.

"We'd probably want Olivia to finish up the school year as well... We could move this summer. I'm serious. I really mean it this time. Can you wait that long?" he asked her.

"Yes," Vivienne said, tears coming to her eyes. "Of course. If you really mean it. Please don't get my hopes up if you aren't one hundred percent serious."

"I'm serious. Where do you want to move to?"

She shook her head, speechless. "I have no idea," she managed to say.

"Let's talk about it tonight at dinner?" Neil suggested.

Vivienne nodded. "Okay." She smiled through her tears. "I'm assuming we're going out?" she asked. Aside from smoothies and bags of salad, they hardly ever consumed any food in their home.

"Well, of course," Neil.

"I'll get ready."

"Wait," Neil said. He wrapped his arms around her. "I love you so much," he whispered. "I'm sorry we didn't do this sooner."

She hugged him back. "I love you too. Thank you for finally realizing how important this is to me."

He took a step back. "One more thing."

"What's that?" she asked.

"What's with all these jars of beads and things?"

"They're for a little project," she said.

"Since when do you do crafts?" he asked her.

"I don't. I'm going to stick it to the Port Elspeth Ladies' Club."

Neil laughed. "I can't wait to see what that means."

Chapter 6

Audra Fleming

Even for someone with frequent social anxiety issues, Audra couldn't remember the last time she'd been so nervous. She'd spent the entire morning shopping for a new outfit and the entire afternoon doing girlish things she didn't normally bother with, like trying out several colors of nail polish and straightening her naturally-curly hair with a flatiron. When she'd transformed herself into someone Ben probably wouldn't even recognize, she realized she was officially out of time for any more big changes. At five thirty, her doorbell rang. In an embarrassed panic over how hard she'd tried, she removed the four bracelets on her arm, swapped her super-high heels for medium-high heels, pulled her hair back into a school-day ponytail, and opened the door with an impossible-to-hide smile on her face.

"Hi," Ben said. He looked so cute in his jeans and gray sweater. In his arms he held a huge display of flowers. Audra feared she might be dreaming.

Seriously, how is Ben Harrison at my *apartment?* she asked herself. There must have been a glitch in the natural order of things for this encounter to have manifested itself. She'd seen pictures of his gorgeous ex-fiancée. How could he go from someone like that to a tall, thin, bland art teacher like herself? Ben was the kind of guy meant for other girls. Hotter-than-her girls.

"Hi, Ben," she said, finally. The words came after far too long of a pause, but not so long that she'd ruined her chances.

You can bounce back from this! Act normal, she told herself. The inner monologue cheerleading her along was going up against her equally strong desire to close the door in his face. Now that this was happening—this date!—it was so different from seeing him at school. She became painfully self-conscious about her tiny apartment. She wondered if her cat's litter box was clean enough. She suddenly couldn't remember whether she'd put deodorant under both arms or just one.

"These are for you. Obviously," he laughed, handing her the vase of flowers.

"Roses! How lovely," she said. They were a mix of white, pink, peach, and red. This meant either he had *all* the feelings for her or that he'd just grabbed whatever looked pretty. Whichever it was, she'd take it. They were the nicest flowers she'd ever received.

"I'm glad you like them."

"Of course I like them. I love them!" *And you!* cheered the little voice in her head. "Come on in."

Not overthinking it. Not overthinking it. Not overthinking it, she repeated to herself as she set the vase on her countertop and pressed her face to the petals, inhaling.

"You look beautiful," he said.

Beautiful, beautiful, beautiful. It took over, bouncing around in her skull, making her barely able to even nod in reply. "Thank you. You look great, too," she managed to say.

"So. We're going to see Christina in her crazy play," he said.

"Yeah," she laughed.

"Do you know where you'd like to eat first?"

"I have a couple ideas," she said. "Is there anywhere special you were thinking of?"

"I've got a few ideas, too," he said. "We can talk while I'm driving, if you'd like."

"Sure," she said. Then she was grabbing her purse and leading them out into the hallway. She was locking her apartment behind her and zipping up her coat. Smiling. Breathing.

Oh my God, she realized. *I'm doing it! I'm going on a date with Ben Harrison and I'm even behaving like a normal human being! Look at me adjusting my scarf like a regular person.*

"You've probably seen my car before," he said. "I call it The Great White Whale. I hope you can handle driving around in a giant station wagon. It was a hand-me-down from my parents and it just won't die."

"It sounds like you're describing my car," she laughed. "I'm sure I'll love it." Was Ben Harrison actually embarrassed about his car? They'd seen each other's cars parked in the teachers' lot hundreds if not thousands of times. She couldn't believe that now he was embarrassed about his. If only he knew that, in her eyes, he could probably do nothing he'd ever have to apologize for.

"Can I just say again, you look absolutely beautiful," Ben said. "And I know this is supposed to happen at the end of the date, but I've been wanting to do this every time I see you in the teacher's lounge for weeks. Months, probably." And just like that, he stopped, turned to her, wrapped his arms around her, and kissed her.

Just. Like. That.

Chapter 7

Cadence Sommerset

"Ahhh, would you look at that?" Dave Sommerset said to his wife. He gestured out toward the deep blue water and then turned in his chair and blew an emphatic kiss to their sprawling home. "All ours! Luxury and success as far as the eye can see."

"Amazing," Cadence said.

"So, Babe, for dinner tonight I was thinking we could try that place the Humphreys have been talking about." Irving and Marlene Humphrey lived up the road from them about a half a mile. Dave had met them earlier that week when he'd been out for one of his early morning power walks. The Humphreys were in their sixties and were, apparently, a very big deal around Port Elspeth.

"That steakhouse on the water where they light Chinese lanterns every Friday and Saturday night?" Cadence asked him. It was just up the way from them, where the coastline jutted out into the ocean a bit. They'd had the pleasure of watching the little lantern show the week before from their Adirondack chairs, snuggled up with blankets.

"Yeah. I think D'Angelo's is the name of it."

"Sure. That sounds fine." She'd actually been in the mood to stay in and have sandwiches or a frozen pizza since they'd been busy all week entertaining dinner guests.

First the Humphreys, then Dave's new boss and his wife, and then Dave's new business associate and his wife and teenage children (on Valentine's Day!). But, even more than he loved entertaining and showing off his home, Dave loved being seen at fancy places. Especially on the weekends. Cadence had hoped their relocation could make them anonymous, but they'd barely settled in and she already felt the pressure of having to be 'on' at all times. Now she regretted sending out that jewelry party invitation. Even more snooty new people in her life was the last thing she wanted.

"Sweet! I was afraid you were going to be lame and say we should stay home," Dave said. "Why don't you get yourself dolled up. If we leave soon, we'll have time to head into town and see a play."

"A *play*?" Cadence asked.

"Yeah," said Dave. "I saw that the community center is putting on something called..." He picked up his phone and checked his notes to himself. "It's called *Little Johnny Jones* and it's at eight o'clock tonight. We need to start supporting these local events."

"It seems like we've already been doing so much," said Cadence.

"Marlene Humphrey warned us that if you want to do things like take part in that jewelry fair, you have to make connections."

"But I'm already taking part in it. I sent out a notice about it and several people responded. The booth is reserved. I'm already in."

"But they could bump you," said Dave. "Marlene warned you."

"Why would they do that?" asked Cadence.

"Because we're not in Arkansas anymore. It takes more than buying the right house and my having the right job. We need to fit in with the right people. On that note,

I'm going to join the Port Elspeth Men's Club and I think you should apply for the Women's Club."

Cadence sighed. "I'm guessing they both cost a lot."

"We'll make it up in connections," Dave promised.

"I'm not even sure that makes sense to me."

"We can talk about this more at dinner. Quietly. Why don't you wear your black dress? You always look so pretty in that."

"Okay," Cadence said.

"One more thing, Babe."

"What's that?"

"No wine for you. If we're going to get serious about making a baby, we need you to be healthy. Right?"

"You're joking."

"I'm serious," he said. "Sometimes when you drink, you act like a fool."

"Doesn't everyone?"

"I don't," he said.

"Is it a health thing or am I embarrassing you?"

"It's a health thing," he assured her, "since we're trying to start a family."

"Then you should quit drinking, too," said Cadence. "So your sperm stay sharp."

Dave laughed. "You got me, Babe. Fine. I'll lay off on talking about your drinking. For now. But the second you're pregnant, you'll stop. Right?"

"Of course," Cadence said. "And I'm not at all insulted that you'd expect otherwise from me." She got up and headed toward their bedroom to get ready for the date she'd rather not go on, already having decided she'd be wearing her green dress, not her black dress, that evening.

Chapter 8

Audra Fleming

"Front row seats?" Audra asked, aghast.

"That's right," Ben said. "So we won't miss a minute of the action."

"The tickets must have cost at least twelve dollars apiece, considering the more desirable, farther-away-from-Christina tickets were thirty dollars each," she joked. Ben was so charming and funny that she had relaxed enough to break out of her shell a little bit.

"You're pretty funny," he said.

She beamed and shrugged modestly. Did guys like funny girls? He seemed to.

"I guess I ought to explain," he said to her. "Christina arranged for us to be in the front row. She was so excited that we were coming to see her tonight that she got an upgrade for us."

Not so excited that we *were coming to see her, so excited that* you *were coming to see her tonight,* Audra thought. She didn't really care, though, whether or not Christina was going to be happy to see her. As far as she was concerned, this was only her and Ben's night.

"An upgrade. That was sweet of her," she said. All through dinner, she'd temporarily forgotten that they were going to be watching Christina singing and prancing around the stage, and not just going to some random play or movie.

But she wasn't about to let anything that might happen during the second half of the evening take away from what was shaping up to be a perfect date.

She and Ben had shared a pizza and bottle of wine at a cozy little café. Talking together had been easy. They'd chatted about things going on at school, their families, stories from college. They'd laughed at each other's jokes and he hadn't checked his phone once. (Audra had been on just one other date in the past year, and she'd felt like a third wheel to her date's phone.) After dinner, she and Ben had made two stops on their way to the theatre—one for after-dinner truffles at a candy shop, and a second stop in a doorway to make out for a few minutes. Nothing could turn this evening in any direction other than perfect.

They settled into the red velvet seats of the old theatre. Everywhere they looked were chandeliers and sconces.

"Port Elspeth really *is* nicer than Middleford, isn't it?" said Audra.

"It's the Eagleton to our Pawnee," he agreed.

"I loved *Parks and Recreation!*" she exclaimed. "I never missed an episode." Now she felt like they had a topic to make endless inside jokes about. Their connections were quickly multiplying and strengthening their bond. She got a little jittery thinking about it.

"Port Elspeth might be a little fancier, but Middleford's got its own wholesome charm that's worth exploring," said Ben. He put his arm around her shoulder.

"Excuse me, but I think you're in our seats," said a short beefy-looking fellow with a Southern drawl.

"Do you mean these seats?" Ben asked him.

"Yes, sir. My tickets say A-7 and A-8. And you and your ladyfriend are sitting in A-7 and A-8. We got four butts and two seats." The small blonde woman beside him looked mortified. She brushed a loose curl from her face with her hand, the sparkling swish of a giant diamond catching the light. She and her stocky, muscle-bound husband were both extremely dressed up. More than anyone else in the entire theatre.

"I'm a little confused," said Ben. "If you don't mind, I'll just check my email. I'm sure I was told that these are our seats."

"You don't need to check your email, my friend," said the man. "I've got the proof right here." He held up two tickets, each clearly displaying the seat numbers A-7 and A-8. His smiling face abruptly turned menacing as he leaned in closer to Ben. "If we spend much more time talking about this, we're going to start cutting into other folks' enjoyment of this fine evening. I hate to make a scene. The curtain's going to go up anytime. You and your ladyfriend need to leave now."

"Sweetie, please," the man's wife said to him.

"I'm sorry," Ben said to Audra.

"It's okay. It's not your fault," she said. Honestly, she'd rather do anything else with Ben than watch Christina's play.

"Excuse us for the misunderstanding," Ben said to the man.

As he and Audra walked away, they could hear the man talking to his wife about how they were freeloaders and had been trying to watch the play without paying for it.

"I swear to you, that's not what happened," Ben whispered to Audra as they shuffled past everyone in the dim theatre.

"I know," she whispered back.

"I'm so embarrassed," he said.

"Don't be! I really just want to spend time with you.".

"Should we talk to the guy at the ticket counter?" Ben asked when they'd reached the lobby. "After all, I *did* purchase tickets, but I left them at home. Once Christina told me we were upgraded to better seats, I figured she'd done whatever she needed to do for them to be aware of it and not sell them to someone else."

"I actually bought tickets, too," Audra admitted. "I thought *I* was taking *you*. But once you told me *you* were taking *me*, I left my tickets at home too."

"It kind of feels like seeing this play wasn't meant to be," said Ben.

"For sure! To buy four tickets and still get kicked out of our seats?"

"We could go back to Middleford and go to a movie," said Ben.

"You must have read my mind," said Audra. "That sounds wonderful. Let's go!"

Tuesday, February 20, 2018

The Inaugural Meeting

Chapter 9

Cadence Sommerset

"I'm so nervous," Cadence said to Dave.

"What do you have to be nervous about?" he replied. "We've got the best house in the whole area, I have a great job, you can look right out our window and see the ocean. If that doesn't tell people we've made it, I don't know what does. We're the beautiful people. What's that saying? 'The sun always shines on us.' And it's true. Just look," he said, grinning and gesturing out at the sparkling ocean.

Don't, don't, don't... Cadence silently willed him.

And then, as she'd been afraid he was going to do, he blew the ocean a kiss. It had become his trademark move. "Mmmmmuh!" he said. "I love it!"

"It *is* beautiful," she agreed.

"It sure as hell is! What could you possibly have to worry about?"

"I don't know. Just... all kinds of things," Cadence said, not mentioning that everything he'd just listed that she should feel confident about related to him and his well-paying job.

"Like what?"

"Well," she said, "Like, do you think red and white wine will be enough, or might these ladies be expecting cocktails as well?"

"Wine's enough. You bought the good stuff, right?"

"I don't know. I tried. I picked bottles that were twenty dollars or more like you taught me to do."

"Good girl. What else are you worried about?"

"I'm wondering how they're going to feel about my Arkansas accent."

"Heck, I don't think we hardly have accents."

"Really, Dave? I think we do."

"There's nothing you can do about how you talk, so quit worrying about it."

"Okay. Do you think I'm going to be stylish enough?

"Just be yourself," said Dave.

"I'm not sure that I know who that is," Cadence said.

"What are you talking about?" Dave asked. He looked seriously unamused.

"Never mind." Cadence flipped the switch to turn on the outside lights. Her entire front yard became a flickering sea of gold. "Everyone's going to be here in five minutes. This isn't the time for a serious conversation."

"What you just said sounded anything but serious. It sounded *stupid*."

"Shhhhh," she said to him.

"Don't shush me!" he said. "A woman ought to know better than to shush her husband. It's disrespectful."

"I only did it because I'm afraid someone's going to show up right now and hear you talking to me like that."

"I can talk to my own wife in my own home however I please," he said.

"I know," she said, smiling and doing her best to diffuse the rapidly-escalating situation as quickly as possible. "I know, Sweetie. And I know you're just teasing, but I've noticed people are more formal here. Husbands don't make comments like that to their wives."

"*Now* what are you trying to say?"

"That people from around here might not get that you're joking. They might not think it's funny."

"Then you shouldn't make comments about how you don't even know who you *are*. As far as I'm concerned, that's grounds for an argument."

The doorbell rang.

"Would you like to meet everyone?" Cadence asked him.

"No. I'll go downstairs and watch a movie. If it turns out anyone high caliber is in attendance at your little soiree, let me know and next time you do this I'll hand out some artichoke dip." Dave got up from his chair and went through the kitchen to escape to his media room.

Cadence took one last look around, decided that everything looked perfect, and answered the front door. A woman who looked like she was in her sixties or seventies stood on the wide front porch. Beside her was a thin, elegant woman with short dark hair and a beautiful, worldly look that Cadence was immediately intimidated by. The woman was wearing a camel-colored coat over a striped t-shirt and worn-in skinny jeans. Her lips were bright red, but otherwise she appeared to be wearing no makeup at all. She looked like she was about thirty or thirty-five.

"You must be Pearl and Margo," said Cadence.

"That's right. I'm Pearl and this is my daughter Margo. Nice to meet you, Cadence," said the older woman.

"Come on in," Cadence said. "Let me take your coats. They'll be right here in this front closet. Please help yourselves to some drinks and snacks from the buffet."

Her entire dining room, which was adjacent to the foyer where they stood, was loaded up with buckets of chilling wine, platters of cheese and fruit, and slices of smoked meats formed into tiny seashells. There was enough food for thirty people. Pearl and Margo got right down to business filling up their plates.

Two more cars pulled into Cadence's driveway. One was a white beat-up Subaru Outback. The other was a Mercedes-Benz GLS. The Mercedes looked exactly like her own. Something told her that Dave was going to be interested in its owner.

Seconds later, a perfectly-coiffed woman who looked to be a well-maintained fifty years old or so got out. The passenger door opened and a miserable-looking teenager with scraggly green hair stepped out of her side.

"What an unlikely pair," Cadence murmured to herself.

The driver of the Subaru was a blur through her fogged-up windshield. Cadence could just make out the silhouette of her chatting animatedly on her phone.

"Olivia, I need you to behave yourself tonight," Cadence heard the driver of the Mercedes say through gritted teeth to her teenage companion.

"I don't even understand why you brought me here," said the teenager.

"Because I cannot trust you," the woman sing-songed to her daughter. By this point they'd just about reached Cadence's front step. The woman stuck out her hand. "Vivienne Van Heusen-Prescott," she announced to Cadence. "And this is my daughter Olivia. What a beautiful home you have!"

"Thank you," Cadence said.

"We're on the water, too. Just a couple miles down the road," Vivienne quickly explained.

"Wonderful!" said Cadence. "It's so nice to meet you both. Won't you both please come inside?"

Just then the door of the Subaru opened and a tall woman with a bright pink stocking cap stepped out. She was still chatting on her phone. She looked ecstatically happy. Cadence could barely remember a time in her life when she'd felt as light or joyful as this young woman looked.

"Help?" Vivienne said.

"Excuse me?" Cadence asked, momentarily thinking Vivienne was suffering from some kind of medical calamity.

"Is she here to help with your party?" Vivienne asked, nodding toward the young woman in the pink hat.

"No," Cadence said, still standing in the open doorway, waiting for the young woman to finish her call and come up to the door. It would have felt rude to close the door on her, but it felt just as awkward to hover here, waiting, when she was clearly in the middle of a consuming conversation. "I believe she's one of the guests. I think she must be Audra."

"How many people will be attending this meeting tonight?" Vivienne asked, taking off her coat and handing it to Cadence.

"Well," Cadence said, "I only received a handful of RSVPs, but you never know if more people decide to show up."

"Did any Mortensons respond?" Vivienne asked Cadence. Before Cadence could answer, Vivienne pivoted to her daughter and barked, "Olivia, take your coat off. You're going to overheat like a popcorn kernel and get sick if you keep it on."

"Mom, I'm taking it off. Jeez! And please stop grilling her," Olivia said.

Cadence gave up on waiting for the woman in the pink hat. She closed the door, hung up Vivienne and Olivia's coats in her front closet, and walked over to the dining room where Pearl and Margo were each piling designer paper plates with olive tapenade, cubes of Gruyère, and gluten-free crackers.

"Pearl and Margo," she called brightly to them, "we've got another mother and daughter pair here for you to meet. These are Vivienne and Olivia Van Heusen-Prescott."

"My last name is just Prescott," Olivia said.

"Pleased to meet you both," Vivienne said robotically to Pearl and Margo. Her expression gave away that she was already bored of them.

The final guest, finished with her phone conversation, rang the doorbell and Cadence answered it, happy to escape from the intensity of Vivienne. The young woman wore a colorful ski jacket and a purple and blue ikat print scarf. She looked puzzlingly familiar to Cadence. By the process of elimination, Cadence knew this must be Audra Fleming, the art teacher from Middleford. But why did it seem that they'd already met? Cadence had never even been to Middleford. And why would someone who looked so happy and friendly evoke a feeling of embarrassment and dread in the pit of Cadence's stomach?

"Welcome," Cadence said to her. "You must be Audra."

"That's right. Nice to meet you, Cadence..." Audra's voice trailed off. It appeared she also recognized Cadence.

"I'm sorry that I can't remember where we've met before, but I'm sure I know you from somewhere," Cadence said. "I'm new to Port Elspeth and I've met so many people lately that I can barely keep them all straight. Have I seen you at the Java Junction on Emory Road?"

"No," Audra said.

"Were you getting your hair cut next to me at City Trends Salon last week?"

"No," Audra said, "it was the play."

"The play?" asked Cadence. And then it dawned on her. "Oh. Oh, no! That was you and your boyfriend who were sitting in our seats. That was *such* an embarrassing incident. I'm so sorry... Wait, why are you smiling even more now?"

Audra sighed. "Because you just called Ben Harrison my boyfriend. And it's true. He is."

Cadence smiled. She'd been expecting a much worse reaction. "Can I take your coat?" she asked.

"Sure," Audra said, still smiling.

"Come on in," said Cadence, "and help yourself to some snacks from the buffet."

Chapter 10

Cadence Sommerset

Forty-five minutes later, the six women ranging in age from sixteen to seventy-three were all seated around Cadence's kitchen table, chatting and enjoying the elaborate snacks Cadence had spent most of her afternoon laboring over. The table was covered with spools of thread and wire, tiny tools, and thousands of beads. Cadence couldn't help noticing that Vivienne, in particular, had really contributed to the stash of supplies. She, alone, had brought enough supplies for their small group to make hundreds of items to sell.

"Thank you all for joining me," Cadence said. Despite being nearly maxed-out on socializing, this group didn't feel nearly as snooty or intimidating to her as the people Dave kept inviting over. Vivienne seemed tightly-wound, but everyone else at the table had a laidback attitude that felt like a breath of fresh air. Pearl was a riot. Cadence had expected Olivia to be a sullen, snotty teenager, but she was actually quite sweet and silly as well. Cadence wondered why her own mother didn't see any charm in her.

"Thanks for arranging this," Margo said. "And for all the wonderful food."

"Oh, of course," said Cadence. Margo was so sophisticated that every time she spoke, Cadence got a little flustered and had to refocus. She wasn't intimidating like Vivienne or the Humphreys, though. They seemed like they *wanted* to be seen as superior, whereas Margo came across as humble and friendly yet of a different league.

"I hope I have something to add to this," Pearl said. "I think whatever jewelry I create we might have to pay people to take off our hands."

"It's not hard at all," Audra said. "You'll see. We'll all be making beautiful jewelry in no time."

"This is fun," said Olivia. "It's so much better than hanging out in my room alone."

"As if you ever hang out in your room alone," Vivienne said crisply, glaring at her daughter.

"So," said Cadence, after everyone had gotten a chance to try some food and chat a little, "I'm not a very artistic person, but I've always wanted to be, so I figured it was time to go for it. I'm so glad you've all decided to join me. And it looks like most of y'all have some experience crafting your own jewelry. We're going to have a great time!"

"Cheers to that," said Pearl, holding up her glass of wine. The ladies all toasted, but all Cadence could think was *Y'all! How could I have said y'all?* And when she was making such an effort to not talk with her Arkansas drawl.

"You'd think since I'm an art teacher that I'd get my fill of these kinds of activities during the day," said Audra, "but my students are too little for this type of thing. These are the kinds of projects I dream of doing!"

"Audra, since you're the self-professed *expert* of the group, why don't you take the lead on teaching us what to do," Vivienne said, in a haughty, showy voice. Cadence saw Olivia roll her eyes in embarrassment.

"I wasn't trying to steal the show," said Audra, "but I'm happy to teach you all what I know. We could start with some simple dangly earrings. Maybe a practice pair or two. Lord knows, we have enough materials here to make some mistakes along the way." She poured out a small plastic bag filled with the pre-made wire portion of earrings. She grabbed a couple pairs of matching beads in graduated sizes, a tiny pair of pliers, and a spool of wire, and as everyone watched, she fashioned the bits and pieces into a perfectly-matched pair of dangly earrings. It only took her about four or five minutes.

"Amazing," Cadence said. "I can't believe you just turned those little parts into a gorgeous pair of earrings."

"Here, a gift for the hostess," Audra said, dropping them into Cadence's palm.

Cadence put them on and admired her reflection using the mirror app on her phone. "Nice!" she said.

"If we had all this stuff," Olivia said to her mother, "how come we never used it before? I could have been making earrings with Ada and Lila all the time."

"Would you quit interrupting everyone?" Vivienne said to her daughter. "If you're going to come along to grown-up functions like this with me, you need to behave like an adult."

Everyone else at the table exchanged a look of shared discomfort.

"I think what we want to do," Margo suggested brightly, clearly trying to change the subject, "is to come up with a fun name for our booth and design a logo for it. All the jewelry we make can have a tag on it with our booth's name. It will make it more like a little shop."

"That's a great idea," Cadence said.

"If you'll all trust me to do it, I think I can handle designing something for us," said Margo. "I have a lot of graphic design experience and plenty of time on my hands right now. It'll be a good way for me to keep busy."

"Sure," Cadence, Olivia, and Audra all said in unison. Vivienne didn't respond, but she had a look on her face like she had something to say.

"What should we call our booth?" asked Pearl.

"It needs to be the perfect name," said Vivienne.

"How about Just Jewelry?" Audra suggested.

Vivienne shook her head emphatically. "No, no, no," she said to Audra. Then she turned to Margo and said, "Before you start willy-nilly designing some logo, you need to have a plan that we've all agreed on. You can't design a logo if you don't even know what we're going to call our booth."

"Oh, of course. I agree," said Margo.

"It's really important to me that we get this entire project done right," said Vivienne, now addressing mainly Cadence.

"Mmm hmmm," Cadence replied.

"You don't know me yet," Vivienne continued, seeming to be speaking only to Cadence, "but if I'm going to be associated with something, it has to be done right."

"I think we all agree that we want to have a nice booth," Cadence said.

"Not just nice. Great," said Vivienne. "We need to have the very best booth. You're new to Port Elspeth, so you don't really understand how it works. You probably think I sound a little fussy."

"Oh, no! Not at all," said Cadence. *You sound downright nuts,* she thought to herself.

"But," Vivienne continued, "you're going to learn fast that the reason Port Elspeth is as picture-perfect as it is, is because everyone who's anyone thinks like this."

"Like what?" Audra asked, genuinely looking confused.

"Everyone here has high standards!" Vivienne said, her tone verging on a shriek. "Everyone here always does their best. They never settle. So, please, tell me that you all agree we're going to have the *very best* booth."

"We'll all try to do our best," Pearl assured her.

Vivienne smiled tightly and shook her head. It was clear to Cadence that she was working hard to calm herself back down. "That doesn't sound very convincing," she said softly, her tone deliberate and measured, a zany smile temporarily forcing her grimace to the shadows. "Some of you are new to town, so you may not be aware that Port Elspeth is a city of achievers."

"And we'll all do our best," Cadence said firmly, but trying to sound reasonable and encouraging. She reached out and patted Vivienne's hand—it was the kind of thing that one of her old friends back in Springwater would have done if another friend was upset—and Vivienne yanked her hand away as if she'd been bitten by a snake. Cadence felt her cheeks flush hotly in embarrassment over the public rejection.

"Estelle Mortenson-Aul lives up the road from me," said Vivienne. No one else at the table looked particularly impressed by this. Cadence suspected no one even knew who Estelle Mortenson-Aul was. "She *always* has a booth at the craft fair. She sells her miniature oil paintings. Her booth is called *Pastoral Scenes by Estelle*. So, there's an idea."

"If we were selling farm scenes and our name was Estelle," said Olivia.

"Would you knock it off?" Vivienne said to her daughter. She turned back to the others, again, focusing mainly on Cadence, and said, "Estelle's niece Phoebe Mortenson-Jones and her daughters are always there selling their family's secret-recipe caramel corn," said Vivienne, "and they call their booth Corny Candy."

"I used to baby-sit for those Jones kids," Olivia said sadly. "They were actually nice back when they were babies."

"I went to high school with Phoebe," said Margo. "I'd rather not see her again. I suppose I'm going to have to face a lot of people from my past at this fundraiser."

"So you and your mother *are* from around here," said Vivienne, a look of newfound interest in Margo and Pearl coming over her face. Just as quickly though, her expression soured back up as she let what Margo had just said sink in. "But you're not interested in the Mortensons?" she added.

"I'm really not," said Margo.

"You don't like seeing people from your past?" Cadence asked. She couldn't imagine why someone who seemed as kind and personable as Margo wouldn't want to keep in touch with old friends, or why they wouldn't want to keep in touch with her.

"I didn't have much in common with the people from around here. When I graduated I went off to college in Chicago, and then when I was twenty-four I moved to Paris. I lived there for just over ten years. I've only been back since a couple of weeks ago."

"Paris," Cadence breathed. She and Dave had been there once. She'd loved it, but they'd fought the entire time. He'd been disgusted by everything from the food to the cigarettes to the toilets that cost a few coins to use and the dog poop no one seemed to ever pick up after. When she'd tried to speak to shop owners and people and their hotel staff in French—after all, she'd minored in it in college— he'd told her to knock it off because she was embarrassing herself. "Their English is better than your French, so why make the effort?" he'd reasoned. He'd been too busy looking down at everything to find one nice thing to say about it. After how badly it had gone, Cadence was fairly certain she'd never get to return there.

"When Margo was growing up, we didn't have the money to afford all the local country clubs and sailing clubs that are such a big part of living here in Port Elspeth," Pearl explained to Vivienne. "And, anyway, none of my husbands were into the social scene," she added.

Olivia snorted in laughter over Pearl's casual mention of 'none of her husbands.' Her mother shot her a dirty look.

"I was married four times," Pearl explained.

"You had four chances and married someone poor every time?" Vivienne laughed.

"It wasn't just that we were poor that I didn't fit in," Margo said, coming to her mother's defense. "It's because I'm a lesbian. The snobby kids gave me such a hard time about it. I just wanted to grow up and move away." She laughed rather nervously. "I'm almost talking myself out of being back here."

"People change as they get older," Cadence said, trying to ignore the look of horror on Vivienne's face.

Vivienne pushed her chair back a few inches from the table and took a deep breath. She began clawing at a hive that had popped up on her cheek.

"At that time, people weren't ready to accept that I'm a lesbian," Margo continued. Every time she said the word 'lesbian,' Cadence saw Vivienne's right eyebrow tic up. "I remember teachers telling me that I was going through a phase and advising me to keep it to myself. I never wanted to lie about who I was, though. Even if it held me back, I had to be honest about being gay."

Vivienne now had hives on her forehead and neck as well. She couldn't seem to figure out which to scratch first.

"I'm sure it wasn't that," Pearl said, coming back to her daughter's defense. "Not taking part in all those clubs was probably what made it hard for you to make friends."

"I really was an outcast," Margo said. "The only club I was ever in was Drawing Club."

"Hey! That's the one club I'm in!" Olivia exclaimed.

"Would you please excuse us?" Vivienne said, standing up. The small array of beads she'd selected went rolling over the table edge and bouncing away across Cadence's polished wood floor. Vivienne didn't bother pretending to care. "I just remembered that my daughter and I have somewhere else we're supposed to be," she said to Cadence.

"We do? Where's that?" Olivia asked.

"I'm so sorry to dash off like this," Vivienne said, already on her way to the front door. "Our coats were in this closet here? Yes? Oh, here they are. Olivia, chop chop! Put those pliers down and get moving. Now. Time to go."

"Would you like to take your materials with you?" Cadence asked, following after Vivienne and trying to downplay her shock. None of the other guests followed after them to see Vivienne and Olivia out.

"No," said Vivienne. "You can hold onto it. I have plenty more at home."

"All of it? Are you sure? There's so much."

"No, that's really not that much," Vivienne said, stuffing her arm into the wrong sleeve and trying to put on her upside-down coat. "What the heck?" she muttered to herself.

"It's upside down, Mom," Olivia said.

"Oh, of course. Silly me," she said, putting it on the right way.

"Are you coming back next week?" Cadence asked.

"I don't think I can. I just remembered something's also going on then. I have *such* a busy social calendar," Vivienne said to Cadence before turning to her daughter and snapping, "Olivia, put your coat on. Now. We need to go!"

"Then I insist you take your things back. I can't keep all of it. There must be hundreds of dollars' worth of beads and tools here," said Cadence.

"Use them for your booth."

"Are you sure?"

Vivienne nodded aggressively and then called out in a ridiculously sweet voice that echoed through Cadence's two-story foyer, "Nice to meet you all! You were all dolls!" She then turned back to Cadence and told her, "Lovely smoked turkey conch shells. From Divinity Fine Foods? I love those. Buh-byeee."

"No, I did all of them myself," Cadence said softly as the door closed behind Vivienne and her daughter and the foyer stood empty, save for one small rolling red bead.

Chapter 11

The Jewelry Makers

"I think I got them all. I'm used to picking up after upset children," Audra joked as she stood up and brushed off her knees with her left hand. In the palm of her right hand were Vivienne's runaway beads. "What the heck was that all about?" she added.

"I'm not sure," Cadence admitted. She'd picked up a couple more bottles of wine as she'd passed back through the dining room. She set them on the kitchen table in front of her guests. "But I guess now there's more room for the rest of us to work and more wine for us to share."

"I think it was my saying I'm gay," said Margo. "I didn't realize anyone in this town didn't already know that about me, or that anyone would even care."

"I'm sure that wasn't it," said Cadence, although it had certainly seemed to be the trigger to Vivienne's sudden need to exit.

"Actually," Pearl said, "I think Vivienne Prescott might be fighting some of her own demons that have nothing to do with what's happening here tonight."

Margo looked over at her mother and gave her an 'Are you sure you want to go there?' look that Pearl promptly dismissed with a little shrug and a wry smile. Pearl Quincy loved her gossip. She always had.

"I didn't realize you knew her that well," Margo said to her mother.

"I don't know her *well*, but I know *of* her," said Pearl. "She and her family used to be all over town. I'd see her face in the newspaper and on the cover of *Port Elspeth Ladies Quarterly*. Then, about five years ago, everything changed. I guess you don't remember this, Margo, since you were living in Paris at the time."

Cadence inadvertently sighed again and whispered, "Paris."

"And," Pearl continued, addressing Audra and Cadence, "you two wouldn't know this since you're not from Port Elspeth, but it was quite the scandal about town. Vivienne's son Oliver was a senior in high school. He was dating a girl named Evangeline Maddingly…"

"Oh, Evangeline Maddingly," Margo said, instantly understanding where the story was going. Even in Paris, she'd seen the news from her old contacts on Facebook about Oliver Prescott and Evangeline Maddingly's shocking, untimely deaths.

"Who's Evangeline Maddingly?" Cadence asked, sensing she was someone important.

"She was the youngest daughter of a very, very wealthy family in town," said Pearl. "The Mattingly family's ancestors were some of the original founders of this town. You know that big house about two or three miles out of town? The tall brown Colonial house with the cedar shake shingle siding?"

"I know which one you mean," said Cadence. She and Dave had just driven past it a couple days earlier. It was perched high on a cliff east of town, overlooking both Port Elspeth and the rocky coastline far below. It was hard to miss it.

"That was their house," said Pearl.

"They don't live in Port Elspeth any longer?" asked Audra.

"No," said Pearl. "They moved away right after everything happened. It was too devastating, I suppose, for them to want to stick around here any longer." She leaned in toward the other three women around the table and told them, "The Prescott boy and Evangeline Mattingly had been dating for a year or two. From what I've heard, though, they'd been close friends ever since childhood. I think Vivienne may have been friends with Evangeline's mother, as well. Oliver and Evangeline were both about seventeen or eighteen years old, and they were both about to graduate from high school and go on to college…"

"Wait, wait," said Audra. "I really need to picture them. What did they look like?"

"Evangeline was beautiful," said Pearl. "She had long, dark, wavy hair and bright blue eyes. Her picture was on everything all summer from the time she went missing, so it's hard to forget. I don't remember much about the Prescott kid. I guess you could just picture his mother, but as a young man."

Margo snorted. "Oh, Mom."

"I'll look her up," said Cadence, pulling out her phone and googling the young woman. Evangeline's senior picture popped up immediately along with tragic headlines Cadence chose to ignore, in honor of the story Pearl was clearly enjoying telling. Cadence held up the phone to show Evangeline's photo to Margo and Audra.

"How sad," said Audra. "She looks so young and sweet."

"Back to the story," said Pearl. "These two kids had been going out for a while, and it was getting to be time for them to go on to college. Evangeline had gotten into Harvard—everyone in the Maddingly family went there— but the Prescott kid wasn't getting accepted anywhere. Apparently, he'd been goofing off at school for years and just about flunked out of all his classes, and he'd lied to his parents. They believed he was doing great. A real golden child. I guess the school had some way for the parents to have been logging in and checking up on him, but Vivienne and her husband had trusted him. They'd never even bothered to log in. He started telling everyone he was going to go to Harvard too. His parents believed him and were all excited about it, only he hadn't been accepted anywhere."

"Uh oh," said Cadence.

"The Prescotts went so far as to throw their son and Evangeline a joint-graduation party. I have no idea how it went this far. Again, I only know what I've read in the papers and overheard at the grocery store. The graduation party was Harvard-themed. They went all out. They even dyed their swimming pool water crimson red, in honor of Harvard. They invited all the local teachers, and that's when everything fell apart. Well, the first round of falling apart, anyway. Things, of course, got much, much worse later."

"More wine, please," Audra whispered, enthralled in the story, not taking her eyes off Pearl. Cadence passed one of the open bottles of Merlot around the table.

"You can imagine," Pearl continued, "how embarrassing and disappointing it was for the Prescotts to discover that their son wasn't going to Harvard. That, in fact, he wasn't going to college at all."

"Ugh! Horrible," said Cadence.

"How could the Prescotts have believed Oliver was going to Harvard when they must not have filled out any paperwork or done any kind of official business relating to his enrollment?" asked Margo.

"I guess maybe they figured it was all going to happen that summer," said Pearl.

"Sometimes people believe what they want to believe," said Cadence.

"The graduation party was just the beginning. It was the catalyst for everything else that soon followed," said Pearl. She was trying to look somber and serious, but the sparkle in her eyes gave her away. She was so clearly in her element, loving being able to dish out all this juicy news to a captive, listening audience.

"I can't get over dying the pool red," said Audra.

"From what I've heard," said Pearl, "Oliver didn't even really graduate from high school."

"Then why did his parents have that graduation party for him?" asked Audra.

"I'm sure the party was already planned long before graduation," said Pearl, "and I've heard that the school let him wear his graduation cap and gown like everyone else, and they let him walk in the ceremony. They even handed him an empty diploma case, with the understanding that he'd retake the classes he was failing at summer school. Not that that ever happened."

"Wild," Margo said, as she passed a clumpy-looking necklace to her mother. "Can you fix this?" she whispered.

"I'll try," said Pearl, adding some more beads to it and making it look a little worse.

"Maybe these will help dress it up a little," said Cadence, threading some old buttons on it.

"I think it needs more pearls," Margo said, taking charge again.

Audra quietly sat back, like she did with her kindergarteners, biting her tongue and letting them find their way.

"So, he didn't go to summer school," Margo said. "Then what happened?"

"Well," said Pearl, but she was interrupted by Cadence's cellphone vibrating. It was sitting right in the middle of the table since she'd just used it to look up Evangeline Maddingly. Dave's texts began flying in, bold and clear, for everyone to see:

Movie is over. Those jewelry hags still there?? You gonna make me hide out down here all night?

Anyone of our caliber show up tonight?

Make me some pizza rolls and bring 'em down when you get a minute. Wasted night! Movie was stupid.

"My, he's a fast texter," Cadence said, reaching across the table to grab her phone. "And such a joker," she added.

"I didn't realize we displaced your husband," Pearl said. "He's more than welcome to join us!"

"That is, if we're of the right caliber," Margo added, smiling sweetly.

"I guess it *is* coming up on ten o'clock," Cadence said.

"Ten o'clock? I haven't been up later than nine in years. Where did the time go?"

"I promise I'll take better control of the class next time," joked Audra.

"I don't mind if we don't get much done, as long as I get one new jewelry item to add to my collection each time we meet," Cadence joked, tossing her head to show off her new earrings Audra had made.

"I really *can* control an art class," Audra laughed. "We'll have heaps of jewelry made before you know it."

Pearl stood up. "Alright, then. Let's call it a night. Cadence, Audra, it was lovely to meet you both. I'm already looking forward to our next meeting."

"But what about the rest of the story?" asked Cadence.

"I'll tell you all the rest next time we meet," said Pearl. "Because you really haven't heard anything yet."

Wednesday, February 21, 2018

The Next Morning

Chapter 12

Audra Fleming

"I still can't believe I got you two losers front row seats to my play, yet somehow you didn't even manage to see it," Christina pouted.

It was ten o'clock in the morning and Audra, Ben, Christina, and Sandra were back in the teacher's lounge, enjoying a break since all their students were taking part in an in-school safety demonstration with the local fire department.

"We'll come to your next play," Ben promised. He sneaked a quick look at Audra and rolled his eyes in exasperation. His arm was around Audra's shoulder and he gave her a little squeeze. They'd gone public with their relationship that Monday. As far as Audra could tell, everyone except Christina seemed happy for them.

Audra gave Ben's knee a little return squeeze that was meant to say, "No kidding! She drives me crazy too!" She couldn't believe how connected to him she felt. Dating Ben was like waking up and finding out she'd married some famous movie star and was now part of his amazing life, and having everyone accept it as normal. She had no idea how she'd gotten so lucky.

Ben glanced at his watch and gave her another squeeze before standing up. "I've got to make a quick call before the next drill starts again," he told Audra.

"Okay," she said, missing him already.

"So," Sandra said to Audra after Ben had left the lounge, "did you decide whether you're going to join that jewelry making group or not?"

"I joined it," Audra said. "In fact, the first meeting was last night."

"How was it?" Sandra asked.

"Pretty interesting. We didn't get much done in the way of actually making jewelry, but I did learn a lot of fascinating local gossip."

"Now you've piqued my interest," said Sandra. "What were they saying about my sweet little town?"

"Does the name Evangeline Maddingly mean anything to you?" Audra asked.

The color drained from Sandra's face. "Of course," she said quietly. "Everyone knows about the Maddingly tragedy." Her voice trailed off as she stood up to make herself another cup of tea.

"*I* don't," said Christina. "Somebody please fill me in."

"It's a terrible story," said Sandra, her back to them as she fussed with her tea.

"Great!" said Christina. "I can't wait to hear it."

Sandra turned back around to face Audra and Christina. She sighed, crossed her arms over her chest, and then picked up her mug and took a drink of tea while they all stared at her expectantly and waited. She then turned back around to fiddle with the sugar bowl on the countertop.

Christina quickly got bored with Sandra's unwillingness to talk. "Audra," she said, "*you* fill us in on what you know if Sandra won't."

"From what I learned last night," said Audra, "Evangeline Maddingly was a beautiful young woman from one of Port Elspeth's wealthiest families. She was about to graduate from high school, but something happened with her and her boyfriend, and—I didn't get the whole story yet—but it sounds like they both ended up dead."

Sandra spun around. "That's not the story at all. *Three* people ended up dead, not just two. And Evangeline Maddingly wasn't the victim. Not at all. If anyone should be blamed, it's her. Everything that happened was her fault."

Just then the fire alarm went off.

"Oh, God! Not this again," Christina moaned. She stuffed her feet back into her scuffed high heels that she'd kicked off beside the love seat she was sitting on.

"It's just another drill, let's skip it," Audra said. She stayed planted on the couch. She wanted to hear what else Sandra had to say.

"We'd better go," said Sandra. "Come on," she said. They'd all received clear instructions ahead of time to take part in the drills as though they were real events. Sandra pointed out the window to where Ben was hurrying toward the school's meeting point. "Your man's on the move," she told Audra.

"My man," Audra said with a smile.

Christina just shook her head contemptuously.

"I need to hear the rest of this," Audra told Sandra as they exited the teacher's lounge. Through the windows in the hall they were walking down, she saw Ben standing under the flagpole, right where he was supposed to be. She liked that he'd rushed out there. It made her trust him and feel safe with him. He was ridiculously attractive but not too cool to play by the rules. She couldn't help feeling flushed with excitement and happiness over her good fortune and the rush of falling in love.

"I shouldn't even be talking about it," said Sandra to Audra as they made their way outside.

"Why not?" asked Audra.

"Because it's wrong to speak of the dead like this."

"Okay," Audra said, thinking that sounded kind of superstitious coming from a science teacher.

"Not to mention, I only know what I've heard. I'm just repeating gossip. I never even knew Evangeline Maddingly or that Prescott kid. I might be from Port Elspeth, but that's not the crowd I'm in with."

"Okay," said Audra. "But, just so you know, I like gossip." She smiled at Sandra and Sandra's pensive look softened a little.

"I do too," Christina said. "Really, who doesn't?"

"How'd your jewelry club ladies get on that topic anyway?" Sandra asked Audra. "It seems like kind of a negative topic for people who'd all just met one another."

"One of the women who was there last night is Oliver Prescott's mother," said Audra.

"No! You're kidding," Sandra said as she, Christina, and Audra all lined up out in the part of the parking lot where teachers who didn't have a homeroom were supposed to go.

"Seriously," said Audra, catching Ben's eye and giving him a little wave before turning back to continue talking with Sandra. "Her name is Vivienne. She and her daughter Olivia were there. They left in a drastic hurry, though."

"I can't believe they didn't move away after everything that happened," said Sandra. "They've become social pariahs. Everyone in Port Elspeth knows this, even people like me who have never personally met them. It's actually pretty sad how all her old friends turned on her. I mean, it's not like she did anything wrong. Still, I'm surprised she had the guts to come to that meeting last night. Maybe she's trying to work her way back in."

The school sounded the whistle that meant they could all go inside.

"Inside, outside. Inside, outside. Why do they make us jump through these hoops?" Christina muttered. "My feet are killing me. I'm going to go barefoot on the grass. It's shorter," she said, yanking her shoes off and running away.

"The ground's all slushy and muddy," Audra said, shaking her head.

"At least she's entertaining," Sandra remarked.

"I guess. Anyway, I was thinking maybe you should join the jewelry club too."

"I don't think so," said Sandra.

"Are you sure?" asked Audra. "After all, you're right in the same town. Even if you don't like making jewelry, there's a lot of good food and wine, and there's plenty to talk about."

"No thanks," Sandra said. "I'm happy to stay at home with my husband and kids. Tuesday night is Boggle and homemade pizza night at our house."

"That does sound pretty nice," Audra agreed.

Ben had caught up with them and found Audra's hand.

"I'd like to play some Boggle with you," he whispered in her ear. She had no idea if he actually meant the word game or something else, but either way, she turned pink and nodded.

"You were the first one out there," Audra said to him.

"I like to lead by example," he told her. "But I never got a chance to make that phone call. It's about basketball."

"Oh, cool!" Audra said. On top of everything else that was wonderful and out-of-her-league about him, he was athletic.

"I'll catch up with you later," he said, taking off and sprinting back to his classroom.

"Sandra," Audra whispered, grabbing her friend's wrist and looking into her eyes with emotion bordering on anguish, "can you believe Ben Harrison is going out with me? Like, seriously. Is this really happening to me? I'm so afraid it's going to end. It seems too good to be true. Can you even *believe* it?"

"You're so excited about him," Sandra said. She looked a little skeptical.

"Why are you looking at me like that?"

"Just be careful about rushing in. I can see you're head-over-heels for him and that's how people get hurt."

"I'll be fine," Audra laughed.

"Okay, just don't jump in too fast."

"Don't ruin it for me," Audra, said, trying to sound light-hearted but meaning it.

"I'm sorry. I'm not trying to. Back to the Port Elspeth Tragedy, this is the last thing I'm going to say about that sad topic," Sandra said to Audra, "and then I really have to let it go."

"Yes?" asked Audra.

"If Vivienne Prescott is going to be a part of that jewelry making club, you might want to consider finding a different club to join."

"But I thought you said that everything that happened was Evangeline Maddingly's fault?"

"I meant that, but it doesn't change that Vivienne Prescott is a person to avoid. From what I've heard, you don't want to have anything to do with her."

"I don't think we're going to see her again," said Audra.

"Then consider yourself lucky."

Chapter 13

Cadence Sommerset

"I told you to relax and take it easy for a while since you don't have to work anymore, but this is ridiculous," Dave Sommerset said to his wife. Normally, he was out the door and on his way to work by seven thirty-five, but today he was going in late since he had a dinner meeting with some new clients that evening.

"What do you mean?" Cadence asked, looking up from her cup of coffee and the word search puzzle she'd been working on.

"It's almost eleven o'clock in the morning and this place is still trashed from your party last night. Is this how you always spend your mornings? Drinking coffee and wasting time?"

"Well," she said, "we haven't lived here long enough for me to say how I *always* spend my mornings, but no. Normally I get an earlier start on things. I've got a little bit of a headache from the wine last night."

"You're getting a little old for hangovers," said Dave.

"You don't need to keep reminding me how old I am. And what's the big deal about whether or not the house is a little messy? You know that when you get home tonight it'll be put back together exactly how you like it."

"How *I* like it," he scoffed. "So now you don't like our house?"

"I love it," she said flatly.

"Cleaning up after your friends come over, when you have nothing else to do all day, is the least you can do."

"And obviously I'm going to do it," Cadence said, "so why are you giving me such a hard time?"

"No reason," Dave said, yanking a coffee mug out of the cupboard and then spinning the Keurig displayer over and over again with a scowl on his face. "Are we out of Cinnamon Roll Surprise?" he asked.

"I haven't been able to find it anywhere here in town. I ordered eight boxes of it online so you never run out again, but it hasn't arrived yet."

"What am I supposed to drink? Plain coffee? I like my Cinnamon Roll Surprise. You *know* that!"

"I found you some non-dairy creamer at the grocery store called Cinnamon Scone. Why don't you try adding that to a regular cup of coffee?" Cadence reasoned. *This is why I don't need children,* she told herself. *I already have this big, crabby, fat baby to care for.*

"Cinnamon Scone creamer?"

"Yes."

"And it's pre-sweetened?" he asked, scrunching up his face to make it clear that he was considering this possibility but was gravely disappointed to have to do so.

"Yes," said Cadence.

"Okay," Dave said. "I guess I'll try it."

"I'm sure you'll like it," Cadence said, forcing herself to smile at him.

"Maybe." His dour mood was relenting like a storm passing in the distance, before it would peter out to a cold dreary couple of days of rain.

"Do you want me to make it for you?" she asked him.

"No, I've got it," he said, now refusing to make eye contact with her.

Cadence got up and began collecting the dirty wine glasses to handwash in the sink. For a few moments they were both quiet, consumed with their small projects. As Cadence dried the last wine glass and put it back on the shelf, Dave settled down on the barstool across from her, his cup of coffee on the counter between them. There was so much creamer in it that it was pale tan. Three cinnamon sticks were in the mug as well.

"Looks like eggnog," Cadence teased gently, trying to get things back on track.

"It's pretty good. I can make do until my usual kind gets here," he admitted.

"Truce?" she asked.

"Now that you're cleaning up after yourself, what do I have to complain about?" he joked.

"Great," said Cadence. She smiled. There was no reason to share how hollow and empty she really felt, or how his moods hurt her. After all, telling him never made things better.

"So," Dave said, "I took a look outside when you gals were doing your crafts, and I saw that someone has a Mercedes just like yours. I thought it was yours at first and I wondered why you'd parked it outside. I thought you were trying to show off. Then I looked at the license plate and saw all those asinine yoga stickers all over the bumper and window and realized it belonged to someone else."

"Mmm hmm," said Cadence.

"Whose was it?"

"It belonged to a woman named... Hmmm. Now, what *was* her name?" Cadence stalled. She found herself feeling the strong inclination not to share anything about her jewelry club with him. Especially not the juicy local gossip about Vivienne Prescott.

"You don't even remember her name?" asked Dave.

"She left right away. Honestly, I don't think she's coming back. I think she realized right off the bat that my little jewelry club wasn't for her."

Behind Dave's left shoulder, the kitchen table was still overflowing with the prior evening's craft supplies, including over a dozen small, fancy jars of beads and an oversized craft carrier bearing its own little luggage tag that, even from where she stood by the sink, Cadence could clearly read *If found, please return to Vivienne Van Heusen-Prescott, 8555 Wild Rose Circle, Port Elspeth, Connecticut. (Red brick house with portico, black shutters, and four-car garage.)*

"Did *anything* interesting happen?" Dave asked.

"Well," said Cadence. She was only going to bring this up because the odds were good that someday Dave would meet Audra. "This was kind of weird. And unfortunate…"

"What was?" asked Dave.

"You know those people who were in our seats at the play the other night?"

"Oh, yeah. Those two grungy-looking kids who were trying to sneak in for free?"

Semantics, thought Cadence. "Yes, them," she said.

"White trash," Dave said.

"Actually," she said, "I don't think so."

"*Babe*," he said, in a tone that implied he'd just about had it with her, "why are you starting something with me again?"

"I'm not trying to! What I want to say is, it's such a small world. As it turns out, one of the women who was here last night is named Audra and she teaches art at the grade school over in Middleford…"

"Never heard of it," Dave interrupted.

"It's a little town about a half hour from here. I think it's northwest of here. Anyway, she was here last night, and we recognized each other right away. It turns out that it was her and her boyfriend whose seats we took."

"We didn't take their seats, we *bought* them. Those were our seats, bought and paid for, and those two scumbags were sitting in them. Get your facts straight. We bought the tickets and they were trying to freeload."

Cadence rubbed her eyes and nodded.

"You're telling me she was here, in our house?" Dave began looking around wildly, as though he expected to find that some precious home décor item of theirs had been stolen by her.

"Mmm hmm. It's kind of a funny coincidence, right? I really do think, even if the seats were ours, that the whole thing with the play was truly just a misunderstanding."

"You're so naïve."

"I'm not," she said.

"You are," he said. "You're like a child."

"How?" Up until six weeks ago, she'd run a division of a multi-million-dollar company and been in charge of a team of twenty-two people.

"Don't get me wrong, Babe, that's what I like best about you."

"Anyway, she was really nice and will be a great help to all of us in the club. She actually knows how to make jewelry."

"I don't want some delinquent in our home, scoping out things to take," said Dave.

"She wasn't like that at all. She seems like a nice person with a full-time job as a teacher. She's certainly not a delinquent! I'm telling you, the whole ticket incident was just a mix-up."

"I've got to go to work," Dave said, dropping his half-full coffee mug into the sink of warm soapy water. Cadence had been about to wash off the serving platters, but now the water would be too sticky.

She sighed. "Okay. Have a nice day."

"You don't have to say it yet. It's like you can't wait to get rid of me. I haven't even showered yet. You can say it to me when I'm walking out the door."

Cadence nodded. "Sorry," she said.

"It's no big deal," Dave said as he made his way up their back staircase with each fall of his feet on the steps making it loud and clear that it *was* a big deal.

Chapter 14

Vivienne Van Heusen-Prescott

"I'm not kidding," Vivienne said to Neil. She didn't call him at work often, but such an urgent matter required it.

"Sweetheart," he said, "give me a second. I need to close my office door. Okay, that's better. Now, listen: I love you, but I think you might be overreacting."

"Don't tell me I'm overreacting," she said. "That woman last night, that *Margo* woman, she's a Port Elspeth native, but she never took part in any of the local opportunities like sailing club and dressage camp or the Port Elspeth Young Actors' Guild. She took part in just one club. You want to hear what it was?"

"Sure," Neil said warily.

"Art Club. Freakin' Art Club! Sound familiar?"

"I've never heard you say the F word before," Neil said. He sounded a little impressed.

"Neil, you're not listening to me! Who does it sound like I'm describing?"

"Olivia?" he guessed.

"Bingo! Olivia. And this *Margo* woman..."

"Why don't you just call her Margo?" he interrupted.

"Fine. *Margo*. Whatever. The point is, Margo is..." Vivienne lowered her voice and looked all around her, concerned at what kind of effect saying this word aloud could trigger with Alexa or Siri or any of the other dozens of constantly-listening security and tech-help devices that filled her home.

"Yessss?" asked Neil.

"This Margo woman," Vivienne hissed into the phone, "is a lesbian."

Neil was silent.

"Aren't you going to say anything?" Vivienne asked him.

"I'm sorry, Punkin, but I just got an IM from the girls at the reception desk wondering if we should order chicken salad or turkey sandwiches for today's lunch meeting. Which one sounds better to you, if you had your choice?"

"Chicken salad," Vivienne seethed. "I guess you're not concerned about how our daughter turns out."

"I'm having a hard time seeing the correlation," Neil said, "but it is nice catching up with you on a workday. Are you ready for some good news?"

"Always," Vivienne said, sinking down onto the chaise lounge in her sunroom, defeated. Even in February, it was usually warm and bright and toasty in this room. The vitamin D she absorbed in here was probably the only thing keeping her from a complete depressed meltdown. She hadn't had an episode for years, but the threat of it happening again constantly loomed over her.

"Neil," she said, resorting to her baby voice that he always responded so well to, "before you tell me your good news, there's something I have to get off my chest."

"What is it, Punkin?"

"I wanted the jewelry booth to be my *comeback*. I wanted it to be my chance to stick it to everyone. I don't think it's going to work out that way. I can't rely on those other women to take it as seriously as I need them to. They're a bunch of drips! They're just a big bucket of drips."

"Well, you can't rely on other people to carry out your vision," Neil agreed.

"Story of my life," said Vivienne.

"Quit the jewelry club if it's not right for you."

"But it was my ticket back into Port Elspeth society!"

"You won't need to be part of this society much longer. Listen up, Punkin. Here's some news you're going to like: I had a long talk with Bob and Allen today and I put in my notice. My work here will be done at the end of May. Start thinking about where you want to go. If we play our cards right, and if you're ready to cut back a little on some of the luxuries, I could retire early."

"Are you serious?" Vivienne gasped.

"Yes," said Neil.

"But you're only fifty-five."

"Hard work pays off."

"We can finally move away from here?"

"That's right," said Neil.

"Wow," Vivienne said. She brushed tears of happiness from her eyes. "I can't even believe it's going to happen."

"Well, it is. Before you know it."

"Thank you," she said.

"You're welcome. It will be a fresh start for all of us. I'd better get back to work now. Anything else you had to unload about last night?"

"No," Vivienne said. Her concerns about Margo's lifestyle now seemed overblown and silly.

"Okay. Have a good day," said Neil.

"You too," she said.

She set her phone on the table beside her and sighed. She dabbed at her damp cheeks and stood up, already contemplating the vacations she and Neil could go on if he wasn't tied down with work.

"Madrid," she murmured to herself as she went to the refrigerator to pull out ingredients for her smoothie; she'd gotten a late start that morning since she'd spent much of the night before tossing and turning, worrying about what that Margo person's high school habits and resulting sexual orientation implied about her own daughter's sexual orientation. Was it normal that Olivia was sixteen and had never had a serious boyfriend? Was it appropriate that she spent her time just with Ada and Lila doing ridiculous things like dying their hair and painting every fingernail a different shade of purple? All the restlessness and worrying had kept Vivienne from falling asleep until after three o'clock, which had caused her to sleep in until after ten o'clock.

Now happier thoughts were displacing her recent sorrows. She pictured the new-and-improved version of herself that European vacations would bring. She'd be tan and glowing, and she'd look ten years younger. She'd make Neil start dying his mousey-brown, graying hair a lovely shade of blue-black. She could imagine herself in Madrid, wearing an off-the-shoulder dress and some hand-tooled leather sandals. She'd carry a market basket instead of a purse and make Neil wear a nice, tight-fitting tracksuit. Olivia could spend her summers with her grandparents so Vivienne and Neil could relish this new, leisurely lifestyle that they so desperately needed.

"And then on to Venice," she said to herself, as she crammed another handful of kale into her blender. She had to use her old smoothie maker today since Nona, their cleaning lady, had called in sick the previous afternoon and the Robot Coupe was still sitting next to the sink, filthy and beginning to smell of rot. Vivienne sighed at the inconvenience of it all. Making a smoothie this way felt so old-fashioned, plus, it ended up a little chunkier than she liked.

"You're a tough cookie," she whispered to herself, sprinkling in a handful of flaxseeds. Now and then, throughout each day, she told herself affirmations of encouragement. She had to. After what she'd been through five years ago, it took all the self-love she could muster to keep herself functioning. That and endless forgiveness. Every night before she went to bed she wrote the following passage in her little blue leather journal:

I, Vivienne Van Heusen-Prescott, forgive myself. None of what happened was my fault. I'm a good person. I can move on. I can still be a good mother and wife. I can still be a valuable, beloved part of Port Elspeth Society. May I have sweet dreams. May I wake tomorrow stronger, better, and happier than I was today.

Then she'd write the next day's date, so her journal was all set up for her to make her personal vow to herself again.

Normally, her handwriting was big and confident and showy. Or, at least, it once had been. Not so in this journal, though. She'd written this exact passage over seventeen hundred times in tiny, slanting handwriting and the journal still wasn't filled. When she filled it someday, she would file it away and start a fresh journal that was just the same. She had a compulsive belief that she must do this every evening if there was any chance of the next day not being disastrous. If she missed it even once, she was afraid that her precariously-balancing life might spin out of control again. So far, her plan was working and she was safe. She wasn't going to test her luck.

Vivienne opened her cupboard and shifted some jars of spices around. She'd just heard that red pepper increased metabolism, so she figured she might as well add some to her concoction. There it was, right next to the black pepper. She decided she might as well use a little of that, too.

She wasn't great with geography, but she was pretty sure Madrid and Venice were only a couple of hours apart. As she recalled, everything in Europe was basically right next door to each other.

After adding ample amounts of both peppers, she sprinkled some dried ginger on top of the kale. Her tears had dried and she realized she was humming an old, familiar tune. It was *That's Amore* by Dean Martin.

"A true Italian classic," she said to herself, smiling.

Those Venetian gondoliers were so sexy! Once, when she was nineteen years old, she'd been on vacation in Venice with her parents and her sister. During that vacation she'd had a two-day affair with a gondolier named Giuseppe. He'd first sung *That's Amore* to her and her sister and parents when they'd met him on their touristy jaunt down the Grand Canal, and then he'd hummed it in her ear all three times they'd made love in his tiny apartment near the Bridge of Sighs.

"Ahh, good times," she said to herself, smooshing some blueberries on top of everything else and forcing the top on the blender.

Olivia had actually gone to school, apparently, since no one from the principal's office had called her yet.

She hit the SURGE button and watched enough produce to feed a class of seventh graders turn into one perfect glass of spicy, nutrient-rich slime, just for her.

"Blessed," she said, lifting it up and taking a long, satisfying sip. "I am blessed."

Chapter 15

Margo Carlton

"I guess I might have left it at Cadence's house," Margo said to her mother. She'd been looking for her phone for an hour. "Could I use your computer to email her?"

"Of course," said Pearl.

"Thanks." Margo took a seat at her mother's desk, shot off a quick message, and a moment later received a response:

Hi Margo!

Yes, I just cleaned up my kitchen table a second ago and saw that someone had left their phone here. I was about to email you all to see who was missing it. I'll be around all day if you want to stop by and pick it up.

Cadence

"Yes, I left it there," Margo reported to her mother. "Which means…"

"You want to borrow my car?" asked Pearl.

"Yes, please," said Margo, feeling more like a sixteen-year-old than a thirty-five-year-old.

"Go ahead," Pearl said. "The keys are on the hook by the back door. But would you do me a favor and pick up a couple things from the store while you're out?"

"Sure," said Margo, "In fact, I'd be happy to. It makes me feel less guilty about borrowing your car."

"You can borrow my car all you want," said Pearl. "Especially if you'll fill it with gas. I hate doing that!"

"Thanks," Margo said. She stood up and was about to get the keys and go on her way when Pearl stopped her.

"I hate to say it, but are you going out like that?"

"Like what?" asked Margo She had on some stretched-out track pants and an old black hoodie.

"You wouldn't know this since you've been away for so long, but all the grocery stores in town have turned into *Emporiums*."

"I'm not sure what you mean by that," said Margo.

"They're all owned by the Mortensons now and they're all like mini-malls. Inside each one, there's a flower shop, a wine shop, a coffee shop, a little daycare section..."

"So?" asked Margo.

"And there's a dress code."

"You must be joking."

"I'm afraid I'm not," said Pearl. "If you want to wear yoga clothes, which I guess your outfit, if I was being generous, could be categorized as, you have to go through their drive-up window."

"If you just need a few things, then fine. I'll do it that way."

Pearl shook her head. "It's not that easy, of course. If you want to use their drive-up window, you need to place your order ahead, but that means creating an account and going through a whole rigamarole I've never been able to figure out. And it requires an app that you have to set up on your smartphone."

"Fine. I'll just do that," said Margo.

"But your phone is at Cadence's house," Pearl reminded her. "Honestly, Margo, it's easier to just put on clothes that fit with their rules."

"Can I wear jeans to their *Emporium*?" asked Margo, exasperated.

"Ummm. *Probably*. Get changed and I'll tell you if I think you'll pass or not," said Pearl.

"This town is ridiculous," said Margo.

"You might want to consider washing your hair as well," Pearl called after her. "That's not part of their dress code, but they have a whole set of rules called 'Health Code' too."

"Unbelievable!" yelled Margo.

An hour and a half later, Margo was dressed in Pearl-approved jeans and a plain blue sweater, ringing Cadence's doorbell.

Ding dong donggg! Ding dong! Ding dong! Sounded the chime from beyond the heavy wooden front door, reverberating in a rich baritone.

Cadence pulled the door open, smiling warmly, Margo's phone in her hand. "Hi Margo! Nice to see you again so soon," she said. "Here's your phone."

"Thank you," said Margo. "I'm sorry I forgot it here. I'm not usually so scatterbrained."

"It's been a lot of trouble to keep track of. I mean, I *did* have to move it from the kitchen table to the counter top, and then carry it up here to the door," Cadence joked.

Just then, a stocky, red-faced man came around the corner. "I thought I heard the doorbell ring," he said. There was a big grin on his face. He took one look at Margo and immediately lost interest. The disappointment that registered on his face was so blatant that Margo, despite having an equal lack of interest in him, couldn't help but feel embarrassed.

"Dave, this is Margo. She forgot her phone here last night. Margo, this is my husband Dave," said Cadence.

The two of them shook hands.

"I've got to get going," Dave said to Cadence. He gave her a quick kiss on the cheek and called, "Nice to meet you, Margaret," over his shoulder.

"Do you have time to stick around and have a cup of coffee?" Cadence asked Margo.

"Do I have time? Well, yes, I have time," Margo laughed. She had nothing but time. "Sure, I'd love a cup of coffee."

"Great," said Cadence, leading them back to the kitchen. "Pardon the mess."

"I helped you make it," said Margo, "so you don't need to apologize. Would you like some help cleaning it up?"

"Nah, I'll get it later," Cadence said. "Let's just have some coffee for now. Take your pick of whatever kind you'd like."

They cleared a spot at the kitchen table and sat down. Just then, Cadence's phone lit up with a text from Dave:

Get that kitchen cleaned up. I might want to bring the new clients to our house tonight for dinner instead of going out. So go to the store and get groceries, in case. I'll send a list soon.

Cadence flipped the phone over. She would have never said such a disloyal thing back in Arkansas, where nearly every person she knew had as strong of a connection to her husband as they had to her, but she heard herself say to Margo, "Please, forgive me for my husband's behavior."

"Oh," said Margo. "Just a moment ago at the door?"

"Yes," said Cadence. "I realize he was a little dismissive there. It was because he was running off to work. He's trying to fit in at his new job. He's stressed."

"I don't need to be interesting to him," Margo said lightly. "After all, he's your husband and I'm not even interested in men."

"I don't want him to be *interested* in you," Cadence laughed, "but he didn't need to be so rude. Clearly, you're beautiful and well-traveled," Cadence continued—Margo's heart took a tiny, unforeseen leap of surprise over Cadence's casual flattering words—"but it isn't the kind of beauty or sophistication that he understands. He likes women who look like me," she said. Cadence was small, blonde, and girlish. Dainty. Pulled-together. Even just sitting in her kitchen with jeans and a t-shirt on, there was a sweet, catalog-perfection to her look. "I'm his type, and every other woman who looks like me is his type." She laughed hollowly.

Margo nodded and took a sip of her coffee, unsure why Cadence was divulging so much information to her. Not that she minded.

"Enough about me," Cadence said.

"Enough about Dave," Margo corrected her.

"Fine, enough about me and Dave. Tell me about Paris. Tell me everything. Don't leave out anything."

Tuesday, February 27, 2018

The Second Meeting

Chapter 16

Audra Fleming

"Okay," Audra said to the group of women around the table. To her shock, every member from the previous meeting, including Vivienne and Olivia Prescott, was there. "Today's lesson is perfect for beginners. We're going to be able to churn out dozens of pairs of earrings tonight. No tools needed! I remembered seeing a whole package of clip earring backings last time, so that's what we're going to make tonight: Clip-on earrings."

"Which tools will I need?" asked Cadence. Her cheeks were flushed. She'd clearly been hitting the wine for some time before the party started. Her face also looked puffy and her eyes were bloodshot, as though she'd been crying.

"No tools are needed for this project," said Audra. "Seriously, it's as easy as it gets. You'll need superglue though. I picked up several tubes and a disposable tablecloth at the dollar store on my way over here. All you have to do is find two matching buttons or stones..." She quickly found two beautiful old enamel buttons in one of the jars Pearl had contributed. She held them up for everyone to see. "Then," she said, "you glue them each to their clip-on backings... and *voila*! You've got a pair of earrings." She held up the pair she'd just created. They looked like something that could be found in one of the specialty boutiques downtown for thirty or forty dollars.

"Those are amazing," said Cadence, slurring her words a little. "Sold! I'm going to want to buy everything you make!"

"This looks like a project even I can handle," said Pearl. She selected two flat blue stones she found in a plastic sandwich bag and turned them into an awkward-looking pair of stud earrings. *Five dollars,* Audra thought to herself. Still, it was a decent first attempt.

Audra, and probably everyone else around the table, noticed that Vivienne and her daughter were being awfully quiet. It appeared they were in a fight and not talking to one another. As if Vivienne could read Audra's mind, she suddenly spoke up.

"It's *so* wonderful to be here. Connecting with like-minded women! Making good things happen for the community! It's *so* wonderful. I love giving back to this town. This is all to raise money for new parks, right?"

"That's right," said Cadence.

Vivienne nodded. "That's what I thought. Isn't it just great that we're doing this?"

"It sure is," said Margo.

Vivienne's face hardened. Apparently, she'd meant for her little display to be for the benefit of everyone except Margo.

"So," Margo continued, "did any of you think of a name we could call our booth?"

Vivienne locked eyes with her daughter, who'd been about to respond to Margo, and shook her head slowly and firmly one time. Olivia's mouth clamped back shut.

"Anyone want more wine?" Cadence asked suddenly. She picked up a nearby bottle of Cabernet and began topping off Olivia's glass of cranberry juice.

"I can't have wine," Olivia said. "I'm sixteen."

"Oh, I'm sorry," Cadence said. Her face fell. "I'm so embarrassed. Of course you can't have wine; you're in high school. Ugh." She set the bottle down, her face immediately blotching up. She fanned herself. "I look terrible when I cry," she said beneath her breath. "Let's hope that doesn't happen."

"I shouldn't have said anything. I wouldn't have minded having some wine," Olivia laughed.

"How would you even know what wine tastes like?" Vivienne asked her. When Olivia ignored her, Vivienne said it again, this time grabbing her daughter's wrist in her own vice-like veiny grasp and giving her a little shake when she said it.

"I *don't* know what it tastes like," Olivia snapped back, pulling her wrist away from her mother. "That's why I wouldn't have minded trying some."

Cadence shook her head. "I think I've had a little too much to drink. I was getting everything ready for tonight and I thought it wouldn't hurt for me to have one glass of wine. One turned into two. Then Dave came home and we got in an argument. He left to go over to a meeting the Port Elspeth Men's Club is having. He's a guest of Irving Humphrey. I don't know if any of you know him, but he lives up the road from us…"

Audra saw Vivienne's eyebrows raise and her eyes bug out of her head a little at that news, but she kept right on sorting beads and buttons into matching pairs for the women at the table, pretending she hadn't noticed Vivienne's cartoonish reaction.

"Anyway," Cadence said, "I guess I overdid it."

"So, the Humphreys live around here?" Vivienne asked.

Cadence nodded. "Just a little up the road."

"How's Marlene doing?" asked Vivienne.

"She's good," said Cadence.

"Good for her," said Vivienne, with a sniff.

Audra felt her phone vibrate in her pocket. Figuring it was probably Ben texting her, since very few other people ever did, she excused herself to go to the bathroom so she could cherish this exciting little moment in private. As soon as she was inside with the door locked behind her, she pulled her phone out and took a look.

At first it took her a second to realize what she was looking at. She'd been intimately acquainted with the body part in the picture the night before, but the room had been very dark. She'd never seen it in such detail before. It was, however, without a doubt, Ben's penis. Not much else. Just a close up of his manhood, standing at firm attention.

She cringed.

"What the heck?" she said out loud. Was this supposed to turn her on?

She bit her lip, considering how to respond.

Before she could make a decision, another text came through from him:

You want some of this?

"Ugh," she whispered. "Really?"

She began to type ***Kind of***, but then deleted it.

She cracked her knuckles and pulled on her shirt collar and paced in tiny circles, trying to figure out how to handle this peculiar turn of events. Her phone went off again.

Come on. Show me yours.

Everything about this felt totally off.
Just weird.
To her, it wasn't hot at all. It was making her feel awkward and sad.

She flushed the toilet and ran some water, stalling for time in case anyone else was waiting to use the bathroom.

Finally, she yanked down her pants, took a picture of herself in her pale yellow Hanes cotton briefs, her legs primly clamped together, and sent it to Ben.

She stalled, waiting for a response. She ran some more water, blew her nose, and peeked inside Cadence's medicine cabinet (so many expensive face creams!).

"I hope that was the right response," she whispered to herself, wondering whether he was going to do something back or if that was the end of how this worked.

Finally, after a couple more minutes had gone by, she told herself, "You sexted! You're now an active, normal part of 2018, Audra. Good job."

She didn't like it one bit, though.

As soon as Audra returned to the kitchen, Cadence stood up and said, "Could you all please excuse me for a moment?" Then she left the room.

"As I was saying," Vivienne said, picking back up in her grand, haughty voice, "I positively *adore* doing nice things for other people, and it's so wonderful to be with other women who feel the same way. I think you'll all have to agree that it's particularly generous of my daughter and me to donate our time to efforts that will result in money being raised for the Port Elspeth Parks Department when we're about to move away from here."

"Oh!" said Pearl. "Where are you moving to?"

"It hasn't been decided yet," said Vivienne with a sly smile on her face. "I wouldn't be surprised, though, if we choose a few different locales. You know, have a few different homes throughout the world."

103

"Wow. How exciting for you," said Margo. "If you'll all excuse me, I think I'm going to check on our host."

"A few different homes," Pearl repeated, rolling her eyes just enough to show how unimpressed she was.

"Mom, please," said Olivia. "Quit bragging. You're embarrassing me."

"I'm not bragging, Olivia," said Vivienne. "I'm just sharing news about our lives. Your father worked very hard for us to have a nice life. So what if now we'll get to enjoy some well-earned peace and relaxation. Finally!"

"So, Vivienne, where are you planning to move to?" asked Audra.

"Stateside, we're not sure yet. We have so many friends around the country, and so many fabulous connections, that it's tough to choose one or even two perfect spots," said Vivienne. "But as far as vacation homes go, I've got my heart set on Venice. I've got old friends there I'd like to reconnect with. One in particular. And who knows where else we may go!"

"Are you excited about moving, too?" Audra asked Olivia.

"I don't really care. I'm sure it'll be okay," she said, though she looked sad.

"That's a brave attitude," said Pearl. "You young people are so resilient compared to us old fogies. I don't know how Margo up and moved all the way to Paris on her own. When she first went there, she could barely speak French. I never could have done it."

"When my dad told me the news that we're going to move away," said Olivia, "I felt bad at first about leaving my best friends, but then my dad pointed out that there are so many ways to stay connected, and those are the ways I spend a lot of my time with them already, so it might not be that big of a change."

"That's a great attitude," Audra said. "Very mature." She wondered if maybe she'd be happier teaching older kids instead of little ones.

"Yes, you're sure a brave girl," Pearl said to her. "Just like my Margo."

"I know what you're trying to do," Vivienne said to Pearl. The tone of her voice made Audra look up from the buttons she was gluing.

"What do you mean?" asked Pearl.

"Quit comparing my daughter to your daughter," said Vivienne. "They have nothing in common whatsoever."

"I certainly didn't mean it as an insult," said Pearl. "I think it's a compliment for someone to be compared to Margo."

"Shut up! You're trying to make me angry! It's not going to work! I'm not falling for it, so knock it off!" Vivienne yelled at Pearl, jumping out of her chair and slamming her fist on Cadence's kitchen table.

Cadence and Margo came running back into the kitchen to see what was the matter.

"There they are!" Vivienne hollered, pointing at them. "The drunk and her girlfriend! Are you two done making out now? Don't think I can't see right through you. You're as transparent as ghosts. *Lesbian* ghosts!"

Cadence pressed her palm to her chest in shock.

"Oh, what an actor you are! Yes, you Cadence. You! With your sweet little Southern drawl and your tiny little Tory Burch jeans. Living here in this perfect house with your perfect life. I'll bet your husband is perfect too, isn't he? Then how come you're so *obviously* miserable?"

"Mom, stop it," Olivia begged.

"It's that obvious that I'm unhappy?" Cadence whispered.

"Honey, you might as well be a billboard. Anyone can see it from a million miles away!" Vivienne screamed in Cadence's face. "It's plain as day that nobody loves you. That's the one thing I can say. My husband loves me. *My husband loves me!*"

"Calm down," Margo said, reaching out to lay her hand on Vivienne's flailing arm.

"You! You repulsive, androgynous street hussy. Get your hands off me. Olivia, get your things! We're leaving."

"No! Not this again," said Olivia. She stood up from the table and handed her half-finished project to Audra. "Sorry. Here you go."

"Vivienne, don't ever come back here," Cadence had the wherewithal to say to her.

"I wouldn't dream of it," said Vivienne.

Chapter 17

Audra Fleming

"I understand if you all want to leave now," Cadence said. "In fact, this jewelry club has been a terrible idea. I'll let them know that we won't be needing our booth."

"Sit down," said Pearl, pulling out the chair Cadence had been sitting in earlier. "We don't have to let what just happened change our plans."

"I've never been screamed at like that in my life," said Cadence, collapsing back into her chair. She held out her jittering hands for the women around her to see. "Look at me; I'm shaking! I don't know what just happened."

"She's clearly a miserable person," said Audra, doing her best to focus on her present situation instead of her non-vibrating phone. "Did you smell her perfume? It smells like ice. I didn't even know that was possible. No one good could want to smell that way. She hates herself and she's taking it out on the people around her."

"I'd say 'Have another glass of wine and relax,'" Margo said to Cadence, "but maybe I could make you a cup of tea instead?"

"I can get it," Cadence said, starting to stand.

"I've got it," Margo reassured her.

"Okay. Thank you. Tea would be nice," said Cadence.

"And the tea kettle is…" Margo scanned the kitchen.

"Right on the stove," said Cadence.

"Right on the stove," laughed Margo. "Anyone else want a cup of tea?"

"If there's some herbal tea that doesn't have any caffeine in it, then sure," said Pearl.

"It's all in that cupboard on the left," Cadence said to Margo.

"I'll take one, too," said Audra. "Any kind is fine with me."

"I suppose," said Pearl, "this is my opportunity to finish the story I started last week."

"I'll admit," said Audra, "I've been grilling my co-worker for details, but I haven't gotten very much information out of her. I've tried googling it, but I can't find anything about this story. Just a few local headlines with very vague, short stories attached. That's all."

"The Maddinglys or the Prescotts probably found some way to pay to remove the information from the internet," said Pearl. "Some people!"

"Oh, Mom," said Margo, "I don't think that's possible."

"If you're rich enough, anything is possible," said Pearl, shaking her head in disappointment at the corruption of Some People. She looked around her then at the huge house they were in and turned to Cadence, "No offense, dear."

"None taken," said Cadence.

"Okay," said Pearl. "Where did I leave off? Oliver Prescott was having the graduation party of his dreams and half the high school was invited, including teachers. Teachers who knew that he hadn't even graduated. I don't know who had the nerve to speak up and say something, but the truth came out that night. From what I've heard, if you think his parents were mad, you should have seen how the Maddinglys reacted. Right there, right in the middle of the party, they told their daughter to break off her relationship with him."

The tea kettle began sputtering and then erupting into a long whistle. Cadence got up to help out, but Margo stopped her.

"Sit! I've already got it taken care of," she said. "Working off and on in some of Paris's busiest cafes over the years made me an efficient waitress."

Audra looked over and saw that Margo wasn't kidding. She'd already whisked away their empty wine glasses, washed them all, and set four mugs, several boxes of tea, a sugar bowl, and a pot of honey on the countertop next to them on a tray.

"Everyone good?" Margo asked, after placing the tray on the table and filling everyone's cups with hot water.

"Now we are," Cadence said.

"Perfect," Margo said, settling down at the table with them.

"If I could run my kindergarten class like you just handled this, I'd get ten times more done in a day," Audra laughed.

"Okay, Pearl, back to the story, please," Cadence said to Pearl, as soon as each of them had gotten her tea fixed how she liked it.

"Now, remember, this was a graduation party for both of them," Pearl continued. "Lot of the gifts were things for both of them to share, like camping gear and gift cards for restaurants. As you can imagine, nothing was inexpensive. Evangeline was in shock that Oliver had lied so successfully to her and wouldn't be coming along to Harvard, but her parents were just disgusted. You'd think they would have simply left, but no. They started gathering up all the gifts and hauling them out to their car. It was very out-of-character! Definitely not their usual dignified behavior."

"Maybe they'd had a little bit to drink," Cadence said, understandingly.

"Vivienne got physical with them," Pearl continued, "if you can imagine that, which I sure can, now that I know her a little bit, and she started wrestling them for the gifts. I guess it was a real show."

"Tell me someone ended up in the blood-red pool," said Audra.

"That would have been good," Pearl mused, nodding. "I never heard if that happened, but let's just say it did."

"Mom," said Margo. "Really!"

Pearl shrugged and continued, "So, this party happened in the late spring of 2013. Actually, I remember the date, because I read about it and heard about it so much, and it's the same day as my sister Tilly's birthday, rest her soul. It was June fourteenth. Flag Day. It's hard to believe it's been almost five years already!"

"Could I borrow that?" Audra asked Cadence, pointing at a blank yellow legal pad resting on one of the barstools nearby.

"Sure, it's just one of Dave's for work. He has a million of these. He won't miss it," Cadence said, handing it to Audra.

"I'll only need a sheet or two. You can have it back when I leave," Audra said, writing *June 14, 2013 ~ Oliver and Evangeline's graduation party* on the top line of the notepad. "I'm going to write down the facts of the case," she explained.

"As you can imagine," Pearl continued, "Oliver Prescott recognized that his perfect life was falling apart right before his eyes. The Maddinglys took their daughter and whatever gifts they could load up, and they went home. Once Evangeline Maddingly had a couple of days to sleep on things and her parents had calmed down enough to quit yelling in her ear about getting rid of Oliver, she realized that she didn't want anything more to do with him. I don't know whether she invited him over to break up with him, or if he invited himself over in the hopes of working things out, or what, but either way, I think the last time anyone saw them alive was that following Sunday night, a couple of days after the party, at the Maddinglys' home. I know that for sure because the papers all kept saying *Last Seen Sunday Evening.*"

Everyone paused and took a sip of tea. Audra felt a shiver run down her spine. *Last seen alive together at Maddinglys' house, Sunday after graduation party,* she wrote.

"Rumor has it, Claire and Mitch Maddingly were out to dinner that evening, and when they came home, Oliver was there trying to patch things up with their daughter. They told him to leave, so he did, but Evangeline went with him, against her parents' will. They went off together in his car."

Pearl cleared her throat and took a long sip of her tea.

"And then what happened?" Cadence asked, unable to bear the wait.

"For several weeks, nothing happened. Both of them were simply gone. No sign of Oliver's vehicle, and since it was a few years old, it didn't have any kind of tracking device built into it like I guess some cars have nowadays. Their phones had been found in the Maddingly's bushes by their front door or some shrubs nearby, I think."

"Both of their phones?" asked Audra.

"Yes. And there was nothing happening with their credit cards. It was like those two kids went away that night and disappeared off the face of the earth."

"The part about their phones makes me think someone kidnapped them. Who would leave behind their phone?" asked Audra.

"Or maybe it just proves Oliver snapped and kidnapped her and then later killed them both," said Margo.

"Everyone had a theory about what happened," said Pearl. "It was all anyone talked about. You have to understand, the Maddinglys were the most important family in town. Everyone felt that way."

"More than those Mortensons or Van Pelts that Vivienne is always bringing up?" asked Audra.

"Even more than them," said Pearl. "And as you can probably all imagine, all the blame was on Oliver Prescott. He'd ruined his reputation with that Harvard lie. Plus, he was never in the same league as Evangeline Maddingly, no matter how hard he and his family had tried to get there. Some folks thought both those kids had been victims of foul play, but the majority of the people in town believed it was all Oliver's fault, and whatever had happened to them was his doing."

"Wait a minute. Did they ever actually find their bodies? Maybe they aren't even dead. Maybe they ran off together and they're somewhere out there, still happily together," Cadence said hopefully, sadly. The tone of her voice showed she didn't really believe it.

"No, I'm afraid not," said Pearl. "On the morning of the Fourth of July, some people were returning to their summer cottage in Hillpoint. That's a little town about an hour and a half from here. They pulled into their driveway and saw a vehicle parked there that they didn't recognize. It turned out to belong to Oliver Prescott." She paused dramatically, taking a drink of her tea.

"What was his vehicle doing there?" Audra asked.

"He and Evangeline must have broken into the cottage. Maybe they thought they could hide there or live there. Or maybe he took her there with the intention of killing her and then killing himself. Who knows? This couple who owned the cottage, they were the ones who made the grisly discovery. They found them both inside, dead. They'd been dead for some time. A week or two, I think."

"That's horrible," gasped Cadence.

"Who were the owners of the cottage? Did they have ties to either family?" asked Margo.

"I don't know," said Pearl.

"How did they die?" asked Margo.

Pearl took a long sip of her tea. "You know," she said, "I forget that part."

"It's kind of an important detail," said her daughter.

"You're right. I'll have to see if I can dig up some more details," said Pearl. "At one point, I think I knew."

"I'm confused," Audra said.

"Confused about what?" asked Pearl.

"Were there more people involved in this story?"

"Well, there was Oliver and Evangeline, and everyone connected to them, like their parents and families and friends," said Pearl.

"Was someone else connected in a *major* way?" asked Audra. "I guess what I'm trying to say is, did anyone else die?"

"Not that I'm aware of," said Pearl. "Why do you ask?"

"Just something my co-worker said to me," said Audra. "Never mind."

"Would you look at the time?" said Pearl. "I must have really talked your ears off! It's almost ten o'clock again!"

"I better get going," said Audra. "It's a little bit of a drive back to Middleford."

"Thanks for trying to teach us to make earrings," Cadence said to Audra. "I swear, next time we'll get some work done."

"And we'll get to the bottom of this story," said Pearl. "I'll call up my old friend Gladiola Peabody. She used to be the Maddinglys' cleaning lady. She'll fill me in on all the details I'm forgetting."

"I can hardly wait," said Cadence.

"Here's your notepad back," Audra said to Cadence, tearing off the top sheet. There, exposed to everyone, was the name *Tiffinie* and the phone number 247-6258, followed by a heart.

Cadence snatched the notepad from Audra's hand, studying it with a perplexed frown. All the color was rapidly draining from her face. She took a deep breath and flipped the notepad over, face down on the table.

"I'm sure that's nothing," she murmured. "Thank you all so much for coming," she said abruptly. And then she walked them all to the door.

Friday, March 2, 2018

School Days

Chapter 18

Vivienne Van Heusen-Prescott

"Hello, Mrs. Prescott. How are you this morning?"

Vivienne pulled her phone away from her face and looked at it to see if it was broken or if someone had put some kind of translating device on it. Joan Benson hadn't spoken so kindly or formally to her in years; she figured something must be amiss.

"Hi, Joan. I'm fine. Is there trouble with Olivia again?"

"No. Not at all. In fact, Principal Davies and I are calling to invite you to a special meeting about your daughter."

"A special meeting?" Vivienne nudged her half-unrolled yoga mat open the rest of the way and sat down on it. A special meeting, no matter how Joan Benson was trying to sell it, couldn't be good.

"Yes, a very special meeting," Joan said pleasantly.

"Oh, now it's *very* special. I'm not falling for this," said Vivienne.

"Excuse me?" said Joan.

"*Excuse me,*" Vivienne repeated, in a mocking tone. "I'll have you know, Joan, that Olivia won't be part of your school system much longer. That's right. Surprise! Ha, ha, ha! Jokes on you! How do you like *those* apples?"

"Pardon me?"

"What? Did I stutter? Do you need a hearing aid?"

"Please, Vivienne, I don't appreciate this. You know I have a hearing-impaired son," said Joan.

"I don't know that! I don't know or care anything about you! All I know about you is that you *love* pouring salt in my wounds and kicking me when I'm down. Well, listen up, Joan Benson! Neil and Olivia and I are packing up and moving out of town as soon as the schoolyear is over, so whatever 'special meeting' you want to throw at me, forget it." Vivienne was too worked up to keep sitting. She stood back up and began pacing the smooth, shining floors of her yoga room. All the tiny Buddha candles and authentic Tibetan incense cones were burning and her lavender eucalyptus diffuser was puffing away at full-blast. She'd been just about ready for yoga hour when Joan's call had ruined everything.

"Vivienne, wait. Please listen! There seems to be a huge misunderstanding happening here."

"I don't misunderstand anything. I can see right through you! Just like I can see through lots of people. You can't trust anyone. And that's a fact." Vivienne spun around and accidentally swept a couple of Buddha candles off their shelf and onto the floor. They promptly started her imported sheer jacquard curtains on fire, engulfing her south-facing wall in a roaring eruption of flames. Not missing a beat, she raced over to her gurgling in-floor fountain, scooped up a huge vaseful of water, doused out the fire, and yelled, "Alexa, text the handyman! Tell him I've got a small repair in the yoga room he'll need to handle ASAP!"

"Vivienne, please listen to me," Joan Benson tried again.

"You're still there?" snapped Vivienne.

"Yes. The meeting I'm calling about isn't because of anything that your daughter did wrong. It's about her artwork."

117

"I'm so tired of hearing about that silly habit of hers," said Vivienne, scrutinizing the huge smoldering burn mark on her wall. "She'll outgrow it soon, I'm sure."

"With all due respect, Mrs. Prescott, she's quite talented and it's a skill that she should be very proud of."

Vivienne yawned and checked her Fitbit. She had, basically, no steps in yet today. She could *feel* the tingle of love handles starting to spout right below each kidney.

"There's a special program happening this summer that we thought she'd qualify for," Joan Benson continued. "It's a very elite program."

"Elite program?" Vivienne repeated. This got her attention.

"Yes. It's *very* hard to get into. Honestly, I think you'll want to come in today and hear about it."

"But we're leaving Port Elspeth soon," Vivienne reminded her.

"I know. I heard you say that, but even if you're moving away, it doesn't affect that she's eligible for this program and it could have a big impact on her future."

"Aren't you even going to ask where we're moving to?"

"Where are you moving to?" Joan asked. To Vivienne's annoyance, she sounded bored instead of interested. She almost let it get to her until she realized it must be fake boredom, which is twice as good as genuine interest, and that Joan was terribly, bitterly jealous of her.

"Venice. Venice, Italy," Vivienne said defiantly. "I have old friends there who are *dying* to see me again. One in particular."

"How wonderful for you. And for them," said Joan. "So, should I pencil you in for two o'clock today?"

"Welllll, let me think," Vivienne said, taking as long as she possibly could before responding. "I *suppose* I can fit a quick stop into my schedule. Fine, see you at two o'clock," she finally said, before ending the call without bothering to say goodbye.

Chapter 19

Audra Fleming

Her class of second graders was absorbed in their paper-weaving project, so Audra discreetly took a moment to break school rules and text Ben:

I miss you! This place is so boring without you ☹

She made herself busy cleaning out her desk drawer. He texted back a couple of minutes later:

Home is boring too! Being sick is no fun!

She glanced up at the kids. They were all still behaving themselves, so she sent off another text:

Are you feeling better? Anything I can bring you after school? Maybe some soup?

He responded:

Still feeling pretty bad. No need to bring me anything. I don't want you to get sick too!

She replied:

That's sweet of you, but I wouldn't mind your germs.

As soon as she hit 'send' she shook her head in self-loathing. "What a dumb thing to say," she whispered to herself. He replied:

_Ha ha_

Just _Ha ha_, without even any punctuation or bother of capitalization. She waited. She tried to think of something else to say, but everything running through her mind sounded sad and desperate. It was Ben's second day in a row being out sick. They hadn't gotten together since Monday evening and now it was Friday. They had no plans to get together that weekend.

They'd never spoken about the sexting episode that had taken place on Tuesday evening when Audra was at Cadence's house. It was as if it had never even happened. She'd seen him Wednesday at school and he'd been friendly yet distant and said nothing about it. He'd avoided being alone with her all day, and then he'd left for the day without even stopping by her classroom to say goodbye. And because of all that, she had the most unsettling feeling that the picture he'd sent had never been meant for her.

How had something that started so strong fallen apart so quickly? The flowers he'd brought her were still in her kitchen at home, about half of them not even dead yet.

If only she'd played harder to get.

"This is all your own fault," she whispered to herself.

"Miss Fleming, are you talking to yourself?" one of her second graders hollered, giggling.

"No, Louis," she said, smiling at him. She put her phone away and got up to walk around the class to inspect their weaving handiwork, but she couldn't stop analyzing everything that had happened between her and Ben recently.

They'd had sex for the first time Monday night. It hadn't been great. She had thought he was falling in love with her. She knew she was falling in love with him. But when they were having sex, she could tell he wasn't feeling it for her. When he was done, it turned out, apparently, they were both done. They'd watched a couple shows and he'd stayed over, but nothing about it had felt comfortable or good.

Then the weird sexting thing the next night.

Then a distant Wednesday.

Then two days of him calling in sick.

It had been the worst week Audra had gone through since some of her junior high school days. The days back when she was the odd girl out at the lunch table, enduring lonely, embarrassing days on end.

I never should have become a teacher, she decided. It often reminded her too much of her own unpopular, unhappy childhood.

She sat back down at her desk and pulled her phone back out of her purse. There was nothing new from Ben.

I guess we were moving too fast? she typed.

She took a deep breath and deleted it.

What if he really was just sick?

But she knew better.

She recognized this feeling. The hollowness that filled a person when all the oxytocin their body had just breathlessly learned to accommodate began to clear out as rapidly as it had come in. From her cheeks to her windpipe to her stomach to the marrow of her bones, loneliness and emptiness were once again taking the place of love.

"Miss Fleming?" one of her students called out.

"What is it, Antonia?"

"Could you help me?"

"Sure," she said, taking one more look at Ben's sad little *Ha ha* and then dropping her phone back into her purse.

Chapter 20

Vivienne Van Heusen-Prescott

When Vivienne arrived at her daughter's school at 2:05 that afternoon (there was *no* way she was going to do them the favor of being exactly on time), she was irritated to find that there were no available parking spots in the guest lot and she had to park across the street in the student and staff lot. This was of particular annoyance since she was wearing her new Manolo Blahnik Hangisi Crystal-Buckle Shimmery 115mm Pumps (in Gold, naturally) with her pantsuit and the heel on them was a bit of a killer if you had to walk more than twenty or thirty paces.

At 2:29, after getting lost a couple of times and stopping off at the restroom to take care of a few things she'd neglected to do at home, Vivienne made it to the conference room where Principal Dana Davies, Vice-Principal Joan Benson, some shaggy man who must have been the art teacher, and her daughter Olivia were all seated around an oval teak table.

"We were starting to wonder about you," said Principal Davies, though it sounded as though she was attempting to be light-hearted about it.

"If anyone had been thoughtful enough to reserve a parking space for me or had given me clearer instructions about where this meeting was being held," said Vivienne, "I would have been ten minutes early."

"Mom," said Olivia, "there are screens right there showing the parking lot and everything else going on around here." She pointed to the wall.

"Welcome to the technological age," said Principal Davies. "We just got them installed."

Olivia added, "We know you didn't get here until five after two, and that you spent almost ten minutes in the bathroom. I guess that's when you put your hair up in that French twist?"

Vivienne took a seat at the table. "Let's get down to business," she said. "You have some elite club for gifted students that my daughter has been requested to join?"

"Well, something like that," said the shaggy man. He held out his hand to Vivienne. "Woody Willworth," he said.

"Willy Wood-what?" spat Vivienne, ignoring his outstretched hand.

"I'm your daughter's art teacher," he said, "and I've been very impressed with her. This is my first year teaching at Port Elspeth, but at my old school back in New York, I was on a committee for students who wanted to fight for equality by expressing themselves through art."

Vivienne snorted and laughed.

"Did I say something funny?" asked Woody.

Vivienne turned to Joan Benson and Dana Davies. "You dragged me in here for *this*?"

The art teacher's face fell. He looked at the principal and vice-principal and then back at Vivienne.

"Olivia has been struggling with her grades," Principal Davies said, "but we believe she's very intelligent and that it's not too late for her to get focused and still go to college."

"Still go to college?" said Vivienne. "*Of course* she'll go to college. Why wouldn't she?"

"Well then," said Principal Davies, glancing at Olivia, "—and I'm not saying anything I haven't already said to your daughter, Mrs. Prescott—if Olivia plans to go to college straight after she graduates, she's going to need to make some immediate, serious changes to offset the poor grades and attendance issues she's been having."

"But those are just signs that she's bored," said Vivienne. "What does high school have to do with college?" When Dana Davies, Joan Benson, and Woody Willworth all simply responded with dropped jaws, Vivienne lowered her voice and leaned in conspiratorially. "Right? Who cares about anything happening in this place, right?"

"Mrs. Prescott," said Woody, regaining enough composure to speak, "this program I'm talking about is very important. Only about a dozen students are selected to participate in it each year, and it's a great honor. Being part of this project makes a big impact not just to the people the students are helping, but to the students themselves. The program started five years ago, and over half of the participants who've graduated from it have gone to Ivy League schools. Wouldn't you like your daughter to go to a school like Harvard?"

As soon as he said it, the faces of Joan Benson and Dana Davies both contorted into grimaces. Joan Benson shook her head desperately at Woody and waved her fingers at her neck in the universal *Stop Talking! Stop Talking Now!* gesture. It was too late to go back, though.

"Harvard? *Harvard?* You want to talk to me about Harvard?" Vivienne screamed. "I buried my son because of Harvard!"

"Excuse me?" asked Woody, looking helplessly around the table for some kind of explanation or support.

"You stupid fool!" Vivienne continued, jamming her finger right in his face. "You greasy, French fry-scented hippie!"

"Mom," Olivia begged. "Please! Not everyone can handle your abuse."

"I *did* have fast-food for lunch today," Woody admitted under his breath, shaking his head in shame. "I usually pack a very healthy lunch. Today was a fluke."

"You think you're gonna get me interested in your feel-good socialist program by talking about Harvard?" Vivienne yelled. "I'll tell you what: Olivia's a big girl and she can make her own decision on this. I'm done talking to all of you. I wash my hands of this. The disrespect! I can't take it anymore!"

"But, Mom," said Olivia. "I can't make the decision myself. It costs twenty-five thousand dollars, which I don't have since I always spend each week's thousand dollars as soon as you give it to me."

"You don't save any of that?" asked Vivienne.

"I mean, how can I? It barely covers lunch for me and Ada and Lila and anyone who joins us every day at Noodle Hut. You want me to have friends but I'm not supposed to buy everyone in line lunch?"

"Whatever," Vivienne sighed.

"Back to the art program," said Olivia, "if I do it, I'll have to live in New York next year."

"It means you'd have to live in New York?" Vivienne couldn't hide the delight that overtook her face.

"Yes," said Olivia.

"Well," she said, feeling the peace that an hour of yoga could not have delivered, "I fully support you. You're very mature for your age."

"I *am*?" Olivia asked, scratching at the Hello Kitty bra she was wearing over her turtleneck.

"And," Vivienne continued, "just like your teachers are saying,"—she flippantly gestured toward Dana and Joan—"I think it's exactly what you need to get a good start in life."

"You think that?" asked Olivia.

"Sure," Vivienne said, already imagining how great her upcoming year was going to be. Without Olivia around to worry about and get in their way, she and Neil could make love two or three times a day. Sex was such a great calorie-burner.

"But Mom, you were telling me to drop out of Drawing Club just last night."

"Shush, Olivia Jane. No I wasn't. Art! I always say, it's the way to make money and gain respect."

"Okay," said Olivia. "Do we need to talk to Dad about this?"

"No," said Vivienne.

"Cool," said Olivia.

"Is there anything else you need from me?" asked Vivienne to the table in general. "Or are we finished?"

"We're done here," said Principal Davies. "Vivienne, we'll have Woody prepare the information about the program and I'll email you everything including the invoice."

"Peachy," said Vivienne.

"Thanks, Mom," said Olivia.

"My pleasure," Vivienne said, already halfway out the door. "You all have a fabulous day!" she exclaimed, and sauntered away, taking her nearest exit outside. They all watched on the wall of security footage as she stepped in a drainage grate in the parking lot and broke off the heel of one of her shoes, but no one said a word.

Chapter 21

Audra Fleming

It was almost four o'clock on Friday afternoon, and Audra was still sitting at her desk. She'd texted Ben at quarter to three, asking him if she could stop by after work to see him. She'd told him she'd be happy to pop by after work, that it was no trouble at all. 'Pop by.' She'd used that exact expression. It didn't sound like her at all. She wasn't sure where she'd come up with it. She supposed she'd been trying to sound casual and light, but it now, rereading it, it just sounded nerdy.

As the clock ticked to four o'clock, she heard the squeaking mop bucket on wheels edging down the hall. A moment later the janitor stuck his head in her room.

"Hi, Fred," she said.

"You're working late for a Friday, aren't you, Audra?"

She nodded. "I'm about to head home. Do you and your family have any fun plans for the weekend?" She stood up and began gathering her coat and scarf and mittens from where they were piled on the radiator behind her desk.

"A birthday party for our youngest. That'll take up most of the weekend, I'm sure. What about you?"

"I think I'll catch up on cleaning my apartment. Maybe read a book." *More likely, I'll cry and sleep all weekend*, she added silently in her head.

"I heard you and Ben Harrison are an item," said Fred. He gave her a funny look.

"Well, sort-of," she said. "I mean, yeah, we've gone on a few dates."

Fred nodded and took a deep breath, as though he had something he was about to say, but then he closed his mouth again and shook his head.

"Were you going to say something?" asked Audra.

"Just going to tell you to drive carefully. Freezing rain is starting to come down out there. The parking lot was pretty slick already when I got here an hour ago."

"Thanks. I'll take it slow," she said.

"That's what I was going to say," he said.

"Excuse me?"

"Take it slow." He smiled rather sadly and she realized he meant with Ben Harrison.

"Have a good weekend, Fred," she said.

"You too, Audra," he said. "See you Monday."

As soon as she was done scraping the ice off her windows, Audra got in her car and called Sandra.

"Hi," Sandra answered. "Weren't the roads horrible? Gaahh! I'm so glad I made it home alive!"

"I wouldn't know," Audra said. "I'm still in the parking lot at work. Is there something I didn't know about Ben?"

"What do you mean?" asked Sandra.

"I just had the strangest exchange with Fred, the janitor. I felt like he was trying to warn me that Ben's a player."

Sandra laughed. "*Everyone* knows Ben Harrison is a player! I've tried to warn you about that myself."

"No, you didn't."

"I did! I told you not to rush in."

"I thought that was a general warning," said Audra. "I didn't realize it was Ben-specific."

"I really thought everyone knew about his reputation," Sandra said.

"*I* didn't know that. I thought he was engaged until just a few months ago."

"He was. And that entire time he was screwing around on his fiancée. You didn't know about him and Christina?"

"*Christina*? The Christina we know, from school? No!"

"Sorry, Audra, but it's true. They were hooking up last year all the time. There's even a rumor that he was dating the mother of one of his students a couple of years ago and she left her husband for him, but then he told her that he had gotten back together with his fiancée. In reality, I don't think they'd ever broken up in the first place."

"This is terrible news. I thought he was so sweet."

"He's like a sexaholic. I've heard he's into guys, too."

"That explains that picture."

"What picture?" Sandra asked.

"Never mind. How could you let me date him?"

"I thought you were just having some fun. And I figured you knew all this about him."

"I didn't know any of this," Audra said. Her voice broke as she began to cry.

"Oh, Audra," said Sandra. "You poor thing. I had no idea you liked him so much. If it makes you feel any better, I think he and his fiancée really have broken up this time."

"Why do you think this time it's real if he lied about it before?" Audra asked through her tears.

"Wishful thinking on your behalf," said Sandra. "He *does* seem to really like you though. Maybe a leopard can change his spots."

"He's been avoiding me all week," said Audra.

"That's not a good sign," Sandra admitted. "But hasn't he just been out sick?"

"Maybe he really *is* sick. Do you think I'm overreacting?"

"Honestly, Audra, I have no idea."

Audra sighed. She turned on her defroster since her entire car had fogged up while they'd been talking. "Thanks for listening."

"Of course."

"I'd better get going. I'm sure the roads are just getting worse and worse."

"Is your apartment close to the school?" asked Sandra.

"Not really. I'm on the complete opposite end of town. I'm thinking of going to Ben's place. He's only a few blocks away."

"Sure, stop in and see how he's doing."

"For safety's sake, I think I should," said Audra.

"What could it hurt? He's probably bored out of his mind. Just do it," Sandra agreed.

"That settles it," Audra said. "I'm going there instead of home. I have to. It's too slippery right now to make it home."

"Alright. Good luck. You can call me later if you need to."

"Thank you," said Audra.

"One more thing," Sandra said.

"What's that?" Audra asked, playing with the vent in her car, switching it from the windshield to her face to her feet and back again.

"I thought of something else about that Maddingly girl."

"Oh? What's that?" Audra asked, though she really didn't care. All she could think about was Ben.

"There was a rumor going around that she had a secret boyfriend."

"A secret boyfriend?"

"That's what I heard."

"Is he the third person you were talking about?"

"What do you mean?" asked Sandra.

"I thought you told me that there were three victims," said Audra.

"I said that?" asked Sandra. Her tone had changed. She suddenly sounded nervous and hesitant. "I guess it's just some rumor I heard."

"Did two people or three people die?" asked Audra.

"Now I'm not sure. No, I mean, of course just two people died. I mean, I don't know," she said. "Uh, I'm pretty sure it was just the two of them. Just Oliver and Evangeline."

"Do you have any idea who the secret boyfriend was?"

"I don't," said Sandra. "You know, I really shouldn't even be talking about this, considering that I know nothing except bits and pieces I've heard repeated around town."

"Do you think the secret boyfriend was involved in their murder?" Audra asked.

"I have no idea," said Sandra. "No one ever talks about any of this anymore. Before you started talking about it, it had probably been a couple years since I'd even heard it get brought up. It's as if no one in Port Elspeth cares any longer. It's not a subject that gets discussed. The whole town wants to pretend none of it ever happened."

Audra watched the icy sleet sliding down her windshield, piling up on her wiper blades. "No one in Port Elspeth may want to talk about it, but *I* do," she told

Sandra. "I'm going to get to the bottom of what actually happened."

Sandra laughed. "If you can do that, you'll be quite the detective, considering no one else has ever been able to."

"I'm going to do it. First, though," said Audra, "I need to solve the mystery of whether or not Ben Harrison cares about me. Unfortunately, I think I already know the answer."

Chapter 22

Vivienne Van Heusen-Prescott

Neil set down his snifter of brandy and frowned at his wife.

"Why are you looking at me that way?" she asked him. Normally he knew better than to challenge her.

"Vivienne, my darling, you know I love you…"

"Yes?"

"But I'm a little upset."

"Don't be upset with me!" she warned him. This was, basically, a household rule Neil needed to follow.

"Alright then, Punkin. I'm confused."

"What part of the story didn't you understand? According to her principal, Olivia is gifted and should be going to an elite, special, hard-to-get-into school."

"Is it a special school she'll be going to, or is it a special program she'll be in?" Neil asked.

"Neil, I don't know. It doesn't matter. The point is, she's gifted and special. I always knew it! Everyone in this town can put that in their pipes and smoke it! And you and I will *finally* have some peace and quiet. Our life has been *so* hard. It's been work, work, work. Climb, climb, climb. And then…" She shook her head. "What I went through is more than any woman, any mother, should ever have to go through."

"What *we* went through," said Neil, reaching out to take her hand in his own.

"Yes. Of course. What *we* went through. Though it was harder for me. I've told you before, I'm not going to get into it with you, but it was harder for me."

Neil nodded. "Of course, Punkin,"

"Our marriage *needs* this, Neil. After all we've been through, we deserve this time to ourselves."

Neil sighed. "I guess it *is* in Olivia's best interest, but she's only sixteen. I'm just trying to say that I would have appreciated you talking to me about it before telling her she could do it."

"There wasn't any time," Vivienne said sadly. "I told them I needed to discuss it with you, but they bullied me into making a decision. I was really under pressure! They needed an answer immediately."

"Why?" asked Neil.

"Because it's *that* big of a deal. If I hadn't said yes at that moment, some other kid would have gotten her spot."

"Oh," said Neil. He picked up his brandy, swirled it, and took another sip. "Well, in that case, kudos to you for acting decisively in a tricky situation."

"Oh, my pleasure," Vivienne said, with a modest little laugh.

"Olivia's excited about it?" he asked.

"Very much so," said Vivienne.

"Where is she?" asked Neil, glancing at the Rolex Vivienne had given him for Christmas the prior year.

"Still at school, I guess," Vivienne shrugged.

"It's getting very slippery out there," said Neil. "I had a bear of a time getting home."

"She'll be fine," said Vivienne, brushing off his concerns and settling down on her husband's lap. "Let's do it in the yoga room quick before she gets home," she said.

"I started a fire in there today and the smell kind of turns me on."

"There's not a fireplace in the yoga room. Is there?"

"No. I literally started the room on fire. It was just a little accident."

"I *thought* it smelled like fire in here when I walked in the door earlier," said Neil.

"I *like* it," said Vivienne. "It reminds me of the arson phase I went through when I was about fourteen."

Neil laughed nervously. "You're okay?" he asked her, looking her up and down.

"I'm fine! Are you checking for burn marks? Oh, Neil. You're a hoot."

"All these years together and you're still surprising me," he said.

"I'm still surprising myself," she replied.

Just then his phone rang. "It's Olivia," he reported.

"Ugh! Ignore it," said Vivienne.

He shook his head and answered it. "Hi there, Cupcake! Are you out there on those slippery roads?"

Vivienne got up. It had always irritated her that she was "Punkin" while Olivia got to be "Cupcake." Aside from some ground-scurrying, disease-infested rodent, anyone would prefer a cupcake to a pumpkin.

"Hang up on her," she mouthed to her husband, miming an old-fashioned phone getting set down on its cradle. "Focus on me, instead."

"Ha ha, very funny," he mouthed back.

She began unbuttoning her silk blouse. She was still wearing the little suit and broken heels she'd had on at the meeting earlier in the day and she fancied herself to look incredibly sharp.

"What's that?" Neil said into the phone. "You're with who? Who's Woody?"

Vivienne shook her head. "He's nobody. Just her gross hippie teacher," she said to her husband. "Watch this!

She ripped her shirt open, showing off her black lace bra. Neil gave her a thumbs up. Ever since she'd sent him the topless picture of herself a couple of weeks earlier, their love life had been on fire.

"I realize the roads are dangerous, Olivia, but maybe I should come and get you. Okay. What's the address?" Neil leaned over and scribbled something on the back of a magazine laying nearby. "Oh, is that right? He's a nice guy and you'll need to work with him a lot on this new project? I don't like that."

"Just hang up," Vivienne whined. She took off her open blouse, threw it on the floor, and straddled him.

"I'm coming to get you now," Neil said to his daughter. "As for future meetings with this Woody character, you're going to have a chaperone. Yes, I said chaperone. ...No, Olivia, I'm being serious."

"Jingle Bells, Jingles Bells," Vivienne began singing in a sultry tone into her husband's ear. Christmas songs, delivered properly, had always turned her on.

"Yes, Olivia," said Neil, "your mother is singing. ...I don't know who's going to chaperone you, but we'll find someone. ...No, it doesn't have to be either one of us. I'm sorry if this is embarrassing you, but that's what parents do. They embarrass their kids. ...Uh, sure, I'll talk to him."

"Is she putting Woody on the line?" Vivienne asked. Her husband nodded. She got up and put her shirt back on. All the buttons were gone from the little show she'd just put on for Neil.

"Alexa, listen up! Reorder that blouse I just bought last week," she yelled.

"Hi, Woody. Neil Prescott here. ...Yes, yes. ...I understand that everything about this is on the up-and-up, and that you've worked with students at your old school on similar projects in the past, but..."

Vivienne grabbed the phone out of her husband's hands. "Woody, shut *up*," she interrupted. "If my husband says my daughter needs a chaperone, she'll have a chaperone. Now put Olivia back on the line."

"Hello," Olivia said a moment later.

"Olivia, this is your mother, taking control of the situation, as usual. Call that art teacher from that tedious jewelry club we've dropped out of."

"I never dropped out," said Olivia.

"Suit yourself. Anyway, call her and tell her she's going to be sitting in with you and that creep."

"He's nice," said Olivia. "Why do you want that lady to be my chaperone?"

"*Duh*! Because she's an art teacher and she'll know better than anyone if he's behaving like an art teacher ought to."

"What if she doesn't want to be my chaperone?" asked Olivia.

"We'll pay her whatever we have to pay her," said Vivienne. "Anyone will do anything. Just about anyone, anyway. You just have to name the right price that gets them to take notice. Your father is on his way to get you." Vivienne gave Neil a look that said *Why haven't you left yet?* At that, Neil leapt out of his chair, grabbed the magazine with the address written on it, and dashed away.

"Okay, I'll try texting her and see what happens," said Olivia.

"Don't text her, call her," said Vivienne.

"Why?"

"Because I said so."

"What's her number?" Olivia asked.

"I don't know. You'll have to figure it out."

"How?"

"If you can figure out Cadence's number, maybe she can give it to you," Vivienne said.

"What's Cadence's last name?"

"Sommerset," said Vivienne. If she'd been talking to anyone other than her daughter, she would have pretended she was too disinterested to know it. "Now quit with the questions! You're exasperating me!"

"How is this *exasperating* you?" asked Olivia.

"You're supposedly so smart that you have to go to a special school in New York, so the least you can do is figure this out. But for now, get ready to be picked up soon. Your father is on his way and you'd better be waiting at the door when he arrives."

Chapter 23

Audra Fleming

Audra rang Ben's buzzer for the third time. Still no response. She turned and looked out at the gleaming parking lot. The roads were so slippery that she'd barely made it to his apartment. She had no idea how she was going to make it to her own apartment. She thought of her cat, all alone at home, and how, after having nothing but boring dry food and water all day, he was going to be expecting a can of tuna fish tonight. It was his Friday night treat.

"I'm coming for you, Flippy," she said, turning to brace herself against the cold, pelting sleet. She'd just gotten back into her car and started it back up when she saw Ben pulling into the parking lot, on his way to his apartment's parking garage. She waved at him, but it was too treacherous out for him to look her way. The parking garage opened and gobbled up his car, closing after him. She looked up toward his windows, waiting. After a couple of minutes, the lights in his apartment came on.

A large part of her was saying, "Audra, just go home," but, of course, she didn't.

She turned off her car, got out, and ice skated in her sneakers back to his front step. She rang his buzzer again. A moment passed and he pressed the intercom button.

"Hello?" he asked.

"Ben! It's me. It's Audra."

"Whoa! What are you doing out in this awful weather?"

"Can I come up?"

He responded by buzzing her in.

She went up the two flights of stairs to his apartment, expecting him to be waiting to greet her with the door open, but the door was closed and she had to knock on it. So she did. After a moment, he opened the door. He was wrapped in a blanket and his hair was messy, but he smelled like he was wearing cologne.

"How are you feeling?" she asked him.

"Ugh! Not good."

"What do you think you've got?"

"The flu," he said. "For sure, it's the flu."

"Terrible," she said. "Have you gone out and picked up any medicine or been to see a doctor?"

"No," he said. "I've felt too bad to even leave. I've just been catching up on about five hundred seasons of *The Office*."

"Oh, how boring and sad," she said, looking over at his clean coffee table. There were no signs of tissues or coffee mugs or bed pillows or any of the usual paraphernalia that typically accompanied a person who'd been sick all day. "Just sitting right there on the couch, all day, not going anywhere. You poor thing," she said.

"It's been the worst. I've slept most of the day."

"Hey," she said. "I got you something."

"I told you I didn't need any soup," he said, smiling the smile that had gotten her into all of this to begin with, "but if you got me some, I'll eat it."

"Actually," she said, "I got you something for your car."

"For my car?" he asked.

"Yeah," she said. "A little surprise for inside your car. It's right here in my pocket, but I can't show it to you because it's a surprise for the next time you get in it. Let me borrow your keys and I'll run down to the parking garage and put it in there for you."

"Ohhh kaaaay," he said. His hands closed on his keys laying on his coffee table, and then he froze.

"What's the matter?" asked Audra.

"Nothing's the matter," he said. "But you don't have to go all the way down there. Why don't you just give it to me now? Or put it in there later?"

"Because it's a surprise and I want to do it now."

"It'll still be a surprise if you give it to me right now, up here, instead of putting whatever you have in my car," he said.

"It'll be more fun if I actually put it in your car," said Audra.

"You don't have to," he said.

"But I want to," she said. "In fact, I insist." She reached out her hand that wasn't hiding behind her back and put it palm up for him to place his keys into.

"I get it," he said.

"What do you get?"

"Just come out with it," he said.

"No, I want *you* to say it," she said.

"You saw me coming home just now. If you go down there, you're going to see that my car is wet. There, are you happy?"

"No," she said. "Not at all. I'm very, very sad. Where were you?"

"I just went out to get some cold medicine."

"You're telling me this after you just said you were home all day."

"Aside from that, I was home all day."

"Right. And that picture the other night? That wasn't meant for me, was it?"

"Uhhh…" He made a noise that was somewhere between a laugh and a cough and a sigh. "Yeah, you were never supposed to see that," he admitted.

"Way to lead by example," she said.

"What's that supposed to mean?"

She shook her head. "Goodbye, Ben. Let's try not to make things too awkward at school."

She let herself out of his apartment.

Chapter 24

Audra Fleming

As she got back into her car, Audra felt her phone vibrate. She assumed it was Ben, but it wasn't. Instead, it was a number she didn't recognize.

"Hello?"

"Hi. Is this Audra the art teacher?"

"Um, yes. Who's this?"

"It's Olivia from the jewelry making club. Remember me?"

"Sure, of course I remember you."

"I have kind of a weird question for you."

"What's that?" asked Audra, brushing away the tears that were running down her face. She started her car. She could see from the dim, dancing blue light of Ben's apartment that he'd turned on his television. *Way to move right on*, she thought.

"I'm going to be working on a special art project for the rest of the school year and then I'm going to move to New York sometime this summer. I guess. I don't really know all the details yet. My parents want me to have a chaperone so I'm not alone with my teacher. They're going to hire you. I mean, if you'll do it."

"To move to New York?" Audra asked, confused. Moving away sounded kind of wonderful, right about now.

"No. You don't have to move to New York with me. I just need you to come up to Port Elspeth for a while on Wednesday nights and maybe some other nights to hang out with me and my teacher. His name is Woody. My parents think he's an evil hippie."

Audra pressed her fingertips to her pounding forehead. "I'm not sure I understand," she said.

Olivia took a deep breath and started over, "I have to meet with my teacher two nights a week to get something called a portfolio ready. He says it's just a technicality and that I'm already in, but that I still have to do it. My parents don't want me to be alone with him because he does some things my mom doesn't approve of."

"Well, Olivia," said Audra, "is this teacher scary or something? If he is, maybe you shouldn't be doing this project with him at all."

"No," said Olivia. "He's not scary at all, but he smelled like fries today and he was wearing a shirt that said *Save the Bees*. And his name is Woody. My mom's kind of a 'three strikes and you're out' sort of person. It's more like two strikes, actually."

"Congratulations on getting chosen to do a project like that," Audra said, wiping her coat sleeve against her nose. "It sounds exciting for you."

"Oh, thank you! So, yeah. My teacher isn't a bad guy, it's just that my parents are weirdos. You've met my mother."

Audra nodded. "Okay, I'll be your chaperone," she said.

"Really? Great! Is a hundred dollars an hour okay?"

"What?" Audra exclaimed. "That's crazy!"

"Okay, what about two hundred dollars an hour?" asked Olivia. "Name your price. They don't care."

"Two hundred sounds fair," Audra said.

"Okay. Super! I'll see you at that jewelry club on Tuesday night. Bye!"

Audra set her phone down and began carefully navigating out of the parking lot.

"What just happened?" she whispered to herself. Between everything that had just gone down with Ben and the exchange she and Olivia had just shared, she felt a little like she was losing her mind.

That bizarre, unexpected request couldn't have come at a better time. It gave her a little something to think about besides the broken heart and damaged ego she was nursing.

When she finally arrived to her apartment nearly thirty minutes later (it was normally just a ten-minute drive), Flippy greeted her at the door, meowing.

"I'm glad I'm home with you," she told him, going straight to the cupboard to get him his Friday night tuna fish. There on her countertop, beside the dying flowers she was about to toss out her window, was the page torn from the yellow legal pad. She set the unopened can of tuna fish down, picked up the sheet of paper, grabbed a pen out of the drawer beside her stove, and wrote *Three people died? Or only two? Secret boyfriend?*

Flippy meowed impatiently.

"Just a second," she told him. "I know your dinner's important, but I'm also going to solve this mystery. Just wait and see."

Saturday, March 3, 2018

Old Friends and New Friends

Chapter 25

Pearl Quincy

Pearl and Gladiola were seated at Pearl's kitchen table, sharing a bottle of wine.

"It's so nice to see you," said Gladiola, smoothing back her tidy silver bob. "What has it been? Almost two years?"

"I think so," said Pearl. "I believe the last time we got together was that time we had coffee at the Beacon Street Diner."

"I heard Margo's back in town," said Gladiola. "You must be enjoying having her around again."

"It's great," said Pearl. "I feel younger again. It reminds me a little bit of back when she was in high school. I hope she sticks around for a while."

"Our Brenna came home one summer when she was about twenty-seven and she was between leases. She stayed with us for three months. It was actually really nice to have her back. She never knew it, but I cried my eyes out when she moved back out. I knew she'd never live at home again."

"Never say never," laughed Pearl. "Margo will be thirty-five this year!"

Gladiola took a drink from her glass of wine and looked at Pearl with one eyebrow raised. "I got the impression from our phone call that you were interested in talking about more than day-to-day chitchat. You mentioned the Maddinglys?"

Pearl nodded, her throat suddenly dry. She supposed it wasn't in the best taste to reach out to Gladiola after all this time just to dig up gossip.

"Uh, yes, Gladiola, that's right," she said, "but, you know, if you don't want to talk about them, I understand. I'm just as content to enjoy this wine and talk about our kids."

"I'm curious what got you thinking about them," said Gladiola, toying with the cuff of her cardigan sweater.

"Margo and I joined a jewelry making club," said Pearl. "Although," she laughed, "we haven't gotten around to making much jewelry. Vivienne Prescott and her teenage daughter also joined the club."

"Really!" Gladiola exclaimed.

"That's right," said Pearl. "I don't know that I'd ever met her in person before, but she's something else!"

"You can say that again," Gladiola agreed.

"Naturally, seeing her there brought up all kinds of questions amongst the other women in the group about whatever happened with her son Oliver and Evangeline Maddingly. But if you'd rather I didn't pry into all that, I really do understand."

Gladiola shook her head. "I don't have any problem talking about it, though you might want to think twice before repeating it."

"Okay," said Pearl, already having a good idea that she wasn't going to be able to keep her mouth shut about whatever Gladiola was about to tell her.

"I warn you," said Gladiola, "it's a very strange story."

"In that case," said Pearl, her eyes shining as she topped off both their glasses of wine, "start from the beginning!"

Chapter 26

Margo Carlton

"I can't believe you've never done this," the redhead seated across from Margo said. "That's cray-cray!" she added.

"I don't think they do things like this in Paris. Things seem to happen a little more... organically there. So, yeah, this is my first time doing this. I guess it shows." Margo wove her fingers together in her lap, trying to calm her nerves. She drew in a deep breath and smiled and shrugged. She was at a furniture store about thirty minutes from Port Elspeth, taking part in a speed networking event for women, which, she hoped, might translate into meeting someone new to date. So far, she was hating every second of it.

"Okay," said the redhead, "you can stop name-dropping Paris."

"I didn't mean to be, it's just that Paris is on my mind a lot since I lived there for so long."

"Yeah, that's obvious, but stop mentioning it. It feels very braggy and annoying."

"Oh."

"I'm here to meet a girlfriend and I can tell you are, too."

"You're right, I am," Margo admitted.

"Well, in that case, I can already tell that you and I have no connection whatsoever, so you might as well let me use the rest of our five minutes to give you some relationship advice."

"Uhhhh, I'm not sure if I like that idea or not," Margo said, caught completely off guard.

"We've got, what?" The redhead checked her phone. "Three minutes left together. I'm just going to do a free-association where I tell you every impression I have of you, and everything you're doing wrong. Okay?"

"I don't know if that's okay or not," said Margo. "I mean, on the one hand, I'm a little curious about what you have to say about me, yet on the other hand, on principle alone, I don't feel like I should just sit back and take..."

"You look too sloppy, for one thing," the redhead interrupted. "Look at *me*. Look at how neat and tidy I look, and look how I'm showing off the goods," she said, running her hands down her ribcage and jutting out her chin. "*Smell* my hair."

"No thanks."

"Clearly, I gave a shit when I got ready this morning. Now look at you. Everything about you is plain, plain, plain."

"This is my style," said Margo.

"You have no style," said the redhead.

"One minute left!" called their event host. "Be sure to get those business cards or digits before you move on to your next encounter!"

"Can I move on to my next opportunity?" asked the redhead.

"Yes," said Margo.

"Good." She stood up from her chair and went to wait behind the person next to them, leaving Margo as the only person in the room who wasn't part of a temporary two-some. Margo soon felt her eyes moistening in frustration and embarrassment. She blotted at them quickly with the napkin her drink had been sitting on and tried to pull herself together before she had to face her next mini-meeting. She looked over at who was coming up next. She couldn't tell if the woman had dark hair or light hair since a silk scarf was wrapped around her head

"Very old-Hollywood," Margo decided, actually somewhat curious to meet her.

"Alrighty, ladies! Whether or not you've met your new best friend, it's time to get on up and move on out!" yelled the host, playing a sound effect of cows mooing. "Remember, those of you in the red chairs stay seated, those of you in the purple chairs get up and move one space to your right. And don't forget, these chairs are all on sale today and you can buy them once we officially open for business at eleven o'clock this morning, at the same time this event ends. Now... Five, four, three, two, one, and switch!"

No one was coming Margo's way. The woman in the scarf was still chatting with the woman at the previous table.

"I think I need to move back to Paris," Margo said to herself. Even if things hadn't worked out with Lisette, Paris had been her home for a decade. Being back in the States was making her realize how much the town and life she grew up with didn't fit her. She leaned over to grab her purse off the back of her chair just as the woman in the scarf sat down across from her.

"I'm sorry," Margo said, as she began to stand up. "It's not you. I've just realized this kind of thing isn't for me."

"Wait!" said her partner for the next five minutes. Their eyes met. "Don't leave! It's me."

Margo sat back down in her chair, too dumbfounded to speak.

"I didn't think it was possible that I'd meet anyone I knew here," said Cadence.

"Cadence! What are you doing here?" Margo exclaimed.

"I had to get out of the house this morning. Dave was driving me nuts trying to put together an in-home gym, so I googled 'what to do near Port Elspeth today' and this came up. I still need to get some furniture for the upstairs guestroom, so I figured I'd kill two birds with one stone. Maybe make some friends and get a new dresser set while I was at it."

"What are the odds? I never do anything like this," said Margo.

"Me either," said Cadence.

"This is a bizarre event," Margo laughed. "I mean, 'Speed Networking for Women at Doug's Modern Interiors.' You know we're desperate if we both ended up here."

Cadence laughed too. "I'm all for skipping out on the rest of this."

"What about your plans to get new furniture?"

"Who cares about that. Should we do brunch?" asked Cadence.

"Absolutely," said Margo. "Let's go."

Chapter 27

Pearl Quincy

"I started working for the Maddinglys in 1990," Gladiola told Pearl. "At that time, Claire and Mitch only had their oldest two girls, Emmie and Edie. Their youngest two daughters, Evelyn and Evangeline, weren't born yet."

"How old were the older girls, back in 1990?" Pearl asked, wanting to get every fact down. She'd considered taking notes like Audra had been doing at their jewelry club, but something told her that would get in the way of Gladiola's storytelling.

"Emmie was," Gladiola thought about it for a second, "a year and a half or two, maybe, and Edie was about six months old. Both of them were still in diapers when I started working there. At first I cleaned their house just on Mondays and Thursdays. Then it went up to Monday, Tuesday, and Thursday. Then Claire Maddingly said, 'Oh, Gladiola, let's just admit it: We need you here every day of the week.' And they really did! It wasn't that she was lazy or a bad mother, but they were so active that it made for a lot of work. Between riding and sailing and attending luncheons and playgroups and music lessons,

155

those girls and their mother had to change outfits about ten times a day and were constantly running here and there. The house always had to be perfect in case some local magazine wanted to drop in for a quick story about how Claire Maddingly arranged some fresh-cut flowers from her cutting garden into a bud vase."

"Fascinating lifestyle," Pearl said dryly.

"It was different," Gladiola agreed, "but I soon learned that being a Maddingly was a full-time job. Not unlike, I imagine, how it would be to marry into British royalty."

"British royalty. Right here in Port Elspeth," Pearl said, nodding. She pushed the platter of cheese cubes and crackers toward Gladiola and took a couple of each for herself, wanting to keep her old friend nice and comfy.

"I'm going to put this out there, before I go too far," said Gladiola. "I knew Claire Maddingly very well for many years, and she was always the friendliest, kindest person. Sure, she was rich and spoiled and all of that, but she was always good to me. It wasn't hard to work for her at all."

"I wouldn't have guessed that by the look of her," Pearl admitted. "She always looked so intimidating."

Gladiola shrugged. "You can never tell."

"No, you can't," Pearl agreed.

Gladiola took a swig of wine and continued, "In 1992 Claire and Mitch had their third daughter, Evelyn, and then in 1995, Evangeline was born. The three older girls were sweet and well-behaved as could be, but I'm going to tell you something."

"What's that?" asked Pearl.

"Evangeline was different. She wasn't like her sisters at all. Those four girls might have all looked similar, all four with dark hair like their father and their mother's deep blue eyes, but Evangeline was never a nice girl."

"I'm surprised Vivienne Prescott didn't say as much," said Pearl.

"Maybe she never knew Evangeline that well, but I did. I knew her better than possibly anyone in the whole world. In fact, she almost made me want to quit my job."

"She was that difficult to endure?" asked Pearl.

"She sure was," said Gladiola. "Those girls had a nanny and a cook. My job was just to keep the house clean. I shouldn't have even had to deal with them too much, and with the older three, I didn't. But that Evangeline!"

"Childish pranks?" asked Pearl.

"I wouldn't say so," said Gladiola. "There was one time, it was the first day of winter break from school, back when she was about four years old, when the *Port Elspeth Daily Talk*—you know, that show that used to air every afternoon?"

Pearl nodded. "I remember it."

"Well, they called around ten o'clock at night and told Claire that they'd like to come by in the morning to take photos of the girls making snow angels and a gingerbread house. Some other story they'd been planning to tape in the morning had fallen through and they needed some last-minute feature, and the Maddinglys, naturally, were on their call list."

Pearl chuckled. "I never knew how things like that worked."

Gladiola laughed. "Me neither, until I worked for them! So, the reporter was even going to bring the gingerbread house kit. All they had to do was to perform some fun activities and get their pictures taken. The house was spick and span. I had it all ready since the Maddinglys had a line-up of holiday parties and guests they'd be hosting."

"Go on," said Pearl, adding some more wine to both their glasses.

"So, this was around ten o'clock at night. I was about to leave for the day—I guess you can see, I worked some very long days there—and Claire and I were in the kitchen talking about them coming the next morning to tape their show. At that point, the girls didn't even know it was going to happen since it had all been arranged so last-minute. We looked up and saw little Evangeline standing in the doorway in her nightgown. 'What are you doing out of bed?' asked her mother. 'Just listening,' she said, and I swear to you, Pearl, she may have only been a tiny little thing, but her smile was pure evil!"

"Evil?" asked Pearl, shivering.

"Evil," Gladiola confirmed. "Claire picked her up to carry her back to her bed and I let myself out. I had to come back early the next morning since Claire wanted me to do some extra holiday decorating before the news crew got there. I let myself into the house—I had a key, of course—and the oldest daughter, Emmie, was up by herself sitting at the breakfast bar, eating a bowl of cereal. Her face was covered in black lines."

"Black lines?"

Gladiola nodded and held out her wine glass. Pearl poured the remainder of the bottle into it and got up to open another bottle.

"That's right," said Gladiola. "Black lines. Like from a magic marker. Right then, her sister Edie came into the kitchen. It was the same scenario. She looked even worse. I couldn't even believe it. They looked at each other and started screaming and laughing. Only, it really wasn't funny. And then Evelyn came in. Evelyn's the second youngest. Back at this time, she and Evangeline shared a bedroom. Her face was also covered in magic marker and a big hunk of her hair was missing.

"What in the world?" asked Pearl.

"At this point," Gladiola, "I thought they'd all been attacked. I know it sounds silly, but I thought someone had broken in and done this to them while they were sleeping. I actually had the terrible thought that maybe something more serious had happened to Evangeline or to Claire and Mitch. I ran upstairs and stuck my head in Evangeline's room and she was sitting up in bed, staring straight at the doorway. It was like she was waiting for me. 'Evangeline! You're okay!' I said to her. She didn't have a mark on her."

"Really," said Pearl.

Gladiola nodded solemnly. "I asked her what she was doing—she was sitting there staring so strangely—and she said, 'Did you see what I did to my sisters?' I said, 'Evangeline! Did you really do that to your sisters? That was very, very naughty!' and she laughed. It wasn't a nice laugh. It was very, very chilling. And then she said, 'I guess the gingerbread house and snow angels story will be just about me today. Oh well. Too bad for them.'"

"That's pretty creepy," Pearl said.

"It gets worse. Much worse," said Gladiola. "I saw the magic marker and the scissors on her bedside table, along with a big pile of her sister's hair. I went over to pick them up and she whispered to me, 'Gladiola, do you know what?' and like a dummy I said, 'What?' She said, 'Come here, I want to say it in your ear.' So I let her. God knows why!"

"What did she say to you?" asked Pearl.

"She said, 'I thought about doing something much worse, but figured this would do for now.' Pearl, she was *four* years old! It sent shivers down my spine. And I could tell you a hundred more stories like that."

"I would have been afraid to be alone with her," Pearl admitted. "I hate to ask, but did the news crew do the story still?"

Gladiola nodded. "Sickeningly enough, they did. Claire lied to them and said the older three had all fallen ill. They went ahead with the story and little Evangeline was the star of it all. She looked like the sweetest little angel."

"Awful," said Pearl. "Do you know, now that we're talking about this, I feel like I can actually remember seeing that segment on the *Daily Talk*. That would be impossible, though, for me to remember something as trivial as that after all these years."

"Not necessarily," said Gladiola. "They ended up turning it into several segments that ran all that holiday season. They showed Evangeline making that God-forsaken gingerbread house from about fifty different angles, they showed her hanging ornaments on the tree, sitting by the fire cuddling their dog, when in reality she hated the poor thing, yada yada yada. They used footage from that shoot to fill in their show for two weeks. I'd be surprised if you *couldn't* remember it."

"Her parents shouldn't have let her be on there," said Pearl.

"No shit!" Gladiola exclaimed. She and Pearl were both rather tipsy and they both began to giggle.

"Oh, Gladiola," said Pearl. "We need to get together more often."

"I agree! Here's a funny little fact. A few days after Christmas that year, I was sitting in the waiting room at the doctor's office and Vivienne Prescott sat down next to me. She had her little boy with her. Oliver."

Pearl's eyes opened wide. "You knew Vivienne way back then as well?"

"Not before that day," said Gladiola. "It was the first time I'd ever met her. She had no idea I was the Maddinglys' housekeeper. She just thought I was some average nobody. Which, I was," Gladiola laughed. "This was back when waiting rooms really were waiting rooms. Do you remember that? How long they used to make patients wait?"

"It has gotten better," Pearl agreed.

"We were sitting there and the *Daily Talk* came on. Once again, they were showing that damned footage of

Evangeline. Christmas was over, but I guess they figured they could still show the snow angels and her building a snowman and all that garbage."

"Ahhh, snow angels and other garbage," Pearl said, laughing. "You're such a hoot, Gladiola."

"At this time, Vivienne was well-to-do, but still an up-and-comer. She and her husband were fairly new to town. They didn't have the famous name or the old-money connections that families like the Maddinglys and the Mortensons did. Boy, did she want in, though! When that segment came on and little Evangeline was on the screen sticking that carrot in the middle of the snowman's face, Vivienne leaned over to Oliver—he was just an ugly, sad, scrawny little thing with duck-fluff hair sticking out all over his head—and she said, 'Oliver, look at the television.' He looked up at it and then went back to playing with his toys. 'Look at it,' she told him again. 'That little girl is Evangeline Maddingly. She's the same age as you. Next year you two will be in the same school. You need to be nice to her. She's going to be your friend. One day, when you grow up, you're going to marry her. Do you understand?'"

"Wow," said Pearl.

Gladiola nodded. "He kept playing with his toys, and his mother got very upset with him. 'Oliver Prescott,' she said—and she really hissed it. It sounded scary as hell—'Oliver Prescott, you need to answer me. Say that you're going to be nice to Evangeline when you meet her. Tell Mommy you're going to be very, very kind and friendly to her.' The poor little guy started to cry. 'I will,' he told her. 'And why is it so important?' she asked him. 'Because I need to marry her when I grow up,' he said. Then she said 'Good boy,' like he was a dog. Then I got called into the doctor's office and that was that. I suppose I would have forgotten the whole incident, but, wouldn't you know it, as soon as Evangeline went off to kindergarten, who do you think her first friend was?"

"Oliver Prescott," said Pearl.

"That's right," said Gladiola. "Evangeline came home after her first week of kindergarten and said to Claire, 'I made a new friend.' Claire was excited because Evangeline didn't seem like the kind of kid who would even *want* a friend. 'What's her name?' Claire asked her. 'He's a boy,' said Evangeline. 'His name is Oliver Prescott.' And right then and there I remembered who Oliver Prescott was."

"Did you ever tell Claire Maddingly about what you'd overheard at the doctor's office?" asked Pearl.

"No," said Gladiola. "Maybe I should have. I suppose I figured that even if Vivienne Prescott had orchestrated for her son and Claire's daughter to be friends, it wasn't necessarily harmful, or didn't mean that he didn't actually care for her."

"I guess they did care for each other," Pearl agreed.

Gladiola shook her head. "Evangeline never cared for anyone. I saw their twisted relationship all through the years. She was very cruel to Oliver. He was always quite thin and wimpy. She had no trouble pushing him around. Now and then he'd give up on being close to her. Get tired of her meanness, I suppose. He'd try to distance himself from her, but then his mother would push them back together. She just wanted him to marry into the Maddingly family. I swear, if they'd had a son, she would have focused on getting her daughter in with them as well."

"You really think so?" asked Pearl.

"I know so," said Gladiola. "When Oliver and Evangeline were in middle school, there was a period of time when I hadn't seen him around for a while. Months. Maybe a year. I figured they were getting to that age where either they just weren't interested in being friends any longer, or maybe their parents thought it was better for them to spend less time together. I figured I wouldn't be seeing him around their house again. It was a summer day and I was outside helping their gardener Earl move some patio furniture so I could vacuum the patio, when I saw Vivienne Prescott's vehicle drive up. She *shoved* Oliver out the door and left him standing there in the Maddinglys' driveway. She drove away. It was the most awkward situation I've ever seen. He didn't know what to do with himself so he asked Earl and me if we needed help cleaning the patio. I asked him if he wanted to go in and see Evangeline and he said that she wasn't really expecting him. His mother had literally *delivered* him there and told him to get back in with her. It was quite the uncomfortable situation."

"It sounds like Vivienne really wanted to keep things going with those two," Pearl agreed.

"You know that Oliver was only flunking out of high school because of Evangeline, right?" said Gladiola.

Pearl shook her head. "No, I didn't know that. Why would Evangeline want him to flunk out? Didn't she want him to go to college with her?"

Gladiola laughed. "Absolutely not. She wanted a fresh, new start without him. She was very, very intelligent and knew that the whole world was hers. There was no way those two were going to have a life together beyond Port Elspeth. It was never going to happen."

"But how can she be blamed for his bad grades?"

"Oliver was at the Maddinglys' house all the time during their junior and senior years of high school," said Gladiola. "By that time, they'd been going steady for a long time. He'd do her homework for her, and then, when it was time for him to work on his own homework, she'd tell him, 'No! I'm bored! That's enough homework for tonight. Let's get out of here.' Then the two of them would drive off together in his car. Sure, he should have stood up for himself, but he never did. I think he felt like every moment with her was too valuable to waste."

"So," Pearl ventured, "everyone in town seems to assume that Oliver killed Evangeline and then killed himself. Do you know if that's what the official report is?"

Gladiola lowered her voice, even though she and Pearl were clearly alone. "The coroner, as you know, has his own connections to the Maddingly family and the other founding families of this town. From what I've heard, his findings were 'inconclusive' but with no findings of foul play."

"Two healthy teenagers don't up and die without there being foul play," said Pearl. "There are two victims and no suspects. Case closed? None of this makes any sense."

"No, it doesn't," Gladiola said. "I've heard one rumor floating around that they were both shot to death. That is was a murder-suicide. I think either the Maddinglys or the Prescotts paid him off."

"Paid off the coroner?" asked Pearl.

"Yes," said Gladiola.

"Could he possibly be that corrupt?" Pearl exclaimed.

"Anything's possible. If you have the right connections in a town like this, you can get just about anything swept under the rug, and no one's going to try to dig it back out. People would rather have it there than out in the light of day. After all, tourism is our number one source of income. We'd hate to scare people away."

"I had no idea we lived in such a crooked little town," said Pearl.

"There's something else you should know," Gladiola said, "and then I ought to be going."

"What is it?" asked Pearl.

"There weren't just two victims. There were three."

"Three?"

Gladiola nodded. "As far as I know, at the time she died, Evangeline Maddingly was pregnant."

Chapter 28

Cadence Sommerset

"Table for two?" asked the hostess.

"Yes, please," said Cadence, nervously scanning the restaurant for any of Dave's new business associates. If it got back to him that she was here, alone, with another woman, and if he discovered it was Margo, he was going to be very, very upset. Years ago, back when they were engaged, she'd made the mistake of admitting to him that she'd had a brief relationship back in college with a woman. She'd thought he wouldn't care that much; in general, he never had much interest in the details of her life before him. She'd also thought that maybe he'd find it a little sexy and surprising. She should have known better. He was furious and disgusted with her. He threatened to call off their wedding and expose her secret to everyone. She'd begged him to forgive her, in large part because her parents had already paid for their entire wedding and honeymoon and the invitations had already been sent.

"Cadence?" said Margo.

"What?"

"She's wondering if you'd rather have a table overlooking the water, which means waiting fifteen minutes, or if you're okay with something else right away."

"Oh. Either. You choose," Cadence said, fearing for a moment that the older woman in the big hat across the restaurant was her neighbor Marlene Humphrey, but then realizing with relief that she was no one she knew.

"If you want a view of the water, you can wait in the bar area," said the hostess. "We've got five-dollar mimosas while you wait."

"That sounds great to me," said Margo. "What do you think?"

"Sure," said Cadence.

"Is everything okay?" Margo whispered to her, as the hostess led them through the restaurant.

"Sure, why do you ask?"

"You seemed really happy when we left the furniture store, but since we got here, you seem upset. Did something happen on the drive over here? Did you get an unpleasant phone call or something?"

"Here you go, and I'll put in an order for those mimosas, too," said the hostess, gesturing to the bar area. It looked like it was from the 1800's, with gleaming wood and nautical touches everywhere.

"This place is really pretty," Cadence said to Margo when they were alone. "I can't get over how beautiful it is being near the ocean. I don't think I'll ever get used to it. I hope I don't, anyway. And, to answer your question, nothing went wrong on the way here."

"I apologize," said Margo. "As soon the words came out of my mouth, I realized they sounded exactly like the kind of thing I would have said to my ex, Lisette, but you and I barely know each other. It was really inappropriate of me to pry so much."

"If that's the way you spoke to your ex, I think it makes you someone who's interested and caring," said

Cadence. She couldn't imagine Dave picking up on a slight shift in her mood unless it was personally affecting him. "If I seem upset, I'm just a little afraid that I might see some of Dave's co-workers, and he thinks I'm shopping for furniture this morning. He wouldn't like it if he heard from someone other than me that I'm here. Like anyone would, he hates it if I lie to him," said Cadence.

"A change of plans isn't exactly a lie, is it?" asked Margo.

"No, I guess it's not," said Cadence. "Dave's just kind of... particular about things."

A waiter set their mimosas in front of them. "They're just clearing a table for you now," he told them. "You came at the perfect time."

"Why's that?" asked Margo.

"Oh, you must not be from here," he said. "We've got a weekly tradition. It happens around this time every Saturday morning. You're going to get to watch the grand dame getting loaded."

"We're going to get to watch her *getting loaded?*" Cadence repeated.

"That's right," he said. "Wine today. Last week it was whiskey. It's quite a scene. It might not sound like that much fun, but I think you'll get a kick out it. To some people, like those two," he said, nodding at a couple who had just walked by, "it never gets old. They're here every single Saturday morning, hoping to catch the show. Anything can be entertainment if you let yourself be entertained by it, right?" he said before walking away.

Cadence turned to Margo, as soon as he was gone. "What in the heck was he talking about?"

"I guess some important old woman's going to get drunk?" asked Margo.

"It doesn't *sound* like it'll be fun to watch, but it must be, or he wouldn't have mentioned it," Cadence said.

"Do you think maybe it's some kind of act, like she gets silly and does a little show?"

"I kind of hope not," said Margo.

"What if she overdoes it and something happens to her? Like, she's dancing and she sprains her ankle?" Cadence asked.

"Yeah," said Margo, "it's kind of inappropriate for some woman's alcoholism to be seen as a novelty or a source of public entertainment."

"Your table's ready now," said their waiter. "Please follow me."

"I don't know that I want to see this," Cadence whispered to Margo.

"I'm going to say something if things get too out of hand," Margo agreed.

"I thought this place was really classy, but now I'm kind of appalled by it," whispered Cadence. "If they didn't have that dessert buffet there," she pointed to a long table overflowing with mini slices of cheesecake and a gurgling chocolate fountain, "I'd suggest we leave."

"And I'd be right with you," Margo assured her.

On their way to the table, the waiter turned excitedly to them and said, "Wait until you see how much wine there is today!"

"You realize it's only eleven o'clock in the morning, right?" said Margo.

"Yes?" said the waiter.

"Is the wine for the grand dame, or whatever you want to call her?" asked Cadence, glaring at him.

"Yes," he said. His smile disappeared when he realized both women looked disgusted by him. "Will this table do?" he asked, showing them to a lovely little round table by the window. It had a white linen table cloth and a bud vase of fresh flowers. It was relatively secluded.

Cadence looked around. "Where's the grand dame? How are we going to see her from here? Or isn't she here yet?"

"She's right there," said the waiter, pointing out the window at a ship in the harbor, docked beside dozens of pallets, each pallet holding a giant wooden wine barrel. *Grand Dame* was printed on the side of the ship in gigantic block letters.

"Oh," said Cadence. "There she is."

"How nice," said Margo.

"Is everything okay here?" asked the waiter.

"Perfect," Cadence said.

Margo nodded. "Couldn't be better."

Chapter 29

Pearl Quincy

"Evangeline Maddingly was pregnant when she died?" Pearl asked, flabbergasted.

"Yes," Gladiola whispered. "And here's how I know she was: I didn't normally work at the Maddinglys' on Sundays or holidays, unless there was some exception, and Easter Sunday was always an exception. They'd have me work for just a few hours in the morning, every year, helping clean up the house and put out the Easter eggs for their annual Maddingly Family Easter Egg Hunt around their grounds.

"Ugh, yeah," said Pearl. "How could I forget about that happening every year?"

"That year, all four girls were home. The oldest three were all either in college or had graduated from college at this point, and I think Edie, the second oldest, had just gotten engaged. Even though they were practically all grown up, they always had to be a part of this yearly tradition. I don't know if any of them had ever missed it. Even the year when Emmie was studying in Italy, I think she managed to still come home for Easter."

"How nice," Pearl said, rolling her eyes.

"They'd all dragged themselves out of bed early— that's one thing about those Maddingly girls—they aren't lazy—and they were all off at the hair salon getting done up for the day. I was going around from room to room, making beds and tidying up and emptying out the trashcans in their bathrooms."

"They all had their own bathrooms?" Pearl asked wistfully.

Gladiola nodded. "Of course they did. I got to Evangeline's bathroom and saw the trashcan was overflowing. I'd just emptied it a day or two earlier. Claire Maddingly liked everything kept up with perfectly. Obviously, or she wouldn't have needed me there so much. I started to pour the trashcan into the bigger trash bag that I was carrying, but I realized it wasn't all going to fit. I started shoving everything down into the bag to make room, at which point I realized her bathroom garbage container was filled with pregnancy tests. *Positive* pregnancy tests. There were probably a dozen of them. She'd taken test after test and tried to hide them and all their packaging in wads of toilet paper."

"No!" Pearl exclaimed. "Could they have belonged to one of her sisters? Or some friend of hers?"

Gladiola shook her head. "I thought at first that they might have belonged to her friend Taylor, who was probably her only real friend besides Oliver, since she'd stopped over to their house the day before. But she'd only been there for about ten minutes, and she'd been hanging out in the kitchen the whole time. No, I knew those tests were Evangeline's and I was devastated for her parents. I may not have cared for her, but I did care for her parents, and I knew this was going to ruin them. Not really, but in their minds."

"So, you're sure it couldn't have been her friend who took those pregnancy tests?" Pearl asked.

"No. In fact, Evangeline had a habit of writing little notes to herself with her purple pen…"

"Yes?" said Pearl.

"Well," said Gladiola. "All over the brown paper bag from Korgan's Drug Store she'd written the F-word over and over again. The paper bag was crumpled up into a little ball, but I saw the writing so I flattened it out to see what it said. She wasn't an empathetic enough person to have been that upset if the tests belonged to someone else. She was worried about herself."

"Do you think anyone else knew?" asked Pearl.

"I have no idea, but I'd think anyone would have a hard time keeping that big of a secret. Especially a teenager. Though, if someone had enough self-discipline, maybe they could keep a secret like that to themselves."

"Having a baby would have ruined her perfect future," said Pearl. "Do you think she intended to keep it?"

"I *know* she didn't," said Gladiola. "Every year for Christmas, her parents gave her a horse calendar. They'd been doing this since she was a little girl, and she always hung it on the back of her bathroom door. She wrote *everything* on there. She probably thought no one else knew it was there. Why would her parents or anyone else use her bathroom when they all had their own? But again, I saw it all the time, and shortly after I discovered those pregnancy tests, I got a little snoopy and flipped through the calendar. It was always good reading. I saw that she'd written *Get Rid of It 2 pm* on Monday, June twenty-fourth."

"Do you think that meant—" Pearl began to say.

Gladiola nodded firmly and continued. "I'll never forget those words in her bubbly handwriting, like it was just another chore, but I knew what it meant. I wondered why she was going to wait so long, and then I remembered that her birthday was June twenty-second, and I realized that she was waiting until she was eighteen years old so she didn't have to involve her parents. Meanwhile, this whole time, her acceptance letter from Harvard was stuck on the refrigerator downstairs and everyone thought she was perfect. You see? You never really know what's going on with anyone."

"Do you think she went through with it? The abortion, I mean."

"No one knows the exact day she died, but I'm guessing it was before June twenty-fourth, because I overheard the coroner talking to her parents and she was still pregnant when she died."

"You actually heard him say that?" Pearl gasped.

"Yes! The Maddinglys have no idea I overheard it, but I did. I definitely did. That's all I heard. I got out of there fast because I didn't know *what* they'd do if they knew I was listening!"

Pearl glanced at the clock on the stove. "Gladiola! Would you believe it's going on two o'clock in the afternoon already? Can I make you a real lunch? Something other than cheese cubes and saltines, I mean?"

"No, no. I don't need a thing. In fact, I've probably bored you out of your mind with this long-winded story," Gladiola said.

"Are you kidding? I've been hanging on every word," said Pearl.

"I think I've told you enough for one day. I'll keep going another day." With that, Gladiola stood up. She was so wobbly that her chair fell over. "Time for me to go," she said.

"Gladiola, I think maybe I should at least make a pot of coffee first," Pearl said, helping her friend pick the chair back up.

"No, no," said Gladiola. "I'm fine. It's just that I don't normally drink very much. I'll get used to it as soon as I get on the road."

"No! That's a terrible plan," Pearl said, feeling quite fuzzy herself. "You need to sober up a little before you go."

The back door opened and Margo walked in.

"Margo, you remember Gladiola Peabody," said Pearl. "Gladiola, this is my daughter Margo."

"It's been a long time," Gladiola said to Margo. "How nice to see you."

"You too," Margo said. She had a small bag of groceries in her arms. She began filling the refrigerator with produce. Gladiola sank back down in her kitchen chair and a flood of relief came over Pearl that she wasn't going to have to fight her friend on driving home just yet.

"What have you been up to?" Pearl asked her daughter.

"An unexpected brunch with a friend and then a trip to the indoor farmer's market," said Margo.

"You sure look happy about it," Pearl said.

"I am," Margo said to her mother. "I'll tell you all about it later."

"Now you really can't leave," Pearl said to Gladiola. "You and Margo need to catch up for a moment. I'll just get some coffee brewing."

"Alright," Gladiola relented, pulling a chair out for Margo. "I can't wait to hear all about your last ten years in Paris."

Margo laughed. "It's going to take me a while to tell you everything."

Gladiola hiccupped and covered her mouth in embarrassment. "Oopsie," she said. "I think I'll be here for a while, so go right ahead. I'm all ears."

Tuesday, March 6, 2018

The Third Meeting

The Port Elspeth Jewelry Making Club

Chapter 30

The Jewelry Makers

"I've tallied your email votes from last night," Cadence announced to the group, "and we have a name for our booth!"

There was a brief round of faux-fancy applause from Margo, Pearl, Audra, and Olivia.

"With five out of five 'Yea' votes, it's unanimous! We're going to call ourselves The Port Elspeth Jewelry Making Club," said Cadence.

"It's a great name," said Pearl. "Nice, simple, to-the-point."

"It's such a great name, in fact," said Margo, "that I designed a logo for us and started making tags and little cards to mount our earrings on. What do you all think?" She presented some mockups to them.

"Those look really great!" said Audra.

"I love them, too," said Olivia.

Pearl beamed proudly at her daughter's accomplishment. No matter how old she and Margo got, she'd never stop being proud of her daughter.

"I hope you're all ready to get a lot of jewelry made tonight, because we're getting down to business," said Audra. "I've made up little kits to help you get started." She distributed a length of wire, the two halves of a clasp, tweezers, and her own pre-selected assortment of fifty-one beads in front of each woman. She'd decided to bring some of her art teacher-ness to this meeting since the past two times they'd met, everyone had spent most of their time just chitchatting and looking through the jars of beads.

"That's right," said Cadence. "We're going to be jewelry-making machines tonight! In fact, I went to the office supply store today and picked up a dry-erase board, and I've charted out the rest of the times we have to meet, and how much jewelry we need to make each time to meet our goal. Sorry to seem so uptight, but the Port Elspeth Women's Club had stringent rules about how much inventory we have to sell, and I agreed to meet their standards in order for us to get the booth."

"Alright," said Pearl, "I'm getting down to business just as soon as I finish this cake you brought, Audra. It's delicious!"

"Best cake I've ever had," Olivia agreed. "Of course, I've hardly ever had cake in my whole entire life."

"You haven't?" Audra exclaimed.

"Why's that?" asked Margo.

"My mom only lets us eat salad and smoothies. I didn't even know a person could make cake. I mean, sure, I've seen boxes of cake mix at the store, but I never thought a regular person could make it. I thought chefs bought those boxes and then made them using fancy mixers they had in their restaurants."

"It's actually really easy to make a cake from a box," said Audra. "I'll show you some time after your portfolio project wraps up."

"Audra, are you helping Olivia with an art project?" asked Pearl.

"Mmm hmm," Audra said, nodding, since she'd just taken a bite of cake.

"I thought you taught younger kids over in Middleford?" Cadence asked.

"I do," Audra said. She took a sip of water, unsure how to explain the unique situation that Olivia's parents had insisted upon.

"She and a teacher from my school are partnering up to help me get into a special program," said Oliva.

"Exactly," said Audra.

"That's great," said Margo.

Just then they all heard the sound of heavy footsteps coming up the stairs. A moment later, Dave Sommerset came into the kitchen. "Oh, look! It's jewelry making time again," he said. "And now your little club starts at six instead of seven so you have even more time together." He was holding a folded striped blanket in his arms.

"Hi, Dave," said Cadence. "Did you come up to join us?" she teased.

"No, I didn't. Cadence, why don't you come outside with me for a second."

"Okay?" she said, picking up her wine glass and giving the women at the table a sheepish smile and a shrug.

They all watched out the window as the two of them made their way down to the twin Adirondack chairs that were illuminated by strings of white lights overhead, facing out toward the ocean.

"Kind of cold out there to sit by the water, isn't it?" said Pearl.

"Maybe they need to talk about something private for a second," Margo said.

"Humph," said Pearl. She turned to Olivia. "Why don't you tell us more about this portfolio project," she suggested. "It sounds exciting! Have you gotten started on it yet?"

"No, Mr. Willworth—I call him Woody, actually— and Audra and I are meeting tomorrow night," said Olivia. "I have no idea how to make a portfolio."

"I'm guessing he's going to want you to put together some of your best paintings and drawings," Audra suggested. "If you have things like that at home, why don't you gather them up and bring them with you tomorrow."

"I already have a big briefcase thing that my dad got me for Christmas a couple of years ago, just for carrying my art around," said Olivia. "It's already filled with all my favorite paintings and drawings I've done. I haven't added anything to it lately, but I'll bring it along with all my stuff."

"It sounds like you've already *got* a portfolio," Audra said. "This whole project might go a lot faster than we thought."

"Great!" Olivia said.

"Okay," Audra said, "tonight's project is to turn these beads and this length of wire into a necklace. We want it to be symmetrical with the biggest bead right in the center, so I suggest you put that bead on first, and then go about adding matching beads to either side of it, growing it out by the middle. You should each have the exact number of beads you need to make a perfect necklace, with plenty of wire left over to easily attach your closure clasps."

Olivia had already gotten started as Audra was talking. "This is so easy!" she said. "I love it. I'm already half done! I could do this all day."

"Fantastic job," Pearl said to her.

"You're all so nice to me," Olivia said, shaking her head.

"How are you doing?" Audra asked Margo.

"A little lost. I'm sorry," Margo said. She still had nothing but a pile of beads and wire in front of her. "I think I missed most of your instructions, Audra. I was a little distracted." She nodded toward the window. The Adirondack chairs had been pushed closer together and Cadence and Dave were snuggled up together beneath the blanket, looking out at the ocean and chatting.

"Glad this little jewelry club isn't getting in the way of their date night," Audra laughed.

"My parents are like that," Olivia said. "If it was up to my mom, she'd never share my dad with anyone. I'm pretty sure she wishes I was never born."

"I'm sure that's not true," said Pearl.

"No, it's true," Olivia said. "It's okay, most of the time. I mean, sometimes it bothers me, but usually I'm used to it. I had an older brother and she didn't care about him either."

"I know the story about what happened with your brother," Pearl said to Olivia, in as gentle a tone as she could, "and I think it must have really devastated her. You can't imagine how much parents love their children, but someday, if you have children of your own, you'll know how much your mother loved both of you."

"That's nice of you to say that," said Olivia, "but I think you're overestimating my mom. She's only interested in herself. And my dad. She's definitely still interested in him. It's kind of gross the way she throws herself at him." She made a face and held up her completed necklace. "Ta da! What do you all think?"

"Amazing," said Audra. "I've never seen anyone work so fast and do such a good job. You're a model student."

"I've only got three beads on mine," Pearl laughed.

"I'm up to four," said Margo.

"I'm going to make another one," said Olivia.

They all kept working and chatting about Olivia's portfolio project and Margo's adventures in Paris, until Pearl squinted out at the Sommersets' yard and said, "How do you think things are going out there?"

"If I had to guess, I'd say pretty cozy," said Audra. "They've been out there for over forty minutes"

The twilight had faded and now the women around the table could only see the silhouettes and faint details of Cadence and Dave. They all watched as Cadence glanced back at the house, started to stand up, and Dave pulled her back down into her chair.

"What's that burning smell?" asked Olivia.

"I think she's got something in the oven," Pearl said. She got up and took a peek inside it. "Oh! Look at that. She made a pie for us. It looks a little dark." Pearl found some potholders in a drawer, took the pie out of the oven, and set it on top of the stove to cool.

"More wine, anyone?" asked Audra.

"Sure, I'll have a little," Margo said.

The four of them continued working on their necklaces and talking more about Paris for another fifteen minutes. Just as Olivia and Audra finished their second necklaces and Margo and Pearl each finished their first, the door opened and Cadence stepped back inside. Her cheeks were bright pink from the cold and her teeth were chattering.

"I'm sorry," she said. "How long was I out there?"

"Oh, not that long," said Audra, checking her phone. "It's quarter to eight."

"Quarter to eight! I'm so sorry!" she said. "Dave wanted to talk about some things that happened today at work and time got away from us." She rubbed her arms. "Brrrrr! It's freezing out there!"

"He's still out there in the cold?" asked Pearl.

Cadence nodded. "He went down by the water. He's got a blanket, though. Oh! My pie! Thanks for noticing that it needed to come out of the oven. I completely forgot about it." She sat back down at the table and reached for one of the bottles of wine to refill the glass she'd brought back in with her. She took a couple of gulps of it and then topped it off again.

"Is everything okay?" Margo asked her.

"Yes. I'm just so embarrassed that we were out there so long and that I abandoned all of you like that. The thing is, Dave doesn't like to be neglected. He isn't happy about watching movies downstairs, either. This club might not work out after all."

"Would it help if someone else hosted now and then, so he can have his house back on Tuesday nights?" asked Pearl.

Cadence took another drink of her wine and nodded. "Yes, that might help."

"I'd be happy to host it next week," said Pearl.

"Thank you," Cadence said. "If that's truly okay with you, let's plan on it."

"It's a plan," said Pearl.

"I'll text or email out our address to everyone," said Margo. "Maybe we should all call it a night," she suggested.

"That's probably not a bad idea," said Cadence. "Could I send you each home with a piece of pie? I spent the whole afternoon making it."

"Sure," said Audra. "I'd love a piece for the road."

"Cake *and* pie, both in one day?" said Olivia. "I've never had so much dessert in my life."

Cadence got up, placed slices of the pie on four paper plates, and wrapped each with plastic wrap. "One for each of you," she said.

As they all made their way to the door, Olivia's phone went off. "Uh oh," she said.

"Is everything okay?" asked Cadence.

Olivia nodded. "It's just a text from my mom. She wants me back at home. That's one big difference from how she treated my brother Oliver. He could come and go as much as he wanted. He was hardly ever home. I'd better let her know I'm on my way before she freaks out." She shot off a quick text, then put on her shoes and coat.

"Drive carefully, y'all," Cadence said, watching as everyone went out to their vehicles. Margo and Pearl drove away, followed by Audra a moment later. Olivia however, stayed parked for some time. Cadence peeked out the window in the dining room, wondering why she was stalling so much when her mother was already worried about her. And then, with her front yard being as well-lit as it was beneath her trademark strings of white lights, she saw that Olivia was eating the slice of pie. Probably, she realized, because she wouldn't have been allowed to do so at home.

"Poor kid," she said aloud. "She's going to make herself sick."

Olivia shoved the last of it in her mouth, folded the paper plate into a tiny chunk of paper, put her window down enough to toss it out onto Cadence's driveaway, and drove away.

Wednesday, March 7, 2018

Secrets Exposed

Chapter 31

Vivienne Van Heusen-Prescott

"Vivienne. Of all people. I never thought I'd hear from you again," said the ice-cold voice on the other end of the line.

"Seriously? That's what you thought?" Vivienne asked, using her saddest, most pathetic tone.

"I was sure of it," was the cool reply.

"That really hurts my feelings," Vivienne said. "There was a time when we were such good friends."

"We were not. Now, looking back, I realize we were merely acquaintances," Claire Maddingly said.

"Acquaintances? You're really hurting me. We were friends. Great friends. And our kids were so important to each other. We had a special bond."

"No."

"Yes. And, for the record, *I* always knew we'd talk again," said Vivienne.

"How'd you get my number?"

"I have my ways," said Vivienne, forgoing the wounded victim act and getting down to business. "Do you think you're the only one who has important connections? I, too, can make things happen and get things done."

"Cut to the chase, Vivienne. After all these years, what could you possibly want from me?" asked Claire.

Vivienne was surprised with how this conversation was unfolding. The Claire she remembered didn't have much of a backbone. Polite to a fault. This new Claire was cold, blunt, and harsh. Vivienne wasn't sure if she ought to be disappointed or impressed.

"I want to catch up, Claire. Just to catch up," she said. "First, I'd like to know where you're living now."

"Your 'connection' who gave up my cell phone number didn't fill you in on that?"

"I was told you could be any number of places. A variety of locations were tossed around as possibilities. New York. London. Copenhagen. Rome." These were all locations that Vivienne remembered Claire mentioning that she and Mitch had homes or where they liked to vacation. In reality, no one had told her anything. She'd run into that old bag Gladiola Peabody at the grocery store a few days earlier and stolen her purse on the off-chance that she'd find information about Claire Maddingly inside it. Sure enough, there had been a tiny spiral-bound notebook with the gold embossed title *Important Names and Numbers to Remember.* It looked like something she'd been carrying around since the 1980's. It was filled with names and numbers, including a new cell phone number listed for Claire that Vivienne had never seen before.

"Why won't you tell me who shared this with you?" Claire asked. "I'd like to know."

"Listen, Claire," Vivienne said, softening her tone considerably. She had no intention of this being a short conversation. Now that she had Claire Maddingly on the line, she wanted to talk all day. "I *miss* you. Just tell me where you're living these days. Old friend to old friend. I'm curious about what you've been up to and how you've been. Is it so bad that I just want to hear about your life? How's Mitch? How are the girls?"

"Everyone is fine," Claire said, after a lengthy pause.

"Great! That's wonderful. I heard Emmie and Evelyn are both engaged now. How exciting! Two weddings to plan! And what about Edie? I saw in the paper that she just had a baby. You're a grandmother now!" Vivienne winced as soon as she said it. After all, Claire had almost been a grandmother years ago, and surely she must know that.

The line went cold for a long moment and Vivienne feared Claire had hung up on her.

How could you, Vivienne? You blew it, she thought to herself. *You mentioned the one thing that was completely unmentionable.* She drew in a deep breath, wondering what she could say to undo the damage. She knew this call was her only chance to patch things up. If it didn't go well, she wasn't going to get another opportunity.

And then, to Vivienne's astonishment, Claire relented. "Oh, Vivienne," she sighed, "I guess it makes no difference if I tell you what city I'm in," she said.

Vivienne smirked. Claire had always been too nice for her own good. Maybe 'nice' wasn't the right word. 'Oblivious' was a more accurate choice.

"Oh, do tell! I'm *so* curious about your beautiful life," Vivienne said, buttering her up.

"We're living in Marseille," said Claire. "We have homes in Italy and Carmel, too—I mean Carmel-by-the-Sea in California—but we spend most of our time here in Marseille."

"Marseille?" asked Vivienne. "You mean in France?" Jealousy quickly began surging through her veins.

"Yes, of course. France," said Claire.

"Of course," said Vivienne. She pictured Claire's swanlike neck and dark blue eyes. Her penchant for wearing tiny diamond-studded barrettes in her bobbed blonde hair. She remembered Claire's classy skinny jeans and pointed-toe flats, and the way she'd instinctively known the myriad of subtle nuances and elegant, natural-looking behaviors Vivienne was forever trying to master. And she almost had mastered them. Before she'd gotten so terribly far away, she'd gotten close.

"Everything back in Port Elspeth seems like a dream," Claire continued, her voice losing its cool edge and gaining the conspiratorial school-girl lilt that Vivienne had once known over cups of tea and afternoon glasses of wine. "And by dream, I mean bad dream."

"There's nothing about Port Elspeth you miss?" asked Vivienne, downplaying how much that stung.

"Not really! Sure, we still have the cottage there; the girls like to use it when they want to see their friends, but we just keep it for them. I haven't been to it in years. Too many bad memories for me. I wouldn't care if I never went back. It's so much nicer here."

Vivienne's mind raced. She hadn't realized that when Claire and Mitch sold their house on the hill and moved away they'd kept their five-bedroom ocean-front farmhouse a few miles west of town. Kept it like an afterthought to use as a holding station for their daughters a few times a year. There had been a time when she'd assumed one day Oliver and Evangeline might live there and raise a family there. She'd been able to picture it perfectly. Before everything had unraveled, she'd been in the habit of buying vintage juice glasses for their kitchen.

"And it's not just the weather, or the food, or the people," Claire continued. "It's everything."

"Well, I suppose France *is* amazing," Vivienne began, but Claire cut her off before she could get her whole thought out.

"How have you stayed there, Viv? I assumed you'd leave. Why haven't you?"

"Neil's job," Vivienne said.

"I just don't know how you've done it. If I was still there, I'd need to be on antidepressants around the clock in order to even get dressed in the morning."

"It hasn't been easy," Vivienne admitted. Claire was the one person in the world besides Neil that she could talk about this with, and she found herself wanting to unload everything. "It hasn't been easy at all," she said, the barrier separating herself from the tears she rarely cried beginning to lift. If it lifted, she had no idea how hard or long she would cry.

"Well," said Claire, "I can't talk much longer. It was nice catching up with you, Viv."

"Oh. You have to go?" Vivienne asked, stunned that Claire was cutting off their conversation just when she thought they were about to bond again.

"I do. Sorry! It's just about dinner time here. Gervais—that's one of our cooks—is going to call us at any moment. I need to get dressed for dinner."

"One of your cooks," Vivienne repeated, forcing herself to push past her desire to chuck her phone against the wall. "Claire, before you go," she said, "there's a reason I wanted to reconnect with you.

"Just a minute, Viv," said Claire. And then, she called out, "Jean-Luc, apporter une autre bouteille de champagne, merci beaucoup." Vivienne heard a man's voice respond back, but she couldn't make out what he'd replied. Still, she was fairly sure Claire had just told someone she needed more champagne for dinner. Their exchange went on for quite a long while. Vivienne began to wonder whether Claire even remembered she was on the line.

She's forgotten I'm here, she thought to herself. *Should I hang up?* The humiliation was so pungent she could smell it. No, that was the aroma of her own sweat.

She muffled her phone into her armpit and whispered to herself, "I hate her," and then pressed the acrid phone back to her ear, just in time to hear Claire say, "I'm back. Sorry, Viv! Are you still there?"

"Yes," Vivienne choked.

"What did you want to say?"

"The reason I called," Vivienne said, "is that Neil and I are going to be leaving Port Elspeth soon."

"Why didn't you say so? Good for you! Where are you going?"

"Venice," Vivienne said, repeating the story that she already was beginning to tire of hearing herself tell. "I have old friends there." She could hardly muster any enthusiasm into her voice about it. "And I have a favor to ask of you before we move away."

"What's that?" asked Claire.

"Everyone blames my son for what happened."

Claire did not respond.

"But I'd like the record set straight."

"I can't help you with this," Claire said.

"I was thinking a billboard. A billboard on the edge of town. Something telling people it wasn't him. You understand, this isn't personal. I love you! I loved Evangeline like a daughter. I just want to clear my son's name. Once we move away, I'll never have the chance to do so."

"We both know you're lucky that Mitch and I got Coroner Phelps to make all of that go away," said Claire.

"You think your daughter was responsible," Vivienne said.

"And everyone else thinks your son was, and we'll never know what really happened up there, so why don't we let it go and move on with our lives?" Claire said.

"I want Oliver's name cleared," Vivienne said. "I want a billboard declaring him innocent, sponsored by you and Mitch."

"I'm hanging up now, Vivienne."

"Don't hang up! Option two, if that seems too heavy-handed, is a statement about how both our families are still hurting."

"Forget it. Goodbye, Vivienne."

"If you don't like the billboard idea, what about a full-page ad in the paper? And no matter what, you and I can still be friends. Maybe Neil and I will move to Marseille, too. We could be neighbors!"

"This conversation is over," Claire said, hanging up on Vivienne.

Vivienne clenched her phone between her palms as if she was praying. It hadn't gone as bad as she'd thought it might. As far as she could remember—the conversation already felt like a blur—Claire hadn't told her no.

She imagined that billboard—she'd already sketched it out on paper, thought about its placement, and spent hours editing the message; Claire wouldn't have to do anything but agree to it and pay for it. A billboard like that, sponsored by the Maddinglys, would turn everything around for her. When she and Neil were driving out of town to start their new life together, the Mortensons and the Van Pelts and every last member of the Port Elspeth Ladies' Club would be chasing after them, begging them to stay.

"If you'd have been nicer, I would have stayed. But now I'm moving to Venice. Or Marseille," she'd yell to them. "Eat my dust!"

Chapter 32

Cadence Sommerset

"I know you're not going to want to hear this," Cadence said, bracing herself for the fight that would surely ensue. "But you really embarrassed me last night."

"Why would you say that?" asked Dave.

"Going outside like that. Forcing me to abandon a houseful of guests. We were out there for over an hour! In the cold! In the dark! Now they all probably think we're crazy."

"It wasn't a 'houseful' of guests," said Dave. "It was an old lady, some kid, some lesbian, and some gangly nerd."

Cadence set down her whisk—she was in the process of making a dessert for the dinner party they were hosting that was scheduled to start in ninety minutes—and took a drink of wine. Then she turned to face her husband. "How are you feeling about things since we moved here?" she asked him.

"I'm feeling good. Never better. We've got a beautiful house *on the ocean*, my job is going great, we're meeting all the who's whos about town, and I just got accepted into the Men's Club. By the way, did you apply for the Women's Club yet?"

"Not yet," she said, "but the booth at the craft fair is connected with their club somehow. I forget how it works, but I think I'm already kind of 'in' with them."

"You have no idea how towns like this work, Cadence."

"You're probably right," she said. *And I don't care.*

"Do you know how many women would kill to be in your shoes?"

"Probably lots," she said. *I don't know any woman who would kill for any reason.*

"You're living the good life, but I can tell you aren't happy. You're never satisfied. You know why that is, right?"

"Enlighten me. On second thought, don't bother." Her hand flew to her mouth. "Oops. I didn't mean to say that second part out loud. I was just kidding!"

"Very funny," Dave said. "See? You're drunk as usual."

"I'm sorry," she said. She wasn't sure if she was apologizing for being rude to him or being drunk. She didn't feel particularly sorry for either, though.

"Why don't you quit drinking from now until when our company comes, and then take it easy during dinner," Dave said.

"Okay, I'll do that," she said.

Dave poured the rest of her glass of wine down the drain and put the bottle in the fridge. "Your problem," he said, "is that you're bored. You need a job."

"You're probably right," she said.

"What about a volunteer position someplace? Find something that's just five or ten hours a week. Not some job that takes it out of you and makes it so you're so beat at night that you can't even host a decent dinner party, but something to keep you busy and get you connected with the right kind of people. This group you've gotten yourself mixed up with is a mistake. You're going to embarrass yourself if people associate you with people like that motley craft crew."

"Motley Craft Crew," Cadence mused. "I like it! That should have been our booth's name."

"I want you to stop hosting that jewelry group," said Dave.

"I already…" she began.

"Effective immediately," he interrupted her.

"I knew you felt that way," she began again, "so last night…"

"Let someone else do it. You can keep going to it, since you don't want to burn any bridges with the Women's Club. Once it wraps up, though, you need to distance yourself from that band of losers you've gotten yourself mixed up with."

"They aren't losers," she said quietly.

"But they are," he said, smiling tiredly at her.

"Hey," she said. "I've been meaning to ask you something."

"Oh? What's that?" he asked.

"It's about something that was written in your legal pad." She could sense him snapping to attention. A sharpening to his senses taking over him as she poured the batter in a pan and placed the pan in her pre-heated oven.

"Something that was written in my legal pad?" he asked, scratching his head.

"Who's Tiffinie?"

"Who's who?"

"Tiffinie."

"I don't know what you're talking about."

"Her name and number were written on a page in one of your legal pads. It wasn't your writing. It looked like she wrote it down herself. Really pretty handwriting," Cadence said, smiling her biggest, fakest, warmest smile at her husband.

"I don't know what you're talking about. Show it to me."

"It's right over there," she said, pointing to where the legal pad was wedged between a pile of magazines. "Right under the latest issue of *Better Homes and Gardens*."

He walked over, pulled it out of the pile, took an over-acted look at it, and set it back down on top of the stack of magazines, shaking his head. "I don't know. Some friend of yours, maybe?"

"No," she said.

"I have no idea who that could be," he said.

"Whoever she is, she wrote her name and number in your legal pad. There's even a little heart."

"I don't know," said Dave.

"Well, let's figure it out together. Where's the last place you took that legal pad?" asked Cadence.

"I don't have any idea who that person is or why her number is on there," Dave repeated.

"What about the heart? Do you know what that could mean?"

"I have no idea," he said.

"Should we call her?"

"There's not even an area code."

"Well, let's give it a try with the local area code," said Cadence.

"I'm not calling anyone," said Dave.

"Then how about if I just give her a call right now and see how it goes?"

"You do that, Cadence, but I have no idea what this number is even about," Dave said, his face getting redder and redder.

"I think we should call her from your phone and see what happens," said Cadence.

"I'm not calling anyone and you're not using my phone. If you want to call the number, you do it on your own phone. You'll just make yourself look like a fool," he said.

Cadence drew in a deep breath. Suddenly she felt very tired. She wondered why she'd bothered starting this fight. Bringing all their troubles to the surface and shedding light on them wasn't going to resolve anything. She ought to know that by now.

"Cat got your tongue?" he asked her, laughing. "Why are you starting this right now when we have dinner guests coming over soon?"

"I'm sorry I'm not better at scheduling talks about what a cheating rat you are," she said.

"Some name and some number—and I don't know where they came from—don't prove anything."

"I don't need more proof than that. Your reputation back in Arkansas is proof enough. I thought Port Elspeth was going to be our fresh start. You said you were going to be good this time."

"I'm telling you for the last time, I don't know where that name and number came from."

"Seriously, Dave. You make me sick. And you break my heart. Why do you do it?"

"At least I've never been a carpet muncher," said Dave.

I'm pretty sure that's not something to brag about, Cadence thought to herself.

"Unlike you," he added.

"I'm starting to think this marriage is never going to work," she said, wondering how she'd ever been stupid enough to have quit her high-paying job to move here in the first place. Of course Dave was never going to change.

"Then pack up and go back home to your white trash family. Of course, once you do that, you'd better find a job again fast or you'll all be out on the streets hungry. I'm not going to have any reason to give money to your mother after we split up."

197

Cadence nodded. She thought about going back home to Arkansas all the time, except the reality of it had just as many pitfalls as being here with Dave. Her mother Dorothy was alone, depressed, and missing one leg due to her diabetes. For the past several years, Dave had allowed Cadence to send her mother eight hundred dollars a month so she could have all the groceries and small luxuries she wanted.

She and Cadence's father had bankrupted themselves paying for her and Dave's extravagant wedding and honeymoon. It wasn't until after it was all over that Cadence realized they'd afforded it all by maxing out credit cards and defaulting on their mortgage payments. It had driven a huge wedge between her and her siblings, since their parents hadn't done anything like that when the others had gotten married. Then Cadence's father had died a year after her and Dave's wedding, leaving Cadence's mother alone, depressed, and penniless.

Dorothy viewed her daughter's supposedly happy, successful life and generous, wealthy husband as her own sole achievement in life, after having lived through her own unhappy marriage and raising two other children who were both still on welfare. On more than one occasion, Dorothy had told Cadence, "You're so blessed to have a good man. Knowing you're well taken care of is the greatest reassurance in my life. Sometimes I wonder what I did wrong with the other two, but then I see you and I know that I didn't fail as a mother."

"Are you at least going to go through with the dinner party tonight?" Dave asked her. "Or are you going to embarrass both of us by making me cancel it at the last minute?"

"Of course I'm going to go through with it," she said. It was easier to have the party and be there than to drive away and go—where? Leaving now would mean dealing with her entire life falling apart immediately, instead of on her own schedule. "If you think I'm going to miss out on all the amazing food I made, you're wrong."

"In that case, you'd better get dressed for dinner," said Dave.

"I know that."

"Don't forget the most important accessory," Dave told her.

"What's that?" she asked.

"A smile."

Chapter 33

Audra Fleming

"Thanks for doing this for Olivia," Woody Willworth told Audra when Olivia went to the restroom. "I don't know whether her parents would have let her be part of this program if you hadn't."

"I'm glad to be involved," said Audra. "It's pretty exciting news for her."

"It is," said Woody. "She doesn't know it yet, but getting into this program will open a lot of doors for her." He smiled at Audra, ran a hand through his gray and blond hair, and then adjusted his glasses. Audra decided he was in his mid or late-thirties. He wore jeans and an old t-shirt covered in faded trees that said Yellowstone on it. He had a sunny aura of warmth and kindness. She couldn't remember the last time she'd met someone she was less intimidated by. He was Ben's opposite, yet there was something rather attractive about him. She wondered whether he was single.

"Nice classroom you have here," she said. It was four or five times bigger than the room she taught in, with a ceramics wing, a gigantic weaving loom in a window-filled alcove, and a whole miniature scene set up on a table on the far end of the room.

"Thank you! Thanks so much," said Woody, grinning. He clearly took a lot of pride in his classroom.

"What's going on over there?" Audra asked him, pointing to the miniature scene.

"Come on over and I'll show you," he said. "Some of my sophomores are making a Claymation movie."

"Did they make all these little figures and the whole town?" asked Audra.

"They sure did," Woody said, nodding excitedly. "The project has been going on all year, and their town has been growing. You can watch their show on the local cable access channel. It's like a Claymation soap opera. They call it *Port Elspeth Troubles*. Each week they do a little show that's a couple minutes long and it airs on Sunday nights around nine o'clock."

"That sounds really fun," said Audra. "I'll tune in this Sunday."

Woody nodded. He looked like he was going to say something, but just then Olivia rejoined them and the three of them sat back down at the table in front of her stacks of drawings and paintings they'd been sorting through.

"If there isn't enough good stuff here to choose from," she said, "I have lots more at home."

"You're so prolific," Audra told her.

"Yeah. I have no idea what that means," said Olivia.

"You produce a lot of work," said Audra.

"Oh, thank you."

Audra picked up one of Olivia's paintings and took a closer look at it. It was an abstract drawing of a young woman. One eye was a few inches higher than the other. The drawing was partially from the front, and partially from the side, combining to make a unique yet familiar portrait. "This is really good," Audra said. "It reminds me of Picasso's Dora Maar paintings"

Woody clapped his hands together in glee. "Oh, Audra," he said, "I'm glad you knew that. This assignment was part of our Art of the Nineteen Hundreds unit."

"I did it just a couple months ago," said Olivia. "I wasn't sure if it was any good."

"It's great," Audra said. "It needs to be included."

"I agree with Audra," Woody said to Olivia. He turned to Audra and said, "It was for an exercise the students did where they took a different drawing they'd done when they were younger and redid it, borrowing inspiration from their favorite twentieth century artist," said Woody. He looked quite proud of himself for having come up with such an assignment.

"That assignment was based on a picture I drew a long time ago of my brother Oliver's girlfriend Evangeline," said Olivia.

Woody nodded. Audra could tell he had no idea the significance of what she was talking about.

"My mom might despise her," Olivia said, "but I have some good memories of her."

"Your mom despised her?" Audra asked.

"She loved her," Audra said. "She loved her more than she loved either of us. It was obvious my whole life long. She was always trying to get Oliver to invite her over to our house. She'd stock the fridge with all her favorite things like Kraft Singles and purple grapes and lemon yogurt, even though she didn't buy most of that kind of stuff for us. But after they both died, she hated Evangeline."

"Sometimes when people are hurting, it comes out seeming like anger," Audra suggested. Woody cracked his back and took a sip from his mug of coffee. He looked confused and uncomfortable about the conversation. Audra knew he'd only lived in Port Elspeth for a year or two, but she couldn't believe none of his co-workers had filled him in on the story of the Port Elspeth Tragedy.

"They were missing for weeks," Olivia said, "and my mom was hardly ever home for the first couple weeks. She was off looking for them constantly. She barely slept. She'd come home covered in scratches and mosquito bites from going through the woods and hiking through fields. When she wasn't looking for them on foot, she was driving all over the place. She was looking everywhere, day and night. I wanted to go out with everyone and look too, but I was only eleven. She made me stay home with relatives or my dad. She was sure she was going to be the one to find them."

"Olivia, I know your mom might seem tough or cold to you sometimes," Audra said, "but the story you're telling me shows how dedicated she was, and how much she cared." Audra tried to conjure up an image of Vivienne as part of a search party, exposing herself to the elements as she traipsed about in hiking shoes and a safari hat. The image was so out of character that, as sad as it was, it almost made her laugh.

"Oh, yeah. She was dedicated," Olivia said. "It was all because of Evangeline, though. Evangeline was like her real daughter and Oliver and I totally came in second and third to her."

"But Olivia," said Audra, "when she was out there looking, she wasn't just looking for Evangeline. She was doing it because your brother was also missing."

Olivia shrugged. "I doubt she would have tried so hard for just him. But, anyway, a few days or maybe a week before those people found them, she gave up. I guess she was exhausted. She got really sick and kind of crashed into a depression. One day she came home from looking, took a shower, crawled into bed, and didn't want to talk to anyone. When those people found them, she could barely deal with it. My dad took care of everything. She had to go to a psychiatrist and take all kind of pills that made her seem like she wasn't even there. She was kind of out-of-it for a year or two. And if I ever brought up Evangeline's name, she told me she didn't even want it spoken in our house."

The three of them were silent for a moment until Woody spoke up and said, "I think you may want to leave this one out, after all." He took the corner of the Picasso-inspired Evangeline project and pulled it away from the rest of the drawings and paintings.

Audra laughed dryly. "Yeah, I think your portfolio might be stronger without it."

Chapter 34

Margo Carlton

"If we're going to host that jewelry club," Pearl said, looking around at her cozy but somewhat-shabby little home, "I'm going to need to spruce things up around here."

"Oh, Mom," said Margo, "your house is nice. I don't think anyone expects it to be as big or expensive as Cadence's house. I mean, really, who else has a house like that?"

"Well," said Pearl, "I still ought to pick up some new dishtowels and potholders. And maybe some new throw pillows for the couch. And maybe a new set of dinner plates. Mine all have chips."

"We could go shopping this afternoon," Margo agreed. "I wouldn't mind doing a little shopping, myself," she added. "I've got an interview on Friday and nothing to wear to it."

"You have an interview?" Pearl exclaimed. "Where?"

"At a graphic design firm. It's for a junior graphic designer position, which I suppose I'm a little old and over-qualified for, but it's better than nothing."

"That's great," said Pearl. "I'm kind of surprised you're interested in it, though."

"Why do you say that?" asked Margo.

"Not even a week ago, I got the impression you were unsure about being back here. I thought you were considering going back to Paris."

"I still am considering it, someday. For now, though, I need a job."

Pearl nodded. "Okay," she said.

"Why are you looking at me like that?" asked Margo.

"Like what?" asked her mother.

"Like you think I'm lying or something."

"I don't think you're *lying*," said Pearl. "Lying is a strong word. But I do think there's a little more to the story."

"What are you trying to say?" Margo asked.

"On Saturday when Gladiola was over here, you came home in the best mood I'd seen you in the whole time you've been home. You said you'd been out with a friend and that you'd tell me about it later, but then you never did. So, spill it: Are you dating someone already?"

"No," Margo laughed. "Nothing like that."

"Who were you with?"

"I was with Cadence."

"Cadence from the jewelry club?"

"Yes, of course. How many other Cadences are there?" Margo laughed.

"I didn't realize you two were spending time together outside of the club," said Pearl.

"It was just by luck. We ran into each other and ended up going out for brunch and to the farmer's market. Cadence asked me not to mention it in front of everyone because it was a different plan than what she'd told her husband she was going to do, and she didn't want it getting back to him."

"*What?*"

"I know that sounds weird," said Margo, "but I'm picking up on the fact that their entire marriage is a little off. He seems to be very controlling."

"Are you interested in her?" asked Pearl.

"*Mom*," said Margo, feeling like an on-the-spot teenager. "why do you have to phrase it like that?"

"Well, are you?"

"Who wouldn't be?" Margo said, wishing she'd never even admitted this much to her mother.

"Well, *I* wouldn't be, for one," said Pearl.

"She's beautiful and funny and cute. But I realize we can only be friends and I'm fine with that."

"Okay," said Pearl. She looked doubtful though.

"Please don't worry about me, Mom."

"Mothers always worry about their children."

"You don't need to worry about this," said Margo.

"Have you spoken to Lisette lately?" asked Pearl.

"Nope, and I'm not planning to," said Margo. "I saw on Facebook that she's moved on and is already dating someone new."

"So that's really over."

"Yes, Mom."

"Just out of curiosity, what's her new girlfriend like?" asked Pearl.

"Thanks for rubbing it in."

"Never mind! I thought you didn't care that much."

"I don't really," Margo said, sighing. "Her new girlfriend is a guy and his name is Julien."

Pearl sighed. "And to think there was a time when I thought *my* life was complicated."

Chapter 35

Audra Fleming

"Oh! I didn't realize anyone would still be here since school's been out for hours," said the young woman in the MIT sweatshirt. She was holding a sketch of a field of flowers.

Olivia looked up from her own pile of sketches and paintings, her face lighting up in recognition. "Taylor?" she asked. "Taylor Van Pelt?"

"Yes," said the young woman.

"You don't remember me? I'm Olivia Prescott. Oliver's little sister."

"Oh! Olivia. You look so... different." The woman in the MIT sweatshirt turned to Audra and Woody, "I'm Annie Van Pelt's older sister. Are you her teachers?"

"I am," said Woody.

"Oh, good," she said. "I'm home for a family thing and my sister has a cold, so I brought her assignment in since she won't be in class tomorrow." She held up the mediocre sketch. Audra guessed it had taken no more than five minutes to do.

"You can set it on my desk," Woody said.

Taylor walked across the room to place it there. Olivia jumped out of her seat and ran over to her. "Taylor," she said. "Come and sit with us. I want you to help me pick out artwork for my portfolio project."

Taylor shook her head. "Sorry, Olivia, but I can't. I'm on kind of a tight schedule. I'm only home for tonight and my whole family's waiting for me so we can all go out to dinner tonight. It's my parents' anniversary. We're all going out to D'Angelo's to celebrate." She set the drawing on Woody's desk, and then, seemingly deciding it was too ugly to look at, flipped it over face-down.

"I thought Annie was sick with a cold," Woody said under his breath to Audra, rolling his eyes.

"Please, please hang out with us for just two minutes?" Olivia begged.

Audra had no idea who this young woman was or why her opinion was so important to Olivia, but she could see it was. "You should really take just a moment to check out her work," she said, pulling out the chair beside her.

"Please hang out with us, Taylor," Olivia said again.

"Two minutes," Taylor said. She sat beside Audra and stretched. "I'm so sore," she remarked. "They just opened this squat bar right down the street from me and I did one of their classes yesterday morning. Now I can hardly walk."

"Squat bar?" Olivia asked. She looked impressed.

Taylor nodded. "You do all these squats and pliés and then drink enough calories in wheatgrass juice and rosé to cancel out all your hard work. It's right between a macramé store and an Anthropologie. My block is definitely designed for women," she laughed.

"A macramé store! Are you kidding me?" Audra exclaimed. There was nothing she liked better than macramé. She'd never dreamed an entire store could be devoted to the revived art of creating rope and yarn wall-hangings.

"I'm dead serious," Taylor said to Audra. She glanced at the time on her Fitbit and then turned to Olivia and said, "So, what are we looking at here?" She peered at Olivia's book of drawings and paintings.

"My portfolio project," Olivia said. "But first, let's do introductions! Woody, Audra, this is Taylor Van Pelt. She was friends with my brother."

"I was Evangeline Maddingly's best friend," Taylor said, her voice heavy, her eyes boring into them all with the importance and significance of that statement.

"Taylor, this is my teacher Woody and my mentor Audra."

Mentor, Audra noted, smiling. It was the perfect term. So much nicer than "chaperone."

"Nice to meet you," said Taylor. She reached over for the pile of Olivia's work and pulled out a picture of a forest. "These are really good, Olivia."

"Thank you," Olivia said. Audra had never seen her look happier. "Taylor used to babysit for me when I was little," Olivia told them. "I'm a grade older than Annie. Annie and I used to play together all the time."

"Olivia, your paintings are as great as your drawings!" Taylor exclaimed, holding up an oil painting of a shimmering dragonfly on a leaf.

"Thanks. I'm glad you like them," Olivia said modestly, her cheeks burning pink with pride.

"You're really talented," Taylor said. Then she pushed out her chair as though she was about to stand up to leave.

"Wait!" Olivia exclaimed. "Tell me something about my brother. Tell me something good. I want to hear what it was like when you were in high school with them."

Audra's heart broke a little at the desperation in Olivia's voice.

"I don't know what to tell you," Taylor said.

"Anything. A story about him and Evangeline. Or… or any story you can think of," Olivia said. She scanned the art room, clearly trying to come up with an idea for a topic. Her eyes fell on a display of intricately cut-out pink and red hearts from her class's Scherenschnitte assignment a few weeks back. "Valentine's Day!" Olivia exclaimed. "Do you remember them celebrating Valentine's Day?"

"I can't even remember my own Valentine's Day back then," Taylor laughed. She bit her lip, thinking. "I'll try. Actually, yes, I remember it. I wasn't dating anyone my senior year, but I can remember that Valentine's Day because your brother got Evangeline a little teddy bear wearing a Harvard sweatshirt. He gave it to her at school that morning."

"Tell me more," Olivia said.

"You know, it's all coming back to me now. It's not a very good story. You probably don't really want to hear about it."

"Of course I do," said Olivia.

"Okay," Taylor said, with an *I warned you* look on her face. "I remember that Evangeline and I were hanging out by her locker. I actually just walked past it a couple of minutes ago, right before I came in here tonight, for old time's sake. Her locker was on that dead-end hall down by the English department. You know what little hallway I mean? There are only about a dozen lockers on it?"

"I know what you mean," said Olivia.

"We were late to class. Evangeline was never late to class, but that day, she wasn't in any hurry at all. Her locker was open and the bear was on the top shelf. I asked her what she and Oliver were going to do that night. Like, were they going out for dinner or anything."

"What did she say?" asked Olivia, her eyes shining.

"She said they were going to go to your house because your mom made them a little cake or something, and then they were going to go out for dinner. I don't remember the exact details about that, but what I do remember is that she was flipping through her notebook, skimming each page like she was looking for something. The thing is," Taylor said, "Evangeline could be kind of... I guess the word is *cool*. If you hear people saying she wasn't nice, it was just that she was so much cooler than the rest of us."

"Okay?" Olivia said.

"I asked her what she was looking for in her notebook, but she just ignored me and kept flipping through it. 'If you need to borrow my notes, you can,' I told her. I'd always let her use my notes. So did Oliver. Anyone would have. She was the kind of person that everyone wanted to be friends with, but she could kind of take you or leave you, you know?"

Woody checked his watch. He clearly wasn't finding Taylor's story as interesting as Audra and Olivia were. "I'll be right back," he told them.

"What was she looking for in her notebook?" Olivia asked.

"I didn't know," said Taylor. "Then she told me, 'You take your notes on your laptop. I *write* mine,' and I said, 'So?' Like, what was the difference, right? She said, 'You retain knowledge better if you write it instead of typing it.' Then she held up her notebook and it was all full of her perfect purple handwriting. She always wrote everything in purple. She told me, 'All of this is in here,' meaning her notebook, 'and in here,' and then she tapped her head."

"She could be kind of a know-it-all," Olivia said to Audra.

"But it didn't come across as uncool," Taylor insisted. "With anyone else, you'd want to hit them if they did that, but with her, it just made me feel like she was smarter and better than me, and like I could learn a thing or two from her. Now, I take all my notes by hand and I get better grades than anyone." She looked up toward the heavens and said, "Thank you, Evangeline." Then she turned back to Olivia. "I still can't believe she's gone. She would have grown up and done anything she wanted. She was the smartest person I ever knew."

"I still wonder what notes she was looking for," Olivia mused.

"So, this is the part I really shouldn't tell you," Taylor said.

"Tell me what?"

"I've never told anyone this before," Taylor said.

"Tell me, please," said Olivia.

"She wasn't looking for any notes. She was stalling."

"She was?" asked Olivia.

"Yes. She told me to go to class without her. She was acting really funny. But I did what she told me to do. I always did what she told me."

"Yesss?" Audra prompted, when Taylor's long pause became so long she feared she'd changed her mind about telling them the rest of the story.

"My feelings were kind of hurt because I felt like she'd dismissed me or something. I was going around the corner and my face was down, and I was trying to keep from crying. And I bumped right into a teacher. A substitute teacher, actually. Our creative writing teacher, Mrs. Swanson, was out on maternity leave..."

"Ugh! I have her. She's the worst," Olivia interrupted.

"Yeah, she is," Taylor agreed, which made Olivia smile. "So, anyway," Taylor continued, "he'd been filling in for a month or so and we all knew him pretty well. He wasn't much older than us. Evangeline had a huge crush on him. She called him Mr. THS. THS stood for Totally Hot Shit."

"Wait a minute. She liked guys besides my brother?" Olivia asked. She looked crushed.

"I'm sorry, but yes," Taylor said. "So, anyway, he put his hand on my shoulder and asked me if I was okay and I told him I was fine. He told me I'd better get to class since the bell had already rung. Then he kind of rubbed at his nose and gave me a funny look. I thought I had a booger or something, so as soon as he left I got my compact out of my tote bag to check myself. By the way, there was no booger. Then I heard this gaspy little laugh coming from down the hallway. I instantly recognized it was Evangeline's laugh. I went back around the corner and there was Mr. Harrison with his arms around Evangeline and his hand up the back of her skirt."

"There was *who*?" Audra asked, her heart suddenly beating loudly enough that she was sure both Taylor and Olivia could hear it.

"Mr. Harrison," Taylor said. "I was so shocked I dropped my compact on the floor and the mirror broke. Talk about seven years of bad luck! At least there are only two more to go."

"Evangeline was making out with a teacher?" Olivia asked, devastation on her face.

Taylor nodded. "I never told anyone any of this, but I guess, what difference does it make now? Evangeline said, to me, 'What are you still doing here?' and Mr. Harrison jumped back and said to me, 'I told you to get to class! You didn't see what you thought you saw!' Well, of course I saw what I thought I saw. I'm not an idiot."

"What was Mr. Harrison's first name?" Audra asked. She realized she was trying to talk normally but her voice was barely above a whisper.

"I think it was Ben," Taylor said. "I walked away from them then because I couldn't even face them. I left my broken compact on the floor. As I was walking away, Mr.

Harrison said to me, 'You keep this to yourself or you'll be very sorry.'"

Tuesday, March 13, 2018

The Fourth Meeting

Chapter 36

Vivienne Van Heusen-Prescott

"If you leave this house, you're grounded," Vivienne told Olivia. It was quarter to six in the evening and her daughter was halfway out the door, a plastic bag from Beads N Baubles tucked under her arm. She was trying to hide it behind a chemistry book, but Vivienne could see right through her little tricks.

"Why?" asked Olivia. "Just five minutes ago you said it was fine if I went to Ada and Lila's house to study."

"Only you're not going there, are you?"

"Yes, I am."

"Don't lie to me! You're going to that repulsive jewelry making club. I know you are. Show me what's in that bag," she said, holding out her hand to her daughter.

Olivia sighed and gave her mother the bag. Vivienne tore it open and pulled out several packets of wire earring parts and a plastic shell case of tiny faux pearls. "Jewelry club," Vivienne confirmed.

"You were fine with me staying in it until out of the blue yesterday."

"I was never actually okay with it," Vivienne said.

"Pretty soon I'm going to be living in New York on my own. You have to stop micromanaging me."

"Where do you learn these expressions? Micromanaging doesn't apply when you're talking about how a mother takes care of her child," Vivienne said indignantly. Just then they heard the sound of the garage door opening. "Aha! Your father's home," Vivienne said. "We'll get his opinion on whether or not he thinks it's appropriate for you to spend your time with that sketchy group of women."

"Dad already *said* he approves. In fact, he told me he was sending Audra a cookie bouquet to thank her for being my mentor."

"I don't like the idea of your father giving anyone but me gifts," Vivienne said.

Neil came through the door then. He looked exhausted. As soon as he saw his wife and daughter, and the expectant looks on their faces, he groaned.

"We've been waiting for you to settle an argument," Vivienne said.

"Noooooo. Not yet. How about five minutes of niceness first," he whimpered. He looked around their house in confusion. It was a complete disaster. "What happened to our house?" he asked.

"Nona quit," Vivienne explained. "I hired a new cleaning lady. She starts tomorrow. I read good things about her on the neighborhood message site."

"Ughhhhh," he said. "Fine. Hi, you two." He gave Vivienne a kiss on the lips and Olivia a kiss on the forehead and then groaned for a few moments, kicking off his shoes and settling down on one of the kitchen chairs. "What a long day," he said.

"Why?" Vivienne snapped. "Usually you aren't home for at least another half hour or so. You're home early, so why was today so exhausting?"

"Some days are harder than others."

"You want a beer or a bottle of water, Dad?"

"A bottle of water would be great," Neil said to his daughter.

"Our daughter," Vivienne began, "thinks it's appropriate to spend her time with people two or three or four or *five* times older than her. As her father, I'd like you to set the record straight," she said to Neil. She crossed her arms over her chest, waiting for him to handle the situation.

"Is this about that jewelry club?"

"Yes. What else would I be talking about?" asked Vivienne.

"Dad, it's harmless," Olivia said.

"Oh, Olivia. You're growing up so fast," Neil said.

"This isn't the time to get sentimental," Vivienne said. "Can you please explain to her the value of having normal, popular friends who are closer to her own age?"

"Here's something you might find interesting," Olivia said. "I spent some time hanging out with Taylor Van Pelt last week."

"Taylor Van Pelt?" Vivienne felt her jaw drop. She clamped her mouth shut and sat at the table beside her husband. "When?" she asked Olivia.

"Hmmm," Olivia said, thinking about what day it was.

"Sit," Vivienne told her. "You're not leaving. At least not until you tell me where you saw Taylor Van Pelt." The Van Pelts were nearly as fascinating to Vivienne as the Mortensons, but, of course, not nearly as fascinating as the Maddinglys. They were another founding family of Port Elspeth. You could always recognize a Van Pelt by their long, pointed noses and droopy gray eyes, and how, despite these sad, obtrusive features, they all shared a pale, waspy kind of attractiveness.

Olivia took a seat at the table. "It was on Wednesday," she decided. "The night I met with Woody and Audra about my portfolio. Taylor came into the art room to drop off Annie's assignment—you remember Annie, right?"

"Yes," said Vivienne, shaking her head. How that little dummy Annie Van Pelt was still reigning supreme, getting elected onto the homecoming court and making it onto the front page of the *Port Elspeth Gazette* for her dressage skills, while Olivia was dying her hair with food coloring and piercing the bits of webbing between her toes was beyond her comprehension.

"Isn't Taylor getting her Master's Degree at MIT?"

"She was home for her parents' anniversary."

"Oh? I wonder what they were doing to celebrate."

"Dinner at D'Angelo's," said Olivia.

"*That* old place?" Vivienne sniffed. "I guess they've never heard of Fig and Breeze or Café Portugal, or any of the new, hip places downtown. Humph." She sure was going to miss keeping up with the Joneses when she and Neil moved away.

"Taylor told me something," Olivia ventured.

Neil pressed the cool bottle of water to the back of his neck. "Go on," he said.

"She was best friends with Evangeline, you know," Olivia said.

"Our Oliver was best friends with Evangeline," Vivienne corrected her.

"I don't think you guys are going to want to hear this," Olivia said. "I kind of wish I hadn't."

"Tell us anyway," said her mother.

"Taylor said that Evangeline wasn't exactly... *faithful* to Oliver."

"Why would you say that?" Vivienne asked, leaning forward and glaring into Olivia's face.

"Please, Punkin. Take it easy on the poor kid," Neil said, gently patting Vivienne on the wrist until she sank back into her chair.

"Taylor told me that Evangeline had something going on with a teacher," Olivia told them.

"No," Vivienne said.

"Are you sure about this?" asked Neil.

"Taylor said she saw them kissing each other. She saw it with her own two eyes."

"That's impossible," Vivienne said flatly. "Evangeline would have never cheated on Oliver. I advise you to stop spreading this rumor, Olivia, and if you see Taylor again, you should tell her the same. In fact, I might do so myself."

"She's not telling it to anyone," Olivia said. "She said it was the first time she'd ever told anyone about it."

"Which teacher was it?" asked Neil.

"Will you stop?" Vivienne shrieked. "There *was* no teacher! It's clearly a lie. Evangeline Maddingly was a good girl from a good home and she never, ever, ever would have *dreamed* of mistreating our son, much less being involved in something so scandalous and inappropriate."

"That's the most I've heard you stick up for her in years," said Olivia. "I thought you hated her."

"I don't hate her. I've never hated her," said Vivienne.

"Dad, do you care if I go to my jewelry making club?" said Olivia.

"It doesn't matter to me," he said.

"Thanks for sticking with me," Vivienne snapped at him.

"Oh," he said. "I didn't realize that the jewelry club was off-limits for her too."

"Just go to that silly club then," Vivienne said. "But don't let anything they say sink in. They're bad influences on you. And when you get home tonight, I want you to park in the garage…"

"Impossible! It's too tight to get in there," Olivia interrupted.

"It is not. You've got several feet of room on either side of you," said Vivienne.

"But, Mom, I can't."

"Say you'll do it or you're not going anywhere tonight."

"Fine. I'll do it," said Olivia.

"And then," Vivienne continued, "you're not going anywhere else for the rest of the week."

"I can drive to school, of course, right?"

"No, you can get there the old-fashioned way."

"Which means what? Ride a horse and buggy?"

"No," said Vivienne. "You can ride the school bus or ask one of your friends to drive you."

"I'm sixteen! I'm not riding the school bus!"

"Then talk to your friends. Those ghastly twins both have their driver's licenses and you cart them all over the place. Let them drive you around for a change."

"Why are you so mean? What about my portfolio meeting?"

"You can still go to it. If you can get Ada or Lila to give you a ride to school tomorrow morning, your Dad will pick you up when it's over. He can come straight from work."

"I can?" Neil asked.

"Yes," said Vivienne. "I'm busy all day tomorrow with yoga and picking out new paint colors for the wall in the meditation room. I'm tired of always being the one to do everything around here."

"But I can really leave tonight?" Olivia asked.

"Yes. Before we change our minds," Vivienne said.

"Thank you, Mom. Thank you, Dad," Olivia said, giving them each a quick kiss goodbye and grabbing her bag of craft supplies. She didn't bother bringing the decoy textbook this time.

"One more thing," Vivienne said, as Olivia was about to go out the door.

"What?"

"You said you're the only person Taylor told that to?"

"About Evangeline and the teacher, you mean?" asked Olivia.

"Yes," said Vivienne.

"Good. Let's hope she keeps her mouth shut about it. I don't need rumors like that going around about Oliver and Evangeline's relationship. After all, we all know it was perfect."

Chapter 37

Cadence Sommerset

"Pearl, your house is so adorable. It reminds me a lot of the house I grew up in," Cadence said to Pearl.

"Thank you," Pearl said, taking Cadence's coat. "I'll just set this on the bed in my room. I don't have a coat closet. Audra and Margo are right through there in the kitchen. You go right on ahead."

"Thanks," Cadence said, taking a good look around at the small, quaint living room. It was extremely lived-in, but cute and clean. Two bright blue pillows, each with a trendy quatrefoil design, adorned the worn sofa. Cadence had a hunch that the pillows were new for this evening.

She went into the kitchen where Margo and Audra both jumped up to give her a hug.

"Check it out," said Audra, gesturing toward Pearl's kitchen table. It was piled up with jewelry.

"What's all this?" asked Cadence.

"I've had some extra time on my hands and all kinds of things to stress me out, so I've really thrown myself into the jewelry project," said Audra. "I made jewelry all weekend long."

"Can you believe how much work she got done?" Margo asked Cadence.

"There's got to be enough here to fill our whole booth. I can't believe you did all this yourself," Cadence said to Audra.

"It was worth it. It helped get my mind off things, plus it leaves more time for us to talk," said Audra.

"Making jewelry has definitely been getting in the way of jewelry making club," Margo laughed.

Cadence took a seat beside Margo, picking up some of the necklaces Audra had made and admiring them. "These are beautiful. They look so professional," she said.

"Cadence, would you like a glass of wine?" asked Margo, offering her the choice of either Pinot Noir or Pinot Grigio.

"What do you think?" Cadence laughed. "How about Pinot Grigio?"

"Coming right up," said Margo.

Pearl joined them in the kitchen, just in time to pull a sheet of chocolate chip cookies from the oven.

"Oh, no!" said Audra. "Chocolate chip cookies straight from the oven are my kryptonite. Am I using that word right? I'm trying to say that I can't resist them."

"Me either," said Cadence. "Cold white wine and fresh-baked cookies. My God. This club is the best thing that ever happened to me." And after the day she'd had, that didn't feel like an exaggeration at all. Dave had called in sick so he could spend the whole day berating her and fighting with her. After several hours of that, she'd called her mother and asked her if she'd mind if Cadence paid her a visit. Her mother had said, "If you're coming into town, why don't you get us a nice suite at the Springwater Bed and Breakfast and we can have some mother-daughter time. Book us massages at the spa, too. And I need to get my hair cut."

Cadence hadn't even been able to explain to her that it wasn't that kind of visit, and that spending money frivolously right now was the last thing she wanted to do.

She'd tried to end the call with a vague, "I'm not sure if a visit right now will work or not, Mom. I was just kind of feeling things out." Then, before she could get off the phone, her mother had broken down crying and asked her for forty-four hundred dollars for surgery for her cat. When Cadence wasn't able to give her an answer, her mother had become irate with her and asked to speak to Dave. Dave had just walked into the room at that same moment, overhead his mother-in-law asking to speak to him, and had grabbed Cadence's phone from her hand. He'd then agreed to send Dorothy an even five thousand dollars.

"You owe me now," Dave had told Cadence, laughing cruelly. "But, hey, that's nothing new."

Cadence sighed now. She took a drink of her wine, hoping she could shut off her racing mind for an hour or two.

"I wonder if Olivia is going to be joining us," said Pearl.

"I think she's planning on it," said Audra. "I met with her last week and she mentioned how much she likes this club. She's probably just running a little late."

"I'm surprised her mother lets her attend it," said Margo.

"Me, too," Cadence agreed. "I hope she didn't forget that we're meeting here instead of at my house. Maybe one of us should text her. I really don't want that poor girl to have to deal with Dave and his horrible moods." She could picture Olivia ringing the doorbell and Dave flinging the door open, his face as red as a beet. "Ughh," she moaned. She realized then just how much she despised him. How was it all hitting her now? She asked herself, for what felt like the millionth time, how she could have allowed herself to be relocated so far from everyone she knew?

"Will it be *that* bad if he answers the door?" asked Audra. "Won't he just tell her we're not meeting there?"

Without warning, Cadence began to cry. "Oh no," she said. "Why am I crying? It'll be fine. How embarrassing."

"You don't need to apologize," Margo told her.

"Margo's right. You can talk to us if you need to," Pearl agreed.

Cadence wiped at her tear-streaked face. "I'm sure I'm overreacting. It's normal for moving to a new place to be really difficult, right?"

"Sure," Audra said.

"Because," Cadence said, "it's been really, really hard. I feel so emotional all the time! I think being the sole breadwinner is stressing Dave out. He makes a lot of money and he's proud of it, but we're in kind of a different situation than we were in back in Arkansas. I used to have a good job. We had a nice life, but it was nothing like how it looks now. We spent a lot of time with our friends and family. I used to see my mother a couple times a week. We'd have dinner every Sunday, no matter what. Aside from when I first went away to college, I've never been away from everyone I knew."

"If there's anything we can do to help you feel more comfortable here, just tell us," said Pearl.

"I appreciate that," said Cadence, wiping at her eyes. "I don't know how I can stand to embarrass myself so much in front of you ladies! I swear, every time I see y'all, I pour my heart out to you."

"Marriages have their ups and downs," Pearl said. "I should know; I had four! But don't throw out the baby with the bathwater."

"Or *do* throw out the baby with the bathwater," Margo suggested. "If it's a stinky, bad baby. You never know. There could be a new, better baby out there for you."

"Babies!" Cadence sobbed. "He wants to have a baby! He can't even be faithful to me. If he can't love me, how does he think he's going to love a baby?"

"He's not faithful to you?" asked Audra.

Cadence shook her head and buried her face in her hands.

"Men are the worst," said Audra. "Just wait until you all hear what I found out the other day about the guy I was just dating. It connects to Evangeline Maddingly. You're not even going to believe it! I'd better tell you all right now before Olivia gets here."

"I'm not very comfortable with a man-bashing session," said Pearl.

"Then we can call it something else," said Audra.

"Please do tell," Cadence said, eager to hear something that would distract her from her own troubles.

"I was with Olivia at her school last week. We were working on selecting art for her portfolio when one of her brother's old friends stopped by to drop something off," Audra said. "This old friend of theirs told Olivia that Evangeline Maddingly was cheating on Oliver with a teacher from her school. And, would you believe, the guy she was cheating with is the same guy I was dating up until a couple of weeks ago?"

"No!" Cadence gasped.

"Does the school district know about this?" asked Margo.

"I really doubt it," said Audra, "considering that he teaches at my school in Middleford. I don't think he'd have a job teaching anywhere if this story was general knowledge."

"Does he know that you know about this?" asked Margo.

"I haven't said a word to him about it. I don't know how to handle it. Plus, it's not like I can prove it really happened."

"He should be fired," said Cadence. "Teachers can't date their students!"

"I know," said Audra. "I've been avoiding even looking at him. I'm sure he thinks it's because we broke up recently. It hasn't been hard to keep away from him; he goes out of his way to avoid me too."

"I hate to even suggest this," said Cadence, "but do you think it's possible that he was involved in Oliver and Evangeline's murders?"

"Oh my God," said Audra. "I certainly hope not! The thought never even crossed my mind. He's a horrible person, but I'm sure he's not *that* horrible. After all, I was almost falling in love with him."

"I watch a lot of television programs about true crime stories," said Pearl, "and when a young woman is murdered, it's almost always her significant other." She shook her head sadly. "Audra, what you're telling us could be very big news. You need to tell the police what you heard and let them handle it how they see fit."

"Do you really think it's serious enough news for me to contact the police?" asked Audra.

"I do," said Pearl.

"So do I," said Margo.

Audra got up and went over to the stovetop. She took one of Pearl's cookies and broke it in half. "I'll think about it," she said, popping a piece of the cookie into her mouth and washing it down with some wine.

"If you don't want to tell the police, one of us could," said Pearl. "Someone needs to, though. He could have been involved in that murder."

"He's a total jerk," Audra said, "but I can't believe he's a murderer. I just can't."

"Are you going to tell the police or not?" Margo asked her.

"Yes. I'll do it. I swear I will," Audra promised, making eye contact with each and every woman in the room, giving them her word. "But for now," she continued, "let's just make some jewelry and try to have some fun. This secret has been safe for five years. Another day or two isn't going to make a difference."

Chapter 38

Olivia Prescott

Olivia had every intention of going to the jewelry club when she pulled out of her driveway. It wasn't until she got to the intersection of Laughing Brook Trail and Meandering Stream Lane that she found herself going straight instead of turning off to go toward Pearl's house.

Ada and Lila had been the new girls at Olivia's school four years earlier, just when the efforts to push her out of the Port Elspeth inner circle were ramping up to full force. Naturally, they'd all been drawn to one another and had become fast friends. They lived about ten miles northwest of Port Elspeth, inland, toward less-desirable towns like Middleford and Bainesfield.

Olivia knew that where they lived was part of the reason why her mother didn't like them. Back before Olivia had her driver's license and Vivienne had occasionally caved in and driven her to the twins' house, she'd made comments about how far away they lived and that they didn't even belong in the acclaimed Port Elspeth public school system. Not to mention, their home was dilapidated and ordinary. A raised ranch, which was Vivienne's nightmare house since it reminded her of the unutterable middle-class upbringing that she'd clawed her way out of.

Ada and Lila's parents were often out of the country since they were both from Poland and just about every relative they had was getting old and dying. They trusted their two older children, Beata, who was twenty-two, and Aurek, who was nineteen, to run the household when they were away. Neither went to college or, as far as Olivia could tell, had any kind of jobs or purpose in life.

The last time Olivia had been at their house, about a week earlier, Aurek had had the most intriguing visitor staying with him. Whereas Aurek was kind of creepy, his friend Harry was super cute, nineteen, and had shown a lot of interest in Olivia. And that was why she was on her way to Ada and Lila's instead of going to Pearl's house. Since it looked like she was going to be stuck at home for a while, she decided to do something fun, dangerous, and unexpected tonight.

She called Ada while she was on her way.

"Ada, it's me. Can I come over?"

"Sure. When?"

"Right now," Olivia said.

"Okay," said Ada.

"Question for you. That guy Harry?"

"Aurek's friend, you mean?"

"Yeah, him. Is he going to be over there tonight?"

"I have no idea. Is that the only reason you're coming over?" asked Ada.

"No," Olivia said. "I want to see you and Lila too."

"Lila's not here."

"That's okay," Olivia said. "I'm coming over anyway, if you don't mind. I'm almost there already."

"I can't believe your mom let you come here again so soon," Ada said. "She hates us."

"My mom hates everyone," Olivia said.

"Here's Aurek. I'll ask him," Ada said.

"Ask him what?" asked Olivia.

Then she heard Ada saying, "Aurek, is your friend Harry coming over tonight? ...He is? ...Is he spending the night? ...Okay. ...No reason. ...No reason!"

"I'm turning onto your road now," Olivia said. "Two more minutes."

"Aurek says yes. He says Harry's going to be here any time. Aurek wants to know why you care."

"I don't care that much," Olivia said. "I was just curious. Can't a person be just curious?"

"Whatever," said Ada.

"I'm just about to your house," Olivia said. "I'll see you in literally one minute. Bye."

When she took the last turn to the straightaway that Ada and Lila's driveway forked off from, she saw a car coming toward her. Just as she put on her blinker to take a left onto the long, narrow dead-end road to their house, the blinker of the car coming her way began flashing too.

"It's him," she realized, as they got closer to one another. She was overcome with nerves and glee. "It's Harry."

He was closer to the driveway and was taking a right, so she let him turn in first and followed his car up the winding, rutted private road leading to their house. At the top, in front of their garage, he parked his junky station wagon and she parked her BMW.

She suddenly felt a pang of embarrassment at having an expensive, clearly parent-bought vehicle. It might have been the norm for most of Port Elspeth's high school students, but she suddenly recognized it as a sign of her dependence and conformity. Some people, she realized for the first time, might not see it as something to be proud of.

Harry got out of his car at the same time she did.

"Hi," she said.

"Hey," he said. He tilted his head, ever so smoothly, and smiled. "Is that my girl Olivia I see?" he asked.

233

"It's me," she said, laughing. Normally, she didn't give her appearance a lot of thought, but the way he was looking at her made her feel tingly and alive. She felt pretty and she realized maybe it was a feeling worth cultivating after all.

"Fancy meeting you here again," he said.

Just then, Aurek stepped out the front door in his usual ensemble of dirty sweats, an old white t-shirt, and black socks.

"Hey," he said to Harry.

"Hey," Harry said to him.

"What are you two doing out here together?" Aurek asked.

"Nothing," Harry said. "We both just got here a second ago."

Aurek nodded once. "Olivia, Ada's in her room. You can go in through the garage door."

"Oh, sure," she said, wondering why she was supposed to go in that door but Harry was going to go through the front door. Still, she started walking the way he'd told her to go.

"We'll catch up later tonight," Harry called after her.

She turned back and smiled. "Okay."

She heard Aurek saying, "What's your problem? Are you here to see me or my little sisters' friends?" as she closed the garage door behind her.

Thursday, March 15, 2018

Unwelcome Surprises

Chapter 39

Vivienne Van Heusen-Prescott

The new cleaning woman was named Shirley and she'd done a little too good of a job. It was a Thursday morning and Vivienne was looking around her house for the basic items she relied on to start her day, like her juicer and her imported foot lotion. Nothing was where it was supposed to be. Shirley had been there until after ten the night before while Vivienne and Neil had gone for a late dinner at Prosecco e Prosciutto, which was only the newest, trendiest restaurant in Port Elspeth. (To hell with D'Angelo's. D'Angelo's was for old people.)

Neil had caved in, as usual, and let Olivia spend the night at the twins' house since either Lila or Ada—they were fraternal twins and looked nothing alike; Vivienne just hadn't ever bothered to learn who was who—had come by to pick her up.

While they were all away, with Vivienne and Neil taking their time over their nine-course meal comprised of tiny plates of cured meats and olives, Shirley had worked her magic, doing what she called an "in-depth, soul-cleansing, reset cleaning." As she'd explained it to Vivienne, "I need to make everything absolutely perfect. Once that happens, I'll just come by two or three times a week—that's up to you—and maintain it."

The Port Elspeth Jewelry Making Club

"I like the sound of that," Vivienne had told her. No wonder everyone on the neighborhood site had said Shirley was the best.

Only, she'd cleared away everything. "Even to me, this seems a little extreme," Vivienne had said to herself. She'd done some mindful breathing and tried to laugh it off, but starting the day by searching for her basic necessities set everything off the wrong way.

She had eventually found her foot lotion stuffed behind a stack of towels in the master bathroom. Her juicer, laid on its side so it would fit, was in the normally-vacant cupboard above the refrigerator.

It was nine o'clock in the morning when she came upon her beloved juicer. She'd been up since six locating things that never should have been lost in the first place. Worst of all, she'd missed *Thursday Morning Port Elspeth*. It was a local talk show that highlighted new local businesses around town. Now how was she going to know where to shop and eat?

"A beautiful juicer like that all taken apart and on its side. I guess she thinks I don't even use it? What a dumbass. Seriously," Vivienne had said, tension mounting, "this is ridiculous." Still, in her opinion, she was doing a good job of remaining fairly calm.

She texted Neil at quarter after nine, needing to fill him in on the incompetence:

I'm going to have a little talk with Shirley. She's the worst!

Neil didn't respond, which ticked her off. She'd been about to send him a scathing message when she remembered he'd told her that he would be in a long meeting all morning and probably wouldn't be able to answer any texts until after lunch. That calmed her down a little bit. She texted him again, deciding she'd be better off

237

smoothing things over and leaving him out of the Shirley situation:

I'm thinking of you! I hope you're having a nice day!

It wasn't until ten fifteen that morning when she was rinsing her smoothie glass beneath the kitchen faucet that she realized her blue leather journal had not been in its usual place beside her bed. When Nona had been their cleaning lady, Vivienne had gotten complacent, hiding it beneath another book or a discarded nightgown.

"No," she said, picturing the master bedroom and the newly-pristine, cleared-off and dusted night tables beside her and Neil's bed.

She dashed off to her bedroom and yanked open the drawer of her nightstand. There was the blue journal, along with her pots of lip balm, flavored massage oils, and the copy of *The Secret* that had all been collecting dust on her nightstand.

"No," she cried, sinking down onto her bed. She flipped the journal open to the last time she'd written in it, confirming that she'd missed writing in it the night before.

"Out of sight, out of mind," she wailed.

Nearly five years without once missing it, all ruined because of Shirley the cleaning lady. She threw the journal against the wall, hard enough to make a small chip in the plaster. Then she called Shirley and screamed at her, "You're fired! Fired! You're the worst cleaning lady I've ever known. You deserve to die. If I ever see you again, I'm going to kill you."

She hung up on her and threw her phone across the room. It hit some dresses hanging in her open closet and fell to the floor unharmed. This only made her angrier. She ran over to it, picked it up, grabbed one of her high-heeled shoes and began hammering at the phone until the screen was shattered. She was breathing so thickly that she began to hyperventilate.

"Lie down. Lie down on the bed," she told herself.

So she did. The room was spinning.

"The things you do, you need to do with calmness and intention," she told herself. "Calmness and intention. Calmness and intention." This was something Dr. Eisley had taught her. Sometimes just repeating these words helped her calm down. She said them over and over until they became sounds without any meaning.

"It's going to be okay," she finally decided. "I'll just write it twice tonight. That's what I'll do. I'll write it twice."

Chapter 40

Margo Carlton

"I might need to quit the jewelry club," Margo told her mother. She set down the window cleaner and crumpled up newspapers she was holding and said, "Also, it's breaktime. Let's eat."

"Why would you want to leave the jewelry club?" Pearl exclaimed.

"Just because I don't want to do it anymore," Margo said, picking the newspaper and window cleaner back up and attacking a spot she'd missed.

"But I just bought those throw pillows and plates," said Pearl.

"I didn't say *you* had to quit it, I just think I should."

"Is this because of Cadence?" Pearl asked.

Margo nodded.

"Margo," said Pearl, "I've never seen you be so unreasonable. You honestly can't accept that she's married and straight, and just be her friend?"

"I like her a lot. It makes me feel really lost every time I see her. Knowing nothing's ever going to come of it is depressing."

"Wouldn't it be better to be her friend than to not even have her in your life?" Pearl reasoned. "Plus, her husband's so terrible and she just moved up here a couple months ago. I think she can use all the friends she can get."

"It's not just the jewelry club and Cadence," Margo said. "It's everything. My job interview last week went terribly and they never even called me afterward, I miss French food. I've started dreaming in English again instead of French, which makes me really sad. I don't belong here. I think I was in Paris long enough that it became my home. Or maybe I don't even have a home. Maybe I don't belong anywhere."

"Oh my goodness," said Pearl. "You're really down in the dumps today, aren't you?"

"I guess," said Margo.

"I understand that it's human nature to be paired off with someone you love—Lord knows, I was four times— but it's not the end of the world to be alone."

"Mom, I don't need a speech about independence. I've made plenty of bold, independent decisions. My mood isn't about being afraid to be alone."

"Speak of the devil," Pearl said, glancing out her front window. "Cadence is here!"

"Don't call her the devil," said Margo.

"It's just an expression," Pearl said, answering the door just as Cadence knocked on it.

"Hello," Pearl said. "Come on in, Cadence. Nice of you to drop by."

"Am I interrupting you?" she asked.

"No," Pearl said. "We're just cleaning the windows."

"I'm sorry to drop in on you like this without calling, but I had a bit of a rough morning and happened to be going just about past your house. I thought some friendly faces might cheer me up. Oh, hi, Margo," she said.

"Hi, Cadence," said Margo.

"We're just about to eat lunch," Pearl said. "Now that my daughter has taught me to be an expert soup maker,

Holly Tierney-Bedord

I've been making a pot of it a few times a week. Why don't you join us?"

"If you're sure I'm not imposing, I'd love to join you," Cadence said.

"You're more than welcome," Pearl said.

"Oh, look at that," Cadence said. "Dave's calling. I'd better take this. Excuse me, please."

She stepped outside, but with some of the windows wide open, Margo couldn't avoid hearing her end of the conversation.

"Hi, Dave. ...I'm shopping. ...That's right, I'm looking for curtains for the bedroom. Then I might get some lunch. ...You're at home right now? ...Lunch together would have been nice, but I didn't know you were coming home. ...I don't know. They must be old. ...No, I haven't renewed my prescription for ages."

"Are you spying on her?" Pearl whispered.

"No!" Margo whispered back.

"Margo, you are too. Get away from that window and come in the kitchen and help me."

"Shhhh," Margo said to her mother. "I'm missing the whole conversation."

"Good," Pearl said. "It's none of your business."

"I'm telling you," Margo could overhear Cadence saying to her husband, "they're old. I'm sure if you look at the back of them they say Springwater Pharmacy and not Port Elspeth. I just brought them along because it seemed like a waste to throw them away. I swear, I'm not still taking them. Why would I do that? I want a baby as much as you do."

"Listen to this," Margo whispered to Pearl, "she's still on the pill but she's lying about it to her husband. He just found out!" Pearl's house was tiny enough that Margo could crouch within hearing distance of Cadence and still carry on a conversation with her mother who was in the kitchen.

"Get in this kitchen," said Pearl.

Margo shook her head. "She also told him she's shopping instead of here with us. Apparently, she's not allowed to have friends?"

"Margo, I mean it. Get in here right now and slice up this loaf of bread. If she comes through the front door and sees you've been hiding out, eavesdropping on her, she's going to be disgusted with you."

"Fine," Margo said. She went into the kitchen and began slicing the fresh-baked bread Pearl had pulled from the oven an hour or two earlier. While she was at it, Cadence came back inside.

"How can I help?" she asked.

"Would you get out the cheese, butter, and jam?" Pearl asked, "since we probably all have a different idea of what we'd like on our bread."

"Sure," Cadence said.

"Is everything okay?" Margo asked.

"Um. No. No, it's not," Cadence said. "He just found out that he's not the only one who has secrets, and he's not very happy about it."

"Do you want to talk about it?" Margo asked.

Cadence shook her head. "Not just yet," she said. "Maybe someday."

Chapter 41

Taylor Van Pelt

I have to go. Someone's ringing my stupid doorbell.

Taylor Van Pelt hit 'send' and stepped over to the mirror that hung in her hallway, checking her teeth. It was nearly one o'clock in the afternoon and she was still waking up. Her hair actually looked pretty good, she decided. She'd slept with it up in a bun on top of her head and now it looked much fuller and wavier than normal. She yawned and groggily squinted at her reflection. She'd just finished a poppyseed bagel. Nothing was worse than having poppyseed-filled teeth.

"Ugh!" she said to herself. "Stupid, stupid little poppyseeds. The bane of my existence." She dug one out with her fingernail as the doorbell rang again.

She lived on the third floor of an old triplex, which meant she had to run all the way downstairs to let in her visitor. She knew it was probably just some delivery guy—she shopped online at least four times a week—but that was an even better reason to get downstairs. Packages frequently were stolen from the porches in the student-filled neighborhood where she lived.

When she opened the front door in the foyer down below, she was surprised to see an old familiar face. It took her a split second to realize who she was looking at. It wasn't an old friend. The visitor standing on her welcome mat was a rather unwelcome sight.

"Hi! Taylor! Hey, how's it going?" her visitor said brightly.

Taylor stayed frozen in place, her suspicions quickly mounting. "Hi," she managed to say. "What are you doing here?" Because it seemed like a mistake.

"I was thinking about you, and I was in Cambridge, so I thought I'd look you up. Your apartment is in such a nice location!"

"You happened to be in Cambridge?" she asked.

"Yes. I had some other things going on here today," her visitor added nonchalantly.

"Funny," Taylor said. "I was just talking about you a couple days ago, and now here you are."

"I know that. I know you've been talking." Her visitor gave her a look of playful admonishment and then glanced at the staircase behind her.

"It took me a second to recognize you with that hat on," Taylor said.

"Oh, this? I always wear a hat when it's cold outside. Gloves, too. Speaking of which," her visitor chuckled, "would you mind if I come in so we can talk inside? It's freezing today!"

"Okay. I guess you can," Taylor said, even though she didn't like this idea. Still, she was raised to be polite, even in uncomfortable situations.

"Oh, good. Thanks."

"It's fine," said Taylor. *Lighten up,* she told herself. *This is kind of weird, but just deal with it.* They started up the stairs. "I'm all the way on the third floor," she explained. "Please ignore my pajamas. I didn't have classes this morning so I just got up an hour ago."

"Oh, how nice that you got to sleep in."

"I'm sorry—I know it takes forever to get up here; it's a lot of steps."

"I'm in good shape. I'll bet you can see the river from up here."

"Yeah, you can," said Taylor, unable to not feel a little smug about the view she'd soon be able to show off. She had her own terrace and her own screened-in porch. All that and a nine hundred square foot apartment with eleven-foot ceilings and its own fireplace. Sure, it was all paid for out of her trust fund, but that was nothing to be ashamed of.

"Have you lived here long?"

"A little over a year."

"Do you have any roommates?"

"No," she said. "My parents wanted to be sure I was able to focus on studying. They thought if I had roommates I'd be partying."

"That makes sense."

"Here we are," she said, opening the door and stepping inside. It was dim inside; her living room light had burned out earlier that morning. Even so, her desire to entertain her visitor—her mother was the same way; she supposed it was an inherent part of being born into a high-society family—began to overtake her gut instinct to avoid this person. "Would you like me to make us some tea?"

"Tea," said her visitor, looking positively dumbfounded. "You really *are* a nice girl, aren't you?"

"I try," she laughed. She heard the nervous edge in her own voice. Some part of her knew all along that nothing about this visit was going to be good for her.

"I don't need anything to eat or drink," said her visitor.

"Do you want to see my view of the river?"

"Maybe later I'll take a look."

"Okay," said Taylor.

"Look at your floor cushions," her visitor said.

"Oh, yeah. They're nice if I have friends over and we all want to play a board game or watch a movie."

"They look absorbent."

"Absorbent?" Taylor asked.

Her visitor nodded, looking pleased. "Do you get to control your own heat?"

"Yeah, I'd go crazy if I couldn't. Sometimes I like it really warm, but at night I turn it down."

"Where's your thermostat?"

"Right there, on the wall by the front door. Are you sure you don't want some tea?" Taylor tried again. "You said you were cold. Tea always warms me up when I'm cold."

"Look at this," said her visitor, picking up a little knickknack from the shelf by the door and pocketing it.

Really? Taylor asked herself. *Did I honestly just watch that get stolen, right in front of my eyes? Why would anyone do that?* "I got that in London," she said. "I got it when I was there with my parents. Are you... keeping it?"

Her visitor nodded. "I think so."

"It has my name on it. Why would you want it?"

"I'm a collector of sorts."

Taylor drew in a deep breath. She had no set of guidelines or rules in place to deal with this peculiar encounter. She went back to talking in the bright, bubbly voice that often moved uncomfortable situations to a less painful place. "London," she babbled. "That's also where I learned to drink tea like the Brits. They drink so much tea it's crazy. Are you sure you don't want to try some? I have some genuine English Breakfast tea that's endorsed by royalty. Or so the sticker on the box says. It's probably a scam for tourists like me," she laughed.

"I'm sure I don't want any tea. Tea would be a disaster," her visitor said.

"How would it be a disaster?" Taylor asked.

"There would be the messy problem of the two cups, telling their little story that someone you knew very well came to visit you."

"Huh?" she asked. Just then she felt a poppyseed she'd missed. How embarrassing! She tried to discreetly dislodge it with her tongue.

"If I was terribly careless," her visitor said, "which, of course, I never would be, there would even be my DNA on one of the cups."

"What are you saying?" Taylor asked, forgetting the poppyseed.

"Basically," her visitor continued, "it's so much better if it looks like you were the victim of some random attack."

"What are you talking about?" Taylor asked, now appropriately horrified. Yet she didn't run or scream. She stood there waiting for this terrible joke to resolve itself.

"You're out there talking about things you shouldn't be talking about," said her visitor. "I have a life and a reputation to protect. And you're trying to ruin everything. Why are you doing that?"

"I'm not doing anything," Taylor whispered.

"I swore I'd never do this again," said her visitor, "but you brought this upon yourself." The gun had a silencer, of course. The first rule in fixing a problem was to not create a new problem in the process.

Taylor's visitor didn't bother checking out the view. There was no more time to waste.

Chapter 42

Audra Fleming

"Welcome to Thursday Night Trivia," Audra told the small crowd gathered at Buck's Bar. "Tonight's theme, which you already know if you follow Buck's on Facebook, is the 1990's. From politics to television to music and movies, all of tonight's questions and answers will take you back to the age of grunge." She was doing her best to keep an upbeat lilt in her voice, but all she wanted to do was go home. Still, she soldiered on: "Question one," she said. "Name the award-winning movie from 1994 that was the top grossing film in the United States, winning forty-five awards and being nominated sixty-five times. For full point value, which is twenty points, please turn your answer in to me before this song is up." She selected *What's Up* by 4 Non Blondes to play while everyone submitted their guesses, and then sat back on her barstool and buried her head in her hands.

"What's the problem?" asked Tate, the bartender.

"Nothing," Audra said.

"Really?" asked Tate. "I'm not sure I believe you."

"It's nothing I want to talk about."

"Love troubles," Tate guessed.

"I wish it were that simple," said Audra.

"I'd be exhausted if I taught school, too," said Tate. He set a beer in front of Audra. "On the house."

"Thanks, Tate," she said. She took a sip of it, nodding as one person after another turned in slips of paper with their best movie guesses on them. She couldn't stop ruminating on the conversation she and Ben had had the previous day.

Woody had called to let her know that he was sick and needed to cancel their portfolio meeting with Olivia. Since her whole evening was open, she decided she had no excuse to not talk with Ben. She'd waited until their school day was over and then she'd caught up with him on his way out to the parking lot.

"Hey, Ben! Wait up," she'd said.

"What's up, Audra?" he'd said. He'd looked anything but pleased to see her.

"I need to talk with you alone. It might take a little while. Do you want to go for a cup of coffee or a beer?" So pathetic of her. Even when she was about to chastise him for being in a fireably-offensive relationship, she was still trying to work a date into matters.

"I don't think so," he'd told her. "What's up?"

"Can we at least sit in your car for a second?" Pathetic strike number two. She was concerned about not embarrassing him or damaging his reputation. Giving him a little privacy.

"Sure," he'd said.

He'd looked so ridiculously cute. He had a new, clean-shaven look.

"Look at your baby face," she'd teased. "I like it."

He hadn't responded. She'd felt like such a fool.

"So, what do you want to talk about?" he'd asked her.

"Oh, yeah. That. Yeah, there's something we need to talk about," she'd said.

"Hey," Tate said, giving her hair a little yank since her head was buried in her arms. "I don't mean to interrupt whatever private moment you're having with yourself here, but the song ended."

"Oh! Sorry," Audra said, jolting upright and snapping back to the present moment. She counted her trivia slips. Two teams were waiting for more clues.

"Okay," she said into the microphone. "This question is still open. For ten points now instead of twenty, here's your second clue: The star of this movie was Tom Hanks. You have until this song ends to turn in your guess, and then we'll move on to question two." She began playing *Jump Around* by House of Pain.

She put her head back down on the bar and went back to rehashing the previous evening's events.

She and Ben had gotten into his car—she'd immediately noticed some girly travel mug she didn't recognize in the console—and then she hadn't known where to begin. After an ultra-pathetic attempt to make small talk, flatter him, and flirt with him, she'd said, "I heard something kind of bad about you last week, and I wanted to give you a chance to explain."

"What did you hear?" he asked. That, of course, made her think he'd done all kinds of terrible things, or why else would she need to identify which one they were talking about?

Jump Around was almost over, so she tallied the votes, stood up and announced that the movie was *Forrest Gump* and seven of the twelve teams had gotten it right, and read question number two: "For twenty points, name the year that Princess Diana was killed in a car crash."

"Make it a high-stakes question!" someone in the crowd yelled.

"Sure," she said. "It's a high-stakes question. If you can name the correct month as well, you'll get twenty-five total points. Correct month and date, you'll get thirty points. But get any detail wrong and you'll get zero points, even if you've got the right year. Good luck everyone.

251

You'll get two songs-worth of time for this one." She began playing *Black* by Pearl Jam and took another drink of her beer.

"I can tell you aren't feeling it tonight," said Tate. He put a bowl of snack mix in front of her. "That's on the house, too. Enjoy," he said before walking away to tend to other customers.

"Thanks," Audra called after him, taking a handful of garlic chips and going back to replaying her and Ben's conversation.

"What I heard," she'd told Ben, "is that you were involved with Evangeline Maddingly."

"Evangeline Maddingly? I don't even know who that is."

"A high school student from Port Elspeth. She was a senior the year you subbed there."

He shook his head. "I don't remember anyone by that name."

"She died under mysterious circumstances, along with another student named Oliver Prescott. How would you not remember a student you taught who died?"

"Oh. Her. I guess I do remember her, but I was never involved with her. Who told you this?"

"It doesn't matter who told it to me. I just want to know if it's true."

"It's a total lie. You need to tell me who's spreading this rumor about me."

"I don't have to tell you anything," she'd responded.

"Why'd you even come to me with this if you didn't want to tell me everything?" Ben had asked her. "You're bringing it up. You need to answer my questions."

"Again, Ben, I don't *have* to answer your questions. I just wanted to get your side of the story," she'd told him.

Then he'd looked her up and down and said, "I can't believe we went out. We're so different."

252

It wasn't even the words so much as the way he'd said them. His contempt had knocked the wind right out of her, as if she'd been punched in the stomach.

Now she felt a tap on the back of her hand. She looked up in surprise.

"Earth to Audra," said Tate. "The song ended again."

"Oh, sorry," she said, getting another one started. "I thought that was a longer one." She reviewed the trivia answers and tallied up everything. Then, feeling like a robot, announced what place everyone was in, read question three, and ate a few more handfuls of snack mix.

When she hadn't been willing to tell Ben that Taylor Van Pelt was her information source, he'd told her to get out of his car. She'd hoped they could talk again today at school—it was sickening how much she hated being in a fight with him—but he hadn't shown up. To further complicate matters, Margo from the jewelry club had sent her a series of texts just as she'd walked in Buck's Bar, asking whether or not she'd told the police about Ben's connection to Evangeline.

She pulled the texts up now, rereading them.

Hi Audra!

Cadence stopped by today. We all got talking about what you told us Tuesday night about Ben and Evangeline.

We're wondering if you contacted the police about their connection.

We still REALLY think they need to know.

If you're not comfortable doing it, I will. Or if you want someone to go with you, I'd be happy to do that too.

Audra sighed and flipped her phone facedown.

"Question four," she said to the roomful of trivia players. She shook her head. "On second thought, I can't do this. I'm sorry. There's something going on that I need to attend to. Team 'Our Brains Are Bigger Than Yours' is the winner, like they are every week. I'll see you all next Thursday night."

With that, she ran out the door.

Chapter 43

Cadence Sommerset

"Hello, Cadence. This is Cindy Lou Mortenson of the Port Elspeth Women's Club. I hope I'm not calling too late."

Cadence glanced at the clock on the kitchen stove. It was eight forty-five in the evening. "No, it's not too late at all. Nice to hear from you, Cindy Lou."

"You too," she said. "So, the reason I'm calling is because I realized that time has been getting away from me and I haven't been keeping up with my craft fair timeline. Silly me! I need to make sure all our booth captains are on track to have enough inventory for sale."

"We're doing great on that," Cadence said. *Thanks to Audra,* she added in her mind, picturing the dozens of gorgeous necklaces and pairs of earrings she'd created.

"Check!" Cindy Lou exclaimed. "Yay! So that's category one. Category two to check off: Do you have a booth name?"

"Yes. We're calling ourselves The Port Elspeth Jewelry Making Club," said Cadence.

"Oooh! I like it. A simple, classic, to-the-point name. Very nice. Check! We're getting right through this list! And who else will be running the booth with you?"

"There will be four others," said Cadence. "Pearl Quincy, her daughter Margo Carlton, Audra Fleming, and Olivia Prescott."

The line went quiet.

"Hello?" Cadence said, making sure Cindy Lou was still there.

Cindy Lou laughed nervously and said, "Where do I begin?"

"What do you mean?" asked Cadence.

"You're new to Port Elspeth, aren't you, Cadence?"

"Um, pretty new still. We moved here at the end of January. Why do you ask?"

"You poor dear. The thing is, there's a lot about Port Elspeth you probably aren't aware of yet. That's exactly why you need to join our Women's Club. You'll get in with all the right people. My husband Dodd told me that your husband Dave just joined the Men's Club. That's a great start, but you really need to join the Women's Club as well. Men don't always 'get' the nuances of society, so it's important for you to be an insider as well."

"Uhhh, yes," Cadence stalled. "The Women's Club. I *am* thinking of joining it. It's just that I've been so busy. You know how it is getting settled into a new home."

"Oh, of course I do," said Cindy Lou. "Now, as far as your booth goes, I'm afraid our Women's Club may take issue with a few of the names on your list."

"Which names do you mean?" asked Cadence.

"To start, Olivia Prescott. That's Neil and Vivienne Prescott's teenage daughter, right?"

"That's right," said Cadence.

"I know who she is, and she's a *very* sweet girl, but she's too young to help out with the booth."

"But I saw photos of it from last year and many of the booths had young girls working in them."

"Those must have been immediate family members," said Cindy Lou.

"Oh," said Cadence.

"It's a safety rule," said Cindy Lou. "No one under eighteen is allowed unless they're immediate family."

"Oh, I didn't realize that," she said.

"Just a little technicality. Sorry about that but rules are rules. Moving on, I don't know Audra Fleming," Cindy Lou continued, pausing so Cadence could explain who she was.

"She's from Middleford. She's their elementary art school teacher," said Cadence.

"Oh! She's from Middleford?"

"That's right," said Cadence.

"But this is the Port Elspeth craft fair."

"Sure, but I didn't know we couldn't include people from nearby towns."

"Middleford isn't exactly nearby. Isn't it forty-five minutes or an hour from here?"

"It's thirty minutes away."

"Well," said Cindy Lou, "I don't really know it. I don't have much occasion to drive out in that direction. Not when everything is so nice here."

"Is Audra welcome to work the booth with me or not?" asked Cadence.

"Mmmmmmmm. I'll have to check with the rest of the committee, but I think not."

"She'll be very disappointed. She made the majority of our jewelry."

"There's still time to make more," Cindy Lou said breezily. "Finally, let's talk about Pearl Quincy and Margo Carlton."

"Let's," Cadence agreed, bracing herself.

"I actually know them fairly well," Cindy Lou said sadly.

"Me too," Cadence said enthusiastically. "Aren't they wonderful?"

"Wonderful?" Cindy Lou repeated. She sighed. "Cadence, I can tell you're a *good* person. I can hear it in your voice. You're probably the kind of person who loves giving anyone and everyone a chance. Aren't you?"

"I am," Cadence said, proudly.

"A real champion of the underdogs, aren't you? Well, I hate to break this to you, but Margo Carlton and her sweet, old, decrepit mother are probably not the best fit for our craft fair."

"Why? They're over eighteen and from Port Elspeth," Cadence reasoned.

"You're right. I can't necessarily disallow them to participate, but for their own best interest, you may want to steer them away from taking part in it."

"Why?"

"I just think they'd be better off not participating in it. I'm afraid they'll realize straight away that they don't fit in, and aren't comfortable or happy, and it will be sad for them. Cadence, I'm a caring person, too, and that's where this is coming from."

"You're asking me to uninvite my entire jewelry making club, and to then run the booth all day on my own. I won't even be able to take a break."

"If you're worrying about someone covering for you when you need to use the restroom, I'll send my daughter Bunny Lou over to cover for you for a minute here and there."

"And what if I don't want to disinvite any of them?" asked Cadence. "They're my friends."

"It will be uncomfortable, but I recommend doing it like you'd pull off a Band-aid. Nice and quick. Get right to the point and then tag on a fresh new invitation to brunch or coffee to soften the blow."

"No," Cadence said.

"What?" Cindy Lou asked, sounding literally shocked. "You're not going to do it?"

"I can't," Cadence said. "I simply can't uninvite them. I don't want to."

"At the very least, you need to tell Olivia Prescott she can't be part of it. Again, and with all due respect, it's a safety rule."

"I'm going to have to think things over," said Cadence.

"What's there to think about?" Cindy Lou exclaimed.

"Whether or not we even want to take part in your craft fair if you're going to be this rigid and exclusionary."

"Are you joking? You clearly have no idea how lucky you were to even get a spot at it. You'd better rethink your stance on things. At this point—and I'm speaking not just for myself but for every woman who's a part of The Port Elspeth Women's Club—we can call this a misunderstanding and move on, or you may be about to burn the biggest bridge of your life."

"The Port Elspeth Women's Club is the 'biggest bridge of my life.' Now I've heard everything," Cadence said, unable to hide her laughter. "Good evening, Cindy Lou." She hung up the phone.

"What's so funny?" Dave asked, coming into the kitchen just then for his nine o'clock snack. Somehow, over dinner, Cadence had convinced him that she was no longer taking her birth control pills, and so, for the moment, they were getting along civilly.

Cadence shook her head in disbelief. "I just got off the phone with Cindy Lou Mortenson. My head's reeling from our conversation. She's quite the snob."

"That's Dodd's wife," said Dave. "Cute little brunette?"

"I don't know if I've ever met her in person," Cadence said. "I can't picture her."

"Be sure to get in good with her," Dave advised. He took the ice cream out of the freezer and rummaged around in one of the kitchen drawers for the heated ice cream scooper. "She has a lot of pull in this town."

Cadence bit her lip and nodded.

"Did you get your Women's Club application submitted yet?" he asked her.

"Not yet."

"What's the holdup?"

"Nothing. I just haven't gotten to it yet."

"You need to do that. You can only get in twice a year and the spring deadline is coming up. I think it's at the end of March."

"It's seventy-five hundred dollars a year?"

"No. Since I already joined the Men's Club, you'd be just six thousand dollars. They knock off fifteen hundred if your spouse is already a member."

"And what do you get with it?"

"Oh, I see. You're going to start nitpicking like you always do. Okay, then, here's what you get when you join." He held up finger number one. "Unlimited access to the Port Elspeth Country Club." He held up another finger. "An invitation to the monthly club meetings." He paused, thinking. "I think they have a recommendations board. You know, where they list pesticide sprayers and people like that." He shrugged and started loading up a bowl with ice cream. "It doesn't matter what you get," he said. "The point is that anyone who's anyone has to belong to it."

"For six thousand dollars, I could start my own club," said Cadence.

"What kind of club would that be and who'd even want to join it?" he asked.

"I don't know. Never mind," she said.

"Big ideas, but no ideas at all. That's Cadence," said Dave. He shoved a spoonful of ice cream into his mouth. "You want to go outside and cuddle up under a blanket?" he asked her.

She shook her head. "I think I'm going to go to bed."

"A lot of fun you are. A real partner in life," he said, taking his ice cream and wool blanket, and going out to watch the crashing waves alone.

Tuesday, March 20, 2018

The Fifth Meeting

Chapter 44

Olivia Prescott

"I can't believe I'm *literally* grounded," Olivia said to her father. She was often grounded, but it was rarely enforced. Especially by Neil.

"Sorry, Cupcake," he said, "but your mom put me in charge tonight since she's sick, and she insists you stay home."

"I don't need anyone *in charge* of me."

"I don't know about that. You're still our little girl."

"I'm practically an adult. Is this all about that dumb dent?"

"It's not just a dumb dent," Neil said. "What happened to your car?"

"I don't even remember," Olivia said.

"How can you not remember getting a dent that huge? The entire passenger side of your car is caved in. You're lucky to be unharmed."

"Someone must have run into it in a parking lot or something."

"If this was the first time it had happened, it would be different," said Neil. "But I noticed just a few weeks ago that you had another pretty big dent in your car. That one was in the driver's side door. This is becoming a regular occurrence."

"That little ding from a few weeks ago was totally not my fault," said Olivia. "Gavin Mortenson opened his car door right into mine in the school parking lot."

"Then you should have said something right away. This is what insurance is for."

"What's insurance?"

"Olivia, I don't know how you're going to live in New York on your own," Neil said. "I have nightmares just thinking about it."

"Oh, boy. Here we go."

"I really do worry about you!" said Neil.

"Ughhh! Please! How did we get on this topic?" she said.

"Okay, if you want to go back to talking about your damaged car instead, I've got plenty more to say about that."

"But it's *my* car," Olivia said. "Why do you guys care if I get a dent or two in it? You're always so concerned about how everything *looks*."

"Olivia, this isn't about vanity. The point is, if you have nice things, you take care of them. If you can't handle having a nice vehicle, we'll get you something junky that you can be more careless with."

"I don't want something junky," she said.

"Then no more dents."

"Fine," she sulked. "I'm just sad I can't make jewelry tonight. If you changed your mind right now, I could still make it there in time." She felt a little bad lying to her dad, but if he ungrounded her, she was going to go visit Harry. He was basically living at Ada and Lila's house since their parents wouldn't be back for weeks. Their brother Aurek might not have liked the attention Harry paid to her, but Olivia didn't care.

"You can make jewelry in your bedroom."

"Fine," she said. As long as she had her phone, she was never far from Harry. That would have to do until she saw him again. She should have known better than to ask this, but she couldn't resist bringing him up: "Hypothetical question for you, Dad."

"What's that?" he asked.

"Do you think a guy who's nineteen is too old for me?"

"Yes," he said.

"That's what I figured you'd say."

"Why are you asking me that?"

"No reason," said Olivia.

"Does he go to high school with you?"

"No. He's out of school.

"Where does he go to college?" asked Neil.

"Ummm. I don't think he goes anywhere. I guess he's taking some time off," Olivia said.

"Where did you meet this young man?"

"Nowhere. I told you, this is all hypothetical."

"Olivia, it's a miracle I'm not completely gray-haired," said Neil. "Why don't you go to your room? I could use a little time to myself."

Olivia sighed and got up. She wasn't used to her dad being crabby with her. The reason she could handle her mother's frequent mood swings and outbursts was because her dad was a constant force, calmly spoiling her.

"Wow. Everyone hates me," she said.

"Don't pout," he said. He looked sad. She could tell he was starting to cave in.

"I'm sick of always being in trouble," she said. "Woody and Audra like me. Principal Davies does too. Vice-Principal Benson has even been nice to me lately. Why don't you guys like me?"

"We like you. Of course we like you," Neil exclaimed. "We love you!"

"Maybe you do, but Mom hates me."

Neil shook his head. "She does not. She's just sad. I think that what happened with your brother made her draw away from you. I think she withholds love toward you as a way of protecting herself. But deep inside, I know she loves you more than anything." He gave his daughter a hug.

"Thanks for saying that, Dad," said Olivia. Even if she didn't believe one word of it.

Chapter 45

The Jewelry Makers

"Did you hear the awful news about that Van Pelt girl?" Pearl asked Audra, as soon as she'd sat down at Pearl's kitchen table.

Audra looked up from the beads she was looking through. "You don't mean Taylor Van Pelt, do you?"

"I sure do," Pearl said. "I was at the grocery store this morning and I heard that she was murdered!"

"Murdered?" Audra dropped the bead she'd been holding.

"That's right," said Pearl. "Isn't it terrible?"

Margo stood up and went over to the oven to check on the baked apple dessert her mother was making for them. She'd been listening to Pearl talking about this horrible news all day, and she wasn't sure how much more of it she could take. Cadence had called to say she was sick and Olivia had called to say she was grounded, so it was just the three of them.

"She's dead?" Audra said. She felt the blood draining from her face and a feeling of sparkly light-headedness overtaking her.

"I can tell you're really upset," said Pearl. "I didn't realize you knew her personally."

Audra just nodded.

"Did you know her well?" Pearl asked.

"I just met her a couple of weeks ago," Audra said weakly. "She wasn't my friend; she was just an acquaintance," she said, suddenly feeling incredibly hot and itchy. Hadn't she told them that Taylor was the one who'd spilled the beans about Evangeline and Ben? Apparently not. "Do you know how she died?"

"Well, her parents and her friends hadn't heard from her for several days. I guess it wasn't that uncommon since she's busy with school. She hadn't been showing up for class, either, but I guess her professors didn't think too much of it. Basically, several people noticed she wasn't showing up for things, but no one did anything about it. When Sunday night rolled around and she never called them, her parents got worried. I guess they talked on the phone every Sunday night. Her mom drove up there yesterday afternoon to check on her, and that's when she found her dead in her living room. I can't even imagine how awful that must have been for her poor mother."

"How did she die?" Audra asked again.

"She'd been shot!"

"No," Audra said.

"I know! Can you believe it?" said Pearl.

"Do they have a suspect?" Audra asked.

"I don't know," Pearl said.

"I can't believe I made it through the whole school day without hearing about it." Audra stood up. "I think I have to go," she said.

"You're leaving?" Pearl said.

"Yes. I'm so upset about this, I don't think I can stay here and make jewelry this evening."

"Maybe you shouldn't drive just yet," said Pearl. "We don't have to make jewelry, but I think you should have a drink of water and calm down. You're white as a sheet."

"Here you go," Margo said, setting a glass of water in front of Audra.

Audra took a long drink of it.

"This is really affecting you," Margo said to Audra.

"Of course it is," Audra exclaimed. "She's the person who I was talking about the other day."

"What do you mean by that?" asked Pearl.

"She's the friend of Oliver and Evangeline who I was talking about. She's the one who told me that Evangeline was dating her teacher."

"Oh, my," Pearl said, gasping.

"Audra, did you ever go to the police and tell them about this?" Margo demanded.

Audra didn't respond. Instead she just took another drink of water.

"Audra, did you?" Margo repeated. "Say you did."

Audra shook her head. "No," she said. "I left trivia early on Thursday night. I meant to go to the police, but I chickened out. I did talk to Ben though."

"When?" asked Margo.

"Wednesday after school."

"How did he handle it?" Margo asked.

"Not good," said Audra. "He flat-out denied being involved with Evangeline. At first he pretended he didn't know who she was, but when he realized how impossible that would be, he admitted he did remember her."

"Did you tell him Taylor was the one who told you about him and Evangeline?" asked Pearl.

"No, but he probably had a pretty good idea it was her," Audra said. She closed her eyes and said, "Oh my God, what have I done?"

"Now are you ready to go to the police?" Margo asked.

Audra nodded. "That's why I was going to leave now. I think I'd better go talk to them right now."

"I think so, too," Margo said. "Let's go. I'll drive."

Chapter 46

Cadence Somerset

"You've ruined everything," said Dave. His face was often an alarming shade of red, but this deep purple color was something new.

"I have not ruined everything," Cadence said evenly. It was Tuesday night and she was skipping her jewelry making club. Dave had thrown such a fit about it when they'd talked during his lunchbreak that she'd decided she was better off not going.

"But you have," Dave said. "I stopped at the Men's Club after work, thinking I'd have a drink with Dodd Mortenson and the guys, and the second I walked in, they all got up and left. Every last one of them. I took a seat at the bar, and even the bartender would hardly look at me. I ordered a gin and tonic, drank it in a hurry, and left. The whole way home I wondered what the hell could have happened. The last time I saw them all, they were friendly as could be to me. And then I realized the answer was obvious. It was all because of you. It had something to do with that phone call you had with Cindy Lou Mortenson the other day, didn't it?"

"I have no idea what you're talking about," said Cadence.

"Did you get in some kind of a catfight with her about that jewelry booth?"

"No, I did not," said Cadence.

"Okay then. Did you get in a fight with one of the other guys' wives?"

"No. I don't know any of them well enough to get in a fight. Contrary to what you think and how we're living our lives, I'm not a person who thrives on conflict."

"If I find out that you did something to hurt my chances here in Port Elspeth, I don't know what I'm going to do," said Dave.

"Are you threatening me?"

Dave's cellphone began vibrating on the kitchen countertop. "It's Dodd Mortenson," he said to Cadence. He gave her a warning look and then answered it.

"Hello, Dodd. How's it going?"

Cadence got up and removed a wine glass from the cupboard. She opened the refrigerator door, debating between Pinot Grigio and Chardonnay. Pinot Grigio, she decided. Buttery Chardonnay seemed too cheerful and festive to have any place in her evening. She poured herself a big glass of the Pinot Grigio and dropped an ice cube into it.

"Oh, your wife made you call?" Dave said to Dodd, chuckling. *You're a drunk* he wrote on the back of one of the pieces of junk mail littering their countertop and passed it to Cadence. She tore it into four rectangles and let them drop onto the floor. She took the rest of the mail and went into the dining room to sort through it, but she could still hear Dave's end of the conversation.

"No! No I hadn't heard anything about it. ...That's terrible news. ...This is the daughter of Bradford and Gigi Van Pelt that you're talking about? ...Sure, I met Bradford just a couple of Sundays ago at that golf outing over at Haverforth Hills. ...That's really terrible news. ...You're kidding. Really. ...Oh, that's awful. Do they know any more than that? ...How are the Van Pelts holding up? Shocked? Yeah, I can only imagine. ...Okay. ...Yeah, of course. ...Thanks for filling me in, Dodd. ...No, I realized it wasn't the cold shoulder. ...No, no. I figured you all had somewhere you had to be. ...Sure, thanks for calling. ...Oh, Friday at seven o'clock at D'Angelo's? I'll check with the wife but I think that should work. ...Okay, Dodd. You have a good night, too. G'bye."

Cadence kept sorting through the mail. A moment later Dave came into the dining room

"So," she said, "they weren't avoiding you," she said.

"Yeah, that was good news. They weren't upset with us after all. But you aren't going to believe what Dodd Mortenson just told me."

"What did he tell you?" she asked, prepared to hear some boring Port Elspeth news that would mean nothing to her. The people around here got upset about ridiculous things like their lawn people coming a day late or their car needing to stay in the shop one extra night, with the only loaner car available being a Honda Pilot.

"The daughter of one of the Van Pelt families was murdered."

"Oh, no! What awful news," Cadence said, feeling genuinely upset. "That's horrible!"

"She was a college student going to MIT. Someone came into her apartment and shot her."

"No!" Cadence said. Even though she had no idea who they were talking about, it was always horrible to hear such awful news about anyone. Especially someone so young.

"That's why the guys left when I walked in. Dodd must have mentioned how they walked out on me to his wife, because she told him to give me a call and fill me in on what happened so I'd realize it wasn't something having to do with me." He chuckled. "What a relief!"

Cadence kept sorting through the mail, making a pile to recycle and a pile to be dealt with later.

"Yeah," Dave continued, "I thought it was something I'd done."

"Or something I'd done," Cadence said.

"Well," Dave said, "I *knew* I hadn't done anything wrong, so I figured it had to be you. The good news is, we're back in with them. We've got dinner plans with them this Friday at seven o'clock."

"At D'Angelo's," Cadence said.

"That's right. Did you overhear me or did you just guess?"

"I'm not sure." In the five or so weeks they'd lived in Port Elspeth, they'd already dined there ten or eleven million times.

"We might as well get there a little early so we can have a drink first," Dave said. "I can get out of work right at five on Friday. Why don't you try to be ready when I get home and we'll go straight there? I can't wait to have their loaded stuffed potato again. You ought to make those at home. I can't imagine it'd be that hard. I think they just mash the potatoes with butter and cheese and put them back into the potato skin and then top it off with bacon, chives, and sour cream. Did you ever try it?"

"Dave! I'm having a hard time focusing on some baked potato after hearing that someone was shot. Do they know who did it?"

"Oh, that. It was probably some transient person who came in off the street or a jealous boyfriend."

"Did Dodd tell you that?"

"Dodd didn't tell me anything."

"Then where did you come up with that explanation?" asked Cadence.

"Common sense," said Dave.

Cadence shook her head and got up to shred a stack of credit card offers.

"Cheer up," said Dave, giving her a noogie.

"Owww! Knock it off! That hurts," she said. "I'm not your little brother, I'm your wife."

"Lighten up," he told her. "Just between us, who cares about some kid you don't know who got gunned down? It's not like this affects our lives in any way. I'm just really glad they weren't shunning me. I need to be in with these people."

Cadence shook her head in disgust.

"Back to that baked potato," said Dave. "You could make something like that here at home if you tried."

Chapter 47

Audra Fleming

"Go over the details one more time," said Officer Johnson.

Audra took a drink of water and cleared her throat. She'd already told them everything she knew twice, but she went through it one more time:

"On the evening of Wednesday, March seventh, from about four in the afternoon to about six o'clock, I was at the Port Elspeth High School with Woody Willworth, the Port Elspeth High School art teacher, and Olivia Prescott. I'm Olivia's mentor for the art program she's in."

"Yes. Go on," said the officer, reviewing her notes.

"Taylor Van Pelt came into the art room to drop off an assignment for her younger sister Annie, who's one of Woody's students. Olivia recognized Taylor and invited her to join us for a little bit, so she did. We got on the subject of Olivia's older brother, Oliver, and his girlfriend, Evangeline Maddingly."

"Then what happened?" asked the officer.

"Taylor mentioned that Evangeline used to be involved with one of her teachers."

"When was this supposed relationship taking place?" asked Officer Johnson.

"On Valentine's Day when they were all seniors in high school. I guess that would have been 2013."

"Yes," said the officer. "And what is that teacher's name?"

"Ben Harrison," said Audra. "He teaches at my school in Middleford."

"And, again, what is your relationship with him?" asked Officer Johnson.

"Until recently, I was dating him," Audra said. This was the part where she'd started crying the first two times she'd told the story. The first time barely counted, though. She'd been babbling so incoherently that none of what she'd said had probably made much sense.

"Were you upset when Taylor said that about Ben and Evangeline?" asked the other officer—Officer Denver—who was sitting across the room from them. His arms were crossed. For the most part, he'd been silently observing Audra as she related her story to his partner. Now, though, he seemed to be waking up, like a bear coming out of hibernation.

"Sure I was upset," said Audra. "I didn't want to believe that the Ben I knew would have ever gotten involved with one of his students."

"Did you talk to him about this?" asked Officer Johnson.

"I did. On Wednesday, March fourteenth I talked to him after school and told him about the rumor I'd heard about him."

"Did you tell him that Taylor Van Pelt was the one who told you the news?" asked Officer Denver.

"No. I refused to tell him that," said Audra. "For some reason, though, I felt like he suspected it was her. Probably, she was one of the only people who knew that secret."

"How did he react when you confronted him about him and Evangeline?" asked Officer Johnson.

"He wasn't happy," said Audra. "At first he pretended he didn't even know who she was. Then he changed his story and said he remembered her, but that nothing had ever happened with them."

"Then what happened?" asked Officer Johnson.

"Not much. We were in his car in the parking lot. He kept denying it. He wanted me to say who had told me. He also said some rude things to me, like how different we are and that he couldn't believe he'd gone out with me. I guess that doesn't have anything to do with the information you're collecting though. Then I got out of his car and he drove away."

"Audra, are you still in love with Ben Harrison?" asked Officer Denver.

"I've never said I was in love with him. We only went on a few dates," she said.

"Why did you two break up?" he asked.

"I don't understand what any of this has to do with anything," she said.

"I'm just trying to gather all the facts," Officer Denver said amicably. He smiled. "You can tell us everything."

"I'm giving you all the facts," she said.

"You must have been upset with Taylor for telling you such terrible news about your boyfriend."

"Ben and I were already broken up when I learned that about him and Evangeline. And I wasn't upset with *Taylor* for talking about it. I was upset about the *news*."

"Why did it take you so long to talk to him about what you found out?" asked Officer Denver. "You said that you met Taylor and heard the story about him and Evangeline Maddingly on Wednesday, March seventh, but you never talked to Ben about it until Wednesday, March fourteenth. What was the holdup?"

"I just didn't want to talk to him about it," said Audra.

"I'm sure you know that Evangeline Maddingly and Oliver Prescott were found dead in 2013," Officer Johnson said.

"Yes, I've heard about that," said Audra.

"Had you heard about their deaths before you met Taylor and heard her story?" asked Officer Denver.

"Yes," said Audra.

"Did you think we, meaning the police department, would be interested to hear about this, considering it related to two students who were found dead shortly after this supposed relationship happened?"

"Yeah, I kind of thought you might want to hear about it," she admitted.

"Why didn't you come to us sooner?" asked Officer Johnson.

"I don't know."

"You must have had some reason," said Officer Denver.

"Because I knew Ben would lose his job," Audra admitted, "and, in a way, I didn't think it was that huge of a deal. Not really. I mean, he had just graduated from college and was just a sub there. He was maybe twenty-three. Evangeline was almost eighteen. I guess I felt like it was annoying but not exactly big news. I definitely didn't think he had anything to do with what happened to Evangeline and Oliver!" She burst into tears again.

"Has Ben missed any work lately?" asked Officer Johnson.

Audra nodded through her tears.

"A lot?" asked Officer Johnson.

"A few days here and there," she said.

Officer Johnson reviewed her notes. Officer Denver slid a box of tissues over to Audra.

"Thank you," she said, taking one.

"What about you?" he asked her.

"What about me?" she repeated, confused what he was asking.

"Have you missed any work lately?"

"Me? No. None at all."

"Have you been in Cambridge recently?"

"Yes," she said, the sound of the word echoing in her head as she felt both officers' interest in her swiftly intensify. They exchanged a glance and then each scooted a little closer to her.

"When were you there?" asked Officer Johnson.

"Last week on Friday," said Audra.

"Friday, March sixteenth?" Officer Johnson confirmed.

"Yes," said Audra.

"What were you doing there?" asked Officer Denver.

"I went to a macramé store," she said. "And to Anthropologie."

"Do you go to Cambridge often?" asked Officer Johnson. "It's pretty far from here."

"It's about an hour and forty-five minutes from Middleford," Audra said. "And no, I've only been there a few other times before."

"So you missed your job teaching this past Friday to drive up to Cambridge?" Officer Johnson said.

"I didn't miss work. There wasn't any school that day. We all had Friday off."

"Your whole school was out that day with no teachers, including Ben, having to work?" asked Officer Johnson.

"Yes," Audra said.

"What made you decide to go to Cambridge?"

"Something Taylor had told me," Audra said. "That day she was in the art room with us, she said she lived near a macramé store. I love macramé and I couldn't believe there was a whole store dedicated to it. I wanted to check it out."

"So, you were near her apartment?"

"I guess I was. I don't know where she lived."

The officers looked at each other, both with grim expressions on their faces.

"Did you see Taylor when you were in Cambridge?" asked Officer Johnson. "Get a coffee or do a little shopping with her while you were there?"

"No!" Audra exclaimed. "I didn't even know her. It wouldn't have made any sense for me to meet with her. The only reason I went there was to visit that store and to get out of town for the day. I wanted a change of scenery and I thought the drive would be nice."

"So you went there alone?" Officer Denver confirmed.

"Yes. What's going on here?" she exclaimed. "Am *I* a suspect?"

"We aren't ruling out anyone," said Officer Denver.

"In that case," Audra said, "I'd like to go. You can't keep me here against my will, can you?"

Neither officer responded.

"If you need to talk to me again, I guess I'd better bring a lawyer with me," she said.

"Innocent people don't talk about bringing lawyers along with them," said Officer Denver.

"I *am* innocent, but you're treating me like I'm guilty!" Audra said, getting up from her chair and going to the door.

"Audra, thank you for coming in and talking with us," said Officer Johnson. "I'll let you know if I have any further questions."

Audra nodded and let herself out. She went down the hallway and out to the front reception desk where there was a small waiting room. Margo was still sitting there waiting for her with an untouched magazine resting in her lap.

"Is everything okay?" she asked Audra.

Audra nodded. Then she shook her head. "I don't know," she said.

"Are they going to arrest Ben?" Margo asked.

"I don't think so. I'll be lucky if they don't arrest me instead. Let's get out of here before they do," she said.

Wednesday, March 21, 2018

Getting Closer to the Truth

Chapter 48

Audra Fleming

"In light of everything that's been going on around town," Woody Willworth said to Audra and Olivia, "I'm glad we're still meeting today. "Thank you, Audra, for making it work with your schedule."

"I'm happy to be here," she said. "It takes my mind off everything else going on." Really, nothing was taking her mind off it. She kept waiting for Officer Johnson or Officer Denver to call her, saying she needed to come back to the police station for another round of interrogations.

"I still can't believe Taylor is dead," said Olivia. "We were all just sitting at this exact same table with her two weeks ago. It's kind of surreal. And sad."

"It sure is," said Audra, squeezing her hand.

"You'd think I'd be used to it by now," Olivia said, "but it's actually bringing all of that back worse than ever. I barely slept last night." Her blue eyes were bloodshot and swollen. "I don't think people ever get used to losing people they care about."

"You've been through a lot in your young life," Audra said.

"You sure have," said Woody, "but for tonight, the show must go on. What do you say we take another look at your collection and see about finalizing the selection?"

Olivia twisted around to where her portfolio case was leaning against her chair and set it on the table in front of them. "I got some work done on this a few days ago, before I heard the news," she told them. "I rearranged the order a little so my best pieces are up front, and then it ends on a final strong note. Also, I found some old drawing pads from last summer that I had completely forgotten about and there was some good work in there. I added two new pieces from there. Let me know if you think they're good additions to the book."

Audra and Woody exchanged a quick glance. Audra could tell they were both thinking the same thing: Who is this new, improved, intelligent, composed young woman? They were both impressed. In that little exchange, Audra also noticed the kind crinkly lines around Woody's eyes and how attractive he was.

"Let's take a look," Woody said, spinning the portfolio around.

"I'm just going to use the bathroom while you guys are looking at it," Olivia said. "I'll be right back."

As soon as she'd left them alone, Woody said, "Can you believe how resilient she is?"

Audra nodded. "I'm glad you saw how talented she is. Celebrating what she's good at is completely changing her self-confidence. She's lucky to have a teacher like you. Honestly, it kind of makes me wish I worked with older kids. I love little kids, but it's great to be a part of a larger, more meaningful project like this."

They flipped through her entire book of work.

"It's a little longer than what we talked about," said Audra, "but I don't think there's one thing she should cut."

"I agree," Woody said. "This collection really shows her versatility."

"Too bad she's not back to hear all these compliments," Audra said, laughing. For the moment, she wasn't thinking about Ben and the police. But realizing she wasn't thinking about it made it all come rushing back. Her smile faded.

"Are you okay?" asked Woody.

"I'm hanging in there," she said.

"Anything you want to talk about?"

"No, but thanks for asking," she said.

At nine o'clock that morning she'd watched as Ben went by her classroom with two plain-clothed officers. One of them was Officer Denver. He'd never returned. She should have been relieved that they were focusing on him instead of her, but the butterflies in her stomach wouldn't let up.

"I'm glad you got involved in this project," Woody said. "Really glad."

Audra smiled at Woody. "Me too," she said.

"So, what do you guys think?" Olivia asked, returning and sitting back down between them, and sliding her phone back into her pocket. She'd looked like she was in a fairly good mood when she'd left the room five minutes earlier, but now she looked glum.

"It's a very strong collection," said Woody.

"Olivia, I can honestly say that this is better than the portfolio I put together for my college graduation," Audra told her, being completely sincere.

"Are you serious?" Olivia asked. She perked up a little at that news.

"Completely," said Audra.

"Do you know what job you'd like to do someday?" Woody asked her.

"I have all kinds of ideas. Is being a graffiti artist a thing?" asked Olivia.

"It might be hard to make a living that way," said Woody.

"Okay, what about someone who paints pianos? We have a grand piano in our house and I'm kind of obsessed with painting it, but my mom won't let me."

"I've never heard of something that specific," said Audra.

"Okay, here's an idea for you. You guys are going to think I'm crazy," Olivia said.

"I doubt that," said Woody.

"My parents tell me that this isn't a real job either," she warned them.

"Try us," said Audra.

"Okay," Olivia said. "When you think it's ridiculous, don't say I didn't warn you. I want to be an extreme stroller designer!"

"What does that mean?" asked Audra.

"Well, you know how there are fashion stylists who make a living by dressing people and choosing what accessories they should wear?"

"Yes," said Audra.

"I want to do that with strollers. I babysat last summer for some of our neighbors and the kids' mom mentioned that her stroller was an Aston Martin, which I had thought was only a kind of car. She said it cost thousands of dollars. To me, it didn't look that special. I thought that if it was made in brighter colors and was more eye-catching that babies would like it better. I realized then I could make a fortune as a stroller designer."

"Interesting idea," said Woody. "It might require some engineering classes in your future. I don't have kids but I imagine that details like shock absorbency are vitally important to creating a good baby stroller."

"Seriously?" asked Olivia. "I might have to rethink this."

"You don't have to decide today," Audra assured her.

"Good," Olivia said, "because I guess I need some more time to figure things out." She put her hand in the pocket of her hoodie. "Someone's texting me," she said. "I hope it's my boyfriend. He's been giving me the cold shoulder all day and I'm *so* sad." She checked her phone. "Ugh. It's my mom telling me to call her immediately. Be right back."

She got up, went over to the ceramics area, and took a seat in front of one of the pottery wheels.

"Hi," Audra heard her saying. "At school. ...Meeting with Woody and Audra. ...Yes, Mom, pretty much every Wednesday until I get my portfolio ready. ...How much longer? Oh, I don't know. Maybe an hour tonight and then I guess we have maybe five more times we'll need to meet."

Audra and Woody exchanged a quick glance. Audra had been fairly certain this would be the last meeting they'd need to have. It was clear that Olivia just wanted to have a reason to leave her house.

She and Woody continued flipping through a pile of Olivia's runner up drawing and paintings, making sure she wouldn't be better off swapping out any of the frontrunners for something in that pile.

"Please don't make me do that," Audra heard Olivia say. "This is so embarrassing. ...Are you serious? ...Ugh. Fine."

Audra looked back down at Olivia's portfolio and then felt a tap on her shoulder. Olivia was holding out her phone to her, covering it with her hand to muffle out what she was about to say. "I'm sorry to do this Audra," she whispered, "but could you talk to my mom for a second? I'm grounded and she wants to make sure I'm doing a school project and that I'm not out with friends."

"Sure," Audra said, taking the phone and bracing herself for Vivienne.

"Hello," she said.

"Hello. Is this Audra?"

"Yes. Hi, Vivienne. How are you?"

"Not bad. Been better. This doesn't sound like Audra."

"I promise you, it's me, Audra Fleming."

"I'm going to ask you some questions only Audra would know," Vivienne said.

"Go right ahead," Audra said, feeling equal parts amused and annoyed.

"Whose house did we meet at and why did we meet there?"

"We met at Cadence Sommerset's house to make jewelry."

"Correct," Vivienne said begrudgingly. "Olivia could have told you to say that, though. This is Ada, isn't it?"

"Do I really sound that young?" Audra asked.

"I'm sorry she's giving you such a hard time," Olivia whispered, shaking her head.

Audra covered the phone and whispered back, "Moms do stuff like this. It's totally normal." Her mother had never been so absurd, but she'd had a friend whose mom was almost this bad.

"Audra, quick as a rabbit and without thinking about anything, tell me where you work and exactly what you look like. Go! Go!" Vivienne spat out.

"I work at Middleford Grade School. I'm tall, thin, my hair is pretty long. Umm… I wear glasses sometimes."

"You're describing yourself like a model," Vivienne scoffed. "People tend to be so delusional about themselves. I think an accurate, non-skewed self-image is about the most valuable thing a person can have."

"Okay, so I guess you believe it's me now?"

"Put my daughter back on the phone."

"Nice talking to you," Audra said, passing the phone back to a mortified Olivia.

"I'm so sorry," she said to Audra before telling her mom, "Yes. Okay, see you soon. Bye." She shook her head and dropped her phone back into her pocket. "I have to go," she said to Audra and Woody. "Thanks again for all your help."

"Olivia," Woody said, "we won't need to meet again next Wednesday. I think your portfolio is ready to be submitted."

"We *have* to meet," she said.

"Why?" he asked. "Aside from getting all the paperwork completed and working out details about your lodging, which we can do some afternoon in late April or early May, you're all set. This went much faster than I expected since you already had so much quality material."

"We have to meet because I like it," Olivia said. "My parents would never look through all my pictures and talk about each one. It would never happen. Even my dad wouldn't want to do that, and he's the nice one."

"If you keep coming to the jewelry making club," Audra suggested, "that'll get you out of the house. And I'll bet the women there would love to see your portfolio."

"I don't know if I should take it places with me," Olivia said. She looked at Woody for his input.

"If you're careful with it and don't spill anything on it, you can take it with you and show it to people," he said.

"Okay, I didn't know. Cool, Woody," she said. Then she turned to Audra. "About jewelry club," she continued, "I'm not supposed to go to that anymore. I'm grounded for getting into some kind of big collision I don't remember getting into. Someone must have driven into me when I was parked someplace. My dad says that a dent that takes off a mirror and caves in the whole side of the car is the kind of dent you'd notice getting, but I don't remember it. See? Someone did it *to* me, so why am I grounded? It makes no sense. I had nothing to do with it."

"Unfair," Audra said.

"Exactly. But maybe my mom'll get distracted or go on one of her stay-in-bed jags for a week. Then I can pretty much do as I please. Who knows? Maybe I'll see you next Tuesday, Audra."

"I'll see you in class tomorrow," Woody said. "Nice work, Olivia."

"Thanks," she said. She waved goodbye and began walking away, forgetting her portfolio and other drawings on the table.

"Olivia!" Woody said.

"What?" she asked, spinning back around.

"You forgot something."

"Oh my goodness! How did I forget everything? It's because my phone and keys are in my pocket and because I have my backpack. Like, psychologically, I thought I had all my stuff. I can't believe I almost forgot *that*, though. It's only the most important thing I've ever done." She slapped herself on the forehead and took her portfolio and leftover drawings that hadn't made the cut, and left for the second time.

"How is she going to manage in New York?" Audra said when she and Woody were alone.

"I don't know," he said. "Sometimes she seems like she's wise beyond her years, but the rest of the time... she's not."

"Do you really think she's ready for this?" Audra asked.

"She'll be with other students her age and they'll have plenty of supervision and guidance. It'll be good for her. She'll be okay," he said.

"I'm glad you think so."

"I think it's a much better alternative than her staying with her parents for the rest of her high school years," Woody said.

"I've met her mom," Audra said, "and she's very wound up, but I would think anyone would be if their child had died under the strange circumstances hers did."

"I probably shouldn't say this," Woody said, "but Olivia didn't get chosen for this program simply because she's talented."

"She didn't?" Audra asked.

Woody shook his head. "The choice to include her in this program, despite that—let's admit it—she is quite immature still, is because Principal Davies and Vice-Principal Benson and I determined that taking part in it and living in New York might be good for her."

"Wow," Audra said.

"I'll tell you more things I'm not supposed to tell you if you want to get some dinner with me," Woody offered.

Audra smiled. "I'm in."

Chapter 49

The Jewelry Makers

"Thank you so much for letting me hang out with y'all again this evening," Cadence said to Pearl and Margo. "Dave's got a dinner meeting with some clients so he won't miss me."

"It's our pleasure to have your company," Pearl said. "When we didn't see you last night, I wasn't sure if we would again or not."

"You didn't think I'd abandon the club I started, did you?" asked Cadence.

"I hoped you wouldn't," Margo said.

"Pull up a chair," Pearl said to Cadence. "Once again, I've made some nice, healthy vegetable soup. With Margo's help and some bay leaves, it's better every time."

"I was hoping soup was on the menu tonight," Cadence said. "In fact, I brought along a baguette and a few kinds of cheese as well."

"Look at that," Pearl said. "You shouldn't have, but I'm glad you did."

"I'm sure you both heard the news about that Van Pelt girl?" Cadence asked them.

Margo nodded. "I was down at the police station last night with Audra. She told them that her ex-boyfriend Ben who she teaches with used to go out with Evangeline

Maddingly, and that—get this, Cadence—it was Taylor who told Audra about Ben and Evangeline."

"Wait a minute," Cadence said, her eyes wide. "That story Audra told us a couple weeks ago, you mean Taylor Van Pelt was the one who told it to her?"

"Yes!" Margo said.

"That cannot be coincidental," Cadence said. "She starts talking about Evangeline and Ben and winds up murdered a few days later?"

"Margo," Pearl said, "maybe we should wait until Audra is here so she can tell us her own version of events."

"Mom, you know Audra would tell Cadence the whole story if she was here with us right now," Margo said.

"Speaking of that," Pearl said, "The local news is starting. Maybe we should tune into that before we eat."

"Good idea," Margo said.

The three women went out into Pearl's living room and gathered around her television.

"Thanks for joining WPTE, Port Elspeth's number one source for local news and accurate weather forecasts," said the familiar face and wide, toothy grin of newscaster Hank Fuggins. The camera panned over to his co-anchor, Tibby Gabbit. Her look was much more pensive.

"And I'm Tibby Gabbit," she said somberly. "Breaking news in the investigation into the death of a young Port Elspeth woman. Twenty-three-year-old Taylor Van Pelt, originally of Port Elspeth and most recently residing in Cambridge, Massachusetts, was found murdered in her Cambridge apartment around noon this past Monday."

"Terrible," Hank Fuggins interrupted.

"Though few additional details of the case have been made public," Tibby Gabbit continued, "detectives working the case are now asking the public to be on the lookout for a white vehicle they believe may have been involved in this crime."

"I repeat," said Hank Fuggins, "the police are looking for a white vehicle they believe may have been involved in this atrocious crime of a beautiful young woman. The Van Pelts are one of the founding families of Port Elspeth."

Margo rolled her eyes. "I can't believe they've still got Hank Fuggins on here. He's such a clown."

Tibby Gabbit took over again, saying, "The outpouring of emotion from the community has been overwhelming. We're learning that Taylor had a big heart and a creative spirit. Her hobbies were synchronized swimming and helping her mother raise show cats. She was on schedule to graduate next year with a Master's Degree in Global Operations."

"An amazing young woman," said Hank.

"If you have any information relating to this case, please contact the Port Elspeth Police Department immediately by calling the number at the bottom of the screen." Tibby Gabbit said, and then turned to her co-host, shaking her head and adding, "What a sad, grizzly story."

"Indeed," said Hank Fuggins. "Indeed."

They moved on to another news story that didn't interest Pearl, Margo, or Cadence, so Pearl turned off the television.

"I wonder what's up with the white vehicle," said Margo.

"Lots of people have white vehicles," said Pearl. "It doesn't really narrow it down much. Let's eat some dinner and take our minds off this for a while."

"Good idea," said Cadence. "The last thing I need is more to worry about."

Chapter 50

Olivia Prescott

"Hi, Ada," Olivia said. She was sitting in the parking lot, trying to figure out what to do with the rest of her evening. Her mother had mentioned that she was going to see her psychiatrist at seven o'clock that night, so she had no reason to hurry home. Usually if she wanted to reach Ada or Lila she texted them, but this time she'd called; she wanted thorough details about Harry.

"Hey," said Ada. "What's up?"

"Not much. I'm finished with my portfolio meeting. We got done a little early. I was thinking of coming over, but it's kind of a long drive to your place."

"It's only fifteen minutes or so. But I thought you weren't allowed to drive right now?" Ada asked.

"I forgot and drove to school this morning, and no one stopped me," said Olivia.

"You're wondering if Harry's hanging out here with Aurek, right?"

"Well, a little. I mean, I wouldn't mind seeing him," Olivia admitted.

"You know he has something going with my brother, right?"

"*Going* going?" Olivia asked.

"Yeah. Obviously. Aurek meets guys on Craigslist. It's kind of his thing. There's always some creeper over here."

"That sounds gross and dangerous," said Olivia. "Especially since your parents are always out of the country."

"You think he'd do this if they were home?" Ada laughed. "At least he only goes out with guys his own age. He steers clear of the super creepers who are older."

"If Harry's into Aurek, then how come he likes me so much?" Olivia asked.

"Because you're cute and you like him back. Harry's not very picky. No offense, Olivia."

"Maybe Harry's just a friend of your brother's. Nothing more."

"Nope. Not possible," said Ada.

"So, is Harry there or not?" Olivia asked. "I haven't heard from him all day, and usually we text constantly. I don't know what happened."

"I don't think my brother's heard from him all day either, which is weird. Lately, Harry's here all night and then he leaves in the morning, but all day they send each other dirty pictures."

"Stop telling me this!" Olivia said. The news was making her stomach hurt.

"Sorry, it's true. But I haven't seen him for a day or two."

"I think I should give up on Harry. It pains me to say that!"

"*Obviously* you should give up on him. He's cute but repulsive," said Ada. "You don't want anyone who's been with my brother."

"No, I probably don't," Olivia said wistfully.

Still, the thought of saying goodbye to Harry's soulful eyes and the way he kissed her neck... The way he said *Hey* when he saw her... All cool and casual. She could hear it now: "Hey."

If the popular girls at school had any idea she was dating someone so hot, they would freak out. Maybe they'd finally show her a little respect. She kind of wished Ada and Lila would tell everyone (leaving out the part about him and Aurek), but the twins were actually good, loyal friends who wouldn't spill her secrets.

"You know something else about him?" Ada said to Olivia.

"What's that?" Olivia asked.

"His name's not even Harry. I think it's really something like Harold or Harris. Aurek overheard him get a call from some guy who plays basketball with him, and that guy was calling him something longer than Harry."

"Same difference. So he has a nickname? My parents used to call me Livvy when I was little."

"Yeah, I guess," Ada said.

"What's his story, anyway? Where's he from?" Olivia asked.

"I have no idea," said Ada. "You know, you could come over and just hang out with me and Lila like you used to. We could watch a movie and make spaghetti with garlic bread."

"I'm supposed to be grounded," Olivia said.

"Then why are you even asking about this?" asked Ada.

"I don't know," Olivia said. "I'm so depressed now! I don't think what you told me is true. About him and your brother, I mean. I don't want to get into it, but when I'm with him, it seems like he really likes me."

"Maybe he likes you but he lusts my brother."

"Stop! It can't be true. I can't even picture it," said Olivia.

"Oh, it's true," Ada said.

"Then I guess it's better this way. I can't come over and watch a movie with you and Lila. I have to go now."

"Okay. Have a good night," said Ada.

"You too," Olivia said.

She sat in her car for a few more minutes, wondering what to do. Then she gave up and drove home.

Chapter 51

Vivienne Van Heusen-Prescott

"It's nice to see you again, Vivienne."

"Is it really, are or you just saying that because you get paid to be my friend?"

"I don't get *paid* to be your *friend*," said Dr. Eisley. He set down his note pad and smiled at Vivienne. "Yes, I'm your therapist and I get paid, but it doesn't mean I don't enjoy seeing you, because I *do*."

"Oh, well, in that case, thank you. It's nice to see you again too."

"How long has it been? Two years? Three?"

"Something like that," said Vivienne.

"I was happily surprised when Nicolette up at the scheduling desk told me you'd called, wanting to get right in. How lucky that my afternoon was free."

"It sure was lucky," Vivienne said. *Because I'm totally losing it,* she thought.

"So, what's on your mind?" asked Dr. Eisley.

"I really needed to see you. I've been keeping up with my yoga, reiki, and chanting therapy, but a few years ago I let Western medicine go."

"You mean…"

"Most therapy. Mammograms. Flu shots," she said. "That's right. I was getting in a really clear space so I said 'to hell' with all of it. But there *is* a place for it."

"Oh, of course there is," said Dr. Eisley. "How are Neil and Olivia doing?"

"Oh, them," said Vivienne, brushing her hand dismissively a few times. "Same old, same old. They're fine. Actually, Neil is finally going to quit his job so we can move somewhere else and Olivia just got admitted into some fancy art program in New York."

"That's fantastic news!" said Dr. Eisley.

"Sure, sure, yeah, whatever," said Vivienne. "I don't want to waste our appointment time talking about them, though. I've got way bigger things on my mind."

"Okay," Dr. Eisley said, nodding sympathetically. "What's bothering you?"

Vivienne's eyes welled with tears. "They're back," she said.

"I don't want to make assumptions about what you mean, but—"

"You *know* what I mean," she said.

"The delusions?" Dr. Eisley asked.

Vivienne nodded. "Yes," she managed to say.

"Vivienne, first I want to tell you that I'm sorry to hear that. I'm sorry to be meeting you again under such difficult circumstances," Dr. Eisley said.

"Thank you," she sniffled.

"How long have you been going through this again?"

"Just a little while."

"By 'just a little while' do you mean days? Weeks? Months?" asked Dr. Eisley.

"Not months. Not even weeks. I don't know, a few days maybe. Maybe a week. I can't remember. The days all run together when I'm asleep."

"Oh, you've been sleeping a lot?"

Vivienne nodded. "Non-stop. I've taken so many sleeping pills I'm surprised I didn't overdose. Oh, just kidding," she added when she saw the look of alarm on Dr. Eisley's face. "But seriously, it's been one thing after another. If I don't sleep, my mind is always spinning. It's partly Olivia's fault. You can't imagine how much trouble she is! She keeps me on edge all the time."

"Oh, yes. Teenagers," Dr. Eisley said, glancing at his own framed portrait on his desk that showed off his wife and young adult children. He gave Vivienne the perfectly-appropriate, been-there-done-that weary smile.

Sometimes Vivienne had the feeling Dr. Eisley was placating her. Then again, that was part of why she liked him.

"And," Vivienne continued, "ever since I started the meditation room on fire, I've been consumed with that project. The painters can't get the color right. How hard is it to find a color that looks nice regardless of the weather or time of day? But they just can't manage it. It'll look good when it's overcast, but then the sun comes out and I realize the color's too warm. So they repaint it and it looks good, but then the next overcast day, I realize it looks too gray."

"These kinds of troubles really can get a person down," Dr. Eisley agreed.

"They can! Thank you for understanding," she said.

"I agree that things like this can be very tiresome to deal with, but do you think they're what brought back your delusions?"

Vivienne blew her nose and spent some time looking out Dr. Eisley's window at the parking lot outside. She wondered which car he drove. She hoped it was something nice. Otherwise what was she doing here? Following the basic laws of the universe, it wouldn't even be logical to take advice from someone poorer than her.

"Vivienne," Dr. Eisley tried again, "Was there something that triggered your episodes?"

301

"Yes, there was," Vivienne said.

"Do you want to talk about it?"

"I guess that's why I'm here, right?"

"Right," said Dr. Eisley, pen poised and ready over his notepad as he waited for the big reveal.

"Okay. You can do this, Vivienne," she said aloud to herself, slapping her face a couple of times and taking a big swallow from the bottle of water Dr. Eisley had handed her when she walked into his office.

"Yes, Vivienne! You *can* do this," Dr. Eisley said encouragingly.

She pulled the bottle of water away from her mouth and took a good look at it. She'd forgotten about Dr. Eisley and his ion-charged drinking water. Later, about five days from now, she'd see she'd been charged eighteen dollars for it as a six-point-font line item on her bill from him. Her insurance would cover it, so she'd let it slide. Over the years, this water had provoked her to feel a smidge of irritation toward him as she sat in his office, drinking it. Each swallow she took was like depositing another forty or fifty cents into his pocket.

"Good stuff, isn't? Electron charged. Do you need another one?" he asked, reaching behind him to his minifridge and pulling one out.

"No thanks. One of these is more than enough."

Another part of her wondered why he didn't charge even more for it.

"Do you think you're ready to talk?" he asked her.

Vivienne nodded. "Yes. Did you hear about the Van Pelt girl?" Vivienne asked.

"I don't think so," said Dr. Eisley.

"Where are you from again?" Vivienne asked.

"I live in Clyde's Bay."

"Oh, that's right," said Vivienne. Clyde's Bay was another seaside town about thirty-five minutes from Port Elspeth. If you couldn't be from Port Elspeth, the next best option was to be from Clyde's Bay. It was liberal-leaning whereas Port Elspeth was conservative, but otherwise it was nice. It had a cute downtown and a sailing club. A small private college known for its useless music degrees. Vivienne could forgive him for being from Clyde's Bay. Still, it was a little hard to believe he hadn't heard about Taylor Van Pelt's murder.

"Don't you read the local newspapers or watch the local news?" Vivienne asked him.

"Usually, I do," said Dr. Eisley, "but my wife and I were out of town until yesterday. We were on vacation."

"Okay," Vivienne said. "It's pretty big news around town. The Van Pelts are one of our founding families."

"Can you tell me a little about it?" He drew in a breath through the little gaps in his straight white teeth, wincing a little in that way that gave her shivers—how had she gone so long since last seeing him? "And tell me about the delusions you've been having?"

Vivienne nodded. "I'll try."

"Take your time. You can do it."

"I hate for words like this to even come out of my mouth."

"They're just words. You're a strong woman. You can face your fears," said Dr. Eisley.

"Thank you," she said. She realized she'd been grasping her hands together into a veiny knot. She pulled them away from one another and shook them out like she was flicking water off them. "I'm so wound up!" she muttered.

"It's great that you came in to see me. That was very brave of you."

"Thank you," Vivienne choked. This was why she came to Dr. Eisley. He was *so* nice. No one ever spoke so kindly to her. She wondered sometimes who she would be if everyone else she encountered was this accepting and gentle. How much softer would she be in return?

"Okay," she said. "Taylor Van Pelt was someone Evangeline and Oliver knew. She was one of Evangeline's best friends. Not her *very* best friend, of course; Evangeline's *very* best friend was Oliver. Taylor went to high school with them."

Dr. Eisley nodded.

"She was a student at MIT," Vivienne continued. "Well, someone gunned her down in her own apartment! And her own mother discovered her body."

"How devastating," said Dr. Eisley.

"Right?" said Vivienne. Saying 'Right?' to anything and everything was a habit she'd adopted from Olivia and her friends. It made her feel a little closer to still being young and hip.

"It's heartbreaking," said Dr. Eisley, shaking his head. "This happened recently?"

"Yes. It just happened," said Vivienne. "And the thing is, Dr. Eisley, this has had an enormous effect on me. I'm trying to hide it from Neil, but it's all I think about."

"Why do you feel you need to hide it from Neil?" asked Dr. Eisley, making a note in his notepad.

"Because he doesn't understand me like you do," she said, her voice husky with tears and phlegm.

Dr. Eisley made some more notes. "Perhaps you'd like to come in with Neil sometime and take part in some couple's counseling?"

"I don't know. I'd consider it, but we're leaving town soon. Venice," she said.

"Oooh! How lovely," said Dr. Eisley.

"Back to the delusions, they're sneaking in constantly. It's so disturbing! I feel so out of control. They make me hate myself!"

"It sounds like you're really having a frightening experience," said Dr. Eisley. "And I can see why. After all you went through a few years ago, and the fragile place you were in, it's to be expected that another terrible event like this would cause some setbacks."

"That's what I'm experiencing? A setback?" asked Vivienne.

"Well," said Dr. Eisley, "It sounds that way to me, though you haven't told me much about the images you've been seeing or the feelings you've been experiencing."

"They're the same as last time," said Vivienne.

"I'm ready to hear specifics if you're ready to go there. You can tell me."

"I don't know."

"Would you rather talk about what you went through before, since that's something we've already discussed together?"

"No," said Vivienne. "I'd rather not talk about that at all. These images are the same, except they're about Taylor instead of Oliver and Evangeline."

Dr. Eisley nodded.

"They're so vivid that they seem real," Vivienne said. At this point, she began full-on weeping. Dr. Eisley's sympathy always made her cave in.

"If you need to go into detail, I'm here for you, and I'll never judge you. I know it's just the illness talking, and that it's in no way a reflection of your true thoughts or desires. You know that, right?"

Vivienne nodded through her tears. "I guess. I don't know." She blew her nose into a tissue and then, for a moment, anger pushed her tears away. She announced through gritted teeth, "I think the person who should really be blamed for what I'm going through is Shirley the house cleaner."

"What do you mean?" asked Dr. Eisley.

"She put my journal away. The blue journal that I write my daily affirmations in. She hid it on me!"

Dr. Eisley nodded. "I think I understand, but if you could explain what you mean…" he said.

"She *put it away*. Every night for years it's been in the same spot next to my bed. I remember to write in it because it's *right there*. But she hid it and then I forgot to do my assignment! She ruined everything! I think that was my breaking point. Yes, I just figured it out now. I think that's about when they started."

"Vivienne, I'll be better able to help you if you tell me about the delusions. I care about you. Do you believe that you can share your thoughts, even the scary ones, with me?"

"I don't know if I shouuuuuld," she said. Out of nowhere, the deluge of tears returned.

"You know this is a safe space, right?" asked Dr. Eisley.

Vivienne shrugged. She was crying so hard she was shaking. Dr. Eisley got up out of his chair and came around his desk. Despite the distraction of her tears, she couldn't help but perk up at this unexpected display of affection. He sat beside her on the couch and put his corduroy blazer-clad arm around her narrow shoulder, giving her a little squeeze.

Humph, she thought, smugly. *I've still got it! This is quite unprofessional of him! I love it.*

"It's going to be okay, Vivienne," Dr. Eisley said.

"I hope so," Vivienne croaked.

"It will be. Believe me; I'm the expert," he joked. He gave Vivienne a reassuring pat on her knee and went back to sit at his own desk again.

Vivienne instantly felt the crushing emptiness of Dr. Eisley's physical absence. "You can stay sitting by me," she said through her tears.

"I'm going to stay right here, but you can keep sharing whatever you need to share with me," he said, smiling his warm, even smile.

"Okay," Vivienne said, feeling dejected.

"Do you think it would do you some good to share your recent delusions with me? Remember, I don't judge."

"If you're sure you can handle hearing them."

"I can handle it," said Dr. Eisley.

"Okay," Vivienne said. She swallowed, unintentionally making a big gulping noise. "Sorry," she said.

"It's okay. Go ahead."

"Well, I keep thinking of how it must have been, and I can totally picture it. I can imagine Taylor in her apartment and how shocked and scared she must have been. I can imagine how the gun would have felt in my hands. You know? The weight of it?"

Dr. Eisley nodded.

"I can picture it all perfectly. It's horrible! I feel like I know exactly how her last moments went."

"Does it scare you to have these feelings?" asked Dr. Eisley.

"Yes," said Vivienne. "Yes!"

Dr. Eisley nodded. "Do you think you're open to going on some anti-psychotics again?"

"I don't know," said Vivienne.

"They really helped you last time. I think it would be a good idea again this time. That, and getting plenty of rest and avoiding stress. I know you're excited about the move you and your family are planning to make, but moving is very stressful. Maybe, all things considered, it wouldn't hurt to push it off a few months until you're feeling a little better."

"No," Vivienne said. "Moving away is all I'm living for."

Dr. Eisley raised his eyebrows in concern.

"Please don't take that to mean how it sounded. It's just an expression. I just meant that I've been waiting for this forever and I want it to happen as soon as it can."

"Fair enough," said Dr. Eisley.

"What should I do?" Vivienne asked.

Dr. Eisley chuckled. "You know I can't tell you what to do, Vivienne," he said, "but I do think seeing me at least once a week—maybe twice—and going back on some anti-psychotics could help. Something else you may want to consider would be to check into a nice facility like Pondering Elms. It's beautiful! They have the best staff, homeopathic care, vegan diet, and gorgeous ocean views."

"That does sound nice," Vivienne admitted.

"I'll email you a pdf of their brochure. If you tell them I referred you, you'll get five percent off and wheatgrass upgrades."

"I'll consider it," Vivienne said, taking the prescription he'd just written up and being sure to let her hand linger on his in the process.

"Vivienne, it was great talking with you today," Dr. Eisley said to her.

"Oh, we're done already? That went so fast."

"It always does," Dr. Eisley chuckled.

"Thanks for listening," she said.

"Just check in with Nicolette on your way out and she can get you set up for your future appointments. Let's go with two times a week until you work through this. Sound good?"

"Yes. Thank you so much, Dr. Eisley," Vivienne said. Then she impulsively hugged him. He reciprocated, but rather pathetically, in her opinion, barely letting their bodies touch.

She got the next several weeks' worth of appointments scheduled and then made her way to the parking lot. When she got into her vehicle and slammed the door, the cocoon of silent, private space made her realize she was whistling a little tune. She felt more at peace than she had in months.

Thursday, March 22, 2018

A Bend in the Road

Chapter 52

Audra Fleming

"Ben hasn't been in school for days," said Sandra.

"Oh, that's right," said Audra. She'd always been a terrible liar. "You're right! Hmm. Weird. I wonder what's up with him."

The two of them were alone in the teachers' lounge getting coffee refills during a rare free moment.

"So, I guess you two never talk anymore?" Sandra asked.

"Barely," Audra said. "Since we broke up he wants nothing to do with me. And he probably never will again." *Going to the cops and telling them that he dated an underage student who, along with her boyfriend, ended up dead, could have something to do with it,* she added in her head.

Despite how bad it looked for him, Audra still wasn't convinced that Ben had anything to do with Oliver and Evangeline's deaths or Taylor Van Pelt's. To her, having the bad judgment to date an almost-eighteen-year-old when he was in his early twenties was a far cry from killing anyone. She didn't want to believe someone she'd cared for so deeply could do something like that.

"I always had a bad feeling about him," Sandra said. "He could be really sweet, but then you'd catch a glimpse of him behaving really arrogantly. He's fine as a co-worker, but he's definitely not boyfriend material."

"*I* thought he was," Audra said.

"Personally, I prefer people with more consistent personalities."

"Where were all these warnings before I started dating him?"

"At least you didn't go out with him for very long," said Sandra.

"Yay, there's an upside to all this," Audra said glumly.

Just then, Christina stepped into the teachers' lounge. "Hey, bitches," she said. It was her usual greeting when she encountered Audra and Sandra together and no students were nearby.

"Hi, bitch," Audra responded, accordingly.

"Did you hear the news?" she asked them.

"What news?" said Sandra.

Christina leaned in closer, for effect, even though there was no one else in the room with them, and stage-whispered, "Ben Harrison isn't coming back. They've *let him go*."

"Let him go?" Sandra gasped. "Why?"

"Oh!" Audra said, doing her best to sound equally surprised. "They're going to have to find someone to sub for his class for the rest of the year."

"Well, obviously," said Christina. "Way to turn gossip into a logistical conversation, Audra. Back to Ben, what do you think he did to get fired?"

"No idea," Sandra said, "but the odds of getting another job teaching anywhere around here, or anywhere at all, aren't good once you've been fired."

"Ben's *such* a good guy," Christina said. "I feel like something must have happened. Like, maybe someone spread a rumor about him. Who knows?" She turned to

Audra and added, "You probably don't know this, but he and I went out, too."

"I knew that," Audra said.

"I would totally vouch for him if I had to. Wouldn't you?" Christina asked her.

"Um, I'm not sure whether that would be appropriate," Audra said.

"You wouldn't be one of his character witnesses if he needed one? He couldn't have been fired for any legitimate reason," Christina said. She turned to Sandra. "Sandra, would *you* be a character witness for Ben?"

"Aren't we putting the cart before the horse? Who says anyone even wants character witnesses?" Sandra asked.

"I thought we teachers stuck together. Nice to see I wouldn't be able to count on you two if I needed you. I'm going down to the principal's office to tell him I want to be a character witness for Ben," Christina decided, letting herself out of the teachers' lounge.

"What do you think he did to get fired?" Sandra said to Audra, as soon as they were alone again.

Audra realized she had her stretched-out t-shirt collar practically stuffed in her mouth. "Ugh, such a gross habit. Sorry, Sandra."

"Oh, I don't even notice that anymore," she said. "Come on, Audra, speculate with me!"

"I need to get to class," Audra said. "Sorry!"

"We should go for a drink after school today and compare whatever details we can dredge up this afternoon."

"Maybe!"

"Okay," Sandra said, topping off her coffee since they'd talked so long that it had cooled off. "I can't wait to see what we both come up with about this."

Chapter 53

Cadence Sommerset

She was a little rusty, but the words were coming back to her. Cadence completed the online application and clicked on the 'submit' button. Then she picked up her phone and scrolled down to Margo's name. She composed the following text:

Hi Margo! It's Cadence. Are you free? Want to meet me for a drink? There's something exciting I want to tell you!

Margo responded a moment later:

Yes I'm free! Just tell me when/where and I'll be there.

Cadence smiled. She didn't know many of the local hangouts yet, so she picked a place she'd driven past that looked like a dive bar. She was fairly certain she wouldn't run into any of Dave's hoity-toity associates at it.

How about Paul and Bev's? Would twenty minutes from now be too soon?

Margo responded right away:

Paul and Bev's in 20 mins works great. See you soon!

Cadence jumped up to get ready. She brushed her teeth, changed her clothes, and took her hair out of the ponytail it had been in and ran a comb through it. She realized as she ran out the door to meet Margo that her heart was racing. She couldn't wait to tell her the news.

Chapter 54

Audra Fleming

As soon as Audra left the teachers' lounge, she felt her phone vibrating in her pocket. She pulled it out and took a look. It was a local number she didn't recognize. She stepped into an alcove by the empty life sciences classroom and answered it.

"Hello. Audra speaking."

"Hello, Audra. This is Officer Bethany Johnson calling. We'd like you to come down to the police station again."

"Why?" Audra asked, feeling her hands go clammy.

"We have some more questions for you."

"Am I in trouble?"

"We'd just like to ask you some more questions," said the officer. Her voice was perfectly even and gave away nothing.

"About Taylor Van Pelt?" Audra asked.

"About that case, yes."

"I'm teaching right now. I have another class starting in just a couple minutes and they're little kids. I have to be in there."

"What time can you be here today?"

"The earliest I could be there is four o'clock."

"We'll plan to see you then," said Officer Johnson. At that, she hung up, leaving Audra holding her phone with a very queasy feeling in her stomach.

Audra quickly skimmed through the contact list on her phone and found Pearl Quincy's home landline. She called it and, mercifully, Pearl picked up right away.

"Pearl," Audra said, trying to get the words out as quickly as they were frantically forming in her mind. "The police. They called me. They need me back there. I think that they think I had something to do with what happened to Taylor Van Pelt."

"How could they think you had anything to do with that?" asked Pearl. "Oh, no, Audra. What a nightmare."

"I don't know any lawyers. I don't know what to do. I think I need a lawyer."

"I think you do, too," Pearl said.

"You must know a local lawyer who can go with me this afternoon? I'm not from this area. I grew up in Ohio. I need someone with me."

"I'll find you someone. What time are you going there?"

"Four o'clock."

"Just go there as planned. I'll find you a lawyer. Someone will be there to go in with you at four," Pearl said.

"Or will that just make me look guiltier? Showing up with a lawyer, I mean," said Audra.

"No," Pearl said sadly. "I think you're safer bringing a lawyer. Stay strong, Audra. It's going to be okay."

Chapter 55

Margo Carlton

"I'm so glad you could join me," Cadence said to Margo. They were seated in a dark booth in the back of one of Port Elspeth's few non-fancy bars. It was the middle of the afternoon and the place was deserted, except for a few old men sitting up at the bar who looked like they'd been there all day.

"Me too," said Margo. She raised her glass of beer to Cadence's glass of wine. "Cheers to fun surprises."

"This *is* a fun one," Cadence said. "Though I'm shaky even talking about it."

"I can't imagine what you're about to tell me."

"I've started applying for jobs," Cadence said.

"That's great," said Margo. "I can be a reference for you if you need one."

"Thank you. I should add, the jobs I'm applying for are in Paris."

"What?" Margo exclaimed.

"I'm looking for a job in Paris," Cadence repeated.

"Are you serious?" asked Margo.

"Completely," said Cadence. Her eyes were glistening with tears of excitement mixed with tears of sadness over the enormity of what this meant.

"Dave is okay moving to Paris?" Margo asked.

Cadence shook her head.

"So," Margo said, "that means… what I think it means?"

Cadence nodded.

"You're leaving your husband?" Margo ventured.

Cadence nodded. "On the off-chance someone actually wanted to hire me, I guess I'd have to. It's not like he'd ever want to go there with me."

"Does he know yet?"

"God, no! He'd have a heart attack if he knew. You're the only person I'm telling."

"Why me?" Margo asked.

"No one else would understand."

"This is really huge news," Margo said. "I had no idea you were thinking of doing anything like that. I was picking up on your marriage troubles, but I didn't know they were *that* bad."

"I think starting over here, away from my family and friends, gave me a lot of clarity. The whole time I've been living here, I've felt like I'm living Dave's life. Like I'm his wife, but not much else. The jewelry club is the only time I've felt remotely like myself, and just about every time it's been a bad version of myself. A crying, drunk version of myself. Your stories about Paris made me realize that starting over someplace new on my own isn't impossible. In fact, it sounds exciting."

"I'm shocked," Margo said. "I'm also really happy for you. I'll do whatever I can to help you get going there. I have plenty of connections. I can tell you what neighborhoods to look at and where to buy your produce. I'll fill you in on everything. In fact, I could even go there with you at first to help you get settled in." At that point, Margo's cheeks flushed. "Sorry. Did I take it too far?" she asked Cadence.

"No," Cadence said. "You can take it as far as you want. In fact, maybe you'd consider moving back there, too?"

Margo set her beer on the table. "Are you asking me to move to Paris with you?"

Cadence nodded. "I guess I am. I mean, it would be a lot more comfortable being there if I had a friend. Heck, your mom could even come with us. She's so sweet. I'd love having her around."

A friend, thought Margo. *She's inviting me to move to Paris with her as friends.* She'd been afraid that was what Cadence meant. Of course that was what she'd meant. How silly of Margo to think, even for a second, anything else. Even so, it still was an exciting, enticing offer to consider.

"Wow," she said. "That's really something to think about."

"This is probably all just a silly dream," said Cadence. "I'd probably need work permits and visas and... I don't know. I don't even know what I'm talking about. But it's exciting to think about."

"It *is*," Margo agreed.

"Okay, so now I feel kind of silly," said Cadence. "Like I had this really big news I couldn't wait to tell you, and I realize it's probably just a dream."

"Do you know how many big moves start with a tiny dream?" Margo said to her. "I think it's going to happen. And when it does, I'll be there with you."

Chapter 56

Margo Carlton

"My mom's calling," Margo said to Cadence. "Do you mind if I take this?" *What horrible timing* she thought, tempted to ignore it so she could instead bask in the moment she and Cadence were sharing.

"Go ahead," Cadence said.

"Hi, Mom," said Margo.

Pearl was speaking so rapidly Margo couldn't understand her at first. Then she realized Margo was telling her that Audra needed a lawyer because the police suspected her in the Taylor Van Pelt murder case.

"Slow down," Margo said. "They're seriously still on that path? How can they think Audra has anything to do with that? It's absurd!"

"I agree, Margo. We need to help her," Pearl said. "We need to get a lawyer for her and go down to the police station with her to offer her moral support. We don't have much time to spare. She needs to be there at four o'clock today. Who's that old classmate of yours who practices law here in town?"

"Danny Dunlevy is who you're thinking of, but we definitely don't want to hire him. Mom, you need to pick someone who's not from Port Elspeth. Everyone here is connected. Pick someone from Clyde's Bay. How are we going to pay for a lawyer?"

"I don't know how we'll pay for it," Pearl said, "but we'll figure it out later. Audra needs our help."

"Okay. You're right," said Margo.

"I'll pay for it," Cadence said.

"I need you to come back and pick me up," Pearl reminded Margo, "so we can go to the police station together."

"I'll be there soon."

"Okay, thank you," Pearl said, her voice shaking.

"My poor mom," Margo said as she hung up the phone. "And poor Audra. This is crazy!"

"I'm going down there with you," Cadence said. "We're going to get her the best lawyers we can find. And then, if the police can't figure out who really did this, we'll have to."

Chapter 57

Olivia Prescott

"Olivia, the first time was a warning…"

"Huh?" She looked up.

"But now I'm confiscating your phone until the end of class," said Mrs. Swanson.

Olivia took a look around her. Gavin Mortenson was clearly in view, playing on his phone, but Mrs. Swanson had blinders on as far as some kids were concerned.

"Nooo! I'll stop. Sorry, Mrs. Swanson," she said.

"It's too late. You know the rules." Her teacher reached down to take it away from her. She froze when she saw the photo on Olivia's screen.

"What?" Olivia asked, sensing that something about the situation had just escalated.

"Olivia," Mrs. Swanson said. She didn't continue. She just looked from Olivia to the phone and back to Olivia. When her eyes returned to the phone again, the screen was dark.

"What's wrong?" Olivia asked.

"Come out in the hall with me."

"Why?" Olivia asked. The whole class was watching curiously.

"Just come with me," said Mrs. Swanson.

Olivia got out of her chair and followed her teacher out to the hallway. Mrs. Swanson closed the door after them. Since everyone was in the middle of class, the hall was deserted.

"What's going on?" asked Olivia.

"Bring the picture up again," said her teacher.

Olivia did as she was told and then turned her phone so Mrs. Swanson could see the picture of her and Harry from about four days earlier. His hair was tousled and his arm was around her shoulder. She'd taken the photo. They'd been at Ada and Lila's house, of course. She'd cropped a glaring, fist-clenched Aurek out of the background.

"Is this your boyfriend?" Mrs. Swanson asked.

"Yes. So?"

"He looks like someone I know."

"Okay. So?"

"What's his name?"

"Harry," said Olivia.

Mrs. Swanson nodded. "How old is Harry?"

"I'd rather not say," said Olivia.

"I'd like you to tell me. He's older than you, isn't he?"

"A little," said Olivia.

"Is he in his late twenties?"

"Gross! No," Olivia said. "He's nineteen. I know that's too old for me, but not by much. In fact, do you know that Casey Ford is dating a guy who's twenty?"

"Can I see the picture again, Olivia?"

Olivia showed it to her again.

"Do you know Harry very well?" Mrs. Swanson asked her.

"Pretty well," said Olivia.

"You two have been dating for a while?"

"No. Just a couple weeks or so."

"Olivia, I'm really not sure the best way to handle this, so I'm just going to come out with it right away. Harry is not who he says he is. That picture you're showing me is the sub who filled in for me when I had my daughter five years ago. I remember him well because he and I had several meetings beforehand to get him up to speed on my lesson plans. He's got to be twenty-seven or twenty-eight years old now. Do your parents know you're dating him?"

"No! And you're not going to tell them!"

"Nothing I just told you concerns you?" asked her teacher. "He's older than you and has told you some huge lies."

"Maybe you're wrong."

"I recognize him. There's not a doubt in my mind about who's in that picture. Do you see him frequently?"

"He didn't talk to me for, like, twenty-four hours, but now he's texting again," said Olivia.

"Can I ask how you met him?"

"I guess."

"Okay. How'd you meet him?" Mrs. Swanson asked. Olivia could tell her frustration with her was just about simmering over. *Her poor daughter,* she thought. *She's got a mom who's almost as bad as mine.*

"He's Ada and Lila's brother's boyfriend when he's not with me," Olivia said. "Personally, I think he's going to end up picking me."

Mrs. Swanson pressed her thumbs to her temples, closed her eyes, and sighed. "Let's go back into the classroom," she said. "First though, I need you to unlock your phone so I can show this picture to Principal Davies."

"No," Olivia said. "You cannot look at my phone!"

"Then will you email the picture to me?"

"Fine," Olivia said, sending it off to the email address where she and her classmates had to send their creative writing assignments each week.

"Thank you," said her teacher. "Please get back in your seat and keep this to yourself. Tell everyone I'll be back in two minutes and they need to keep working while I'm gone." And then Mrs. Swanson hurried away, leaving Olivia standing alone in the hall, trying to make sense of everything that had just happened.

She opened the door to her classroom, went back in, and sat down at her desk. She was a social outcast, so no one bothered to ask her what was wrong. She heard Gavin Mortenson say "Freak!" under his breath. Everyone started laughing.

Olivia put her head down on her desk. Mrs. Swanson couldn't be right. To her, Harry looked like he was nineteen. And he definitely didn't seem like any teacher she'd ever met. She swallowed, trying to stop herself from crying. Nothing about this made any sense at all.

Chapter 58

Audra Fleming

The tiny silver painter's palette charm was dangling from a red thread on Audra's wrist. Woody had given it to her the night before. Two dates in two nights! Playing with the charm gave her some comfort as she sat in the police station with the new lawyer that Pearl, Margo, and Cadence had found for her.

Elaine Schroeder was a tough-looking woman with blonde and steel-gray hair. She had nicotine-stained fingers and a smoker's cough. Having her there made Audra feel about as reassured as she could feel, given the horrible circumstances. Pearl, Margo, and Cadence were out in the waiting room. They all were sure this huge misunderstanding would be sorted out in no time. Audra prayed they were right.

"Can you please describe your car?" Officer Johnson asked her.

"It's a white Subaru," Audra said. "It's out in the parking lot if you want to see it."

"Wait," said her attorney.

"There's not any reason they can't look at it," Audra said to her lawyer.

"I need to have a word with my client, alone," Elaine Schroeder said to Officer Johnson. She and Audra had just met and had barely had even a moment to talk before having to sit down with the police.

"Elaine, it's okay," Audra said.

"I'm here to serve my client, and we need to step outside for a moment. I have to insist on this," Elaine said to Officer Johnson again. "Audra, please, come with me," Elaine said, scooting her chair out from beneath the table.

"Is it the same vehicle you drove when you went to Cambridge on March sixteenth?"

"Yes," Audra said.

"Audra, stop talking," Elaine said.

The interrogation room door flew open. Officer Denver stepped in. "We have a new development," he told his fellow officers. He turned to Audra and her lawyer and said, "Audra, you're free to go."

"I am?" she asked.

Officer Denver nodded.

"Okay!" she exclaimed. She wasn't going to question why. Not to mention, she could clearly read the note written on the notepad he was holding in his hand.

T Van Pelt est TOD per Fitbit: 1:00 pm 3/15/18

She and Elaine stood up and began gathering their things. Audra was no expert, but she was pretty sure that TOD meant time of death, and as the detectives already seemed to know, she'd been in school teaching on Thursday the fifteenth at one o'clock.

Chapter 59

Vivienne Van Heusen-Prescott

When Olivia got home from school that afternoon, Vivienne and Neil were both sitting at the kitchen table waiting for her. Neil looked like his same old self, but Vivienne had changed.

Her hair was pulled back into a small bun at the nape of her neck. Dozens of small silver bobby pins held every last flyaway strand in place. She'd noticed that morning that the bad thoughts originating in her brain were piercing through her skull like crocuses in snow. They sprouted forth like tiny downy feathers, innocently enough, but then they came loose and turned into something dark and dangerous. And when that happened, when they came loose and fluttered out into the world, she could no longer control them. Thus, the new hairstyle.

She could tell Neil didn't like it, but she didn't care. "It's for the best," she'd told him. He wouldn't understand that only if she kept her hair prim and tidy and under control, would the thoughts stay where they belonged. Nice and close with few escapees. And if there were a few that got out, they'd be close enough to catch and squash, like gnats.

Vivienne patted her bobby pin-covered head and said to her daughter, "You're late. It's almost four thirty."

"I stopped and got a shake," she said, holding up the paper cup. "It took forever because they only had one person working the cash register."

"You know you're not allowed to have junk like that," said Vivienne. It was one thing for her daughter to go behind her back and eat junk food. It was something else entirely for her to openly flaunt it. The least she could do was to try to destroy the evidence, like a teenager who had proper respect for her parents. Vivienne noted that this was, potentially, a regrettable turning point for her daughter.

"Let's just cut to the chase," said Neil.

"Let's," Vivienne said. "I got a very unpleasant phone call from your principal this afternoon."

"I know," said Olivia.

"Your mother called me and I left work early," said Neil. "You realize that I'm trying to finish many, many projects right now and, if anything, I should be putting in longer hours than usual."

"Yes, Dad," said Olivia. "I'm sorry."

"Oh, you're sorry to him but not to me?" asked Vivienne. And just like that, the delusions started up. She could feel them trying to slide down her head. They were all getting caught in the bun at the nape of her neck. She could picture her son and Evangeline, and what they must have gone through. Images and scenes that hadn't troubled her for years were vivid again, freshly retouched to include Taylor Van Pelt's fearful eyes and how she'd probably begged for mercy up until the last moment.

"I'm sorry to *both* of you," Olivia said.

"You should be," said Vivienne, forcing herself to come back to the present moment. She patted her bun, deciding a shower could wash bad feelings down the drain, whereas shaking her hair out would scatter the images everywhere.

Olivia began walking out of the room.

"Hold on a minute," said Neil. "Where do you think you're going?"

"I think I might need to take a shower," Vivienne said to no one in particular.

"United front," Neil reminded her. "I came home early from work for this."

Vivienne nodded, trying to play the part that usually came so naturally to her. "Olivia!" she yelled abruptly. "Your father asked you where you're going!"

"To my room?"

"Oh no you aren't! Sit down at the table with us and give us your phone," she said.

Olivia sat down but instead of taking out her phone she crossed her arms and sighed.

"Your mother asked to see your phone," said Neil.

"Don't always make me the bad guy," Vivienne said to him. She was coming back down a little, like someone descending from a hot air balloon. The ground and stability were within reach.

"Fine," Neil said. "I'd like to see your phone," he said to his daughter.

"Why?" asked Olivia. "You can't. It would be an invasion of my privacy."

"I think these pills are too strong for me," Vivienne murmured quietly enough that Neil and Olivia both chose to ignore her. "Or I need to take less of them, or maybe mix them with something else that balances them out."

"Principal Davies told us you're dating a man in his late twenties or thirties. Is this true?" Neil asked Olivia.

"He was only twenty-seven the last I heard," said Olivia. "Anyway, we're not really 'dating.' Except for riding around once to get away from Aurek, we've never even left the house."

"Who's Aurek?" asked Neil.

"Stop everything!" Vivienne yelled. That last part about a man in their home had really struck a nerve with her. "You mean he's been here, *inside* our house?" Beneath her sculpted helmet hair, her mind quickly began darting to all the ways that was creepy and awful. She considered getting Shirley back in there for one more deep-clean and then firing her again.

"No. I always see him..." Olivia trailed off. "Principal Davies didn't say?"

"He has a mustache, doesn't he?" asked Vivienne.

"No, Mom. Yuck."

"Does he drive a Trans Am?" asked Vivienne.

"I don't know what that is," said Olivia. "His car's a big white station wagon. It's ugly. Is that a Trans Am?"

"When you and this pedophile meet, where do you go?" asked Vivienne.

"His name's Harry and we don't meet here," Olivia said. "He's never even been here before. I met him through Ada and Lila's brother Aurek. He told me he was only nineteen. Not that anyone cares, but he's really nice!"

"You're not ready to go to New York," Neil decided.

"Oh, yes she is," Vivienne said. "And the sooner the better. Trust me, it's the right thing for all of us." She stood up from the table, pushed her chair back, and went straight to her bathroom. She heard Neil coming after her.

"Vivienne, come back here," he said.

"Leave me alone," she yelled, locking herself in her bathroom. She pulled open her medicine cabinet and took out two of the pills Dr. Eisley had prescribed. She was only supposed to take one at a time, and she already hated how they made her feel, but she was desperate.

She swallowed the pills and then quickly began removing the bobby pins, a few at a time, as fast as she could. She didn't take out the bun until she was safe with all four shower heads turned to the 'heavy massage' setting, pelting on her. Then she set it free, squeezing it and all the terrible images from her mind.

As the water washed away all the collected atrocities, she began to calm down a little. She tried to force the parts of her brain that were on her side to take back over.

Taylor Van Pelt—a face she'd never dreamed would become so familiar and haunting. The hooded gray eyes and long nose. The porcelain skin, so fair that blue veins showed through. The puzzle of how, when all the unattractive parts came together, they'd made something striking. Something soft from all the hard, wrong pieces. The way she must have looked lying there on the floor. It was so real. Horrific, yet fascinating.

Vivienne's mind kept wanting to return there. She could perfectly imagine the way her blood must have looked seeping from her hair and pooling out around her. This part in particular played like a black and white movie where everything was happening at half the speed it was supposed to.

A touch too slow.

"Tooooo slowwwwwwww," Vivienne whispered. "A touch tooooo slowwwwww."

Taylor's blood was thick and silver. It looked like mercury flowing.

The way Vivienne pictured it, it could almost be called beautiful.

Friday, March 23, 2018

A Visit to Wild Rose Circle

Chapter 60

Vivienne Van Heusen-Prescott

"I'm sorry to drop by unannounced like this," Audra said, speaking over the music.

"It's coming from everywhere. The music! Can't you tell? There are even speakers in the yard," Vivienne said excitedly. She stood in her open front doorway, panting. Her eyes were half-crossed and her lips were formed into a gleaming, crooked smile. About half a spool of fishing line was wrapped around her shirt. An hour earlier when she was organizing her medicine cabinet, she'd found a long-ago misplaced plastic sandwich bag of tiny white pills. She'd taken two along with her morning dosage of anti-psychotics. Now she felt zoomie and incredibly hopeful. There was no other word for it. Hopeful. Hopeful, hopeful, hopeful. Like a spring foal with her heart on fire! Kicking up dandelions and whinnying love songs!

"Hi there!" she exclaimed brightly. She wasn't sure if she'd already said that or not. "It's Audra, right?"

"That's right," said Audra.

"I was just listening to jazz and decorating for Easter! It's been so hectic this spring that I've gotten a very late start."

Everywhere behind her in the foyer, she'd stuck tree limbs she'd picked up from her yard into oversized vases and hung pastel Easter eggs from them. Hence, the fishing line. Four-foot-tall bunny nutcrackers and potted lilies formed a path from her front door back to her kitchen. She was dressed in a blinding neon pink ensemble. Her smile felt great. It felt like a permanent, natural part of her face now. When she blinked her eyes—not that she had in a long, long time—they felt so *right*.

It was the pills. She was sure of it. The zoomie pills. Why had she ever stopped using them? What *were* they? Where had they come from in the first place? Maybe it was the combination of them with the anti-psychotics that was making her feel so wonderful. The little white zoomies had made her gravitate toward the bright colors she was wearing today.

"I'll always wear bright colors from now on," she told Audra.

"Do you mind if I come in?" Audra asked her.

"Come right in! Are you here to see Olivia? She's still in bed. I called her in sick today. I didn't like the way her principal talked to her yesterday. If you're mean to me, you pay for it," she explained with the smile still firmly in place.

"She's still in bed?" Audra asked. It was twelve thirty in the afternoon.

"Right?" Vivienne laughed. "How does she sleep through this music? I guess she's used to it," she yelled. "Have you ever been here before?"

"No," said Audra.

"You're a teacher, aren't you? Oh! I remember you! I'll bet we owe you some money for mentoring Olivia. Come with me into the kitchen."

"That's not actually why I'm here," said Audra, but she followed after Vivienne.

"Don't you have to teach today?" asked Vivienne.

"Today was an early release day in Middleford. It was an early release day here in Port Elspeth, too."

"Oh! So Olivia only missed half a day of school. Even better!" Vivienne exclaimed.

"I was coming up this way to see a friend, so I thought I'd stop in for a minute and visit with Olivia. That's why I thought she'd be here on a Friday in the middle of the day."

"Because it's an early release day," Vivienne said. She opened up a canister on one of the shelves in her kitchen, pulled out five one-hundred-dollar bills, and handed them to Audra. "I don't remember what we agreed on. Just take that. Okay?"

"Sure. Thank you," Audra said, stuffing the money into her pocket.

"Hey, Audra! What are you doing here?" Olivia asked, stepping into the kitchen. Her hair was a mess and she was dressed in a Pokémon night shirt.

"I was hoping we could talk about something relating to your portfolio project," Audra told her.

"In that case," Vivienne said, going back over to the canister and taking out another hundred dollars, "here's some more money for you."

"No, I'm good," Audra said, setting it back on the countertop.

"Just take it. You two talk art and I'll get back to decorating. More nutcrackers coming out of the storage room in five... four... three... two... one! Bye!"

She danced out of the kitchen and then took a running start at sliding across the foyer floor on her socks. Halfway to the front door, her foot caught on a glass vase filled with pussy willows and she tripped and fell on her face.

Audra and Olivia both heard the thud and went running out to check on her.

"Are you okay, Mom?" Olivia asked, crouching down to her side.

Audra busied herself cleaning up the water and broken glass. Meanwhile, Vivienne quietly moaned.

The jazz blared on.

Vivienne sat up, finally, after listening to her daughter and Audra discussing whether an ambulance should be called. She rubbed her head and looked herself over to make sure a rogue bit of glass hadn't cut any exposed skin she worked so hard to preserve. "Coast is clear," she reported, finding herself to be unharmed. "I really wiped out!" she added.

"Why are you still smiling?" Olivia asked.

"Am I?" asked Vivienne.

"Like crazy," Audra said.

"I just feel so good," said Vivienne. "I just feel so darn good."

Chapter 61

Audra Fleming

"Is there a place we can talk alone?" Audra asked Olivia. "Like, maybe in there?" She pointed through the Prescotts' peacock blue front living room to the terracotta tiled sunroom beyond.

"Sure," Olivia said. "What's up?"

Olivia looked around. Vivienne seemed to have disappeared.

"She's in the storage room getting more Easter decorations. Plus, she can't hear us over the music."

"Good," Audra said.

"We can shut the doors so we can actually hear each other, too," Olivia said. She closed the doors and manually adjusted the wall speaker.

"Thank you," said Audra, settling down onto one of the loveseats.

"Is everything okay with my portfolio?" Olivia asked. "Should I go get it?"

"No. I'm actually here about something else. I got a call on my way here and I thought it was my ex-boyfriend Ben. I teach with him and he hasn't been in school lately."

"Okay," Olivia said.

"This is where things get complicated," Audra said.

"I can do complicated," Olivia assured her.

"It's the same Ben who Taylor was telling us about who was involved with Evangeline."

"No way! *That's* your boyfriend?"

"It was," said Audra.

"Why would you go out with him after you knew that?"

"Olivia, I didn't. I went out with him before I knew that."

"Oh. That's a relief! Why didn't you say anything when Taylor told us that?"

"I was too surprised and upset at the time."

"Oh. Well, I'm really sorry for you, Audra. Is that why you're here? You need to talk about it? I'm super honored you turned to me!"

"The reason I'm here is that I got a phone call this morning. I thought Ben was calling me, so I picked up. It turned out it was someone named Aurek who said he lives between here and Middleford."

"Aurek! I know Aurek!" Olivia exclaimed.

"I know you do. Aurek was calling from Ben's phone. Apparently, he's dating Ben..."

"Gross. Aurek dates everyone! He's dating my boyfriend Harry, too. Not dating, just messing around with him. Anyway, small world. What's super weird is that Harry possibly subbed at my school, too. Something like that. My teacher's always picking on me. Everyone always says Port Elspeth is an incestuous community and now I know they're right!"

"Where I was going with this," Audra said to Olivia, "is that Aurek got jealous of Ben's many other relationships, so he started contacting people on Ben's contact list. He told me everyone Ben is involved with, I guess in an effort to sabotage all his other relationships, and your name was on the list. Olivia, do you understand what I'm saying? Ben is Harry. Harry is Ben."

What Audra didn't mention to Olivia was that she had a pretty good idea the *'Come on. Show me yours.'* text and picture Ben had sent her the night she was at the jewelry meeting had been meant for Aurek, not her. It was easy to see how he'd sent them to her instead, considering she and Aurek had such similar names.

"Oooh! Ugh! I get it!" Olivia exclaimed. "Audra, this is wild! We're dating the same guy!"

"I'm not dating him anymore," Audra said. "You shouldn't be either. He's bad news."

"I've only heard this from about five million people lately," said Olivia. "How come I haven't gotten *my* call from Aurek yet?"

"Maybe because he's working his way down the list alphabetically," said Audra.

"Oh, never mind," said Olivia. "Harry must have gotten his phone back from him. He just texted me a little while ago. It's what woke me up."

"Unless it was Aurek texting you, pretending to be him?"

"No, it's him. See? He's eating lunch and he misses me." She showed Audra the photo of Ben and a bowl of cereal. Audra couldn't believe that until just a few weeks ago, she'd seen him as a responsible, cute, cardigan-wearing colleague who she was crazy about. She recognized that he was at his apartment.

"I guess the police released him," she said.

Ever since seeing the note about Taylor's time of death being one o'clock, she'd been racking her brain to figure out if Ben had been in school that Thursday during the middle of the day. She could recall seeing him first thing that morning, and then talking with him in his car after school, but she had no recollection of seeing him any time that afternoon.

She knew his schedule fairly well. Thursday was his light day. From eleven o'clock to one, he was lunchroom monitor for the students' varied staggered lunchbreaks. There were a few monitors on duty at all times, and if one was missing, no one would have thought much of it. Especially someone deemed busy, cute, and popular like Ben. Audra wouldn't have tried skipping a shift on one of her days, but she figured Ben could probably get away with it and the others would just say, "Where is he? Oh well, boys will be boys!"

From one o'clock to one forty-five, it was time for his lunch break. It wasn't uncommon for teachers, especially ones like Ben who lived nearby, to go home for lunch, so no one would have missed him then either. From one fifty to two twenty, he met with his advanced reading students or graded papers. Then he usually hung out in the teacher's lounge for a bit and spent the rest of his day grading papers or working on his upcoming curriculum. Another stretch of time when he could have gotten away with not being at school.

Audra had been counting on the police to sort through this, but she had a sad hunch she'd given it just as much thought, or more, than they had, and she didn't know the answer.

"If that picture of him is truly from today, and he's in his apartment eating cereal, I have to think that means they think he didn't do it. So now what?" she said to Olivia.

"Hmmmm. I guess so," Olivia answered.

Audra gave up on trying to talk to Olivia about this and said instead, "What's up with your mom?"

"I don't know! She's acting weird. She's in the best mood I've ever seen her in!"

"I feel like she's on something. Something really strong," said Audra.

"Should we check on her?" asked Olivia.

"Maybe," said Audra. "First though, will you stay away from Ben Harrison?"

"A.K.A. Harry?"

"Yes."

"I guess so. It's not going to be easy, though!"

Trust me, thought Audra. *I know.*

"Do you think we should tell the police that I was dating him, too?"

"No," Audra said, "let's just go and check on your mom."

Chapter 62

Olivia Prescott

"Hi, Mom," said Olivia. "Done putting out decorations?" Her mom looked so strange that she almost had an inclination to go over and give her a hug, but the two of them never did things like that. She hadn't been hugged by her mother since she was the cute little blonde girl who was on the cover of the gourmet food catalogs.

Back then, when they went on one of those photo shoots and it went well, her mom would give her a big hug in front of everyone and then take her out for frozen yogurt, just the two of them. She'd talk about the two of them in the third person. She'd say "Vivvy and Livvy! Vanilla and strawberry! Mommy-daughter date!"

As long as Olivia didn't get frozen yogurt on whatever dress she was wearing for the photo shoot, everything was great. But that was a long time ago.

"Wow, you really got a lot done out here while we were talking," Audra said to Vivienne.

"The decorations," Vivienne said, nodding. "Yes, I put them up until I ran out! What do you girls think?"

"Pretty," Olivia said. "I had no idea we had such an... *abundance* of Easter décor."

"Very nice," Audra agreed.

"Are you cleaning now?" Olivia asked her mother.

343

"I sure am. Cleaning is so calming. It really helps me focus. I don't know why I've been paying someone else to do it all these years. It's fun!" Vivienne said to her daughter, briefly looking at her with the same scary, zany smile that she'd had when Olivia had first woken up.

"Are you feeling okay?" Audra asked Vivienne.

"Pretty good, pretty good!" Vivienne said. "Why do you ask?"

"Oh, look at those," Olivia said. On her mom's feet were the microfiber cleaning booties Oliver had given her for Christmas when he was about twelve years old.

"Watch me work," Vivienne said, and then took off.

Olivia hadn't seen her mom wear the cleaning slippers in years. Normally Vivienne avoided everything that brought back memories of her dead son. Today, though, while she and Audra stood by as her audience, she zipped around the dining room, toeing dustbunnies out of corners and cleaning the grooves in the backs of her cane-back chairs with swipes of her feet.

"So agile," Audra remarked through a smile that was partially grimace. She looked a little horrified.

"I took ballet for years," Vivienne informed them.

"I know," said Olivia.

"I was very athletic in my day," Vivienne continued. "Olivia, do you remember my power-lifting phase?"

"Kind of."

"What about bowling?"

"No."

"Well, I bowled too." She round-housed the mantle and yelled, "Deep clean, my ass! This is what a deep clean looks like."

"Come with me," Olivia said to Audra. "I think we should look in her bathroom. When I was younger, she got on some pills that kind of messed her up. After my brother

344

died, she had a really hard time. Maybe she's back on them."

"I don't know if I'm comfortable searching through your mom's bathroom," said Audra. "Plus, I'm supposed to meet someone soon."

"Who?"

"I don't know if I should say."

"Is it Woody?"

"Well, fine. You figured it out. It's Woody."

"Yay!" said Olivia. "He's nice. Just come upstairs with me. I don't want to be all alone when I figure out if my mom's a pill-popper!"

"Alright," Audra relented.

They went up the curving staircase together and at the top of it, they took a left. They went past the storage room and the upstairs laundry room, the craft room, and Vivienne's off-season clothing storage room. At the end of the hall was the master suite. Olivia took a quick look back and, making sure her mother wasn't following them, grabbed Audra's arm and pulled her into the room. They walked past Vivienne and Neil's twin walk-in closet and took a right into their bathroom.

"She keeps her pills in there," Olivia said, nodding toward the medicine cabinet that took up the whole side of the wall beside the sink. "Go ahead."

"You're going to make me do it?" asked Audra.

Olivia nodded. "Just open it."

"Fine," Audra said. Inside the medicine cabinet were all the usual suspects. Tweezers and facial rejuvenation oils. Under-eye cover cremes and lip-plumping serums. "Olivia, I don't think she keeps her prescriptions in here."

"Try those little wicker storage containers," Olivia suggested.

Audra took out one of the wicker boxes—it was about the size of a tissue box—and removed the lid. "No pills in here either," she reported.

"Let me have a look," said Olivia. She took the box and peered inside, then she wrinkled her forehead in confusion.

"Do you recognize that stuff?" Audra asked.

Olivia nodded. She scooped out the miniature double-decker bus, the sparkling sapphire necklace, and the pewter bear that used to hang from Oliver's keychain.

"I recognize this, anyway," she said, holding up the pewter bear. "I haven't seen it in forever. I'd forgotten all about it."

"What is it?" Audra asked.

"It belonged to Oliver. It was part of his keychain."

"What about the other things?" asked Audra, still looking for whatever pills Vivienne was high on.

"I don't know," Olivia said. "The necklace looks familiar, but I'm not sure why. And this little bus? I don't know what this is." She rolled it over in her hand, saw what it said on it, and felt a queasy sinking feeling in her stomach. She wished it felt more like surprise and less like she was saying 'I told you so' to herself.

"You okay?" Audra asked her.

She nodded. "I don't think these are anything we need to worry about." She put everything back in the wicker box and set it where they'd found it.

"Well," Audra said, "I don't see any pills in this entire cabinet."

"Then let's get out of here before we get in trouble," said Olivia.

Saturday, March 24, 2018

Tracks Uncovered

Chapter 63

Cadence Sommerset

"We're going to get to the bottom of this," Margo declared, setting her laptop computer on the kitchen table.

"Yes, we are," Cadence said. How they were going to do so, she had no idea. She was just happy to be spending the day with Margo and Pearl while Dave was off golfing with all his new friends. She hadn't gotten up the nerve to tell him anything yet.

"I think the answers to everything lie within that cabin," Margo said.

"The cabin?" Cadence asked.

"Where Evangeline and Oliver were found. Undoubtedly, Taylor's death and their deaths are connected. If we can figure out how Evangeline and Oliver were connected to that cabin, we might be able to solve everything," said Margo.

"Good idea," Pearl said.

"I knew the Port Elspeth Jewelry Making Club was going to be good for something. Even if it wasn't making jewelry," Cadence said, happily distracted by Margo's energy and the way, now and then, her words had a touch of a French accent. Honestly, she didn't even care if they solved any murders. She was content to listen to Margo talk about anything she wanted to talk about.

"So, I looked up the owners of the cabin," Margo continued.

"Good thinking," said Pearl. "You were able to find that out?"

Margo nodded. "The people who own it now are called the Beels. They just bought it four years ago. The people who owned it when the murders happened were the Degans. They had just purchased it a couple months before everything happened. I was able to pull up the real estate transfer report and they bought it…" Margo took a look at the sheet she'd printed out, "on May tenth, 2013."

"Did the Degans buy it as their main residence or as a second home?" Cadence asked.

"As a second home," said Margo. "They were from Poughkeepsie. They hadn't even moved in yet. I read an article where Phoebe Degan, one of the owners, said that aside from moving some furniture in back in early June, they hadn't even spent any time in the cabin. The day they found them, on the Fourth of July, was the first time they were coming there to enjoy it."

"How awful to make that discovery," said Pearl.

"No kidding," said Cadence. "No wonder they turned around and sold it a year later. We should do a little research and see if the Degans have any connection to the Maddinglys or the Prescotts. Or to the Van Pelts."

"I already tried, but I couldn't find anything," Margo said. "No shared contacts whatsoever. And the Degans seem like boring, ordinary, innocent people." She showed Cadence some pictures of them she'd printed out. They looked like tired, plump retirees. Not the kind of people who'd be mixed up in any of this.

"Let me take a look at the cabin again," Cadence said.

Margo put in the address and an old real estate listing came up. The cabin's front door opened to a flat rock patio tapering up to a grassy sprinkling of trees and then denser forest all around. Matching bent-willow rockers sat side-by-side to the left of the front door.

"It's really nice," Cadence said. "I love the snowshoes hanging over the front door. It looks like something you'd see in some rustic-style decorating magazine."

"And very, very secluded," Margo said. "Forty private wooded acres with hiking trails and its own trout pond."

"I've got an idea," Cadence said. She saved a couple of the images of the exterior and interior of the cabin and then did some image searches. Real estate site after real estate site came up, all linking to the cabin's address: 527 Cinnamon Fern Road, Hillpoint, Connecticut.

"Keep scrolling," Margo said. "Stop. Click on that one from the website called Musingswithviv.com."

When Cadence tried they got a warning that said *This webpage has been removed or deleted.* She hit the 'back' button and they read as much of the description of what had once been there as they could.

"*...love this gorgeous little place to live out your boho cabin fantasies! Now for some cocktail recipes...*" The date on the page description read April 3, 2013.

"I've got an idea," Margo said. She googled Musingswithviv.com. They came to a website showing Vivienne and her family, all dressed up for Christmas.

"Wow! This photo must be from about five or six years ago? Vivienne looks so... bulky."

"She sure does," said Margo. "Her neck is twice as thick as Neil's."

"I can't believe how much Olivia looks like her brother," said Pearl. Vivienne and Olivia were dressed in emerald green velvet floor-length gowns. Oliver and his father were wearing maroon velvet tuxedos.

"She's got a certain style, doesn't she?" said Cadence.

This website is closed until further notice it said below the photo. There were no links going anywhere.

"You realize what this means, right?" Margo said to Cadence and her mother.

Cadence nodded. "Vivienne must have seen that cabin when it was for sale. She put it in her blog. In other words, she had it on her radar before Oliver and Evangeline ever ended up there."

Chapter 64

Audra Fleming

"Hi. It's me, Olivia."

"Hi," Audra said. She smiled at Woody. They'd been having lunch at a little restaurant overlooking the water in Clyde's Bay when Olivia called.

"Could you come over?"

"I'm spending the day with Woody. We're having lunch right now."

"It's really important. There's something I need to tell you."

"Can you just tell me now, over the phone?" Audra asked.

"I guess so." Olivia lowered her voice. "Can you hear me, Audra?"

"Barely. Why are you whispering?"

"I don't want my mom to hear me."

"Okay?"

"Maybe I ought to text you instead."

"You can't just tell me right now?" Audra asked.

"I don't know. Okay, I'll try. Can you still hear me?"

"Yes."

"My dad went into work today to catch up on some things. It's just my mom and me at home. I'm not supposed to leave, but she's kind of scaring me."

"What do you mean by that?" Audra asked. "Does it seem like she's been taking pills?"

"Maybe, but that's not what I'm worried about. Things are weird around here today. She had someone here early this morning in our garage, fixing my car. He was in the garage with the garage door closed. She told me to stay in my room. I saw the car guy leave about fifteen minutes ago. What was up with that? Why didn't she have my dad take it into the place where my parents always get stuff done to their cars? No one has ever come here to our house and worked on our cars before. What does that mean?"

"I have no idea," said Audra.

"As soon as he left, she just came in here, right before I called, and told me to put on my hiking clothes. I said I didn't have any. She gave me a box with some shoes, a fleece pullover, and some pants. 'Now you do,' she said. Then she said, 'Can you believe I ordered all of this last night and it came today? Modern technology is amazing.' She said we're going to go on a mother-daughter walk in the woods."

"Olivia, that sounds fun," Audra said. "What's the problem with that?" She smiled at Woody and ran her finger down his thumb. Sorry, she mouthed to him.

"I'm pretty sure she's going to kill me," Olivia whispered.

"What? Why would you say that?" Audra asked, horrified.

"We don't go hiking. We never have. Well, I take that back; we went to Giuffrida Park as a family about eight years ago. We all got covered in mosquito bites and ticks and never went again. Why is she doing this?"

"Olivia, you don't believe your own mother is going to kill you, do you?"

"I had a shake yesterday and I didn't even lie about it."

"None of what your saying makes any sense to me," Audra said. "You're really scaring me. Do you need us to come to Port Elspeth?"

"Yes. Please," Olivia said.

"Okay," Audra said. "Hold tight and stall her. We're on our way."

Chapter 65

Vivienne Van Heusen-Prescott

"This hat is perfect," Vivienne said to her reflection. It was a sludge-colored canvas hat with a cotton cord that hung just below her chin. Paired with her skin-tight cargo pants, baby tee that said *Get on Out There and Hit the Trails, Girlzzzzz,* and *World's Best Mom* fanny pack, she'd never been more ready for anything. "I always knew someday I'd find the perfect occasion to wear this hat."

She added another layer of SPF 30 concealer, in part because it was sunny outside, but also because she needed to be ready for pictures. Then she began trying on sunglasses. Aviators looked too aggressive. Yes, she looked really hot in them, but hot wasn't what she was going for today. Next, she tried on some Dwayne Wayne glasses.

"These are ridiculous. Why do I even own these?" she asked herself. She threw them in the trashcan.

The third time was a charm. Her Warby Parker tortoise shell Kimball classics were the answer. Darkly tinted but not mirrored. Conservative without being stodgy. They pretty much screamed Mom of the Year. And she looked amazing in them.

"Olivia!" she yelled. "Are you almost ready?"

When Olivia didn't respond, she felt her adrenaline kick up another notch. But before she could track her down, her phone went off. She picked it up and took a look. Neil was texting her. She sat down on her bed and read it.

Hi Vivienne, my Punkin! We've had another rough week!

She rolled her eyes and read the next text coming in.

I was thinking the three of us could go out for a nice dinner when I get home tonight. Maybe even go out of town for the night.

"No way," Vivienne scoffed. She began to send him a text back, setting him straight, but then realized that she had no reason to argue with him. She'd let him have his way for once.

Fun! Where are you thinking? she texted and hit send.

Seriously?? Great! I haven't thought much about it. Maybe... I don't know! You and Olivia choose.

Vivienne laughed and texted him back:

Okay. We're going hiking right now. We'll figure it out while we're out and about enjoying nature.

She had to bury her face in the pillow on her bed she was laughing so hard.

You and Olivia are going hiking????? You're joking!

Am not, she texted back. She sent him a photo of herself in her hiking gear. She pursed her lips in a sultry duck-faced pout.

I love you more every day. You and the Cupcake have a great time.

This one kind of ruined her momentum. She read it several times, each time feeling more and more adrenaline leaving her body.

When she didn't respond to it, Neil sent her another one:

Can't wait to see you both tonight. Back to work for me!

She set her phone down and took off her hat, deflated. Questioning everything.

Sometimes, she almost felt like the girl she used to be. The girl who grew up in a raised ranch who spent her summers playing field hockey. Sometimes she wished she'd never come to Port Elspeth. Wasn't Port Elspeth, when everything was boiled down to the bare, simple truth, entirely to blame?

But there were no reset buttons. There was no going back.

She pushed herself up from the bed and began pacing her bedroom. She did some squats and karate chops, trying to get back to where she'd been before Neil had derailed her.

Whatever pills she was on today, she was going to have to stop taking. She'd felt so energized and alive yesterday, but these ones she'd taken today were a downer. They made her feel very honest and very logical and very, very ordinary. She had no use for pills like these.

Chapter 66

Audra Fleming

With Woody beside her, Audra rang the Prescotts' front door. When no one answered right away, Audra turned to Woody and said, "Should we walk in?"

"Try one more time first," Woody suggested.

Just as she pressed the doorbell again, the door flew open. Vivienne was standing before them in a silly getup that included a floppy hat and fanny pack. Her hand rested on a wooden walking stick.

"Hello! Oh, it's you again. And *you*," she said to Woody, not bothering to disguise her distaste. "Listen, if you're here to talk to my daughter about her portfolio project, it's not a good time."

"Hi, Audra! Hi, Woody," Olivia said, coming up behind her mother. She looked very relieved to see them. She, too, was dressed in hiking attire.

"It will only take a minute," Audra said brightly.

"Go ahead then," Vivienne said, crossing her arms and waiting.

"The reason we're here," Audra began, "is because… because…"

"Because there's a really important art show going on downtown today and we thought Olivia should know about it," said Woody. "In fact, we could even take her there to see it."

"You came to my house, again, to see my daughter, and to offer to take her away with you on a Saturday? What's up with you teachers and your lack of appropriate boundaries?" Vivienne said to Audra and Woody. "I've already got some other creeper on my backburner I'm going to have to deal with soon."

"Mom, if you're talking about Harry, please leave him alone."

"Enough, Olivia."

"Please let me go with them to the art show."

"But we're going hiking now," said Vivienne. "And no phone for you. Leave it at home. I want you to be present and in the moment with me. If you want pictures, I'll take them with my phone."

"I don't want to go," Olivia said.

"Is there anything else you need from my daughter, or did you just want to tell her about that art show?" Vivienne asked Audra and Woody, preparing to shut the door in their faces.

Audra looked at Woody helplessly, unsure how to proceed.

"Olivia, are you coming with us?" he asked her.

She shrugged. "I don't know."

"She isn't," Vivienne said. "Good day," she added.

She'd just about closed the door in their faces when Olivia stuck her foot in it to stop it from closing. She turned back to her mom. "One second. I have something for my portfolio I have to give them before they go," she said to her mother.

"Then give it to them. We're leaving."

"I have to run upstairs and get it."

"Then do it. Quickly," Vivienne said.

"I'll be right back," Olivia said, racing up the stairs.

"She's not going anywhere with you," Vivienne informed them. Her phone sounded then. She pulled it from one of the many pockets of her cargo pants and examined it in annoyance. "My husband," she explained. "He can't get enough of me." She shook her head and stepped off into the dining room to respond to him.

Olivia came rushing back to them, carrying a painting of a clown that the three of them had already vetoed. In fact, just a few weeks earlier, she'd declared it to be her worst painting ever.

"What's this?" Audra asked in confusion.

"I should have given this to you when you were here yesterday," Olivia whispered. "I don't know why I didn't." She handed them the painting as well as something else that was wrapped in a ball of tissues.

Vivienne walked over, her eyes still on her phone. "You done here?" she asked her daughter, yanking her back into the foyer.

Olivia nodded.

"They've got whatever they need from you?" Vivienne asked her.

"Yes," Olivia said.

"Good. In that case, goodbye," Vivienne said to Audra and Woody. She shoved the door closed.

From where they stood on the front stoop Audra could hear the door being bolted.

"Now what?" Audra said to Woody.

"I'm not sure," he said.

They hadn't even made it back to his car before Audra saw one of the Prescotts' four garage doors going up and Vivienne's Mercedes backing out. Olivia was sitting in the passenger seat. She waved meekly at them as Vivienne turned around and went barreling out of the driveway and out of sight.

Chapter 67

Audra Fleming

"Do you think we need to follow them, or would that just make us look crazy?" Audra asked Woody.

"I don't know Olivia's mother well enough to know how to answer that," said Woody.

"I don't really think we can chase down a mother for taking her daughter hiking," said Audra. "I feel like kind of an idiot for coming over here at all."

"Then again," Woody said, "Olivia looked downright terrified when they drove away."

"You're right. I think we should go after them," said Audra. "I'd rather look like a fool than do nothing."

"Okay, let's go," Woody said.

They both got in his car when Audra remembered the bundle of tissues Olivia had just handed her. She pulled it out of her pocket and began to open it when Woody said, "Do you know these people?"

Audra looked up, just in time to see Margo, Pearl, and Cadence pulling up to the curb. They were in Pearl's car with Margo at the wheel. They all jumped out and ran up to Woody and Audra in a frantic rush.

"The police aren't here yet?" Margo asked Audra.

"No," Audra said. "Are you expecting them to come here?"

Margo, Pearl, and Cadence were yelling over each other: "We called them and then we came over here," Margo said at the same time Pearl said, "I told them we had to get Olivia away from her mother immediately," and Cadence said, "I thought the police were coming right over here, but I guess we beat them here."

"So, Olivia called all of you, too?" Audra asked them. "About the hiking trip?" she added.

"No," said Margo, "it's about the cabin."

"I'm so confused," said Woody.

"I *told* you two that was Olivia and Vivienne who we just saw go by!" Cadence said to Margo and Pearl.

"Someone, call the police again," said Pearl.

"You saw them? Did you see which way they were going?" Woody asked.

"Who can say?" asked Cadence. "We saw them just a block from here."

"Everyone," Pearl yelled, "let's go! We need to follow them!"

"Is anyone going to tell us what's going on?" asked Audra.

"I could ask you what you're doing over here, too," said Pearl, "but there isn't time. Margo, are you driving us again?"

"Sure," Margo said, running back to the car.

"We'll be right behind you," said Woody.

"Audra, I'll call you once we're driving," Cadence said. "I'll fill you in on everything. First though, we'll call the police again and tell them which way Vivienne's headed. That is, if we can possibly catch up with her."

Audra and Woody jumped back into Woody's car and followed after Pearl's Buick Regal.

"You need to fill them in on what's going on," Woody said.

"I'll wait until Cadence is off the phone with the police and calls me. I'm sure it'll be any second."

"Or just text them all now," Woody suggested.

"Good idea," said Audra. She quickly composed a text to all the women in the car ahead of them and hit send:

Vivienne said they're going hiking. We could head up toward Giuffrida Park. I heard Olivia mention it. What did you find out? Have you been to the police station?

Then she reached back into her pocket and pulled out the bundle of tissues. As she unwrapped it, she recognized the items from the wicker storage bin she and Olivia had found in Vivienne's bathroom the day before: the pewter bear that Olivia had mentioned had belonged to Oliver, the sapphire necklace, and...

"What's that?" Woody asked, glancing over at the pile of mementos in Audra's lap.

"A little bus that says *Taylor* on it," said Audra.

"Taylor!" Woody exclaimed.

"I'm calling the police now, too," she said.

"Okay," Woody said, nodding grimly. They were still keeping up with Margo, Cadence, and Pearl, but Audra was well-aware that Vivienne and Olivia could be headed anywhere. He glanced at the bear and the necklace. "Do you know what the other things are?"

"The bear belonged to Oliver. The necklace, I'm guessing, was Evangeline's. I have the terrible feeling that everything here is a souvenir of Vivienne's last day with each of them."

Chapter 68

Cadence Sommerset

"It's Dave calling again," Cadence muttered. She'd already ignored his first two calls.

"Can't you tell him this isn't a good time?" asked Pearl.

"He wouldn't understand," Cadence said, answering it.

"Hi, Dave," she said.

"What took you so long to answer me?"

"I'm with Pearl and Margo. I'm kind of in the middle of something."

"What are you doing with those two hags? I came home from golfing so we could go to that movie we talked about."

"Movie?"

"Yes. I told you I wanted to go to a movie this afternoon. *Red Sparrow* with Jennifer Lawrence. She's hot as hell."

Cadence's phone lurched out of her hands as Margo took the Buick over a curb. "Up ahead! Way up there. Isn't that Vivienne's Mercedes?"

Cadence craned her neck to see. "It sure looks like it," she said, picking the phone back up off the floormat.

Dave was still talking. "I came back early, just to spend some time together, and you're not even home. Don't you think I would rather be drinking brandy old-fashioneds and making high caliber connections? But—"

"Then go back out with your friends," Cadence told him.

"What?" he asked.

"If that's what you'd rather be doing, then go do it. I'm having a good time with my friends. And, like I already said, we're kind of in the middle of something."

"Making jewelry. Whoop-de-doo," said Dave. "I'm going to call your bluff; I'm going back to the club for another eighteen holes. I'll see you when I see you."

He hung up on her, at the same time Margo said, "Which way did she go?" and Cadence's phone rang again.

"I don't know this number," she said.

"You'd better answer it," Pearl said.

"Hello, Cadence Sommerset speaking.

"Hi, Cade!"

"Hello?" said Cadence, thoroughly confused about who she was speaking to. No one ever called her Cade.

"It's me! Cindy Lou Mortenson. How *are* you?"

"Uh, fine. Sorry, Cindy, but—"

"It was *so* nice having dinner with you and your husband the other night. Dodd and I had the *best* time. Are you all ready for the craft fair?"

"Ummm…"

"I feel like we had a misunderstanding the other night on the phone. I'm afraid you got the impression that you weren't welcome. That's not how I meant for you to feel at all! I just wanted you to be careful to be getting in with the right sort of folks. You know?"

"This isn't a good time, Cindy Lou."

"Okay, I'll make it quick. As you know, the fair is coming up soon. It's Saturday, April seventh, which will be here before you know it. You and all those… friends of yours should all plan to arrive by eight in the morning to start getting set up. We've decided that with Dave fitting in so well with the Men's Club, we'd like to do all we can to make you feel comfortable, too. We can't hold it against you that you're kind-hearted and reached out to some less-desirable people."

"Are you talking to the police?" Pearl asked Cadence.

Cadence shook her head.

"Did someone just ask you if you were talking to the police?" asked Cindy Lou Mortenson.

"No. No, no," Cadence laughed. "Alrighty, Cindy Lou. Got it! See you first thing on the morning of April seventh. Gotta go!"

"Oh, wait," Cindy Lou said. "Another thing. And this is really big. You're going to be so excited! The Connecticut League of Independent Craft Connoisseurs, also knowns as CLICC, is going to be at our fundraising fair doing blind, unbiased judging. They'll be handing out ribbons for best in show! Isn't that exciting?"

"It sure is. I have to go now, Cindy Lou. Goodbye," Cadence said, hanging up. Her phone immediately rang again. "It's the police," she announced, answering it.

"Hello, Cadence speaking."

"Hi Cadence, this is officer Bethany Johnson calling you back. I've got a message here that you and Margo Carlton think you have some information about the Evangeline Maddingly and Oliver Prescott deaths?"

"Yes," Cadence began. "First of all, we need help catching a 2018 silver Mercedes-Benz GLS with yoga stickers all over it. I've got a vehicle just like it, and you should be able to track it with satellites or something since it comes with all the modern technology. Last seen heading north on—"

Officer Johnson cut her off. "That investigation is closed. My sergeant has asked me to pass on to you that no foul play was suspected in that case, and that—"

"Don't you even want to hear what we have to tell you?" Cadence asked, as Margo slowed down to turn around in someone's driveway. Audra and Woody were still behind them, but Vivienne's Mercedes was nowhere to be seen. Margo pulled over to a small abandoned auto shop on the side of the road and Woody pulled off right behind her. Margo put the car in park and jumped out to run back and talk to them.

"Cadence," said Officer Johnson, "I've got the notes here from the call earlier today that you and Margo discovered something relating to a blog Vivienne Prescott had and the cabin where Oliver and Evangeline's bodies were found, and we did visit that website, but it looked like it hadn't been active for years and it had no links going anywhere on it."

"Okay, that's because—"

"Cadence," Officer Johnson said firmly and deliberately, "there really isn't anything to be uncovered about that case. The coroner determined there was no foul play." There was the sound of papers being shuffled. "I think the final conclusion was... it was a bear attack."

"A bear attack? That's the first I've ever heard of that," said Cadence.

"That's all I can tell you."

"We're chasing after Vivienne right now because we're worried about her daughter Olivia. We thought they were heading toward Giuffrida Park to go hiking, but then we lost them. They must have turned off from the highway onto some smaller road. We need your help."

"Cadence, I need to put you on hold for just a moment," said Officer Johnson.

"She just put me on hold!" Cadence exclaimed to Pearl. Margo came running back to the car a moment later.

"Audra's talking to Officer Johnson now," she reported.

"That makes me feel a little better about being put on hold. She doesn't want to hear about what we know about Evangeline and Oliver's deaths," said Cadence. "Someone paid off the coroner to say they died of a bear attack, and this whole town is in on it."

"A bear attack," Margo and Pearl exclaimed in unison.

"I know!" Cadence said. "How is this suddenly the story after five years? I've read every article ever printed about this case by now, and I've never seen it mention anything about a bear attack before."

Woody ran up to their car. "Audra's still talking to them," he said breathlessly.

"Are they listening to her and taking her seriously?" asked Margo.

"Yes, I think so," he said.

"We had huge news and they completely disregarded it," said Cadence. "Meanwhile, Vivienne and Olivia are just getting farther away!"

"We have huge news, too," Woody said. "We sent them a text with a photo of these," he said to Margo, Cadence, and Pearl, opening his hands and showing them the souvenirs Vivienne had collected.

"What the heck?" asked Margo, picking up the little double-decker bus with Taylor's name on it.

"So yes, I think they're finally listening," he said.

Chapter 69

Audra Fleming

"When I told them I'd already spoken to the Cambridge police and sent them the photo, too," Audra said breathlessly, "they really started to pay attention! They said they're dispatching officers to go after Vivienne."

The five of them were standing by their cars outside the old abandoned service station, trying to determine their next moves.

"What are we supposed to do?" asked Margo.

"According to them, nothing," Audra said. "They told me to stay out of it, except for coming down to the police station to hand over that evidence."

"I don't trust them," said Pearl. "After what you've been through, I think you should get your lawyer involved for any more dealings with our local police. And maybe even take the evidence up to Cambridge instead of turning it in here in Port Elspeth."

"Good thinking," said Woody. "She's absolutely right, Audra."

"They might have been able to sweep the Maddingly and Prescott case under the rug," said Margo, "but the Taylor Van Pelt case isn't going to go away so easily."

"Should we keep going toward Giuffrida Park?" Cadence suggested.

"I think Vivienne saw us behind them and they're going somewhere else now," said Pearl.

"We need to do something if they won't," Audra said. "Olivia's in trouble."

"Do you hear that?" Cadence asked. Then they all heard it. The sound of sirens. Seconds later, two Port Elspeth police cars went zooming by them with their lights on. A moment later, two more followed.

"Oh my heavens," said Pearl. "I think they've taken us seriously."

Tuesday, April 3, 2018

The Final Jewelry Meeting

Chapter 70

The Jewelry Makers

"And five hundred," said Pearl, setting the final pair of earrings they'd created in the plastic tote on the floor beside the kitchen table. It was seven o'clock in the evening and she, Margo, Cadence, and Audra were all gathered in her kitchen, splitting a bottle of wine and finalizing their preparations for that coming Saturday. The past week and a half had been a blur for all of them. This was the first time any of them had felt calm or normal in days.

"Why are we even going through with this?" asked Margo.

"For Olivia," Audra reminded them.

"And because we have so much inventory we don't know what to do with it," said Pearl.

"I'm afraid Olivia's going to regret it," said Cadence. "With everything going on with Vivienne, won't it be horrible for her to be there with all her high school friends and their evil mothers gawking at her?"

"She said she wants to do it," said Audra.

"If it's not going well, we'll leave," Margo decided. "I've burned my bridges with this town before. I'm not afraid to do it again."

"Dave will disown me if I leave partway through it, but that sounds more like a reward than a punishment," Cadence joked.

"Ooh," Audra said, "I just got an alert on my phone." She paused to read it, her face turning ghostly white. "Oh my God. She did it."

"We all *know* she did it," said Margo.

"But she confessed. She actually confessed! Oh, now Woody's texting me. He says to turn on the news right now. He says she made some kind of video and they're playing it on CNN."

Pearl, Margo, Cadence, and Audra all rushed into Pearl's living room and turned on the television. There on the screen was Vivienne, all dolled up in a haphazardly-matched ensemble that included a sequined gold track jacket and embroidered choker necklace she must have borrowed from Olivia. Her eyes were glazed over and bugging out. It looked to be a video she'd recorded into her phone.

"...and that's why I'm doing this my way, on my own terms. Because that's how I roll! First, I want to talk to you, Dr. Eisley. I totally thought these were bad memories I'd just imagined, but then it dawned on me when I was mixing pills the other day and I had a moment of enlightenment, that these are just regular memories I've suppressed. I'm still considering going to Pondering Elms to recover from this and if I do that, I'll mention you sent me. Also, Neil, I'm not sure what's going to happen, but please know that I love you." She cleared her throat a couple of times before continuing.

"Okay, here I go: For the record, I didn't want any of this to happen. It only went this way because it had to. Evangeline should have been part of our family. I always wanted to accept her into it.

"My son loved Evangeline. Despite what Claire and Mitch think and what they want everyone to believe, I know Evangeline loved him back. Claire, can you hear me? You, out there on your deck chair in the South of France, are you listening? You should have put up that billboard for me. It's not like I ever asked you for anything. We stocked our fridge with whatever your daughter liked. We bent over backwards for her. The whole family did! All of us. You should have given me that billboard. But that's another story for another day. Today, we're talking about what happened back in 2013.

"So, here's the deal. Back in the spring of 2013, Evangeline was pregnant. Surprise, everyone! Perfect little Evangeline. She had scheduled an abortion for June twenty-fourth, two days after her eighteenth birthday. That way she didn't need her parents' approval. The doctor's office called her and told her she was going to have to pick an earlier date because she'd be too far along on that date. That meant she was going to have to do it when she was still seventeen.

"Who did she turn to? Moi. Little old me. A couple days after that disastrous graduation party, she called me and said, 'Vivienne, can you pretend to be my mom so I can get an abortion? Pretty please!' The irony is, I don't think she ever needed parental approval to begin with. But, she thought she did so I went along with it. I told her sure thing, but that we'd have to come up with a plan to get her out of town for a few days.

"She didn't understand why we'd need to do it that way, so I told her I had a private doctor who would handle it. Honestly, there was no way she was going to break up with my son and abort my grandbaby all in the same month! No way in hell! I figured I'd find a way to talk her out of both those scenarios happening.

"So I sent Oliver over to her house that night—it was Sunday, June sixteenth—to get her and take her to the cabin in Hillpoint. I'd already driven up there and checked it out on my own a couple months earlier just for the heck of it one day when Neil was at work. I'd been thinking we might want to buy it. I told Oliver that we owned it and that he and Evangeline should stay there. I said not to tell his father or anyone else. He never questioned me on anything. I told them if they couldn't get in to just break a window. I knew they were selling it furnished. It was beautiful! I didn't know someone had bought it already. It was still showing up on all the real estate sites." Vivienne paused to scratch her neck. The sequins were creating quite the rash.

"There was hardly any reception up there, but I still wouldn't let them take their phones. Oliver threw them out onto the grass as he and Evangeline drove away from her house that Sunday. Just like I'd told him to do.

"I told Oliver they'd need to stay there and hold tight while I arranged for a doctor to come and take care of things. I brought them everything they needed that wasn't already there. Fancy food to eat. Bottles of water since the water there was shut off—let me tell you, Evangeline wasn't happy about having to go to the bathroom outside— I figured that after a few days in that cozy little abode, they'd patch up their troubles and everything would turn out fine.

"The way I saw it, we'd still get Oliver into Harvard some way or another. Evangeline would have the baby and I'd raise it for them while they were away at Harvard. Claire and Mitch could co-raise it with us! The Prescotts and the Maddinglys were finally going to be one family.

"Just to be safe, I took Oliver's car keys back with me after the first time I visited them. They were sure they'd lost them. I told him I'd bring back another set. And every time I visited, I told them they couldn't use my phone because there wasn't reception, but that I'd been telling everyone they were on a trip to Portugal that Oliver's grandparents had surprised them with. Evangeline was afraid her parents were going to be upset with her since she was supposed to have broken up with him, but she was kind of eating up how jealous all her friends were going to be.

"A few days before her birthday, the doctor was supposed to arrive after about four other supposedly-rescheduled appointments. Of course no one did. Evangeline was really upset and she was getting very suspicious. She wanted to be home for her birthday on the twenty-second. Naturally, she had a big party planned. To get her mind off things, I threw her a birthday party that lasted for days. I bought her all kinds of nice things. A ginger lime bath set. Mmmm, I can still smell that lotion if I think back!

"Well, as you can imagine, Evangeline started pressuring Oliver to get them out of there. And she wanted that abortion! Then, on June twenty-fifth when I was stopping in to give them some pudding with prenatal vitamins crushed into them for my grandbaby, I caught Oliver putting my car keys in his pocket. I don't know what he thought he was up to, but he should have known better than to double-cross me. I got them back from him, and I didn't visit them for three days. When I showed back up on the twenty-eighth, boy oh boy were they mad at me!" Vivienne laughed delightedly at the fond memory. "They'd been living on nothing but bottled water and a rotting basket of fruit for three days. I started telling him a story about how when he was a little kid he only wanted to eat fruit, but he didn't want to hear about it. This is when things got bad between Oliver and me. He was angrier with me than I'd ever seen him.

"I told him to calm down. I said the doctor was really coming this time. I got all serious about it like I never had before, and I told them to clean up the cabin and get ready for it. Evangeline was upset because there wasn't any running water in the cabin and she was sweaty and dirty. I told her to relax because doctors—especially that kind—see everything and nothing bothers them. I put on some music and we all started cleaning things up.

"Then, when things looked nice and tidy around there, I said the doctor had advised us to get Evangeline ready for her procedure. I tried to sound like I was reciting some instructions I'd been given. I told them, 'Put some pillows behind her. Give her two aspirin—As if! That would just make her bleed more—and then secure her hands and feet to the bed,' I told Oliver. Well, she didn't think this sounded normal." Vivienne began to laugh, "but I assured them it was what the doctor had ordered.

"Oliver was getting mouthy with me again, demanding that we all leave if the doctor didn't show up as scheduled. So, once Evangeline was tied up, he and I went for a walk in the woods—really, just up the hill a little ways—it worked out perfectly since there was an air mattress and a blanket he and Evangeline had taken up there and I was really into powerlifting at the time—I could bench press two hundred pounds easily—and I did what I had to do. After the incident with the keys, I'd decided I'd better come prepared. I figured that it was one for one. He was going to have to go away, but now we'd have the baby. With the music still going and the silencer, she didn't even hear it happen. You understand, I didn't want to do it, but he was causing so much trouble and all I could think about was my grandbaby.

"I went back inside and I was thinking, 'How am I going to stall her for another six months?' Don't get me wrong, I was sure I'd figure out a way. For the time being, though, I just kept telling her that the doctor would be there soon. But then she ruined everything. After a full day and a half of listening to her cry and beg and ask where Oliver was, and after she'd peed the bed three times, she said to me, 'You know this isn't even Oliver's baby, right? Don't you know that? This is my teacher Ben's baby.'

"I told her that couldn't be true and you know what she said to me then? She said that she and Oliver had never even had sex. 'What about that air mattress?' I asked her and she laughed in my face and said she'd taken a nap on it. 'Whose baby does Oliver think this is?' I asked her and she laughed in my face again and said he thought it was his and that he was so dumb he didn't even know better. So everything I'd done was for nothing. For nothing! For nothing!" Vivienne screamed.

A banner proclaiming *Breaking News: Confession in multiple murders happening now. Warning: Graphic Content.* scrolled ceaselessly across the bottom of the screen as the four jewelry makers sat by, giving it their rapt attention.

"So I shot her too, and I was smart about it. I wrapped my hand around hers when I pulled the trigger, getting gunpowder all over her. Then I went outside and dragged the air mattress back down to the cabin and got Oliver back inside, right next to her. Side by side. I thought it would look like a nice murder-suicide. Maybe even some kind of mutual pact they'd both planned together. Then I did some more clean up. I got the air mattress out of there since it was covered in dirt and leaves. I cleaned it up nice and tidy since that's how Evangeline liked things. But then the coroner met with me and Neil and Claire and Mitch. You know he's Claire's first cousin, right?

"He said, 'These two didn't die at the same time. Oliver's been dead at least a day longer. Maybe two days.' As you can imagine, Claire and Mitch were stunned to hear that. 'And, you see this,' the coroner said, 'those are gunpowder burns on her arm.' Claire and Mitch didn't like hearing that either. Then he said, 'You know she was pregnant, right?' Even with rope burns all over her ankles and wrists, her parents still didn't believe she wasn't to blame. At that point, Mitch said, 'What happened in that cabin isn't anyone's business but theirs. The town of Port

Elspeth has no need to know about any of this.' Then he and Claire asked Neil and me if we agreed. Neil didn't agree at all. He wanted to get to the bottom of it. But I told him we should let it go. So we tried to. But I realized I didn't want to let it go. I wanted everyone to know how Evangeline was like a daughter to me. Our families were almost one family, and then, just like that, they weren't anymore. How could I let that go?

"Claire, are you watching this? Hi, Claire! Hi, Mitch! Hello, Jean-Luc or whatever the frick your name is!"

"She'll confess to murder but won't say the proper F-word?" Margo said to no one in particular, rolling her eyes.

"Claire, I don't think it's too late for us to be friends," Vivienne continued. "If you move back here, Neil and I won't move away. We could make another go of it. Think about what I've done for you. I got rid of that little talker Taylor Van Pelt. She was certainly getting her fingers in the pie." Vivienne scratched at her raw red chest again. "These sequins are scratchy," she laughed. Then her eyes filled with tears. "I miss you, Claire. I miss everything about those days. Those were good times. If only we could go back...

"So, you probably want to hear about that Van Pelt girl, too. This time was way less messy. No pun intended. It was strangely beautiful and calming. It's those waspy Van Pelts. Everything they do seems so refined. Even dying. I had it all planned out and it went like clockwork. I turned down the thermostat and cracked a window to keep her apartment as cold as possible. But they were on to me from the start. Driving out of there in Olivia's vehicle—mine has too many yoga stickers on it, I figured Olivia's was harder to identify—I sideswiped a parked car and pretty much totaled the entire passenger side of it. Luckily, she's a terrible driver so I convinced her she did it. But my big mistake was keeping that damn bus."

She leaned closer to the screen and said, "Here's my tip to all of you: You can't keep anything. You just can't keep anything. That's all, folks. Buh-bye!"

The screen cut away from Vivienne's video and back to the studio where a panel of newscasters sat waiting to comment with varying expressions of horror and sympathy on their faces.

"Okay, and there you have it," said one. "Where do we begin?"

Pearl stood up. "Have you seen enough for now?"

Audra and Cadence nodded. Margo looked too queasy to respond.

Saturday, April 7, 2018

The Jewelry Fair

Chapter 71

The Jewelry Makers

"Here you ladies go," said Cindy Lou Mortenson, smiling a wide, so-white-it-was-almost-blue smile. She gestured grandly toward the tiny card table in the farthest corner of Ballroom A of the Port Elspeth Country Club.

"Why does everyone else have a table that looks like it's about four feet wide and ten feet long, whereas ours is maybe three by four?" asked Margo.

"It's just luck," said Cindy Lou, pouting on their behalf. "See? Look behind you. That's Noreen Alberts and she also wound up with a three by four."

They all turned to see a hunched-over elderly woman peddling scratchy-looking crocheted baby bibs. As they watched, the old woman picked up a stack of the bibs, slammed them against the table edge, and a small puff of dust rose from them. Then she exhaled and coughed the cloud away toward someone else's booth. She sat down heavily in the lawn chair she'd brought from home with a grunt and gave them all a *What are you looking at?* look. They all quickly turned away.

"If for any reason you decided you'd rather not participate today," Cindy Lou said, looking pointedly at Olivia and back to Cadence again, "just pack up and go. At any time. Just leave. No hard feelings."

"No, we'll be staying all day," Pearl said.

"Okay! Great! In that case, thanks for participating. Have a good one!" Cindy Lou hurried off to report to her friends how ridiculously that had all gone.

As soon as she was out of earshot, Cadence spun around to Pearl, Margo, Audra, and Olivia, and said, "That woman drives me bonkers!"

"She's something else," Olivia agreed.

Cadence gave Olivia a hug. "Are you holding up okay?" she asked her.

Olivia nodded. "But my dad is really sad," she said. "He's the one person who always believed in my mom. I don't know how he's ever going to get over this."

None of the other women had anything in the way of supportive words to give Olivia about this. There was nothing that could be said that would likely soften what Neil was going through. The women all made themselves busy getting their booth ready. When their plastic storage tote was cleared out, they stood back and took a look.

"It looks really great," said Audra.

"All twelve square feet of it," laughed Pearl.

Cadence checked her phone. "We're ready an hour early since we had way less booth to decorate than everyone else and twice as many of us. What do you say we drive over to the coffee shop down the road?"

"That sounds like a wonderful idea," said Margo.

"I'd love that," said Olivia. "Oh! But I just realized I was supposed to check in with my dad about ten minutes ago. I'll just give him a quick call before we go over there. This'll only take a few minutes." She took off for a more private spot across the room, leaving the others to put the finishing tweaks on the booth.

"Do you think we're safe leaving our booth unattended?" Audra asked.

"The ladies of the Port Elspeth Women's Club are a trustworthy group of upstanding citizens," said Pearl.

They all laughed.

"In other words," said Cadence, "who cares if they sabotage our booth? We've bounced back from bigger things."

"Olivia seems to be doing quite well," Margo said.

"She's an amazing kid," Audra said. "In fact, she's part of the reason I put in a request to transfer to the Middleford high school art department next year. She made me realize I might have more fun teaching older kids for a while."

"That's great," said Margo.

"And, I have some news too," Cadence said. "Right before we got here this morning I checked my email and I have a job interview... in Paris."

"What?" Audra exclaimed. "Paris?"

"And I've got a pretty good feeling about how it's going to go," Margo said, "because I know the person who's interviewing her and I've already put in a good word."

"How's that possible?" asked Pearl.

"I set it up for her," said Margo.

"But please don't tell anyone yet," Cadence said to Audra, quickly scanning the room for any high-society snobs that might be listening in, "because Dave doesn't even know yet."

Olivia came walking back to them then. "Ready for coffee?" she asked.

"We sure are," said Pearl.

"I'll drive," said Audra.

"So," Margo asked Olivia, "How's your dad doing?"

"Not the best, but he says at least we've got each other. Also, he's staying with his company now that he doesn't have any reason to quit his job. He told me he likes his job and thought he was too young to retire and do nothing. He said he could stay with their company but transfer to their Hoboken office so I can still go to my art program but live with him instead of having to live on my own."

"That's great news," Audra said. "Woody and I will do whatever we can to help make it easier for you, too."

"You and Woody sure are doing well," said Cadence.

Audra blushed. "He's a sweet guy. I'm falling for him big time. I think it's actually kind of lucky that I had the whole Ben experience, because it helped me realize just how special and wonderful Woody is."

"As far as the whole Ben-slash-Harry thing goes, I'm not quite there yet," said Olivia. "But thanks, Audra. That makes me feel better to know you and Woody will be keeping an eye out for me, too."

The women returned from their coffee run just in time to see Cindy Lou Mortenson yanking a blue ribbon from their booth and stuffing it into the hip pocket of her Citizens of Humanity cropped jeans that she'd paired with Chestnut Tieks. Of their entire little group, only Cadence recognized the status symbols and she no longer cared about any of them. Or the blue ribbon.

"Should we bother saying anything?" asked Audra.

"About that poor, jealous woman stealing our blue ribbon?" asked Pearl. "I didn't even notice it happen."

"Me neither," said Margo. "I saw nothing."

"Tell you what," said Audra. "I think we might as well go shopping at our booth, take everything we want—after all, it's ours—and then go out and get a pizza. Who's with me?"

"That's the best idea I've heard yet," said Olivia.

"I call dibs on those turquoise dangly earrings," said Cadence.

Holly Tierney-Bedord

"And I call dibs on a Mediterranean veggie!" Margo exclaimed.

So they took all the jewelry they wanted, set up an honor-system box that they all had a good laugh over, and drove away in search of pizza.

Epilogue

One Year Later

Love and Marriage

Cadence Bliss-Carlton

"It's kind of strange being back here, isn't it?" Cadence said to Margo. Pearl hadn't made the trip with them. She was back in Paris, enjoying spending time with husband number five and their new puppy, a furry little Miniature Schnauzer named Gustav Klumpf.

"Yes and no. I've come and gone from Port Elspeth so many times over the years that it's not such a huge deal," Margo said. "Is it tough for you?"

"As long as I don't run into Dave while we're back, I'll be okay. I'd just as soon never see him again. I mean, you know."

"I know," Margo agreed. She took her hand and squeezed it. "You know we both kind of love a little drama sprinkled in now and then."

Cadence sighed and laughed. She squeezed Margo's hand in return. "Well, yeah. That we do."

"Ooh, it's starting," Margo said as the music began. "I wonder where Olivia is?"

Cadence checked her watch. "She's not officially late yet. She has another two minutes to spare."

"Oh, there she is," said Margo.

Olivia and a cute young guy neither of them had ever seen before came hurrying into the church and slid into the pew right beside them. Cadence leaned over and gave Olivia a hug. Olivia's hair was back to its natural shade of blonde and she looked breathtakingly happy and pretty.

"It's so nice to see you both," she whispered. "This is my boyfriend Blake. Congratulations, you two. Sorry I couldn't come to Paris when you got married. I was right in the middle of my final project for the year."

"It's okay," Margo said.

"You can visit us any time when your schedule isn't so busy," said Cadence.

"Look at Woody," Margo mused. "He looks so nervous and happy."

The music stopped and there was a long pause. Everyone stood and turned as the bridal processional began. Audra stood at the end of the church with her arm linked through her father's, her eyes brimming with happy tears. Today she looked more beautiful and confident than Cadence had ever seen her. Her wedding dress was elegant and simple. Her long curls spilled over her shoulders and her smile was radiant.

"Isn't it super crazy how all of us found love this year?" Olivia whispered to Cadence.

"Super crazy," Cadence agreed, wiping away her own happy tears.

As Audra made her way past them, Cadence noticed the red thread with the charm on her wrist Woody had given her and the dangly little silver bell earrings Olivia had made. And, around her neck, the necklace that she, Pearl, and Margo had made at their very first meeting when they weren't yet capable of making much of anything. It was loaded down with pearls and glass beads, old buttons and tacky charms, yet Audra wore it proudly on her wedding day.

"I'm so glad I started the Port Elspeth Jewelry Making Club," Cadence whispered to Margo.

"We weren't the best jewelry makers..." Margo said.

"And good thing we weren't," Cadence said, "or we might have missed all our other amazing opportunities."

A Note about the Author

Holly Tierney-Bedord lives in Madison, Wisconsin. She is the author of over twenty novels and stories including *Sweet Hollow Women, Surviving Valencia, Bellamy's Redemption, Sunflowers and Second Chances,* and *The Miraculous Power of Butter Cookies.*

For more information or to sign up for Holly's newsletter, visit www.hollytierneybedord.com.

A Note from the Author

Thank you for reading *The Port Elspeth Jewelry Making Club.* I'd love to hear your feedback. Please consider taking a moment to leave a review on websites like Amazon and Goodreads.

The Port Elspeth Jewelry Making Club suggested book club questions and discussion topics

1. At the start of the book, Cadence is new to Port Elspeth. Have you ever started over in a new place? What struggles did you face?

2. Margo returns home after ten years away and finds that Port Elspeth no longer feels like where she belongs. How common do you think this experience is?

3. Vivienne's obsession with social climbing was her downfall. While Vivienne's character was an extreme example of being socially-obsessed, have you seen this come into play in real life?

4. Which character or characters did you most relate to? Which characters' choices did you most agree/disagree with?

5. How do you think Olivia and Neil will fare in the future?

6. What do you think will/should happen to Ben Harrison?

7. What lessons will you take away from the ladies of The Port Elspeth Jewelry Making Club?

Please enjoy this free sample of *Sweet Hollow Women* by Holly Tierney-Bedord

Chapter 1
Sweet Hollow, Louisiana
Maggie
1962

Margaret Haydel would turn ten years old on June 23, 1962. It was a birthday she had long dreamt of celebrating. The desire to graduate to double digits like her best girlfriends Susan Carter and Lynette Booth had weighed heavily on her mind since winter, when they'd both turned ten. As of late, however, her birthday dreams were overshadowed by a suffocating fear. Three men had recently escaped from Alcatraz Prison, and Margaret—or Maggie, as she was called— was certain those men were coming after her.

Late, late into the thick Louisiana night, Maggie's father Walt and Uncle Winslow sat on kitchen chairs on the porch outside her window, talking about the escape. Some folks said the men had drowned, but Maggie's father and uncle were certain they hadn't. Maggie pretended to be asleep, lying still in her bed as their cigarette smoke and conversation drifted in. Walt and Winslow were small time crooks—really, who wasn't, in some way or form, back when only God was watching—and the story had ignited their imaginations. They went over the details they'd read in the newspaper, again and again, from the heads made of wax to the raincoat life raft.

Most folks saw the Haydel brothers as serious, cool men. Hard nuts to crack, Maggie had heard them called. But when they talked about the Alcatraz escape, they were wide open. Their admiration was blatant. Palpable. Maggie could feel the new life breathed into them by the news of the escape, could feel how inspired they were by it all, and it sent shivers down her spine. She feared what her father and uncle were capable of, and even more so, she feared those three escaped prisoners. She had seen their photos in the newspaper and had dreams that they were hiding in her closet, waiting for her.

Night after night, while the bullfrogs sang their swampy rhythm, Maggie listened. She knew the sound of a match being lit, the sound of a beer can being opened and its small metal tab getting tossed into a pail, the scraping of the chairs on the old porch floor.

First they spoke entirely of the Alcatraz escape, with appreciation, like sports fans recounting a great baseball game, play by play. When they tired of that, they spoke of crimes they had committed in the past. Between the audible, deep drags of their cigarettes and the humming cicadas came the details of the small but substantial decisions they'd made that were the essence of their success. The lift in their voices and the staying power of these conversations scared Maggie, as did the fact that she was privy to all of it. Their conversations were becoming her own personal off-limits radio program, only so much worse. She tuned in religiously each night.

She discovered that years back, before she was born, they had robbed small stores across Louisiana, Mississippi, Texas, Alabama, Arkansas, and Florida. She learned all their tricks. There had been a woman named Birdie who went along with them. She'd been their decoy. A beautiful woman with black hair who flirted and distracted the menfolk as needed. They never hit the same town twice, and they never stayed in a store more than five or ten minutes. They favored Sunday mornings, when folks were at church, or festival days, when there were parades that tied up all the townspeople and policemen, leaving a little shop on the outskirts of town isolated and vulnerable. If things weren't going their way, they weren't afraid to leave with nothing. Not that this had happened often. They knew the back door of the grocery stores were often left unlocked for deliveries. They knew the cash boxes were usually hidden on a shelf beneath the cash register, with some minor obstacle like an old cigar box filled with pencils blocking their view. The more they did it, the more they learned. They never busted a window or did much damage unless they had to, and they were long gone before most folks ever knew what had happened. They dressed like simple farmers or businessmen and had license plates for whichever state they were in, as to not draw attention to themselves. They had never been caught.

Maggie didn't know Birdie, had never heard of her before, and didn't know what had become of her. Did Mama know about this horrible woman? What kind of a lady would help in a robbery, Maggie wondered. Crime, like roast beef and beer, seemed like it was only right for men.

Sometimes they said things Maggie didn't understand but that sounded sinister: "You sure she won't go in there?" from Uncle Winslow, and, "Trust me. She won't. There's no way in hell," from her father, followed by low, awful, conspiratorial laughter.

When they were tired of reminiscing, they spoke of what they could do now, since they were older, wiser, and had this terrible inspiration taking hold of them.

"We should think about the Marianna Bank," said Uncle Winslow. "We could go on a Sunday and be back at work Monday morning. No one would even know we were gone."

There was the sound of a long drag of a cigarette being inhaled, and Maggie held her breath, waiting for her father to tell Uncle Winslow he was crazy. "Naa, I think we'd head toward Texas. Just across the border," he said instead.

Uncle Winslow worked at a service station and Maggie's father was a janitor at the hospital up in Monroe. He drove up there every morning but Sunday, in the family Buick, wearing his navy blue coveralls and carrying a lunchbox filled with sandwiches that Maggie's mama had made for him. His cigarettes were always in his top right pocket and his hair was combed straight back, shiny black and silver. There'd been silver in his hair as long as Maggie could remember.

When he arrived home in the evenings, he looked tired but pleased to see his family. Maggie's little brother Johnny loved to look in his father's lunch box for candy and coins, and what he found he could keep. Maggie knew her father didn't forget these trinkets on accident, as Johnny thought he did, but that he placed them there on purpose. She fancied herself to be an adult, smiling along with Mama and Daddy at her younger brother's innocence. Johnny was just four, and everyone babied him. Their father often brought home larger gifts for them, mainly flowers for Mama that patients had left behind or slices of pie from the cafeteria. When Daddy began working at the hospital, he worked the night shift, but after three years he was promoted to daytime hours and they got to see him more.

Mama always said it was a good job. It was good enough that it afforded them a little house, and enough clothes and food, a car, and toys, and allowed her to stay home and take care of them.

Listening to her father and Uncle Winslow scheming, when as far as she could tell, their family wanted for nothing, Maggie was afraid of what would happen to them if something were to go wrong.

She looked around her in the near-dark, at the murky, familiar outlines of her bedroom. At her yellow rose wallpaper and shelf of horse figurines, and the pom-pom edged curtains her mama had made. She wanted to go outside and tell her daddy and uncle that they didn't need any more than they already had. That their life was perfect just the way it was, and that she loved her daddy so much more when he didn't talk about these scary things. But she knew better.

She was learning that all grownups had two sides. It was difficult to take the side she was used to and the new, bad side, and put them together to form a person who still looked like the person she knew.

She stayed very still. If they could scheme, so could she. She would scheme a way to save her father from being bad, at least so long as the Alcatraz prisoners didn't get her first.

Chapter 2
Memphis, Tennessee
Carasine
2009

It wasn't until she was the new girl, with her former life in Sweet Hollow having disappeared in a wispy cloud of dust last seen from the back of her family's old brown van, that Carasine Busey came to a full understanding of how unique her name was. Yes, she'd been the only one in town with such a name, but there'd been plenty of other humdingers to go around: Velvet Bathwater. Shantilly Cox. Garby Musket. Tawny Dung. The list went on. Even the rich kids had stupid names like Ansley-Maybeth McArdle and Thorpe Witherbottom. Who could say what was a good name and what was a bad name? Weren't all names kind of silly? Carasine had actually thought her name rather beautiful, back in her Sweet Hollow days.

But when David and Rhonda enrolled her in the big, square school in Memphis, before the other students had a chance to mock her style or intelligence, they mocked her name. "You're named after lamp oil," they told her. It had never occurred to her that

Carasine sounded exactly like kerosene. Before that day, Carasine Busey thought she might be special, the way most people, deep down inside, dream they are. Upon finding out she was, in fact, named after an old-fashioned combustible, something inside of her died.

She had always been a flosser, like a girl in *Seventeen* magazine, like a worldly girl who knew enough to pay attention to the details. From the first time the traveling school nurse gave an oral hygiene demonstration, back when Carasine was just five years old, sitting cross-legged on the sweating floor of the school cafeteria, she'd been one of Winn Parish's rare devotees to proper dental care. A keen interest in her own self-worth had come naturally to her, back in those early Sweet Hollow days, when she'd felt like one of the few sophisticates in a world of slobs. She had greedily saved the small plastic boxes from the hygiene kits that the little brick school provided once a year, hiding them beneath a pile of old plaster pearls in the back of a jewelry box Granny Maggie had passed on to her. She'd allowed herself just a snippet of the delicate white ribbon at a time, conserving it, making it last, never wrapping long pieces twice around each finger as the video had instructed. She'd flossed almost daily, always out of sight. It would have made her seem superior if she'd gotten caught.

But in the ninth grade, in the bustling, big-city high school, filled with beautiful, intimidating kids who couldn't possibly *really* be the same age as her, the floss stopped coming; it wasn't part of the way they did things here, and Carasine forgot to notice. She stopped clipping her nails and her split ends, ceased even to wear the Maybelline Great Lash mascara that had been a staple of her appearance since she was in the fifth grade. Once the sixth-most popular girl in her class, no longer was she clean and special. There had been times in her Sweet Hollow days that she'd been invited to parties in the grand mansions of her old-money classmates, when she'd kept her head down, sensing that fifth place or even fourth might be within her reach if she was cunning and stealthy and patient and absolutely, positively never screwed up. Now there was no longer hope of making it to the top.

With the enjoyment of being an example having been taken away from her, Carasine felt no desire to try. Not much about Memphis meshed with her way of thinking and doing things. Her family may have been adjusting to life in the city, but her heart was still in Sweet Hollow, firmly fixed to all she'd started there, and with long, invisible veins still defiantly connected to the heart of LeRoy Buntcher. Somehow, someday, she could feel it in her soul, she'd return to Sweet

Hollow. After all, she had unfinished business there.

End of free sample.

About *Surviving Valencia*:

Twins Van and Valencia Loden are killed in a tragic accident shortly after they start college. Charmed, bright, and beautiful, they held their family together and elevated their family to greatness. In their loss, a shadow is cast upon the family, particularly on the remaining child, who lacks the easy grace and popularity her older siblings took for granted.

As an adult, her life begins to turn from mediocre to amazing when she is saved by cool, artistic Adrian. The kind of happiness once reserved only for others is finally hers, until pieces of the past begin ruining what seems to be a perfect life.

Made in the USA
Lexington, KY
03 July 2018